†HE BATTLE
OF
EVERNIGHT

'Hobbit-fanciers will find much to delight them' *The Times*

'Cecilia Dart-Thornton exhibits strong and authentic evidence of having visited some of the more exotic corners of Faerie . . . Crucially for readers, she proves she's able to bring the unicorn back alive, netted in golden prose' *Washington Post*

'With deep roots in folklore and myth, tirelessly inventive, fascinating, affecting and profoundly satisfying' *Kirkus Reviews*

'Depicts a world that borrows from Celtic mythology but adds a few unique and refreshing twists . . . belongs in most fantasy collections' *Library Journal*

'Readers who crave long and detailed journeys through fantastic lands filled with magical creatures will enjoy . . . Dart-Thornton's world takes many traditional elements of epic fantasy and manages to stir them into something charming and new' *Amazon.com*

'Like Tolkien and many of the best fantasy writers, Dart-Thornton has created a wonderful fantasy world that is a delight to wander through' *Herald-Sun*

'Generously conceived, gorgeously written . . . might well go on to become one of the great fantasies' *Magazine of Fantasy and Science Fiction*

'An enchanting narrative . . . encompasses mystery, magic, technology and romance' *Romantic Times*

'An inventive, elegantly written saga that invites comparison with the best fantasy novels of the twentieth century, it may well prove to be one of the classics of the twenty-first' Elizabeth Hand, author of *Walking the Moon*

THE BITTERBYNDE TRILOGY:
BOOK 1: *The Ill-Made Mute*
BOOK 2: *The Lady of the Sorrows*
BOOK 3: *The Battle of Evernight*

Visit Cecilia's web site:
http://www.dartthornton.com

THE BITTERBYNDE · BOOK III

THE BATTLE
OF
EVERNIGHT

CECILIA
DART-THORNTON

TOR

First published 2002 in Tor
by Pan Macmillan Australia Pty Limited

First published in Great Britian 2003 by Tor
an imprint of Pan Macmillan Ltd
Pan Macmillan, 20 New Wharf Road, London N1 9RR
Basingstoke and Oxford
Associated companies throughout the world
www.panmacmillan.com
www.toruk.com

ISBN 0 333 90757 4 (hb)
0 333 90758 2 (tpb)

Copyright © Cecilia Dart-Thornton 2002

Maps by Elizabeth Alger

THIS BOOK IS DEDICATED TO ELEPHANTS

The conservation of elephants is emblematic,
in many ways, of the conservation of nature.
—Peter Stroud, Elephant Conservation
Royal Melbourne Zoo

AUTHOR'S NOTE:

Some of my proceeds from the sale of this book are being
donated to the Royal Melbourne Zoo's efforts for the
conservation of elephants in their native habitats, such as
Sumatra. However, my donations will not even come close to
being sufficient for the task.

If you wish to make a donation or learn more about the
conservation efforts of the Royal Melbourne Zoo, please contact:
The Director, Department of Conservation and Research, Royal
Melbourne Zoo, Elliot Avenue, Parkville, 3052, Australia.[1]
Website: http.//www.zoo.org.au/

Recommended reading:
When Elephants Weep: The Emotional Lives of Animals,
by Jeffrey Moussaieff Masson and Susan McCarthy (Delta).

---

1 Other than donating some of the proceeds from the sale of this book, Cecilia
  Dart-Thornton is not associated, either directly or indirectly, with the Royal
  Melbourne Zoo and therefore accepts no responsibility and/or liability for any
  acts or omissions of the Royal Melbourne Zoo.

Many thanks to the following writers (in alphabetical order) for their warm welcome into the world of speculative fiction: Kirsty Anderson, Jack Dann, Kate Forsyth, Ian Irvine, Sophie Masson, Maxine McArthur, Sean McMullen, Garth Nix, Janeen Webb, Sean Williams and Lucy Sussex, author of *The Scarlet Rider*, whose kind words won my heart.

**Cecilia
Dart-Thornton**

CONTENTS

THE STORY SO FAR

This is the third book in THE BITTERBYNDE trilogy.

Book I, *The Ill-Made Mute*, told of a mute, scarred amnesiac who led a life of drudgery in Isse Tower, a House of the Stormriders. Stormriders, otherwise known as Relayers, are messengers of high status. They 'ride sky' on winged steeds called eotaurs, and their many towers are strewn across the empire of Erith, in the world called Aia.

Sildron, the most valuable of metals in this empire, has the property of repelling the ground, thus providing any object with lift. This metal is used to make the shoes of the Skyhorses and in the building of Windships to sail the skies. Only the metal andalum can nullify the effect of sildron.

Erith is randomly visited by a strange phenomenon known as 'the shang', or 'the unstorm'; a shadowy, charged wind that brought a dim ringing of bells and a sudden springing of tiny points of coloured light. When this anomaly sweeps over the land, humans have to cover their heads with their taltries—hoods lined with a mesh of a third metal, talium. Talium prevents human passions from spilling out through the skull. At times of the unstorm, this is important, because the shang has the ability to catch and replay human dramas. Its presence engenders 'tableaux', which are ghostly impressions of past moments of intense passion, played over repeatedly until, over centuries, they fade.

The world outside Isse Tower is populated not only by mortals but also by immortal creatures called eldritch wights—incarnations wielding the power of gramarye. Some are seelie, benevolent towards mankind, while others are unseelie and dangerous.

The drudge escaped from Isse Tower and set out to seek a name, a past and a cure for the facial deformities. Befriended by an Ertish adventurer named Sianadh, who named her 'Imrhien', she learned that her yellow hair indicated she came of the blood of the Talith people, a once-great race that had dwindled to the brink of extinction. Together, the pair sought and found a treasure-trove in a cave under a remote place called Waterstair. Taking some of the money and valuables with them, they journeyed to the city of Gilvaris Tarv. There they were sheltered by Sianadh's sister, the carlin Ethlinn, who had three children: Diarmid, Liam and Muirne. A city wizard, Korguth, tried unsuccessfully to heal Imrhien's deformities. To Sianadh's rage, the wizard's incompetent meddling left her worse off than before. Later, in the marketplace, Imrhien bought freedom for a seelie waterhorse. Her golden hair was accidentally revealed for an instant, attracting a disturbing glance from a suspicious-looking passer-by.

After Sianadh had departed from the city, bent on retrieving more riches from Waterstair, Imrhien and Muirne were taken prisoner by a band of villains led by a man named Scalzo. Upon their rescue they learned of the deaths of Liam and Sianadh. Scalzo and his henchmen were to blame.

Imrhien promised Ethlinn she would reveal the location of Waterstair's treasure only to the King-Emperor. With this intention, she joined Muirne and Diarmid, and travelled to distant Caermelor, the Royal City. Along their way through a wilderness of peril and beauty, Imrhien and Diarmid accidentally became separated from their fellow travellers, including Muirne. Later they met Thorn, a handsome ranger of the Dainnan knighthood whose courage and skill were matchless, and Imrhien fell victim to love.

After many adventures, followed by a sojourn in Rosedale with Silken Janet and her father, these three wanderers rediscovered Muirne, safe and well. Muirne departed with her brother Diarmid to join the King-Emperor's armed forces. Recruits were in demand, because rebel barbarians and unseelie wights were mustering in the northern land of Namarre, and it seemed war was brewing in Erith.

Imrhien's goal was to seek a cure from the one-eyed carlin, Maeve, before continuing on to Caermelor. At her final parting from Thorn she was distraught. To her amazement, he kissed her at the last moment.

At last, in the village of White Down Rory, Imrhien's facial disfigurements were healed. With the cure, she regained the power of speech.

Two of her goals had been achieved. She now had a name and a face, but still, no memory of her past.

At the opening of Book II, *The Lady of the Sorrows*, Imrhien realised that Maeve's cottage was being watched and decided to leave secretly, in disguise. With black-dyed hair, gorgeous new clothes, a fake identity and a new name—Lady Rohain Tarrenys of the Sorrow Islands—Imrhien arrived at Caermelor Palace.

There she informed Duke of Roxburgh, Tamlain Conmor, and the Royal Bard, Thomas Rhymer, of the treasure under Waterstair. The magnificent trove became the property of the Crown and Rohain was richly rewarded for her part in its discovery. She was given jewels, an estate, the title of 'Baroness' and the services of a maid named Viviana Wellesley.

Rohain had to remain at Court until she gained an audience with the King-Emperor. The sovereign, however, was busy with preparations for conflict with the barbarian rebels of northern Namarre. Serious trouble was brewing there, and it was feared that the Empire itself was in danger of being attacked and overrun.

The maidservant Viviana turned out to be a friend and ally, and Thomas Rhymer and the wife of Tamlain Conmor, Alys, watched over Rohain. They told her tales of the Faêran, the race of powerful immortals who long ago used to walk the lands of Erith. Another courtier, Dianella, the niece of the Royal Wizard, Sargoth, also appeared to befriend the newcomer.

To Rohain's delight, she discovered that her friend Sianadh had escaped death. She told him about her amnesia, and he advocated returning to Isse Tower in a bid to find out more about her origins. But spiteful Dianella discovered Rohain's identity was faked, and told her to abandon her wealth and leave Court forever, or face the broadcasting of her duplicity. Taking Sianadh's advice, Rohain departed for Isse Tower, accompanied by Viviana.

At the Seventh House of the Stormriders, all that Rohain could learn was that the deformed servant she had once been was found near Huntingtowers, a frightening place inhabited by the Wild Hunt. Rohain set out for Huntingtowers, but her journey was cut short. On returning to Isse Tower, she was reunited with Thorn, only to discover that he in truth held a higher status than she could have imagined.

She returned to Caermelor Palace at Thorn's side. Fearful lest her cup of happiness should break, Rohain concealed from him the fact that she had no memory of her past life before Isse Tower. When her lover had to depart for the conflict in the north, he left her in the safest possible place—the Royal Isle of Tamhania. Before they parted, he gave her a golden leaf-ring as a token.

Tamhania was guarded by enchantments that made it inviolable to unseelie forces. During a violent storm Rohain was tricked into kindling the great Beacon that opened safe passage into the harbour. She unwittingly allowed unseelie entities to breach the security of the island. Soon afterwards, the destruction of Tamhania commenced, and Rohain fled over the sea with her friends. Many boats were lost: the rest were torn from one another.

Rohain found herself washed up on a remote shore not far from Huntingtowers, along with Viviana and young Caitri. Knowing she faced great peril, Rohain decided to assume yet another identity, and took the name 'Tahquil'. Using boiled treebark, Viviana dyed Tahquil's hair brown. Through the cindery air, still filled with the ashes of Tamhania's volcanic destruction, the companions travelled to the caldera of Huntingtowers. On the outskirts of the caldera, Tahquil found a gold bracelet. The sight of it triggered memories . . .

She recalled a time long past, in the land of Avlantia, when the city of Hythe Mellyn had been purged of a plague of rats by a mysterious Piper, who had snared the rodents with his enchanting music. The city had not paid the Piper his due, so in return he stole away the children of Hythe Mellyn, leading them under Hob's Hill.

One child alone had not answered the Piper's call. Ashalind na Pendran had had an injured leg and had been unable to follow. As she grew up in the city of sorrow, she sought constantly for a way into the Piper's realm. Easgathair, one of the Faêran—the immortal race who walked of yore in Erith—took pity on her, and described a way to penetrate Hob's Hill. Once inside, Ashalind was brought before the Crown Prince of the Faêran, Morragan, the Raven Prince. Clever Ashalind was able to answer three questions with which the Prince challenged her. In return, he permitted the children to return to the world of mortals.

However, the relinquished children began to pine and languish. A profound longing for the Fair Realm had gripped them, a deadly yearning known as the Langothe. The wizards of Avlantia declared that there was no known cure. In desperation, Ashalind called on Easgathair to allow the children to pass back into the Fair Realm, this time with their families, so that the longing would leave them, allowing them to survive. Easgathair granted her request. He also announced that the Gates between the Realm of the Faêran and the lands of mortals would soon close forever.

On the Day of the Closing, the citizens of Hythe Mellyn deserted their homes and rode into the Fair Realm. Just before the Gates swung shut, Ashalind discovered that there was in fact a cure for the Langothe, of which the wizards had been unaware. She decided to return to Erith. Due to a last-minute skirmish between Prince Morragan and his brother Angavar, both members of the Faêran Royal Family were locked out of the Fair Realm along with their respective retinues. They were forever exiled to the world of mortals. However, Ashalind had already slipped into a traverse that was known as the Gate of Oblivion's Kiss because of the condition, or bitterbynde, it imposed on all who entered it.

By the time she-of-many-names emerged, a millennium had elapsed in Erith. Through many trials she managed to make her way to Huntingtowers, where, on the haunted slopes of the caldera, she lost her golden hair, her voice and her memories.

The Gate's bitterbynde had come upon her.

THE BATTLE
OF
EVERNIGHT

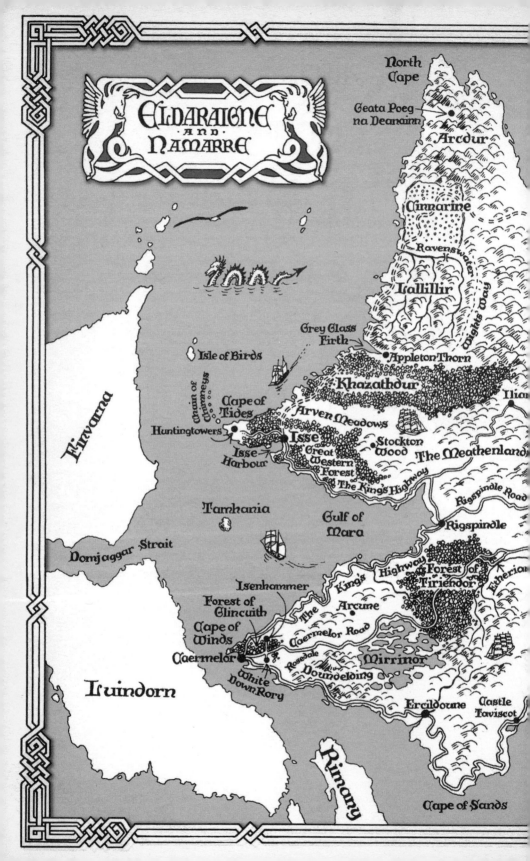

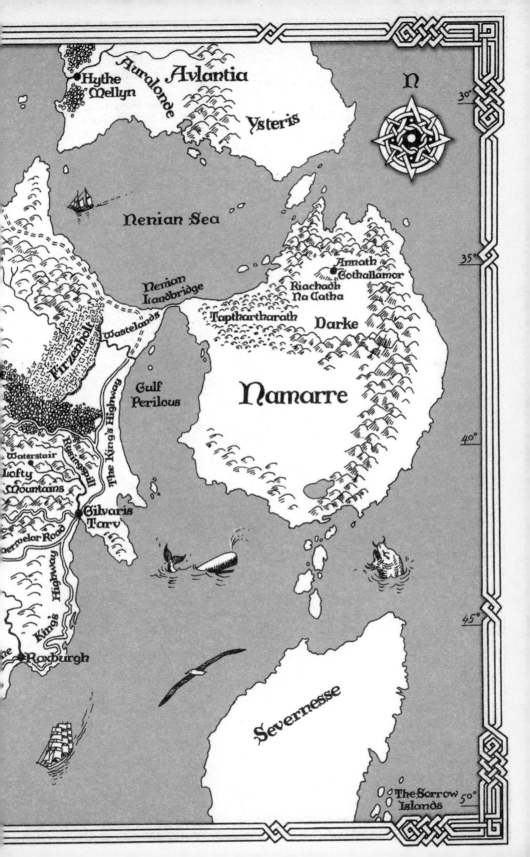

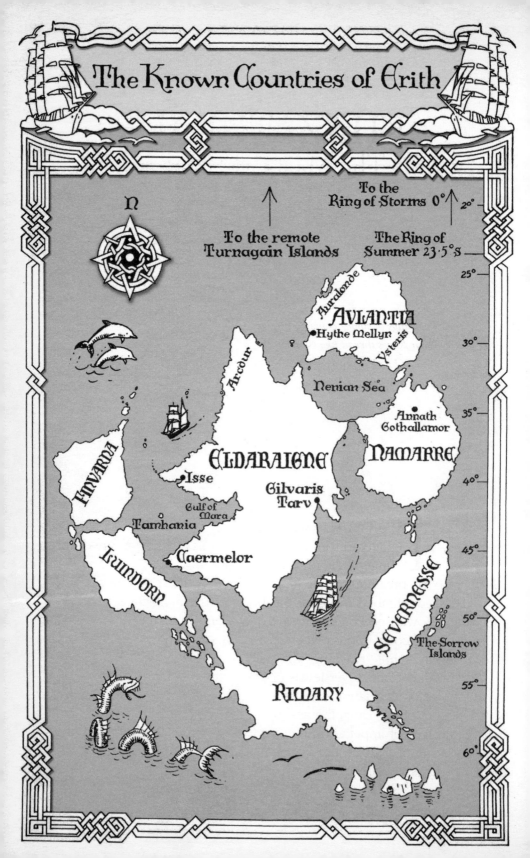

The Known Countries of Erith

N

To the remote
Turnagain Islands

To the
Ring of Storms 0°   20°

The Ring of
Summer 23·5°s

25°

Auralonde

AVLANTIA
Hythe Mellyn

Ysteris

30°

Ardour

Nenian Sea

35°

Annath
Gothallamor

ELDARAIGNE

NAMARRE

40°

Finvarna

Isse

Gilvaris
Tarv

Gulf of
Mara

Tamhania

45°

Luindorn

Caermelor

SEVERNESSE

50°

The Sorrow
Islands

55°

RIMANY

60°

1
KHAZATHDAUR
The Masts of Shadow

Pale rings of smoke come floating through the trees,
Clear voices thread like silver on the breeze,
And as I look towards the west I grieve,
For in my heart, I'm crying out to leave.

MADE BY LLEWELL, SONGMAKER OF AURALONDE

The rain was without beginning and without end. It pattered on incessantly, a drumming of impatient fingers. There was only the sound of the rain and the rasp of breathing while the girl, mute, amnesiac, shorn, and wasted, climbed out over the brink of the mine-shaft. She was alone, with no concept of her own identity, no memory of how she had come to this place. In subterranean darkness she crawled blindly, until, reaching an opening, she tumbled out among javelins of rain. Over levels of harsh stone and through dripping claws of vegetation she drove herself on limbs emaciated by weeks of the Langothe and days of starvation in the wilderness and lack of appetite for the food of Erith after the sight and fragrance of Faêran fare. Sometimes she slept momentarily, or perhaps lost consciousness.

Pleasantly, even the Langothe had been forgotten then.

With stiffening limbs she moved slowly through the mud and wet stone of the abandoned mines, oblivious of their beauties or horrors, blind to obstacles that tore at her. Reaching level ground, she rose onto trembling legs and walked, an action her limbs seemed to remember by some instinct of their own.

The little dog was gone. The girl had lain a long time underground after the cave-in, at whiles licking at water droplets that oozed from the rock. Buried alive, she was presumed dead. The Hunt had been abandoned because the hunters had not known who she was, believing her to be merely some foolish spy, some unlucky wanderer or thief, now punished by death beneath the rock fall. Yet, she had survived, whether due to the Lady Nimriel's mysterious gift or some inherent strength, or something else, unfathomable.

The ground had emptied from beneath her feet. She hurtled downward, to be brought up on a spear-point of agony. Her bracelet had snagged on a dead twig. She released the catch and fell into a thicket of *Hedera paradoxis.*

Hours passed.

Later, lying ivy-poisoned by the roadside, the shorn-haired waif in tattered masculine attire had been discovered by a passing carter. He had stolen her Faêran cloak and delivered her into the hands of Grethet.

Much had happened since then . . .

Now, as memories flooded back like sap rising in Spring, a strange euphoria blossomed within the damsel lying in a semitrance beneath the night-bound woods near Huntingtowers. The experience of recall imbued her with power. She felt like a winged being looking down on the world from an impossible height, while a light of glory crayoned her pinions in gold. So expanded was she in this virtual form that if she held out her hand she could cup the rain. Clouds brushed her cheek with cold dew, and should she raise her arms she could catch the sun like a golden ball. Mankind moved like beetles around her feet, and nothing could touch her. She had endured it all and been borne through, shining. She was winning.

So far.

Her shoulder hurt. It was being shaken in an iron claw. Her entire body quaked. She thrust off the claw, uttering an inarticulate groan.

'Rohain! Mistress!' Hazel eyes in a rounded, dimpled face appeared, framed by bobbing yellow curls with brown roots.

Sitting up, the dreamer took a swig from the water-bottle. Like any warrior, she rinsed her mouth and spat, then wiped her lips on her bloodstained sleeve.

'Via, I told you not to call me that. And cut your fingernails.' She rubbed her shoulder. 'Are we alive?'

'Yes, all three. You saved us.'

'I would like to agree, but I have this ornament on my finger which is responsible for our current state of health.' Her hands wandered up to her face, lightly touching the forehead, the nose, the chin. She examined a strand of dark hair. 'Am I as I was? Am I ugly or beautiful? Boy or girl?'

Viviana and Caitri exchanged meaningful looks.

'Your experience at Huntingtowers has unsettled you—er, Tahquil,' said Caitri. 'Come, let us help you to your feet. We must get away from here. We are still too close to that place.'

As they stood up, the one they called Tahquil swayed, clutching at her heart. Leaning against a linden tree she closed her eyes and grimaced.

'Zooks, ma'am, what is amiss?' asked Viviana, full of concern.

'Ah, no, it cannot be. Alas, it has me again. This, then, is the price.'

'*What* has you?'

'The Langothe. There's no salve for it.' The sufferer gulped down her pain. 'Let us go on.'

I must endure the unendurable.

She wondered how long it would take to destroy her.

It was the second of Duileagmis, the Leafmonth, viminal last month of Spring. In the woods, every leaf was a perfect spearblade chipped from lucent emerald, fresh from the bud. As yet the new foliage was unbitten by insect, unparched by wind, untorn by rain.

The travellers walked through a glade striped with slender silver-paper poles marked at spaced intervals with darker notches that accentuated the clean smooth paleness of the bark. The tops of the poles were lost overhead in a yellow-stippled haze of tenderest green.

The damsel called Tahquil twisted the golden leaf-circle on her finger. Her thoughts fled to he who had bestowed it upon her. *I miss thee. I have come full circle. Here I am once more. And thee, my love, shall I ever see thee again?*

The damsel, Tahquil. Her insides ached. Yearning chewed at them.

Thus she thought: *I am a thousand and seventeen and a half years old. I am Ashalind na Pendran, Lady of the Circle. I come from a time before the shang, before Windships and sildron. The kingdom of my birth has crumbled to nothing. One of the most powerful Faêran in Aia pursues me—but why? Is it simply because I committed the crime of eavesdropping and survived his vengeance, or does he guess I have found a way back to the Realm? Is he after my life or my knowledge? And all the while the other powerful Faêran, his royal brother, sleeps forever amongst a great company of knights beneath some unmarked hill.*

One Gate to Faêrie remains passable: the Gate of Oblivion's Kiss. Only I may enter it, only I might recognise it, if I could recall. But the past has returned imperfectly to me. The most important recollection of all, that of the Gate's location, is still hidden in oblivion's mists—mayhap 'tis hidden forever. Indeed, some other events surrounding my time in the Gate-passage lack clarity.

If I could return to the Fair Realm with the Password 'elindor', the Keys could be released from the Green Casket. The Gates might be opened once more. The Faêran would be able to send a discreet messenger to where their High King lies—for surely they could guess where he would be, or find him by means of gramarye—to tell him to return in all haste and secrecy to the Realm. Yet, if the Raven Prince discovers that the Gates are open and enters the Fair Realm before his brother, he might use his second boon to close them again and condemn the High King to continuing, everlasting exile.

Back and forth shuttle my thoughts, my confusion. This is like playing a game of Kings-and-Queens: if this, then thus, but if that, then the other.

Nonetheless, many matters are now clarified. Now I understand truly who it is that hunts at my heels—it is not the Antlered One, after all. Huon is only one of Morragan's minions. Huon's powers are naught by comparison with his master's. Now I understand whose henchman noticed my Talith hair in the marketplace of Gilvaris Tarv, and who lost track of me after the attack on the Road Caravan, and who found me again when Dianella and Sargoth betrayed me. I understand who it was that ordered the Wild Hunt to assail Isse Tower, who sent the Three Crows of War through the Rip of Tamhania. I know who pursues me with destruction wherever I may go: the Raven Lord, Morragan, Fithiach of Carnconnor, Crown Prince of Faêrie.

Sombrely, as she walked through the birch woods, the traveller with the dark-dyed hair and the festoons of thyme dwelled again on the moment she had first set eyes on him in the Halls of Carnconnor under Hob's Hill.

With eyes as grey as the cold southern seas, he was the most grave and comely of all the present company. Hair tumbled down in waves to his elbows, and it was the blue-black shade of a raven's wing . . . he regarded her, but said nothing.

I dismiss that personage from my contemplation, she said to herself. *He brings sorrow. The Faêran! I have met with them, spoken with them! Sorrow they bring to mortals but delight also, and they are so joyous and goodly to behold as I would not have believed possible.* Again she caressed the golden ring on her finger, smiling sadly, her eyes misted with reflections. *Indeed, had I not seen with my own eyes Thorn wielding cold iron in his very hand, I would have said he must be of Faêran blood. Beloved heartbreaker! I am fervently glad he is no Faêran—but I must banish thoughts of him now.*

When I walked from the Geata Poeg na Déanainn, it was my thought to embark on a quest to restore the Faêran High King to his Realm. I wonder—how long had he reigned in the Fair Realm, the High King of all Immortals, bearded with his pride, swollen with power, overripe with glory in his failing years? For how many centuries did he sit upon his hoary throne in Faêrie, toying with the lives of mortals, before he met his own exile? And would it truly matter to me if this ancient King and his dormant warriors were to lie forever entombed under Erith's eroding mountains?

She sighed. She already knew the answer.

Yes, it would matter. Those who sleep might waken, one day.

In this era, I have heard more tales of the Faêran than I knew in the past. Those tales have illustrated a race that is dazzling, but callous and cruel. Like all mortals I am drawn to them, but now that I recall history, my abhorrence is confirmed. I dislike the Faêran, almost as heartily as the Raven Prince hates mortalkind. I could not endure it if Faêran warriors should awaken and, undying, walk in my Erith. It is the fault of the Fair Ones and their quarrels, and their heartless laws, that I am here now in this perilous place, separated from those I love. I am fully aware of the trouble they may wreak, if they rouse from their enchanted sleep.

She who I once was, Ashalind of my memories—she loved them. I, her future incarnation, am wiser. Oh, they are beauteous, fascinating—it is impossible not to be attracted by them. But I, Tahquil-Rohain, loathe and fear their alien ways, their weird morality, their immutable laws, their arrogant use of power. 'Tis true that sometimes, when it suits them, they may behave with kindness, but the tales reveal them to be haughty, proud, contemptuous and cruel. They are users and punishers of my race. Rightly do folk name the Faêran 'the Strangers'. Strange indeed are they, scorching flames of gramarye. They ought to be shut out of our world.

This is my conclusion: that the Sleepers must awaken and depart. They must go back to where they belong. Every Faêran now in Erith must be repatriated.

If the Langothe is not too swift in its deadly work, I shall go back to Arcdur and seek the Gate. Then I shall return through it to the Perilous Realm and use the Password to unlock their Casket of Keys so that the Faêran of the Realm may go forth and find the hill in Erith where their King sleeps. Some shall waken him and his noble company, and take them away. Others shall take away the beautiful Raven Prince who frets and rails so passionately against his exile. When they and all their shadowy, sparkling, fair and terrible kind are gone, then the Gates must truly be locked forever. I shall not rest until that is accomplished.

This is my predicament and my undertaking.

Coloured spindles of lupins, as high as a man's knee, marched between the boles of the silver-birches. Each one flaunted a different hue, ranging from salmon, peach and apricot to mauve, maroon and lavender. Clusters of flower-turrets sprang from their own green coronas of frondescence. Now at the height of their blossoming they stood so erect, so tapered and symmetrical, each petal so crisp and painted and perfect, that they seemed artificial. Their petals brushed the garments of the travellers as they passed.

'Where are we going?' asked Caitri, not unreasonably.

'Northeast. Then north.' *Nearer to Thorn, in fact. Yet never shall I seek thee my beloved, never shall I bring my hunters upon thee.*

'Did you find what you wanted at Huntingtowers?'

'I did. Tonight, if we find a safe place to rest, I shall tell you everything.'

'Tonight you shall sleep,' admonished Viviana in a motherly manner, 'since you did not do so last night. We thought you were in a trance. We believed you were bewitched.'

'Why are we heading north?' Caitri wanted to know.

'The region called Arcdur lies to the north. I must find something there—a Gate. The first time we see Stormriders overhead, you must wave them down and go with them, feigning that you have not seen me. You two have suffered enough. This new quest of mine is not for courtiers.'

'Your words insult us,' said Viviana.

'I am sorry, but it is true.'

In silence they walked on.

'We will not see Relayers,' said Caitri. 'We are travelling far from the lands over which the Skyroads run, which are their usual routes. Besides, they have searched this coast already. They shall believe us lost, and they will not return.'

'Is there any road to Arcdur from here?' Viviana queried.

'Not that I know of. The King's High Way used to go there, but it has long since been swallowed by the forest, or fallen into the sea. I know only that Arcdur's western shores lie along the north-west coast of Eldaraigne.'

'Then we ought to keep to the sea's margins,' Viviana said. 'If we keep the ocean to our left we will be sure to come to Arcdur eventually.'

'It would be impossible,' said Tahquil-Ashalind, once Rohain. 'The cliffs along here are rugged, pierced by deep inlets thrusting far back into the land. Without a boat we cannot go that way.'

Viviana stopped by some low tree ferns. She plucked out some whorls of fiddle-heads, tightly coiled, like pale green clock-work springs. Other greenery and assorted vegetation hung on lengths of twine from her waist, her shoulders and her elbows, obscuring the articles swinging and clanking from her chatelaine.

'You have not eaten since the day before yesterday, *auradonna*,' the courtier reminded Tahquil from behind her matted, bleached curls. ''Tis little wonder your belly pains you.'

The euphoria dissipated. Tahquil looked at the dead and wilting leaves she herself carried, and the dirty, worm-eaten tubers. A forgotten tendril of something akin to hunger stirred within her. One could not live on memories. The three companions sat beneath the lissom poles of the birches and kindled a fire. Viviana unbound bunches of edible roots, seedpods and herbage.

'Via has become adept at finding food,' explained Caitri with a touch of reproach, 'especially since you went off on your own. She's remembered all you've taught us. She has an eye for it.'

'Even courtiers can learn,' said Viviana haughtily, 'to be useful.'

'Then let me teach you how to cook,' offered Tahquil. It would be a distraction from the hurt within.

These wooded, gently undulating hills were named the Great Western Forest, but, more innocuous than a forest, they were actually one vast woodland of beech, budding birch, oak and rustling, new-leafed poplars, hung with leafy creepers. The trees were interspersed with brakes of hazel and wild currant bushes veiled with a diaphanous lace of blossoms. Rivulets chuckled through leafy dells. Bluebells sprang in a lapis lazuli haze, attractive and perilous.

Directed by a dim, smoke-bleared sun glimpsed through the woodland canopy, the travellers walked on through the reddish-brown smog of the day, and at evenfall, when weariness threatened to sweep Tahquil from her feet, they climbed to shelter in a huge and ivied weather-beech, pulling themselves up on vegetable cables to rest in a scoop at the junction of three great boughs.

Twittering like sparrows in the undergrowth and fallen leaves, a gaggle of small wights came tumbling and capering over the knotted roots below. They were grigs. No more than eight inches tall were they, apple-cheeked, their eyes dark brown with no whites, their small mouths grinning. On their heads perched fungus-red caps, terminating in tasselled points. Their knee-breeches were bark-brown, their coats the fern-green of trooping wights. In this typical eldritch attire they performed cartwheels and other acrobatic feats which they apparently considered hilarious, and which in their audience's opinion were tediously uninspired.

'I should like to throw something at the little uncouthants,' said Viviana peevishly.

Nestling into the spoon of the tree, Tahquil slept. Oblivion descended, total again. She slept through the shang wind when it came, but Viviana, watching, pulled her mistress's taltry over her head lest she dreamed. In the unstorm, the cindery air transmuted to minuscule sequins.

'I shall have to inform her soon,' said Caitri.

A putrid drizzle of stagnant daylight announced dawn, struggling to pierce Tamhania's airborne, incinerated detritus. The travellers stretched their limbs stiffly.

'By the powers!' exclaimed Tahquil, snapping into wakefulness. 'We're lucky to be alive—we didn't set a night watch!'

'*You* did not,' said Caitri primly, crushing stytchel-thyme leaves to release their pungent oils. '*We* did.'

Tahquil smiled through encrusted ash-mud. 'It is well that I have you both with me.'

She rubbed more thyme leaves over her limbs and clothing, and they breakfasted on water. As she stoppered the water-bottle, Caitri looked up at her mistress. Her deep-lidded eyes seemed huge, liquid; her cheeks were paler than usual.

'It is the season to endure,' she said, obscurely.

'What is it, child? Your eyes tell me a terrible tale. I recall, now, you have been trying for some while to impart some tidings to me. Suddenly I burn to know. This time you must out with it—for it is something that concerns me deeply, I feel.'

Caitri swallowed. 'It is this. I should have told you earlier, but I could not. Even now—'

'Go on! Give me the words, quickly, or I shall go mad with the waiting!'

'The reprobate Sargoth, he who was once the Royal Wizard—'

'What of him?'

'He escaped from the palace dungeons and roams freely through Eldaraigne. He seeks you, and has sworn to take terrible vengeance upon you.'

The weather-beech stretched its arms upwards to the sombre sky. Talium-coloured butterflies puppeted through the leaves, like primrose petals on strings.

'How do you know this, Caitri?'

'I overheard, at Tana, the day after the last Watership came bearing news. It was too odious. I could not tell you, and besides, it was forbidden.'

'Whom did you overhear?'

'They were holding converse in the adjacent chamber, Prince Edward and the Duke of Ercildoune. I was arranging flowers in a vase for you—burnet roses, they were. I did not intend to listen. I could not help it—their words carried clearly. The Prince seemed agitated and sorrowful. He was saying that he wanted to leave the island, to go north to the war. He said he felt like a merlin in a cage, pent up, when what he wanted to do was to fly free to fight alongside the other warriors. He said it was not manly to hide on Tamhania when he should be on the battlefields slaying wights, his sword black and smoking with their blood. The Duke, he tried to persuade the Prince otherwise, saying he was too young yet for battle. The Prince replied that at the very least he should be scouring Eldaraigne for the escaped wizard, Sargoth, who by his tricks had slain the soldiers that pursued him, and who had vowed to do all in his power to bring about the downfall of the Lady Rohain, against whom he held a bitter grudge.'

Caitri was biting her lip, uneasy about conveying ill tidings. 'And then the Duke, he told Prince Edward to hush, not to speak so loudly, for doubtless the wizard would soon be recaptured and it would not do to cause undue alarm by revealing this threat, which in fact was no threat at all, because my lady dwelt in security on the Royal Isle. And the Prince after a time, he said yes, he knew that. They did not say more, after.'

'Are you certain of what you heard?'

'Yes. There was no mistaking it. I am so sorry, but I thought it best to warn you . . .'

Tahquil-Rohain stared at the cinnamon rind of the weather-beech. A brightly enamelled ladybird walked across it, a tiny hemisphere of scarlet and black on barely perceptible feet. The fragile insect teetered along the edge of a crevasse in the bark.

'Gramercie, Caitri,' she said. 'It is well done, to inform me that yet another enemy seeks my blood. Nay, I do not mock! I mean every syllable in earnest. Those who know their enemies are better prepared to defend themselves. The disagreeable Sargoth, wherever he might roam, shall not catch me unawares!'

But, having allowed recollections of Tamhania to return, Caitri was weeping now. 'Poor Edward!' she sobbed. 'And dear Thomas!' Her tears were a catalyst. Memories of all they had ever loved and lost sprang clearly to the forefront of the damsels' minds. The impetus of Tamhania's tragedy, postponed during their scramble for survival, now returned to them in full force. Together, they wept inconsolably, until no more tears would come.

As aftermath, a deep tranquillity pooled within them.

Ultimately, Tahquil swung out of the tree, scrambling down the woody creepers to the ground. She landed hard and did not glance up.

'Come.' Her throat rasped. ''Tis time we were away.'

Above the leaf canopy, rain clouds gathered. They let down their silver hair to wash away the grieving ash, the corrosives.

The next morning the air struck clear, wincing, sparkling like polished crystal.

Northeast they walked, keeping about two miles inland from the coastline. A northerly breeze brought the savage scent of the sea. The sounds of wights bubbled all around, especially at night: footsteps, rustlings, occasional bursts of manic laughter or screams, that *sense* of unseen presences that raised hairs, prickling, on the scalp, and choked the throat with a cold hand and hammered at the heart. Either their tilhals or the shining ring or good sense or luck or all four had, so far, kept safe these three inexperienced wayfarers.

From time to time, Caitri and Viviana continued to anoint Tahquil with oil of stytchel-thyme to prevent recognition by her scent, because there were, in the world, things that would not be barred by charms and good fortune. Tahquil showed her companions the gold enamelled bracelet and told them all that had returned to her as she sat in the shadow of the caldera. They were left awestruck.

'After all that has transpired, my lady is *in fact* a lady,' Viviana said, with a courtier's consciousness of rank. 'A right rare one, if I may say so!'

'How is it, my lady,' wondered Caitri as they travelled, 'that you are not dust? In the tales, when mortals return from many years in Faêrie, they crumble away after setting foot on Erithan soil.'

Ashes to dust. 'I know not, unless it were part of the Lady Nimriel's gift, or a property of the Gateway in whose shelter I spent a thousand years.'

'But can you not remember the exact location of this Gateway?'

'I cannot. Yet I think that if I set eyes on it I shall know it.'

'To search for it—that is where we are going?'

'Yes.'

'But should we not instead seek out the King-Emperor so that you may inform him of all you have recalled?' persisted the little girl. 'For, if anyone can aid you in the hunt for this Gate, it is His Majesty! Why, with the Royal Attriod and all the Legions of Erith at his command, he could not fail!'

'His hands are full enough with the conflict in the north,' Tahquil said quickly. She paused, as if reconsidering, then added, 'In all truth, I would fain keep my lord from this perilous business of Gates and Faêran princes and unseelie hunters. Already, he risks his life at the battlefield. I have no wish to bring further danger upon him.'

'In my opinion,' Caitri responded, choosing her words with care, 'a decision against taking your news to His Majesty is unwise. He is our powerful sovereign, and a Dainnan warrior beyond compare. Wizards throng to his summons. He governs great armies of bronze and iron. Does my lady truly believe such a one cannot defend himself against unseelie foes? I say he *can*—and he can facilitate your quest as well.'

'I thank you for your outspokenness,' Tahquil said with sincerity. 'There is much in what you say.' *Additionally,* she reflected wryly, *between my love and myself, who are handfasted, there should be no secrets . . .*

'Surely it is our duty as citizens,' interjected Viviana, 'to acquaint our sovereign with the nature of the disquieting undercurrents that are stirring. Surely it is his right, as Erith's monarch, to be able to name the enemies of the Empire.'

A look of pain twisted Tahquil's features. Racked with indecision, she strode faster, her hands plucking at the air as if grasping for answers. Unable, for the nonce, to decide whether to let the arguments of her companions sway her, she permitted her thoughts to briefly stray.

Indeed, he does rule armies of bronze and iron, she mused. *His own armour is wrought of polished steel, and had I not seen him wearing it, I would wonder—not for the first time—whether Faêran blood flowed in his veins. Yet the touch of cold iron to the Fair Ones is as the touch of flame to mortals. No Faêran lord or lady may brush so much as a fingertip against steel and not be tormented with agony beyond measure.*

No, he is not of their race. It is my love for him that makes him seem more marvellous than other men. 'Love is blind,' they say; rather should they say, 'Love makes heroes of ordinary fellows, princes of commoners, Faêran of mortalkind. In the eyes of all lovers the beloved transcends the mundane, forsakes all flaws and becomes supernatural.'

Besides, how could he be other than mortal? He is the King-Emperor, whose very birth was witnessed by the Lord High Chancellor, not to mention a multitude of midwives and carlins.

Abruptly, Tahquil slowed her pace and waited for the others to catch up.

'Speed is imperative,' she said resolutely. 'If we go looking for His Majesty, much time will be lost. The sooner my plan is put into action, the sooner the Faêran will depart from Erith and leave us in peace. The more we dally, the more chance Prince Morragan has to find the Gate before us!'

'True enough!' Caitri agreed.

Resignedly, Viviana shrugged. 'Then so be it. Against my better judgement I follow.'

'I do not compel you,' Tahquil rebuked mildly.

The courtier smiled. 'Well!' With a flourish of her hand she indicated their wild and leafy surroundings. 'Where else would I go?'

A rill fed a woodland pool; a dark-green stillness flooring a frog-hollow lapped in vernal shade. Here the travellers halted, warily, to bathe their hands and faces. They kept watch for signs of unseelie presences, wights of water, such as drowners, water-horses or dripping fuaths. They dared not venture in, lest pallid hands should shoot forth from submerged lairs and seize them. Nothing untoward took place, save that as they left the pool Tahquil looked back and, in the shifting light and shade, thought she saw something sitting alone at the water's edge, where only emptiness had sat alone before. Pulling her taltry well forward she urged her companions to hasten.

The jade-misted birch woodland gave way to groves of blossoming pear and almond, and now they walked beneath a sea of another kind: foaming acres of exuberant white petals in luxuriant profusion, an aerial wedding-world, zithering with bees.

'The last remnants of an old orchard, perhaps,' said Viviana. 'Like Cinnarine. Oh, to see *those* lands in Spring.'

'Cinnarine is too close to the battlefields for my liking,' said Caitri.

The long, narrow, pointed spear-blades of almond leaves and the shorter, rounded, glossy discs of pear foliage still lay wrapped tightly inside their buds, on the point of unfolding. On boughs bereft of any greenery, only pristine clouds of starched blossom gathered, their white wax petals flawlessly formed. Nebulae of paper-white butterflies steamed among the flowers. Flocks of milky doves ascended and descended like snowy, burst pillows. Thistledown wafted like the ghosts of fallen stars.

The wanderers dined on chicory leaves and silverweed roots. Contrarily, the astringent flavours evoked for Tahquil a contrasting picture of Oswyn's honeyed pears poached in cardamom and anise sauce, and her almond bread, rolled into buttery crescents, last tasted a millennium ago but seeming only a short span of time. Yet even the memories of these dainties could not put zest into her appetite, already dulled by the Langothe.

As the dusk chorus of birds had foretold, the sky bloomed like a grey-blue pearl, dim but faintly luminous. Treetops were suspended, dark against its satin. From the finest end of the finest overhanging bough, silhouetted, a tiny possum let itself down delicately, slowly, quietly, by its tail. Its hands grasped the twig below. It swung sideways and was gone.

That night, waiting for sleep, hammocked high in a natural web of ivy strung thickly between almond boughs, Tahquil lay and listened to the rustlings of the possums. As her eyes began to adjust to the moonlight, she became aware that she was staring at one of them, and it was looking back at her. She saw it, dark against the pale black sky. Its shy partner had dashed away in panic, crashing down into the ivy net. This one regarded her solemnly then unhurriedly melted into the night—a wild thing, courageous, inquisitive. Untouchable.

She fancied, for an instant, that if she did but turn her head she would find Thorn lying beside her. And so she did not turn her head, lest he was not.

Her companions slept soundly. Caitri's triangular face, surrounded by its abundant cloud of wavy, brown hair, was at peace. Her thin, pale limbs sprawled among the leaves and her neat, bow-shaped mouth was relaxed, slightly open.

Next morning the companions journeyed on. On the other side of the snow-lace orchard the trees became sparser. The spaces between them allowed glimpses of a sky the pastel blue of a wild bird's egg, striped with wind-raked ribbons of cloud. The orchard dwindled and dropped away altogether, giving way to rolling grasslands pricked with soft colours like a sprinkle of dyed sugar crystals.

These borderland tracts were like wild gardens, bursting with colour at the height of their flowering. The hard rain of Tamhania's destruction had scarcely touched them. Deep bosks of rhododendrons filled them, and callistemons thrusting forth their startling scarlet bottlebrushes, and mauve magnolias, and bright-baubled hakeas. Towards the middle, the flower meadows were drowned in cataracts of wisteria, a profusion of purple tassels rich with heady scent, a rain of delicate flowerets hanging in chains and dripping with petals and bees.

The travellers gazed out across the meadows. To the north, a dark ribbon crossed the horizon from east to west. From this distance, it looked to be a sheer cliff wall or escarpment, or a front line of giant warriors standing elbow to elbow.

'Ahead of us lies the mighty forest of Timbrilfin,' said Tahquil, forcing her thoughts away from Thorn to recall the lessons in mapping she had learned as a child. 'I have never come close to it, but in my time I learned of it and once, from a boat, I glimpsed the final reaches of its western arm. We are come to the Arven Meadows in the Marches of Timbrilfin.'

'I have heard of a vast forest in these parts,' said Viviana, 'but I have not heard the name you call it by. I do not remember what I have heard it called; however, I think 'twas not so pleasant to the ear.'

'Perhaps the name has changed over the years,' suggested Caitri.

'Many things alter, over time,' said Tahquil. 'The forest itself may not be the same.'

'I do not want to enter it,' said Viviana. 'It looks dark and eldritch, even at this distance.'

'That's as may be,' replied Tahquil, 'nevertheless we must go through, for there is no way around. Or if there is, it would take us many leagues out of our way, for the forest stretches right across the west to the rocky cliffs of the coast, and equally afar into the east.'

'In *your* time perhaps,' said Viviana, 'yet its mightiness may well have dwindled these thousand years.'

'Think you?' asked Tahquil. 'I see no end to it at either side.'

After carefully scanning the dark line across the horizon, the courtier had to agree.

Lumpy with bundles, the travellers made their way through the flowers. To a casual observer they might have looked like three taltried peasants in stout boots, the leader tall and slender with greasy brown locks overshadowing the face, the second shorter and plumper with straw-coloured curls straggling from beneath the hood, the last small and slight with hair combed neatly back from a clean-boned child's face. Thigh-deep they waded in a rainbow of tulip goblets, silk-petticoated peony and ranunculus, long perfumed trumpets of daffodils and bonnets of freesia, hyacinth's grapes and bells, the earnest blue lace of love-in-the-mist, the innocent faces of primula and the filaments of crocuses dusted with saffron powders. Knee-deep the travellers splashed through little boggy streams or wandered amid armies of flag-lilies waving like proudly borne standards—a blaze of amethyst banners tongued with yellow flame. At nights they looked for islets or forks in these rivulets, sleeping between two arms of running water so as to be safe, at least from minor wights.

For this land was riddled with eldritch manifestations.

When the evenings drew in, humpbacked, small, bogle-like mannikins with beady eyes and snouty, wicked faces would cavort among the flower stems. They pelted the travellers with tiny stones, hurling abuse in high-pitched voices. They turned somersaults, rolling themselves into balls, and as they rolled along they were no longer mannikins but hedgehogs which uncurled before snuffling out of sight. The flowers swished as though invisible legs stalked through the Arven Meadows.

The urchens were annoying and their aim was accurate, the cause of painful bruising and cuts. It seemed that the more their three victims shouted, waved their arms and tried to chase them off, the more the urchens delighted in inflicting torment. Guffawing with derision, they pitched more stones and wheeled away.

'Leave off,' Tahquil said to her friends at last. 'Attention only encourages them. Ignore their pranks and perhaps they'll grow bored.'

Eventually the wights moved off.

'Beastly urchens, giving hedgehogs a bad name,' said Caitri, wiping blood from her cheek where a sharp stone had gashed it. 'It must be centuries since mortals have passed this way for them to harass.'

'I don't suppose they have much else to think about,' said Viviana.

'I don't suppose they have much to think *with*,' said Caitri scornfully.

The urchens returned on one or two other occasions, in case the travellers should languish for spiteful company.

'Where do they find all those pebbles?' pondered Viviana.

Stars hung overhead like burning snowflakes.

One sunfall, while gathering dead twigs of rhododendron for kindling, Viviana screamed. Gibbering with terror, she came splashing across a beck to the island campsite. Snatching up knives and sticks, Tahquil and Caitri stood back to back with Viviana folded between, preparing to defend themselves.

'Should something powerful come, we have no chance,' murmured Caitri to Tahquil beneath Viviana's hysterical, unintelligible gasps.

'I know.'

They scrutinised the meadows. The flower heads nodded, skimmed by a zephyr and the enchanting flute-like calls of a pied butcherbird. The great, wild garden appeared guileless.

'What saw you, Via?' Tahquil asked without turning her head. Every nerve hummed like ship's rigging in a sea storm.

'It came at me. It had a face, like a man's but shaggy, horned. It was naked from the waist up, ten feet tall with goats' legs . . .'

'Goats' legs? Are you certain it was ten feet tall?'

'Well, perhaps nine. Maybe eight. No less than five or four—'

'An urisk.'

'But you should have seen it! It was horrid!'

'It sounds like an urisk, Via. Did it look like the marble figures supporting the Duke of Roxburgh's mantelshelf in Caermelor Palace?'

'Why yes indeed, it did resemble those, only—'

'If it is an urisk you saw we have nothing to fear.'

'Maybe it was. Maybe it wasn't. But 'twas most fearsome.'

The Arven Meadows now lacked any sign of wights. As the travellers kindled their little fire, the book of night opened, upon whose dark pages were printed the runes of constellations spelling out a huge, slow language as old as evolution.

'There are trows about,' said Tahquil next day as they picked their way across the confetti-stippled uplands. 'Each night I see them, moving under the starlight.'

'The Grey Neighbours,' said Viviana. 'Harmless mostly, but vengeful if offended.'

'In the Tower we never saw any wights at all,' said Caitri. 'Only if we returned late from gathering in the forest beyond the domains, someone might glimpse movement or the flash of eyes in the darkling, but not often. I heard only the tales.'

'We had a bruney at Wytham,' said Viviana. 'He was called Billy Blind—a very reliable little domestic who kept the house spick and span. And there was my lady's household wight at Arcune, which used to sing with us and swing on the pot-hook. But I'd never seen unseelie wights except from a distance,' she shuddered, 'until I met with hobyahs on the road to your Tower, Cait. That was a meeting I could well have done without.'

'And now you have met an urisk,' said Tahquil, 'and what is more, I suspect this urisk is following us. Upon reflection, I think it has been trailing us ever since we stopped to wash in that pool under the birch-woods.'

'What might it be after?' asked Viviana nervously.

'That I cannot say.'

That night, Viviana unhooked her sewing implements from her chatelaine and stitched up a rent in the leg of her breeches. A watch was kept all night, but in the morning her silver thimble was missing.

'I left it here by the fire,' she exclaimed, 'and now it is gone! Stolen.'

'Trows,' said Tahquil darkly. 'They are silver-thieves.' Fleetingly, a vision returned to her—a memory of a happier time spent amongst trows and henkies, when eldritch music played. *They danced, then, the Dainnan and the girl—so close, so very close but never, ever touching. Neither did a lock of his hair flick her shoulder nor the hem of her dress brush against his boot, that was how precisely they danced. Later, looking back on this night, Imrhien could not clearly recall the slow beauty of the inhuman harmonies or her wonder at the clear eyes that smiled down on her, only the way the wind lifted his long, dark hair like spreading wings.*

'Guard well your chatelaine, Viviana,' she said, thrusting aside the knife that twisted in the wound.

The courtier checked over the ornate clasp holding together the medley of chatelettes; the scissors, the manicure set, bodkin, spoon, vinaigrette, needle-case, the looking glass and spike-leaf strainer, the faulty timepiece, the workbox, the portrait and tilhals, the anlace, penknife, snuff-box and pencil.

'This motley collection seems sorely out of place in the wilderness,' she sighed.

'It may yet come in useful,' Tahquil assured her.

She lay back to rest against dulcet grasses, and closed her eyes. Dimly, through sombre veils of yearning, the conversation of her companions drifted into her awareness.

'Do you not long for home and hearth?' Viviana softly quizzed the little girl.

'I miss my mother,' admitted Caitri, apparently surprised at the question, 'but life in Isse Tower was disagreeable—never the life

for me. Now I am bound to my lady's service, and gladly do I follow her. This is the way I was taught. I follow, I serve, I learn. It
is enough for me to walk outside the walls of the House of the
Stormriders. Being content, I crave no more. And you?'

Viviana deliberated. 'I am fearful of these wights that haunt
our surrounds,' she said eventually, 'and I would wish we might
find ourselves safe within walls.'

'Walls may not guarantee safety, necessarily,' Caitri reminded
her.

'Yet they *appear* secure, which is reassuring.'

'Then, do you wish you might not accompany my lady on this
quest?'

'No I do not wish that, but 'twould make my heart lighter were
I convinced that our venture stands a good chance of success. I
fear the dangerous regions lying across our path might ensnare us,
and drag us to our doom.'

Next morning they journeyed on.

The land undulated in folds and banks and wooded shoulders
from which toppled the pewter braids of rills. Ever as the travellers
approached the thick, dark border of Timbrilfin, leaving at their
backs the flowery lea, the outlying trees grew higher and stouter,
closer together. For fourteen cool rain-misted days they trudged
along, although there were no visible paths. Few words were
exchanged between them. Food was scant. Half a month had
elapsed since they had left the slopes of the caldera, when they
came under the forest fence.

The sun shone from the northwest, still making its annual
zigzag journey to the southern tropic. Away from it fell the heavy
shadow of the fence of trees, casting a chill, grey gloom all along
the boundary.

A dim and mysterious place, it certainly felt eldritch.

There the travellers halted, tilting back their heads to look up.
High above, the straight boles of massive autarken trees leaped a
hundred and fifty feet up to a distant roof of leaves. In the spaces
between these magnificent pillars dusk gathered—a hollow
absence of light, a curdling of twilight.

'Timbrilfin, Land of Mighty Trees, uninhabited by mortal men,' said Tahquil aloud. Instantly she regretted having spoken. Caterpillars seemed to be crawling across her shoulders.

'Something is *listening*,' said Caitri, voicing the opinion of them all.

As one they turned and moved away. When they considered themselves out of earshot of whatever lurked in the darkness beneath the trees, they stopped to talk.

'I had supposed that Timbrilfin would be like the fair Forest of Tiriendor,' said Tahquil quietly, 'but I was mistaken. Tiriendor possessed its dangers, but at least it was filled with light and air. Those overshadowed vaults ahead of us give out an ominous look. It may be that in the centuries since my time hosts of unseelie wights have gathered within those sunless arbours. Now horrors unguessed might well dwell therein. We are not Dainnan knights. The three of us, alone, are no match for any truly fell beings. It is unlikely we would pass unscathed through their domain.'

'What is to be done?' asked Viviana. 'As you have said, to the west the forest meets the ocean, while to the east the trees stretch mile after mile. Are we to turn back at this barrier, after coming so far? Must we return to Court after all?'

A note of hope might have chimed in the courtier's tone.

Tahquil chewed a stem of grass, squinting thoughtfully at the sky.

'No,' she said. 'But I need time to think and we all should rest. That spring we passed not far from here, soaking out of the hillside—let us sojourn there.'

The spring was not much more than a boggy patch, vivid green, fringed with rushes and iris. Here, dragonflies of metallic emerald-gold or ruby iridescence froze in midair on almost-invisible wings of diaphane. Abruptly they froze in another place, kissing the reeds and the water. Midges droned, frogs *creeked* in the last of the butter-yellow afternoon light.

There the companions rested while the sun's rays lengthened, reaching long warm fingers across the land. The fingers withdrew, clenching into a hot fist which punched out of sight behind the horizon. Further up the slope, the forest stretched taller, blacker, more menacing. Indeed, it seemed to have advanced a few yards down the hill while the travellers were not attending. They fastened their eyes on it.

Dusk crept over the landscape.

A sad wind searched over the grass, in and out of the trees. Leaves moved with a soft fluttering sound which possibly included a light footfall.

Tahquil stood up.

'Wight,' she said loudly. 'Urisk.'

There was no reply. The staccato dragonflies had vanished. All was still.

'Urisk,' she repeated, 'show yourself.'

Viviana and Caitri sat utterly motionless, save that the lips of the former were moving in some kind of chant. Water waited, lurking darkly amongst plaited bog-grasses.

'*Obban tesh!*' muttered Tahquil. 'How may I persuade?'

Viviana raised her head.

'Urisk,' she quavered helpfully, 'pray come forth.'

An encouraging frou-frou rustled in a nearby clump of parallel, tasselled stems.

'In the name,' said Tahquil, 'of the King-Emperor of Erith. In the name of Nimriel of the Lake and Easgathair of the Gates. May it please you, urisk, to appear!'

They stared at the clump of tasselled reeds. In a moment, Tahquil swung around. At their backs, woven into the gloaming, there existed a small dark-skinned chap with a pointy face which concluded, appropriately, in a goatee. Two stubby horns stood up from a nest of curly brown locks. Thick hair covered rounded haunches tapering to neat, cloven hooves. His waist was strung about with a belt of braided rushes, from which dangled a syrinx.

His voice hooted tragically, like wind whistling through hollow wood.

'Duck,' he honked.

Stones whizzed past their ears from the clump of reeds, followed by shouts of laughter. The urchens made off, leaving Tahquil daubing a fresh graze on her chin and Caitri massaging a sore elbow.

The urisk remained.

Tahquil cleared her throat. She thought, *I have summoned a wight. I have invoked an eldritch thing. Such a summoning may be onerous, may become a burden to the summoner. It must be followed through rightly. What do I know of these goat-legged wights? They are seelie. Someone whose very name pierces my heart once told me that urisks crave human company, but their appearance frightens people. Should they be thanked or does thanks drive them away?*

'You honour us,' she stammered. 'We request your help.'

'But,' whistled the wight, 'ye be afeard o' me.'

'Oh no, not at all,' Viviana assured him, her eyes like saucers. 'I am sorry I screamed in the rhododendrons. You took me by surprise, that is all.'

'I'm accustomed tae it by noo,' mourned the urisk. 'Your kind want nae part o' me since my ain hoose fell tae ruin.'

'Be that as it may,' said Tahquil, 'now that we have invited you to converse with us, will you help us find a way through Timbrilfin?'

'Och, I've nae heard the forest called by that name that this many a lang nicht,' said the urisk squatting down on his hairy haunches. 'That is an auld kenning, that is, from the nichts langsyne when the forest was young and Themselves that named it were wont t' gae on their Rades or a-hunting through its green aisles. Green no mair are the lofty halls o' *Arda Musgarh Dubh,* but grey as sowen-pats.'

'Is that its title now?' asked Tahquil, not attempting to pronounce it. 'A formidable one!'

'For a formidable wood,' said the urisk. ''Tis the name my folk ken it by, one o' many names. *Bolr Sceadu* the bogles call it; the Great Ones say *Axis Umbru,* while to the swans whose speech is still close to the Faêran, it is *Urlarliath.* But the Men of the Grey Glass Firth title it *Khazathdaur,* meaning the Masts of Shadow.'

'Can you show us a safe path through?'

'Och, that be axin somethin', that be. Safe? There's nae sich thing as safety for mortals in that kittle foggie roughness yonder. Ye dinna want tae gae in there, ye three lassies. 'Tis a muckle greet tree-tangle, that one. D'ye no' ken what abides in its glaury lairs?'

They shook their heads.

'Wicked things,' said the urisk. 'Powerful things. 'Tis ever dark and shadowy on the forest floor. The trees grow high and the leaves block out the sun's rays, so the light o' day never reaches doon there. 'Tis always twilight or black nicht, and in the shadows stalk unseelie sorts. Skrikers lurk there, and pixies that mislead travellers.'

'I thought pixies were nice little wights, like fanes, but with wings,' interposed Caitri.

'Nae lass, not *nice* at all, pixies. With their wee lanthorns, they'll lead mortals like ye intae bogs until ye stick fast in the muck and droon. They'll feign voices and call ye frae up ahead until ye walk over a cliff. They'll invite and draw ye from your road and lose ye in the wilderness.'

Tahquil interposed, 'Skrikers and pixies are dangerous, but if one keeps one's wits, one may confound these minor wights. Begging your pardon,' she added, in case she had offended him.

'Bide—I hae not told the worst o' it. Hae ye no' heard o' Grim?'

'Many tales tell of him,' said Viviana, shuddering. 'A shape-shifter he, and a stealer of merriment.'

'Aye, a shape-shifter who has taken to haunting the tall timbers o' Arda Musgarh Dubh. And Black Annis, she dwells there too, the hag o' cats, the eater of mortal children. And speaking o' cats, grey malkins hunt through the forest as weel.'

The travellers exchanged glances. No charm would fend off grey malkins, for those were *lorraly* beasts—efficient, feline killers.

'And if ye escape Grim and Black Annis with the malkins and the rimfire and the rest, ye may have tae deal with another which visits the dark floors of Arda—the Cearb himself.'

'The Killing One?' Tahquil asked, her mouth suddenly dry.

'Aye.'

'Then, is there no chance of crossing Khazathdaur safely without Windships or eotaurs?' she asked.

'Och, there might be a way,' hooted the wight.

They looked at him expectantly but he spoke no more. Over his shoulder, the moon was rising, outlining his horned, disquietingly alien silhouette. Yet in the glimmer of night his face was gentle as he gazed at the small mirror on Viviana's chatelaine like a miniature moon at her waist.

'I hae moved in the forest,' he said at last, 'and in its fringes, since I lost my hame in the braes o' Ishkiliath, which Men call the Grey Glass Firth. I ken the ways o' the forest, and I ken its kindreds, and I keep out o' the way o' most. But there's a race o' folk that lives high in the leaves, far frae the ground, and their paths hang in the air, up where the light sieves through. With their nets and their iron they keep themselves safe frae malkins and all. They might let ye use their roads, if I ax them.'

'If they use iron, then surely these folk are not of eldritch.'

'They be a mortal race but what kind I cannae say. This verra nicht I shall axe them, for 'tis kittle for ye here. There's sonsy hurchins in them spretty bushes.'

'Kittle?'

'Dangerous.'

The urisk became part of the environment again.

'Bide awee,' his voice fluted back. But he was gone.

'Can it be trusted?' Viviana wanted to know.

The moon edged twenty-seven degrees higher. The three travellers sat beside the spring, maundering in and out of a light doze. Tahquil dreamed that the touch of the breeze on her cheek was Thorn's breath. In the gathering dew frogs chanted monotonous lullabies, setting the brain buzzing with broken fragments of thought which subtly changed into incoherent half-dreams.

A sharp cry jolted Tahquil back to wakefulness. Viviana was on her feet, rummaging in the folds of her cloak, casting about.

'Hens' bells!' she cried. 'Stolen, right off the chain, my timepiece!'

Near the forest fence a leaden stirring could be detected.

'There they are!' shouted Viviana triumphantly. 'Trows—the thieves!'

She dashed forward before anyone could stop her. As her companions hurried after, a pale glow opened from Tahquil's finger.

'The ring warns. Something unseelie is near,' Tahquil said urgently to Caitri. 'Something worse than trows.'

They caught up with the courtier right under the overhang of Khazathdaur's black boughs. Grey faces peered out from between the trunks just inside the forest, their large eyes baggy, their noses long, with rounded, drooping ends. The foremost of these was a small trow-wife wearing the traditional grey headscarf. In her hand she carried the silver timepiece, in its case inlaid with ivory and bronze. From the shadows the trows glared at the mortals. A hundred and forty-three feet above their heads, a leaf became detached and fell, eddying like a flake of soot in the moonlight.

'Give it back, wretched wight,' demanded Viviana angrily, holding out her palm. ''Tis mine. 'Tis all I have in this olc wilderness. Give it back.'

The trow-wife made no reply. Somewhere, a fox barked, harsh and grating, not like a sound from a natural fox's throat. The ring pulsed with a brighter light, like a warning.

Then the trows' bulbous eyeballs bulged. The corners of their malleable mouths turned down in a strange reversed rictus and they all retreated further back into the shadows.

'No!' Viviana stepped forward. 'You must not go—'

With a last grimace, the trows fled into the forest.

'It takes more than the pulling of faces to frighten us,' Viviana called after them.

'Odd,' said Caitri, 'I could have sworn that they suddenly took fright.'

'Yes, but not from us—*from something coming behind us*,' said Tahquil, spinning on her heel.

It was moving—walking or gliding—tall and straight as a chimney. At first she could not make it out between the tree trunks on the lower slopes. Two triangles flapped—the corners of a long, black coat. Was it a man?

If it were, something was horribly wrong with his head.

Tahquil felt her insides turn to water. The ability to move drained from every limb. The head of this approaching man-thing was wrenched over to the left side, lying horizontal on the shoulder. It was twisted back in a position which would have been impossible unless the neck had been wrung. It was the head of a hanged man.

A mote of moonlight splashed down.

The skew-polled apparition glided on, reeling itself in unerringly on the thread of the travellers' paralysis.

Then, a hooting: 'Tis Wryneck! Dinnae just stand there ye ninnies, run for yer lives!'

At this, the thread snapped. The supernormal energy of panic surged through their limbs. Released from the vice of terror the mortals took to their heels in the direction of the urisk's call—'This way, this way!'

As they ran into Khazathdaur's submerged glades the autarken trees, like iron towers, closed in at their backs. They blotted out the moon.

The smell of fear was darkness. In the darkness there was no speed but instead a pressure, as though the hunted mortals ran futilely into a sponge. As if it had sensed a need for camouflage, the ring's light had dimmed.

'Over here! Over here!' The urisk's hooting was fainter now.

'A trick,' shrieked Viviana. 'We're being pixie-led.'

'No!' shouted Tahquil.

They swam through shadow paste. It blinded their eyes, stoppered their noses and mouths. It suffocated.

A horizontal beam of wood slammed against Tahquil's face.

'Climb!' It was the reedy voice of the goat-wight.

Groping in the dark she found a series of slats in parallel—a ladder.

'You first.' Roughly she hauled on Caitri's elbow and felt the little girl pass her, ascending energetically. The ladder wriggled like an eel.

'Your turn, Via.' The courtier needed no second urging. She swung up behind Caitri, then hesitated.

'My lady—'

'Go on, if you love life. It hunts after us yet!'

Indeed it did. Fungous parasitic growths on the ramrod tree boles gave off enough corpse light to show a more intense black in the blackness—a chimney gliding nearer, swifter. With Viviana's boots out of the way, Tahquil grabbed a rung, hoisted herself up, hung in space, scrabbling for a footing, booted a toehold and began to climb the serpentine rails.

But too late.

An extrusion of darkness came forth; a long, hinged jaw. With one rapid movement Tahquil pulled out her knife, aimed and threw it. The blade flared cobalt as the weapon vaporised. It was destroyed instantly. But her attack had been enough to cause a hesitation, and in that instant she climbed beyond the reach of that long, toothy jaw. Clambering on as fast as strength permitted, she unintentionally rammed her face up against Viviana's boot heels.

'Get up!' she screamed. 'It is still coming!'

Inexorably, the twisted head was moving up the ladder. Tahquil flung down a second knife. It blazed up like the first, obliterated. The pursuer's hook-jaw reached for her ankles to pull her down.

A pipe tune puffed through the forest like smoke.

It stopped short, replaced by yelling:

'Yer greet laithron doup, yer hawkie's hurdies Wryneck, ye couldnae catch me if ye had wheels on.'

The insult was not stinging enough to provoke retaliation perhaps, but sufficient to bring on another pause. Additionally, the chimney-thing was tugged by the power of its spoken name. In that instant of reprieve, Tahquil surged upward to find an astonishing emptiness on the ladder. Viviana's boots were no longer there, but hands gripped Tahquil firmly under her armpits and heaved her up sideways, up and over onto a platform. With a rattling swish the ladder dropped, collapsing back to the forest floor, still bearing its singularly nightmarish burden.

Sucking in great draughts of air, the companions reclined with their backs to the tree-trunk, alone on the platform. Somewhere nearby a stream of gibberish broke out, burbled on for a while then bleated off into the distance.

It seemed that for the moment they had reached safety.

'How did you cut down the ladder?' gasped Tahquil.

'We did not,' panted Viviana. 'Some *things* did. They were

here with us but I had no chance to look at them. They helped us get off the ladder, then they dashed away.'

Their unidentified rescuers had apparently deserted them. Tahquil crawled to the side of the wooden floor. Savage spikes of iron protruded horizontally from its edge. Grasping one for security, she peered down through the gloom.

'We're only about twenty feet from the ground. That *thing* may be able to get up here, given time. We ought to climb higher.'

'We have no choice,' said Caitri, gazing at the overhead murk. Flush with the treetrunk, another ladder led upwards. Meanwhile, down on the leaf-mould, ill-boding footsteps went pad-padding purposefully.

'Wryneck made only silence. Others are on the move down there,' said Viviana, easing her bundles where the strings cut into her flesh. 'The higher we go the better pleased I'll be.'

But the aftermath of fear was enervation. They remained drooping against the treetrunk, procrastinating against further ascent, overcome by lethargy.

Not a lateral shoot, twig or limb branched out from these autarken pillars. They stretched sheer-sided from the ground to the canopy one hundred and fifty feet above. There they burst into multiple bifurcations, forming an interweaving grid, a huge, mottled ceiling whose girders supported a natural roof thatched with layer upon layer of leaves and other types of fruition. The canopy linked all the trees of the forest, yet up there the slender twigs were so fragile that only birds and the lightest arboreal creatures might cross it.

Heavy breathing and a kind of intermittent tearing effect erupted beneath the travellers' feet. Between a pair of jutting iron spikes, two green flames were rapidly approaching. Beneath this pair of eyes, a snarl widened. Black lips everted on shiny red gums embedded with sickles of gleaming enamel.

Amazed at the previously unsuspected depths of their strength reserves, the mortals shinned up the next ladder. Before they had attained the platform above, a yowl of white rage seared their ears. Looking back they saw a massive paw, its talons unsheathed, swipe up over the edge of the recently vacated platform.

Destructive, poison-coated needles of steel that could rip open a man's belly with one clout now scored furrows across the planks, generating a chilling screech. The interstices between the spikes were too narrow—one of the claws, impaled, tore off. The wood-work shuddered from a mighty blow to its underside. Part of it gave way and tumbled slowly into the gulf, revealing the cat's rabid maw, saliva-dripping fangs, flattened ears, slitted eyes and powerful, switching tail. The three birds it hunted did not wait to inspect it further. Reaching the precarious safety of the higher perch they pulled the ladder up after them.

By now, six or seven well-thewed felines were swarming up the surrounding trees. With an agility belied by their size, they leaped from trunk to trunk, twisting in midair to present themselves belly-first to their destinations, claws hooking deep into the bark as they closed on each tree stem. The forest giant supporting their human quarry stood somewhat apart from the rest—the space around it was just a little too extensive for the grey malkins to bridge it with their aerial manoeuvres. One, having hitched its way to a higher level than their platform, sprang out and across, performed the spine-wracking twist and, by inches, missed landing right beside them. It plummeted, contorting.

Their tree was protected from malkin attacks by its spiked platforms, its wide separation from sturdy outreaching boughs, and the provision of wide, rusty metal bands which clasped the circumference of its trunk at regularly spaced intervals. Claws could not penetrate these deflective bands. Higher climbed the fugitives now, forsaking the clamour of the frustrated hunters. Bundles and bottles banged between their shoulder blades. Every twenty or thirty feet the ladder passed through a cutout in a higher platform fastened against the huge trunk. Each time they reached such a haven, they rested a moment, gathering strength.

At last they could go no higher.

The reason for this was twofold: they had in truth exhausted themselves with their exertions, and there were no more ascending ladders. The light-emitting growths were sparser in these upper regions but a silver-of-blue tinge to the air hinted of moon-light behind foliage laminae. Some ropes, anchored to the tapering bole with hooks and pulleys, projected sideways in a graceful curve. Their opposite ends were lost to view. Hot and flushed, the travellers drank deeply from their water supply and sank down to wait out the night like a trio of wooden dolls, too alert for danger to fall comatose.

Tahquil laid her head against the tree bole and thought she heard the hydraulic pumping of green blood within that cortex as though it were the pulse beat of her own life. Her mind, as always, turned to Thorn.

From the moment she had first espied him beneath the trees of Tiriendor, the kernel of her thought had been always with him, so that at times she felt detached from the play of life, as though she were an onlooker viewing her physical surroundings from somewhere at his side. Since the Langothe's return, another yearning had been added to love's anguish, and now, faced with the possibility that they might never meet again, that somewhere in the world Thorn might be slain in battle and lost to her forever, the two agonies combined as one. She felt they hammered out her blood to thinness until it was but silverwater in her veins, and she with bones of crystal, so drained as to let the light through, was a wafer, a leaf of glass to be blown away in the bitter south wind.

Yet she clung on, as her hand clung to the ridged and whorled bark of the giant autarken—for within that crystal burned a poignant flame not yet extinguished by despair. Fancy bore her far from Khazathdaur and somewhere within her skull she stood in a starlit glade of Faêrie beside a tall knight. His dark head was crowned with sharp white stars like thorns.

Always, shadowing every word and deed, sweet sorrow and terrible longing desolate my heart.

Sounds carried long distances and rose up high, in Khazathdaur. From far below fountained a busy whirring as of spinning wheels in motion. This carried on for a while until, without warning, jolly music struck up as though a band of fiddlers and pipers played accompaniment to a rollicking peasant barn dance. Yet there was a queer element to it. It seemed only a copy, a hollow attempt to emulate the orchestrated merriment of such an occasion—even a parody. It stopped as suddenly as it had started, chopped off in the middle of a bar.

'Sooth, this *is* no picnic,' remarked Viviana. Her face, in the gloom, looked pallid as dead flesh.

The platform swayed ever so slightly with the slow dance of the tree. It moved in rhythm with winds far above, blowing among the massed leaves. The forest's lullaby soothed the weary travellers into a slumber so profound that a slight creaking of ropes and a sigh of cloven air could not waken them.

Silver-of-blue diffused, becoming a dense green twilight. The morning sun filtered through translucent tiers, millions upon millions of leaves whispering and murmuring continuously. Khazathdaur could never be truly silent. Leaves rustled in upper winds that never seemed to ruffle the airs below the leaf canopy, bringing a sound like the sifting of fingers through a coffer full of tiny crystals. Hundreds of thousands of leaves glided slowly down as though threaded on invisible filaments.

In Tahquil's breast the hard ache for the land beyond the stars drew salt water that quivered in her eyes, reflecting leaves.

By the morning light the travellers saw, on the platform's opposite side, freshly heaped vegetation. There was a dazzle of white blossoms with luteous centres, and fruits like leathery gourds with skins striped and speckled in what might have been, in another light, shades of madder. There was a leafy bough from which some of the outer rind had been stripped, and three dried, hollow gourds filled with pure water, and a small woven-twig cage packed with spun-silk cocoons like bonbons, pastel pink, softest saffron, palest pearl. From the calyxes of both fruit and flower trailed long beards of cellulose fibres.

Out of the blossoms arose a honey fragrance so intense as to be almost intoxicating. The travellers discovered these nectar-brimming blooms could be eaten. The crisp autarken leaves proved edible also, tasting of sweet angelica. Slashed open, the fruits revealed dark red flesh like a wound—a meaty, palatable pulp. The bark's inner cortex, when peeled away from the core, tasted like strips of chewy bread. Caitri slit open one of the long, oval cocoons. A pale, blind grub wriggled there, rearing its blunt head. Flinching, Caitri dropped it as if it had scalded her.

'Oh, poor thing.'

Instantly remorseful, she scooped it back into the cage. They made no more attempts to dine on the cocoons.

'''Tis a wonder they didn't bring us dead birds,' said Caitri.

'Here no birds sing,' said Tahquil. 'Have you not missed them?'

'Not I. I am sated on sweetmeats,' said Viviana with her mouth full of honeyed blossom. 'Who ever would have thought that one could eat *flowers*!'

'We eat cauliflower,' said Caitri. 'At least, others do.' She wrinkled her nose.

'And Sugared violets, and rose petals,' added Tahquil, biting a fruit.

Caitri looked up at the high canopy, dim and grey, sparsely raining leaves.

'I see no such flowers or fruits as these within reach. I fancy they all sprout in the higher regions. I wonder how the Tree-Dwellers get them down.'

'I cannot imagine,' said Tahquil. 'But I do imagine that the urisk asked those Tree-Dwellers to aid us by dropping one of their ladders. After all, it *was* his voice calling us and not some pixie counterfeit luring us into Khazathdaur to meet our doom.'

'Yes, the little fellow proved trustworthy,' said Viviana, 'I'll grant that. The trows unintentionally aided us also. If they had not stolen my chatelette we would have been still sitting beside the soak when that thing called Wryneck came upon us. He might have cut us off from the forest and the Tree-Dwellers' assistance.'

They fell silent at the mention of this horror.

In the jade twilight the forest world was all perpendiculars tapering down to vanishing points in darkness far below; a vertiginous perspective. On the ground, peril waited. Overhead swayed slender boughs and twigs too fragile to bear the weight of anything heavier than a possum. To either side stretched reeling chasms of air so vast that merely to look into their depths was to feel oneself falling.

It seemed there was nowhere to go.

Tahquil examined the apparatus of ropes and pulleys tied to hooks nailed into the trunk.

'These ropes are made of the fibres growing from the bases of the fruits and blossoms—strong, tough, coarse cordage, twisted together. Ropes would be useful in our situation. Perhaps we could manufacture some . . .'

'We shall have no use for ropes or anything else if we remain perched up here forever,' said Viviana. 'I wish those Tree-Dwellers would return to help us.'

'The urisk said they have highroads of their own up here,' said Caitri, tracing the outward-leading cables with a forefinger. 'I believe this is the beginning of one, and another leads out from one of the platforms below.'

Tahquil unhooked a thick rope tied in a massive knot near its free end.

'The Tree-Dwellers' gear is cleverly designed,' she said, inspecting it. 'Simple and effective. This is what I know as a flying fox. Pryderi used to have one rigged. It led from the balcony of his house to the bottom of the hill. He would let me ride it when I was a child—I liked to think I was flying. If my father had known he'd have had an apoplexy.' She pulled hard on the rope to test it. 'It is secured firmly. And see, by this mechanism this knotted ride rope can be pulled back to its starting position when the rider has disembarked at the other end.'

'Yes, but where *is* the other end?' pondered Caitri.

The cables swayed almost imperceptibly, pale lines passing into an indifferent gloom beyond which a jungle of tree pillars could be dimly glimpsed.

'There is only one way to find out.' Tahquil gave the ride rope one last tug.

'I shall go first,' she said. 'If all's well, I'll send back something tied to the ride rope as a token—a bunch of these dried stytchel-thyme sprigs, since it appears I am adorned with so many of them. This retrieval cord will follow me. It must be allowed to unroll freely as I go, and it must be coiled neatly when the ride rope is brought back, or the whole operation may fail. Should the retrieval cord snag and the flying fox be halted abruptly in midflight, the passenger would be flung off. There is no safety cord to hitch us on.'

'You are not going to jump off this ledge on that contraption!' Viviana cried. 'What if you fall? 'Tis a long way down—I cannot even glance over the edge without feeling swoony.'

'Take heart, Via,' said Tahquil bracingly. 'There's nothing else for it.'

''Tis always the same saw,' desponded Viviana. '*There is no choice.* Are we naught but flotsam on this quest, to be tossed about at the whim of contingencies not subject to our command? Methinks the only choice I have made so far was to accompany you, my lady, and yet even that was not a choice, for I could not in all conscience do otherwise.'

'Speaking from experience,' said Tahquil, 'I would say that perhaps I have only ever made one true choice in my life and that everything else I have ever wrought has been a result of causes beyond my choosing. I searched for the stolen children for seven years but how could I not seek them? I entered the Fair Realm but how could I resist the chance to save them? I chose to leave the Fair Realm at the last moment but even then, if I examine my heart, I know I *had* to leave and in truth it was no choice. Perhaps you are right.'

'True choices,' said Caitri sagely, 'are made all the time—the small decisions. If we have no say in where the road takes us, at least we can decide how to place our feet and what to look at along the way.'

'The Duke of Ercildoune used to argue that we choose our own destinies—' began Viviana.

'This conversation is becoming too allegorical for me,' Tahquil broke in, changing the subject. 'When I reach the other end, I shall tug on this thick cable, the slide cable, three times. That will be the signal for you to start hauling. Fare thee well.'

Seizing the rope with both hands she swung forward. As she left the platform she tucked her feet up on top of the knot, wrapping herself around the thick ride rope. Over her head the pulley squealed, running along the main slide cable down into darkness and the unknown.

She rolled down the cable's incline at exhilarating speed, her hair and taltry and cloak streaming out like banners. To either side the forest flashed by as though she flew along the middle of a columned canyon.

The cable stretched a long way, as far—it seemed—as Summer's end.

At last the flying fox's terminal rushed at her with alarming rapidity out of the gloaming—another platform on another tree. Just before the end station, the pulley reached its lowest point and turned uphill, slowing the headlong rush of the ride rope and its rider dangling underneath. Tahquil's boots clipped the shelf's edge. She yelped in pain, let go with one hand and was dragged unceremoniously onto the ledge by the ride rope before she remembered to release her grip. The pulley having reached the apogee of its swing, it lost the last remains of momentum and succumbed to gravity's seduction. It reversed direction and slowly began to slide back down. Righting herself, Tahquil seized the rope just before it swung off the edge and out of reach. It would have pulled her over the edge with it, except she flung her weight backwards, hauled hard and quickly hooked it over a peg jutting from the trunk.

She found herself on the second highest platform of a tree which appeared identical to all the other trees in Khazathdaur. From the ledge directly below, the cables of a flying fox ran back towards the first tree. From the platform immediately above, a profusion of funicular cordage radiated in three other directions. This tree was an aerial crossroads.

Tying the sprig of dried thyme to the pulley she tugged three times on the slide cable, sending a quiver along its length. This cable was so thick and long that the quiver dissipated before reaching the end of the visible section. Vigorous repetition of the exercise was eventually answered by a sudden tension of the retrieval cord. Unhooking the pulley she hurled it forth and watched it disappear behind curtains of shadow. It occurred to her that she ought to have checked the upper platform for danger before sending for her friends. Now there was no time for it.

Presently, the slide cable tautened and began to hum. Out of the half-light hurtled Caitri. Like a fruit on a vine she was tightly clenched in around herself, eyes shut.

'Open your eyes!'

The pulley slowed on its final short ascent. Caitri's boots touched the stage. She released the rope too soon—borne forward by momentum she toppled over the further edge. Tahquil grabbed two handfuls of clothing and pulled her back with all the force she could rally and they both sat down hard, the ride rope pendulating about their ears.

'Horns of the Ant!' expostulated Caitri, white with shock.

They sent for Viviana who arrived with speed, propelled by proportionally greater inertia. Swinging her legs down, she alighted gracefully, as though well practised.

'That was easier than I had expected.'

Her companions blinked at her.

'Where to from here?' Viviana asked. Oblivious of their astonishment she surveyed the forest. 'From the platform above us, the highways lead in three different directions.'

'North. We must ever go north,' said Tahquil. 'But as to which direction is which, I have no notion. I lost my bearings during the confusion of the flight from that lop-headed creature, and now the sun cannot push its beams through these leaves to show us its path.'

High up, a sweet, soft rain began falling in a long sigh, a gift of clear water to swell buds, soothe parched leaves and rinse the long green hair of the forest. No drops yet penetrated the canopy.

When the shower had passed, the companions climbed the spindly ladder to the higher platform.

'See!' said Caitri. 'Flowers bedeck the anchor point of the central cable, and its carrier rope is here, too. The carriers are missing from the other two flying foxes.'

'A clear directive. 'Tis obvious,' said Tahquil grimly. 'No matter which way is north, the Tree-Dwellers have indicated the path they wish us to follow. Let us hope they are as benevolent as the urisk has told.'

'But we could use the retrieval cords to haul back the other ride ropes,' suggested Caitri sensibly.

'I have no wish to offend these forest denizens. We move within their domain—never forget it. Over us they have the power of life and death. We must bend to their will for now, yet remain wary.'

They negotiated the second flying fox in the same manner as the first. It brought them to a similar tree in similar surroundings.

'This sameness proves irksome,' said Viviana. 'I feel as though we go nowhere, or in circles.'

''Tis impossible that we should be going in circles,' declared Caitri. 'Take note—we have travelled in a straight line, so far.'

As if to mock these words the next garlanded flying fox veered off on a diagonal, bringing them this time to a platform within view of other enshelfed autarkens which were strung together by rigging. As they went deeper into Khazathdaur repeating these flying performances, they became more adept at takeoffs and landings. Also, the number of rigged trees multiplied.

''Tis a veritable spider's web,' marvelled Viviana.

Having traversed about a dozen spans, each measuring a good forty yards, they stopped to rest on the subsequent platform. Their arms and legs ached with the unaccustomed strain of clinging tightly to the ride ropes, urged by the knowledge that no safety cord was attached. Nothing could rescue them from a certain fall, should their grip loosen.

In the gloom far off to the right, a geometry of long triangles could be discerned indistinctly. It appeared to be an interweaving of lines strung between the tree pylons at great height. Once or twice it seemed to the travellers, peering into the dimness, that small figures moved along these lines.

After reaching the next tree they looked across to discover that the distant webs had become more complex, and traffic on them had increased. Instead of a flying fox, suspension bridges led off from this platform. They were made of wooden slats tied across a pair of parallel cables, with a single handrail of rope. The entrances of two were barred with slender cords. Through the handrails of the third, nosegays of leaves had been stuck.

'Upon my word,' exclaimed Viviana, 'this is more like it! I never thought I would joy in walking upon such a rickety affair, but after dangling from those fox ropes, this appears to be safety.'

'Mayhap 'twill lead us to the Tree-Dwellers' city,' said Caitri, glancing to the right. 'I'd as lief behold it, and them.'

To run the gamut of the suspension bridge was no mean feat, as it turned out. The whole creaking contrivance wriggled and shook like an angry watch-worm the instant the travellers set foot on it. Under the differing rhythms of their footsteps it bucked out of synchronisation and was as like as not to suddenly smack up jarringly at their boots as they put them down, or to drop away under their steps so that they stumbled. Haltingly they made their way, careful not to glance down. Between the slats a great nothingness opened to the forest floor, far below and dark-mantled. One single fortunate shaft of sunlight momentarily struck down like a gold pin through the bridge as they crossed, and the leaves continued to shower down all around, and the forest breathed uncountable sighs.

Now they could see, over to the right, what might have been a tree city. Amongst the long bridges and flying foxes and cat-walks, the elevated walkways and flyovers, the autarkens supported wider, more solid platforms. Some of these were walled. Small dwellings perched there, built close against and around the tree boles. Small oblong windows and doors showed black against the grey of the structures, and a rumour came to the ears of the companions, almost below the reaches of hearing— voices on the static airs, and perhaps the sound of singing.

'We are being led away from the tree city,' sorrowed Caitri. 'Why should they fear us?'

'Or scorn us,' said Viviana, 'or be sending us astray.'

'Why should they provide us with victuals only to lead us to ruin?' Tahquil asked.

'Perhaps they wanted to fatten us up for their larders,' responded Viviana gloomily.

'Methinks,' said Caitri, ''tis neither scorn nor fear, but a desire for privacy tempered with goodwill. They wish to speed our passage, that we might not stumble into their midst and trouble the patterns of their lives.'

'Scorn,' repeated Viviana.

A loud screech made them all jump; the bridge heaved and

undulated. From everywhere or nowhere resounded a guttural pronunciation:

'I walk with the owl
And make many to cry
As loud as she doth hollow.'

Wings juddered forth like squeaking hinges. They flapped away, to be swallowed by darkness.

'I thought there were no birds here,' said Viviana.

'That *was* no bird.'

Gingerly, with trembling knees, they set out to cross the next beflowered bridge.

It seemed that the day was closing. Pale grey leached to dark grey around and over and under the swaying, airy road. The wighting hours approached. Already, maniacal laughter tore through the trees, punctuated by simpering giggles and tortured groans.

Almost sumptuously, the next platform was surrounded by a low wall. It was laden with fruits, foliage, flowers and rain-filled gourds.

'Here we may sleep without fear of falling,' said Viviana gratefully.

They feasted, sipping a drop of the seemingly inexhaustible dragon's blood as the evening drew chill. Taking turns to stand watch that night they saw, further off, tiny lights moving, up in the remote heights away to the right, which they had begun to call the east. The Tree-Dwellers' city.

Closer at hand, the forest's emanations were more eldritch. Sweet, wild music came spiralling on the cool draughts, a music that tugged at the heartstrings, its cadences evoking lost loves and lonely mountain tarns in the moonlight. At the same time, way down below, something out of sight went clanking across the forest floor, shuffling, as if chained and gyved and fettered in iron.

In the pit of night the lights of the tree city blinked out, one by one. Silence settled in, except for the incessant susurration of leaves. Tahquil, who was on watch, remembered a place where harps and flutes resounded, and sweet voices sang—yet, trying to recapture the fleeting images of the Fair Realm was as hopeless as trying to hold water in a sieve, as vain as trying to fashion ropes from sand, as futile as reaping with a sickle of leather.

Tirnan Alainn—Faêrie.

How should I so love a place? she thought. *A land of dream and legend, perhaps no more tangible than dreams and legends— a land which lies beyond the stars, and which is no more suited for my dwelling place than the sea is fit to be my abode. Why should I waste and weary and pine for a shining jewel that can never be grasped? Surely the rough homespun and coarse bread, yea, even the cool silks and Sugar-cakes of Erith ought to be enough for me. Yet, the Langothe overrides both my aversion to the Faêran and my love for my native land. It pulls the tide of my blood and that I cannot change. Something in the very core of my being responds to its call—a recollection that seems to come from before my birth. It is like some powerful race-memory that awakens and reaches forth and, unavailing, mourns. For when I first set eyes on the Fair Realm, it seemed I had always known it. I recognised every tree and cloud, every lake and mountain as my heart's desire. Now would I go thence, if I could, like a shotten arrow.*

She wondered again how long it would take for the Langothe to claim her life. Some of the children of Hythe Mellyn had succumbed within weeks of their return to Erith. Others had lingered for months, slowly fading. She, Tahquil, endured constant pain, and victuals held no relish for her. Yet her strength had not yet waned. Perhaps it was some property of Thorn's ring, or maybe part of the arcane gift Nimriel had bestowed on her in the Realm. Whatever the reason, the Langothe did not seem to be killing her as swiftly as she had expected.

On her finger, the gold ring tightened.

The sharp smack of a whip sliced the darkness. Tahquil peered over the edge of the stage, between the armouring of flabellate spikes. Shrunk by distance and lit by its own ghastly luminescence, a coach and four raced through the trees. The driver on the box wore a three-cornered hat and a short cape. What rode within the black coach Tahquil could not discern. The conveyance slowed to a halt and then rolled slightly backwards, in the manner of all wheeled vehicles finding their point of rest. In that similarity was the only commonality between the black equipage and more *lorraly* turnouts.

A door opened.

A boot weighed heavily on a step. A second dented the dank mould of the forest floor. Now a statue stood beside the coach. Motionless, the horses stood also, and the driver sat ramrod straight on the box. Then, as a sphere gyrates on a swivel, the statue's head turned. One expected to hear the sound of machinery in motion.

Tahquil held her breath. Oddly, she could perceive all this quite clearly from her perch, even through the gloom. It was spread before her like a miniature scene, like clockwork figures on a table, lit by a soft, eerie radiance.

As silently as it had appeared, the sculpted form was gone. The coach rocked with the motion of a weight settling inside. The door closed, the horses moved off with an echoing clang of harness, and the whip's crack shot upwards to explode beside Tahquil's ears.

Whether this unseelie manifestation had been tracking her and her companions she could not say, but such a powerful wight, so close by, could hardly fail to pinpoint its prey. It might be supposed that, fortunately for the mortal damsels, the creature had been hunting something else; that it was not aware of mortal watchers close by, or even of their presence in the forest. Tahquil knew the carriage for the same vehicle she and Muirne had seen before the attack on Chambord's Road-Caravan. She knew it now, with the certainty of recall, to be the coach of the Cearb, that unseelie slaughterer of Men and cattle they called the Killing One.

Day after day the three wayfarers travelled along the highroads of Khazathdaur, leaving behind the mysterious village or city of the Tree-Dwellers. Sturdy, numerous bridges leading to every quarter gave way to less numerous flying foxes. The arms and shoulders of the travellers ached from the tension of gripping ropes; their sinews transmuted themselves to agonised cables of steel.

When the shang came, the autarkens took on the mellow burnish of aged gilt; a sombre sheen like the last rich rays of vintage Summer lingering languidly on sated bronze. Every falling leaf became a spangle, each rope a chain of fireflies; the canopy turned into a shimmering galaxy of green-gold. The only tableau the travellers saw was of two children gathering flowers on the forest floor where no light-loving petals had bloomed for centuries, their images existing beyond harm there on the leaf carpet which now buried them to their waists. There was no other evidence of the psychic debris that haunted scenes of passion.

Each night the forest sprang to renewed vigour with queer sights and sounds. Far below, a heartbroken sobbing would start up like a millwheel, or weird, high singing would weave resonating glass rods through the forest, or eldritch knockings and tappings would echo through the lofty vaults, emanating from down among the roots. Sometimes strange smoke rings came floating; blue-grey wreaths of vapour that moved slowly through the trees. O, O, O, they made, before some transient breath of air deformed them, like buckled wheels. High on their airy perches the travellers would shiver, bearing witness to these phenomena; however, they sensed also that they were watched over by the elusive Tree-Dwellers. Food and drink, though monotonous, were never in short supply.

Yet ever and anon they felt *other* eyes upon them. Other beings bided here in Khazathdaur, amongst the serried wooden towers, the attenuated vaults, the fluted shadows like widows' veils trailing from every soaring bough, the endlessly falling leaves drowning in a watery twilight. It was ancient, this world of neck-breaking heights and breathtaking depths unknown by wind or sunlight, and it was filled with secrets. Gnarled roots dug deep below centuries-old layers of leaf mould imprinted only by the strangest of footprints or wheel ruts, a soft, yielding compost that covered up many curious things and out of which many curious things grew . . .

In the far reaches of the forest where stands of massive oaks began to mingle with the autarkens, the smell of aniseed came pouring like a rich oil upon the air. Grey malkins were about.

Their eyes made the night into an aiode of emeralds. On the wide bands of iron nailed to the tree boles, the claws of the great cats could find no purchase. The predators yowled their frustration. Sometimes the night was further troubled by a loud ululating wail like theirs, yet almost human—Black Annis howled her dismal hungers in a cave somewhere down beneath the mould and stones. Once upon an eve there came a muttering, in a low monotone:

'Ellum he do grieve,
Oak he do hate,
Willow do walk
If you travels late.'

'Zounds,' whispered Viviana, 'was that Black Annis, d'you think?'

If travel by bridge was slow, rope and pulley was faster. Fourteen days after coming under the stasis of Timbrilfin-Khazathdaur, there came a time when, alighting skillfully on a rather unkempt and shaky platform with frayed edges, instead of being greeted with a highway signposted by leaf or flower, the travellers found that they had reached a dead end.

In any event, there was nowhere to go but back into the forest's heart or down the rickety ladder which swung against the trunk and vanished away towards the ground. It appeared that this tree was the furthest outpost of the network rigged and maintained by the Tree-Dwellers. All around, mighty tree stems continued to plumb the distance from canopy to floor in slatted hues of grey and black. Yet there was an end to the aerial roads.

A last offering of forest fare awaited the travellers, but their dismay at this turn of events blunted their appetites.

'Where to now?' mused Caitri, staring down over the crumbling, barbed edge to where perspective falsely indicated that the bases of the surrounding trees huddled close together.

'Down, by my reckoning,' replied Tahquil. 'Let us go swiftly, before night draws in—and we would be well advised to carry some of this fare with us. It may be long ere we find any other provender now that we are leaving the auspices of the Tree-Dwellers.'

'Conversely,' said Viviana, 'it may be a short while before we personally provide provender for the grey malkins of Black Annis. The claws of the lovely Dianella are seeming ever more amiable by comparison.'

'Do not underestimate that lady's weaponry,' said Tahquil.

Down the long, long ladder they went, past the iron bands that deflected predators' claws. Twenty feet from the ground the stair of rope and wood stopped short at a narrow ledge. On hooks there, a rope had been coiled, one end of which was belayed to the tree. This last distance must be descended by rappelling, with this rope passed under one thigh and over the opposite shoulder so that it might be paid out smoothly and gradually.

'I shall go first,' said Viviana. 'I am practised at this trick, for my brother and I used to clamber upon the oaks in Wytham Park when we were children, although our parents were kept ignorant of our vulgar behaviour. My lady has first braved every enterprise thus far, and it is now my turn. Should you not allow it I shall not be able to countenance myself.'

'So be it,' said Tahquil, smiling wryly at the courtier's determination. 'During my journeys in the wilderness I too have been taught somewhat of the art of rope-descent. Caitri, watch and learn. Viviana, should you spy danger, shout loudly and we will try to haul you up, although I fear there's not much leverage on this thin shelf.'

Viviana took the rope in both hands. Cordage made from the silk-smooth beards of autarken blossom did not burn the skin. She let it slip slowly through her fists. Nervously she set her boots against the trunk, gritted her teeth and leaned back with a display of confidence she scarcely recognised in herself. Pushing from the ball of her foot she walked backwards down the tree into the dreariness of everdusk. Her shoulders felt almost wrenched from their sockets. Her tensed forearms suffered a dull, sustained pain as though bruised; they trembled and threatened to lose all sensation, all power. At the last they betrayed her. The rope shot skywards through her fingers and she fell into a great drift of leaves which sprayed up like water.

Scanning the depths, her companions could see nothing.

'I am hale!' Viviana called, spitting out a leaf. 'Haul away!'

Tahquil and Caitri pulled up the rope. It occurred to Viviana that the bank of dead leaves in which she was sitting might be home to things with which she would prefer to avoid close contact. Hastily she waded out of it, thigh-deep. Tahquil came swinging down, then Caitri. By the leaf-ring's glow they looked at each other.

'Should we simply leave the rope dangling?' wondered Tahquil. 'Fain would I withhold from ground-dwellers access to the highroads of the Folk of the Trees.'

They tried tossing the rope's end back up to its hook, to no avail.

'We beg pardon,' Tahquil called softly skywards. 'We cannot close your gate.' Mindful of not thanking their benefactors in case, like wights, they took offence, she added, 'Your kindness is gratefully acknowledged. May your trees be forever fruitful.'

From the jade demi-dusk came no answer.

'Let us move on,' said Tahquil, shaking leaves from her hair. 'We can do no more, and must flee before the coming of night.'

They set off. Thick shadows were fastened like webs in the hollows between the ancient trees. All that could be seen was the light of the leaf-ring shining on their three faces. The companions could not know where they were going—only intuition guided them, a sense that they should continue to progress in the direction they had been shown by the Tree-Dwellers.

Now that they were down on the ground their sense of unease quickly turned to dread. All around, the pit of Khazathdaur festered with unclean things. The whispers of the mortals fell dead on the dank compost underfoot. As they blundered forward their feet dragged as though weighted with stones, and they became certain some sightless horror came in pursuit, reaching out to seize them.

Viviana held the chatelaine fast folded in her cloak, so that it would not clash and ring. Their boots sank to the ankles in the top layers of leaves. Underneath, decomposed mould had compacted to form a springy firmness. They waded through piles and mounds built up by the steady sibilant showers cascading gently from a canopy now so far above it was lost to view. Tiny spores of apprehension came clinging over them and took root and grew into a clammy terror which burdened their limbs until it seemed they could no longer go forward but must sink down on the forest floor, doomed to perish in the damning weald.

Then from afar, a call. It was the winding of a horn.

At once, as though at a signal, the air stirred. A light breeze had entered the forest. Down this new airstream it came again—the long, clear note that seemed to come sweeping over open hills under wide skies.

A third time it sounded. The travellers pushed on with renewed hope and vigour.

At last, grey light filtered through a thinning of the trees. Undergrowth sprouted in the wider spaces between the boles. Harpoons of red-gold light pierced the leaf canopy and strayed down to the murky floors, here and there picking out a quill of copper, a nib of russet, a sickle of mellow gold among the fallen leaves. Clumps of juniper bushes and crepe myrtle added a dense dark green. The travellers' morale lifted at the thought of reaching the outskirts of Khazathdaur, of being able to look up and see the clear sky again and feel the wind combing their hair. Faster went they, eagerly. Now through the trees streamed the long, amber light of sunfall. Joyousness seized them—they had almost made it to the far edge of the forest!

Tahquil's hand flew up. A shock went through the ring, and a '*ping!*' as though a sharp blow had struck it. Almost simultaneously, Viviana jumped sideways with a shouted exclamation, losing her grip on the implements hanging from her belt.

'Something hit me! It hit my knapsack!'

An agitation whipped the bushes all around. Like vengeful wasps, invisible projectiles shrilled through the air. Puffs and eddies of leaves showed where they were hitting the ground. Disturbing the undergrowth, red caps like tall mushrooms poked up. Beneath them were the sly faces of tiny archers.

The travellers bolted. Sharp points whizzed past their ears. Unseen darts struck their thick cloaks, and deflected off Tahquil's ring. One ricocheted off Caitri's belt and another off Viviana's chatelaine. The soft mulch hampered their running feet like sludge, weighed down their boots, stuck to their leggings. It seemed certain, after all, that they would never get out of Khazathdaur, when abruptly the tree stems diverged and fell back on either side. They burst forth into the open.

Caitri uttered a sharp cry and fell sprawling.

'Get up! Come!' her companions urged, endeavouring to drag her to her feet. Ælf-shot whistled all around. Caitri writhed on the ground, clutching her shin. Tahquil threw off her pack, heedless of scattering foodstuffs. She hoisted the little girl under the armpits and dragged her away. Viviana snatched the knapsack and followed, using both packs as a shield against the darts that zoomed from the forest.

Down a grassy slope they struggled. Caitri now hung limp in Tahquil's arms, a dead weight. The shooting decreased as the targets drew out of range, and finally, when for the space of about fifty yards there had been no more *thumps* of eldritch arrows hitting bundles, Tahquil heard Viviana cry, 'Hola! The attack is over. Stop, so that I may help you.'

Beside dense low clusters of yellow-flowered gorse Tahquil gently laid Caitri down on the grey-green grass and leaned over her.

'She has taken a stroke!' wailed Viviana. 'She will be paralysed!'

'Cait, can you hear me?' Tahquil said tenderly.

Caitri's eyelids fluttered open. Her face was grey and drawn.

'I am hale,' she whispered thickly. She tried to rise, but collapsed with a groan. 'There is no feeling in my leg, my arm . . .'

'Bide,' said Tahquil. 'We shall lift and bear you.'

She did not mention that one side of the little girl's face was dragged down and half her mouth remained slack when she spoke. The child looked like a doll fashioned half of porcelain and half of rags, limp down one side. Tahquil knew they must bear her away from the dangers of the forest. But where could they go?

Against the slanting, nasturtium-tinted rays of the westering sun Tahquil stood, shading her eyes with her hand. A light, fresh breeze raced across the grassy hillside. Rank upon rank of silvery grass blades bent their backs to it in waves tumbling down to a wide vista below.

Tahquil looked to the north. From her feet the land ran down in a gentle slope towards a long, narrow inlet. Here, the sea sliced into the land from miles away on the western coast, cutting a deep valley filled with still waters the colour of steel. Half tinged gold in the fallow afternoon, clean flinty rock-cliffs fell steep and stark from the heights into the firth. Seabirds glided on outstretched wings, in the shape of *margran*, the M-rune. Low hills rose to the east and west and also across the firth to the north. At the head of the inlet the land rose gently to a marshy vale watered by rills which fed a fast-flowing brook chattering down out of the hills to the ocean.

Near at hand, towards this vale, the countryside was chequered with little verdant meadows. They were bordered by blossoming hawthorn hedges, screened by sallows and alders. Clotted with the flowers of late Spring were they, and so lush that already the grass stood high. Down along the inlet's edge a few thatched roofs peeped from dark-smudged lines of trees. Smoke issued from chimneys like wisps of wool, and were teased out by the breeze.

'A village,' croaked Tahquil, hoarse with relief. 'An abode of Men in the wilderness. We must go there—I'll warrant they sustain a healer—a carlin or a dyn-cynnil.' She glanced back and up at the tall, sinister eaves of the forest from whose dominions they had so narrowly escaped. The trees leaned forward.

'Via, we must cross our hands over and grasp each other's wrists, in this manner, to form a seat. We must hold Caitri's poor arms about our shoulders and thus we may bear her down the hill.'

Just then the sun sank into the dyed ocean far beyond the hills and a deep, throaty voice said, 'Stay!'

The admonition issued from a large, hairy creature like an oversized bruney. He was dressed raggedly, like a household wight, but about five feet tall, deep-chested, massive across the shoulders. His superb physique indicated enormous strength.

'Run!' contradicted Viviana. Starting forward she began to drag

Caitri along, a helpless burden. Without appearing to move, the wight barred their path.

'They call me seelie,' he said. 'Down by Ishkiliath, they do. I can cure the ælf-stroke, I can. Give me the girl.' He grinned a gaping, thick-lipped grin.

'Set her down, Via,' said Tahquil, deliberately avoiding the use of her friend's full name. She did not take her eyes from the wight as Viviana lowered Caitri to the grass.

To him she said, 'Can you in truth do as you say?'

'Aye, that I can.'

'Do not let him touch her,' hissed Viviana.

Tahquil hesitated. 'What else do they call you, down there in the village?'

The uncouth fellow bowed.

'Finoderee at your service, miss. I plough, I sow, I reap, I mow. I herd cattle and sheep, I thresh and rake and carry, I build stacks. I can clear a daymath in an hour and want nothing better than a crockful of bithag afterwards. I work all night, but at the top of Glen Rushen, above the curraghs, that's where I curl me up in my hiding place each day. I can heal a weal and cure an ill too, and I can cure this mortal girl.'

'Well sir, you give a thorough account of yourself and no mistake,' said Tahquil guardedly. 'A strong fellow I see you be, with a kindly feeling towards humanity. If I let you cure her, what will you ask in return for your pains?'

Finoderee's chunky jaw dropped open, his eyes widened in shock.

'Alas, poor Finoderee, don't send him away! He only wants to help!'

'No reward, then,' said Tahquil quickly, alarmed at his unpredictable distress. 'Howbeit, if you can cure her and not harm her in the process . . .'

'I'd like a word wi' ye if I may, lassie,' politely said the urisk, who was sitting beneath a gorse bush. Tahquil, taken aback at the unexpected appearance of their friend, approached him while Viviana stood guard over Caitri, glaring at Finoderee. He was shuffling his huge, hairy feet in the grass.

'Och, the cure is simple,' murmured the urisk confidentially. 'Ye mun find the piece o' ælf-shot that struck the lassie and gie it her, and she'll jump up as sonsie as ever. They dinnae lodge in the flesh, those bits o' shot. It'll be lying aboot somewhere. Dinnae let Finoderee find it first—that is my rede. He cured Dan Broome's red cow all reet but carried it off afterwards. But yon linkin' birkie's mightier in thew than in brain, ye ken? He will do your biding gin he is able, and a mollymawk the likes o' he might be easily gulled.'

Tahquil nodded gratefully to the urisk.

'Finoderee,' she said clearly, 'we do need your help. Please take this,' she unhooked the silver spike-leaf strainer from Viviana's chatelaine while its owner spluttered indignantly, 'and fill it with water from that stream and bring it back.'

Energetically, Finoderee loped off across the hillside with the chatelette in his hand.

'My silver sieve!'

'Quickly, Viviana—we must find the arrowhead that gave Caitri the stroke.'

Backtracking up the hill, they crawled about on the long tussocks. The urisk joined the search.

'What should it look like?' asked Tahquil, on all fours, fossicking.

'Bother, I cannot see anything anyway, 'tis too dark,' said Viviana. 'And you've sent that Finoderee fellow on a fool's errand. When he realises the task is impossible he will return in wrath!'

'Not he,' rejoined the urisk. 'T' only thing that gets him of a pother is criticism of his wark. If that happens ye must look to yourself, for he can be spiteful. If ye've put him tae summat he can no' do then it can be no' criticised, eh?'

'Here's something,' said Viviana. 'Ouch, 'tis a gorse prickle. Nay, I have it, I think!' She held up a triangular shard of flint, its edges dighted as thin and sharp as any metal blade.

'Weel done,' approved the urisk. Viviana ran down and gave her find to Caitri, who received it in her sound hand and touched it to her paralysed leg. Hope changed to despair on her face and a dewdrop tear squeezed from the corner of her eye, catching mercurial reflections of the first stars.

'Tith no uthe,' she lisped.

'Dinnae be fashed,' said the urisk encouragingly. 'We shall just luik wi' a stronger e'e—that's all there is to it.'

'You have night vision,' Tahquil said to him, 'have you not?'

'Aye, but I cannae see through thick tuffets o' bent. I'm no' of Faêran bluid, ye ken!'

'That nuggety wight will be coming back any moment now,' wailed Viviana, 'and if he finds the right flint he shall carry off Caitri. If nobody finds it Caitri shall be maimed for life!'

Scrabbling around, the urisk came up with a handful of arrow-heads. He galloped to the side of the prostrate patient.

'Here ye go, lassie!'

Caitri tried them all, again and again, to no effect.

'I think I could hop down the hill, if I might lean on thome-one,' she said.

'Nonsense,' said Tahquil. 'The thing must be hereabouts, somewhere.'

She gave Caitri a sip of *nathrach deirge*, and in doing so touched her left hand to Caitri's side. A pressure exerted itself on the leaf-ring. Walking up the slope, Tahquil let the pressure direct her hand, into the dry, soughing grass stems. Down among their roots her fingers met a fragment, hard and cold.

'I have found another,' she said. She placed it in Caitri's hand.

No moon showed on the horizon on this the last-but-one day of the month and also of Spring. From the curraghs at the head of the valley, nocturnal marsh birds hooted. More stars came out, scattering their reflections like flaws over the glassy waters of the firth below. The leaves at the eaves of Khazathdaur rustled and the trees soared, uninviting, black against the stars.

'The forest wakens,' softly said the urisk.

Tahquil was watching Caitri intently. The little girl smiled. She stood up.

'It was the one,' she said, opening her fist to show them the piece of ælf-shot. 'Oh—it has crumbled to sand!'

'All tae the good,' said the urisk briskly. 'It can harm naebody else.'

Viviana laughed with relief. She and Tahquil embraced Caitri.

'Feater advice was never given,' said Tahquil tactfully to the urisk, wanting to thank him but bearing in mind that he might be insulted by thanks, as wights apparently were.

'You came in goodly time, but how came you here?' Caitri asked the little goat-man.

'I hae no head for heights. I came along byways through the forest,' he hooted. 'I have wandered it lang enow that I ken it weel. Howsoever, the lands of Ishkiliath are my real hame, or they were once.'

'And those who dwell in the village down there—would they be kind to three wayfarers?'

'Mortal strangers hardly ever come tae Appleton Thorn by land. The only foreigners they meet are sailors coming by boat, up frae the sea. The villagers will squint at ye sideways but most o' them be reasonable sorts of folk.'

A couple of lights stippled the night, down amongst the lines of trees along the cliffs.

'Now,' continued the urisk, 'get along wi' ye. Ye're standing on the banks o' Creech Hill and a bullbeggar haunts here sometimes. Besides, ye're still on the borders o' Arda Musgarh Dubh and its tall population has lang roots.'

'Yet its small archers are bad shots,' said Viviana. 'Fortunately.'

Tahquil wondered about the village. *Should I walk down there amongst humankind? Will there be spies of the Prince Morragan, to recognise and betray me? Few wights dwell within human settlements—mainly domestic solitaries, usually seelie and untravelled, for they do not willingly stray from their Places. I might be safer in that village than anywhere, and yet . . .*

At their backs, the black curtain of the ancient forest stood silent, like an unvoiced spell. The helpful Fenodoree remained a small blob in the starlight, still kneeling beside the stream. His tuneless singing wafted across the slope:

'If ye call me imp or elf
I rede ye look well to yourself.
If ye call me fary,
I'll bait ye long and weary.

If good neighbour ye call me,
Then good neighbour I will be,
But if ye call me seelie wight
I'll be your friend both day and night.'

The three travellers picked up their belongings. The night wind plucked at their hair and the corners of their garments. Now four, they strode down the hill towards Appleton Thorn on the high cliffs of the Grey Glass Firth, and the slender grasses sighed at their passing.

2
ISHKILIATH
Field and Fen and Mortal Men

In mountain caves the bat-winged worm, a thousand époques old,
With furnace breath and jewelled hide lies coiled around his gold,
While on the ocean's gleaming foam a giant shell unfurls.
Behold! A mermaid sleeps within, more marvellous than pearls.

With passion warm as dragonfire, with benthic mystery,
They kindle mortalkind's desire—the silkies of the sea.

OLD SONG OF TAMHANIA

The piquancy of the salt sea and the pungent aroma of seaweed cast up on the rocks stung the wind. Straggling atop and down the cliffs, sheltered by hardy firs and rowans, the village of Appleton Thorn was protected on the landward side by a semicircular fence. This was no ordinary fence, but a mighty fortified palisade of oak and ash, studded and barbed and bound with iron. Eleven feet high it stood, overlooked by small watch-houses built in the treetops just inside the perimeter.

'There is an East Gate and a West Gate,' said the urisk, leading the three travellers to the left. 'The heathery coast road runs frae the West Gate. The road to the east leads tae the rigs and the corries of the Churrachan, the sykie risks, the heigh gowan banks and the foggie braes. No gate has ever been made in the southern wa' o' the Fence. There's nae road rising to the glaury choille-rais.'

'We ken only the Common Tongue,' said Tahquil. 'Make plain your meaning, prithee sir.'

'Och, I'm forgettin'. *Rigs* are what ye might call fields, a *sykie risk's* a marshland, a curragh. *Banks* and *braes*, them's slopes and dales to ye. I must mind my tongue—things hae changed since last I spoke wi' your kind.' He sighed. 'And as to the rest—there's no road up Creech Hill to the forest because naebody frae the village goes there and most things that come frae out o' Arda's shades are no' welcome among Men.'

'I see no Mooring Mast either. Why do they choose to dwell in such a remote and forsaken place,' asked Caitri, 'and so close to Khazathdaur?'

'The forefathers of the villagers lived here in greater numbers once,' replied the urisk. 'As years went by and things o' unseelie ilk pushed deeper into these regions, many o' the villagers departed. Those who remained did so because this is their land, or mayhap because of the Thorn.'

Tahquil's heart hung static over a beat.

'What Thorn?' she said quickly.

'The Noble Thorn they title it—a lone tree growing in the Errechd, at the heart of the village. 'Tis said it is the only one of its kind. It puts forth flooers only once a year, at middle-night on Littlesun Eve. At that season, sailors sometimes come in their boats up the firth to see it.'

The travellers arrived at the Fence and followed it around to the West Gate without being hailed from the lookout posts in the trees. Only a rumour of conversation emanated dimly from the village precincts.

'Tomorrow's Flench Ridings Eve,' remarked the urisk. 'They're likely all clatterin' at the tavern this night, singin' cuttie-muns.'

The gate was as tall as the Fence, a grille of wood and steel bars.

'Here I'll leave ye,' said the urisk. 'The haunts o' Men are dear to me but I walk them in my own way.'

'Oh, but shall we see you again?' stammered Viviana.

'Aye, if ye wish it.' The urisk seemed shyly pleased.

'Farewell,' they said.

He bowed and trotted away through the darkness into a stand of feathery peppercorns.

Caitri turned suddenly and looked over her shoulder, back towards the forest. 'I thought I heard footsteps following,' she said.

Tahquil took a deep breath and shouted towards the gate, 'Hallo! Please let us in—we are benighted wayfarers seeking hospitality!'

This announcement was greeted by sudden tumult on the other side of the gate. It sounded like someone heavily armed, falling out of a tree. This cacophony was followed by a subdued cursing and a clanking of metal.

'Who goes there?' a man's voice eventually shouted.

'Three wayfarers seeking hospitality,' repeated Tahquil.

'Stand back nine yards from the gate!' came the order.

They obeyed. From a wooden boxlike affair nesting above the Fence in the fork of a tree, a figure wearing a brightly polished open helmet surveyed them. This figure exchanged remarks with a party on the ground near the tree's foot, then a large nose appeared through the bars of the gate.

'Advance and be recognised!'

Forward now they stepped again. They could hear the guard in the tree saying, 'Certain, are ye?' and the guard on the ground mumbling unintelligibly.

'Are ye wights of eldritch?' challenged Big Nose, peering through the gate.

'No. We are mortal damsels.'

'All of ye?'

'Yes.'

A further raucous clangour ensued; a laborious unbolting, unlatching, unchaining and unlocking up and down the length of the mighty gate. With one last crunch, a small portal in the gate swung open. Big Nose's head popped around it and he jerked his chin in the direction of his shoulder, a gesture the travellers interpreted as permission to enter.

'Look lively then,' he said. 'Can't leave the door open all night.'

Ducking their heads under the low lintel, the visitors entered.

Big Nose quickly shut the postern after them, securing it again with much fuss. Meanwhile, Bright Helm hurried down his ladder, which was missing a few rungs, and stood looking at the new-comers with undisguised awe.

Both the gate guards were clad in loose-fitting tunics belted at the middle, taltry hoods with camails and cross-gartered breeches tucked into boots. Over this they wore half-armour; thick leather tassets and epauliers. One had on a worn leather brigandine dec-orated with bright studs where metal plates were riveted to the interior; the other sported a mail hauberk of antique design. Thick and brown, their hair straggled to their shoulders. They were armed with falchions, broadswords and halberds, and a thorn tree sigil was emblazoned on their gear.

At their backs, some forty paces off, stood an ivy-covered tav-ern—it was from here that the sounds of conversation had issued. Tangerine lamplight glowed from its leaded casements. The sign over the door bore a painted image of a thorn tree, black-boughed and spiky.

The mouths of the guards hung open. Tahquil shifted uncom-fortably under their stares, until one man elbowed the other in the ribs and they recovered their composure. Their eyes slid briefly over Tahquil's companions but kept rolling back to her like ball bearings to a lodestone.

Bright Helm cleared his throat.

'Well I'll be jiggered,' he said, scratching his ear. 'I never seen the like. Three young maids a-traipsing over the countryside on their own—well I never. I suppose you heard the Forest Horn a-blowing.'

'You'll be here for Flench Ridings,' surmised Big Nose, 'and the Bawming of the Thorn on the morrow, with Burning the Boatman. You'll have come up the coast road, off a ship. Will you be stay-ing for the other Summer celebrations?'

'Regrettably, no,' replied Tahquil without depriving him of his assumptions. 'We are but travelling through.'

'Ah.' Bright Helm tapped the side of his nose with a stubby fin-ger and winked knowingly, in the manner of one who is privy to knowledge so common it need not be questioned further. Tahquil guessed he had no idea why three damsels might be 'travelling through', but presumed that everyone else did, and was loath to reveal his ignorance.

'Are rooms available at the inn?' she inquired.

'Most assuredly, mistress!'

Bright Helm flew along the path ahead of them, to be the first to announce the Arrival of Strangers. Big Nose stolidly brought up the rear with the air of a seasoned campaigner who would not allow Unexpected Visitors to interfere with Duty.

'Burning the Boatman?' Caitri whispered nervously in Tahquil's ear. 'Are these folk so barbaric?'

'I think not,' Tahquil replied. 'I suspect it is a title for some less excessive custom.'

The uproar triggered by Bright Helm's advance warning instantly broke off when Tahquil and her companions entered the yellow torchlight of the tavern's common room.

Dirty, stained and ragged the travellers appeared, this being partly self-inflicted for purposes of disguise and partly imposed by the exigencies of travel. Before them, the room presented a motionless tableau: drinkers poised with tankards upraised, folk sitting, standing, immobilised in the act of turning around, jaws dangling loosely, eyes protruding.

All at once Tahquil felt very weary and wished they had not entered there.

'What's amiss, lads? Ain't ye ever seen a *miss* before?'

The pun-maker, a doughty man, sun-browned, stood with his thumbs hooked through his belt. In contrast to the snuff-brown locks of the other patrons, his silky mane of hair was a soft shade of grey, streaked with silver as though it had aged before its time, for his face was that of a young man of perhaps eight-and-twenty Winters.

Laughing but shamefaced, the patrons buried their noses in their beer. The hum of talk and the clatter of tavern business resumed. Now covertly, the customers observed the three visitors, squinting sideways, as the urisk had augured.

The doughty man nodded affably.

'Wassail and welcome to Appleton Thorn by Grey Glass Firth,' he said with a cheerful grin. 'I hight Arrowsmith, Master of the Village and Lord of the Hundred. Will you sup this night?'

'That is indeed our wish, sir. Gramercie.'

While Arrowsmith called for meat and drink, places were found for the newcomers. After guardedly introducing themselves as 'Mistress Mellyn', 'Mistress Wellesley' and 'Mistress Lendoon', they sat down, unnerved by the excess of attention. It was not long before every customer at the inn had found a reason to gather around their table. Big Nose, his post forgotten, was saying authoritatively, 'They have come for Flench Ridings and the Bawming of the Thorn. They have come up the coast road, off a ship.'

Everyone contributed.

'We don't get many ships these days—I reckon only two or three a year.'

'And after that storm, the terrible one when the sky went all black for days and the waves came up big, right to the cliff tops like never was seen before, well, we ain't seen a single ship since.'

'Give us tidings—what news from the world?'

'The Royal Island of Tamhania has been destroyed by unseelie forces,' the travellers said. 'Its downfall was the centre of the storm. Meanwhile the armies of the King-Emperor amass in the east. Skirmishes and small engagements have been fought, but as yet no great battle, when last we heard.'

By the time the taverner's wife planted heaped platters on the table, the audience was packed tightly around. Arrowsmith waved them away.

'Allow our guests to dine in peace, gentlefolk. Give them room to lift their elbows! You, Wimblesworthy and Ironmonger, are you not on guard at the West Gate tonight? Hasten back to your post. Bowyer, give us a song by the chimney.'

Sheepishly, Big Nose and Bright Helm hurried out. Enthused at being called upon to entertain the guests, Bowyer stepped up on a three-legged stool, tidied his jerkin, puffed out his chest, waited for the talk to subside and began to sing:

'All was hushed in the Mountain Hall as the Jester told his tale
But outside in the bitter cold a voice began to wail.
The Jester told of the Great High Road that goes forever on,
Winding by the greenwood trees and past the Ring of Stone.

'Through the rocky mountain gate, along the jagged ridge
Past the dark well of the fire, across the iron bridge.
And who would travel this long road with lamp and staff in hand?
'Tis Jack the soldier seeking for the Door to the Lost Land.

'Three coins within his pocket and a raven on his shoulder.
The rival's sword hangs at his side—the South Wind's blowing
    colder.
And when at last he reached Road's End, 'twas at the eleventh
    hour.
The storm raged in the darkling sky ahint the blackened tower.

'"And who art thou," the Watchman cried, "that knocketh at
    my door?
For now that thou hast raised your hand thy fate is sealed for
    sure."
The soldier raised his sword on high—a rune was writ thereon.
The thunderstorm fled swift away, and a bright star shone.'

When Bowyer finished, everyone applauded and called for
another. The words '. . . *seeking for the Door to the Lost Land*'
unsettled Tahquil, but in the noisy tavern there was no opportunity to ponder them further. Bowyer had a second ditty well under
way when, without warning, the door crashed open.
Wimblesworthy rushed in with a frightened look and asked for the
loan of a crossbow—
    'To shoot a Shock which hangs upon the West Gate!'
    'A Shock, is it?' cried the inn patrons. 'That's what comes of
leaving the gate unattended!'
    They all poured out of the Thorn Tree, following
Wimblesworthy to the gate. Out of curiosity Tahquil joined them,
Arrowsmith striding close at her side.
    A thing with a donkey's head and a smooth velvet hide hung
on the wooden middle rung of the grille. Beyond it hung the dark,
with which it seemed to merge. Holding aloft their blazing torches,
the onlookers stood in a semicircle regarding this phenomenon
from a few yards away.

'What *is* a Shock exactly?' asked Bowyer, frowning at the apparition.

Nobody knew. They could only say that things like that were called Shocks.

'Why don't ye use yer falchion?' suggested someone.

'*You* use yer falchion!' said Wimblesworthy aggrievedly. 'You get close to it then!'

'You're such a maukin, Wimblesworthy,' said a drinker who had carried his tankard out with him and still had it in his hand. 'You'd be frightened of a chicken. What's the use of having a whey-blood like him on guard, Arrowsmith?'

'I'll show you *maukin*!' growled Wimblesworthy. 'I'll sneak up and grab it and take it to the inn to get a good look at it. Then you'll find out what a Shock is.'

'Aye, go on Wimblesworthy,' they all encouraged, since there was little entertainment to be had from a Shock that did nothing but hang on a gate. 'Do it!'

Emboldened by the support of his companions, Big Nose crept forward. As he seized the thing, it turned suddenly around, snapped at his hand and vanished.

Wimblesworthy bellowed. He jigged about, cradling his hand to his chest. His friends ran to his aid, lifting him bodily and carrying him back to the inn with all speed. Arrowsmith ordered that the gate guard be relieved and doubled.

The last of the crowd trailed back to the Thorn Tree.

'What a night!' said Ironmonger, shaking his helmeted head in wonderment. 'First Strangers, then a Shock. Well I never. What next?'

'What next indeed?' cried Arrowsmith. 'With all these goings-on it would be safer for these three young ladies to stay in a well-protected house such as my own. My good sisters shall see that they are comfortable. What say ye, Mistress Mellyn?'

Tahquil noticed some of the men nudging each other.

'It would not be meet,' she demurred. 'Gramercie, sir.'

'Meet? I myself shall sleep in the stable, if 'tis propriety you are thinking of. You shall share the house with my sisters and no one else.'

'Except of course *tomorrow night*,' said one of the men significantly.

Arrowsmith stood as if a sudden thought had struck him.

'Aye, tomorrow night. Well, we shall take that as it comes. I insist that you accept my offer of hospitality—after all, it would be less costly for you.'

In her turn, a sudden thought struck Tahquil. How much money did she and her companions carry? Did they have enough even to pay for the food they had eaten that evening?

'Well sir, if your sisters agree—'

'Of course they shall agree!' laughed the village's Master. 'Now we shall fetch your companions from the inn and wend home forthwith!'

At the Thorn Tree, the wounded man sat with his hand plunged in a flagon of beer while the taverner's wife mopped his brow.

'Let's see what's to be done,' said the wife.

Bravely, Wimblesworthy lifted his damaged extremity. Beer, mixed with blood, dripped down his sleeve gaily, like red feathers.

'Ah, look at that!' admired the inn patrons. 'He'll bear the scar of that bite on his thumb for the rest of his life, no doubt.'

Discovering that he lived yet and furthermore was branded with a badge of courage, the hero managed a watery smile.

'Who's a maukin now, Cooper?' he sniffed.

No sooner had Tahquil, Viviana and Caitri stepped out of the inn door accompanied by Arrowsmith and several others, than one of the new gate guards came up to them wearing a puzzled look.

'Finoderee's at the West Gate, Arrowsmith,' he reported. 'Says he's got summat for these misses here.'

'A busy night at the gate.' The Master of the Village turned to his protégées. 'Can this be?'

'Yes,' replied Tahquil. 'It is possible.'

They returned again to the West Gate. Through the bars, Finoderee held up a muddy, dripping object in his huge paw.

'I did it!' he said triumphantly. 'Though 'tis only a drop. Had to put a bit of clay-mud in the holes first. It wants mending, ye know.'

Viviana grabbed the silver spike-leaf strainer.

'Don't spill the water,' warned the wight.

'Well done,' said Tahquil. 'We now have all we require. Goodnight.'

Finoderee did not leave the gate. He stood nodding at Caitri. Tahquil saw that the men were laughing silently.

'You gave Finoderee a little sieve to bring water?' Arrowsmith said. 'Best jest I've heard since last Peppercorn Rent!'

'Hallo Master Arrowsmith,' said Finoderee. 'I'll be mowing your alder-meadow tonight.'

'Aye, and I'm sure I don't know what I'd do without your help,' said Arrowsmith.

'I am the hardest worker you've ever seen, ain't I?' said Finoderee.

'Surely,' agreed the Master. 'Well, you'd better be getting to that meadow now. The night's wearing on and cock-crow's not long away.'

'I don't mind cock-crow. I'll toss the hay to the fading moon or the star of morning and care not a whit for the rooster's alarm.'

'Finoderee is the wonder and no mistake,' eulogised the men.

Satisfied, the brawny wight loped off.

After the exciting events of the evening, the travellers spent a restful night at Arrowsmith's house, an oak-timbered building with a thatched roof, high gables, low side walls and mullioned windows. His sisters, Betony and Sorrel, welcomed them as he had guaranteed; he had sent a message on ahead and they had bade the servant air extra featherbeds in preparation. Their brother slept in the stable, keeping his promise.

As usual the Langothe would not permit sleep to come easily to Tahquil. While she lay in her bed looking through the window at the moon-sheen of the night sky she was reminded of the colour of Thorn's eyes.

On the morrow, it was so pleasant to wake upon goosedown, to bathe in hot water and to be served with cowslip wine, barley bread, fried kippers, and ducks' eggs—boiled with a handful of gorse flowers to dye them yellow—instead of cold forest leaves, that Viviana and Caitri begged Tahquil to consider staying in the village for a day or two. Added to these pleas were the blandishments of the villagers, who insisted that their guests remain for their forthcoming annual celebrations. Under such pressure, Tahquil yielded, although it cost her dearly and the Langothe had its cruel say. In her heart, the last Gate to Faêrie called.

Moreover, the east itself called, for she hoped with the fervency of life itself that Thorn remained safe and well. She prayed that he had not fallen victim to the wiles and treacherous glamours of unseelie wights, who would be certain to target the leader of their foes. Despite herself she constantly pictured him as he might appear at the fields of conflict, if he lived; James XVI, King-Emperor, mounted on his armoured war-horse Hrimscathr, the sword Arcturus scabbarded at his side and its damasked quillons catching the sun's rays. Thus he came to her mind's eye, shining in the steel field-armour of the era, with its slender, elegant lines and cusped borders and shell-like rippling, damascening glinting on the lames; with studded metal roses connected by riveted laminations to shoulder, elbow and knee, and adorning the breastplate. The Lion of D'Armancourt roared upon his breast—a great golden lion, gorged with an antique crown. His open-faced burgonet was crested with a panache of herons' hackles threaded with gold. A lambrequin of purple sarcenet hung down from the back of the helm, embroidered with tiny gold trefoils. Beneath the steel nose-guard there would be a glimpse of high cheekbones, the strong chin, the eyes as keen as knife blades. Perhaps he would smile at one of his captains and then the lean lines of laughter would appear at each corner of his mouth. The Royal Attriod in their plumed splendour would surround him, armoured cap-a-pie, light splintering off richly ornamented chausses, vambraces, coudieres, genouilliers, tassets, gauntlets. Flanked by standard-bearers, a trumpeter, the Legions of Eldaraigne and battalions from the armies of every country in Erith with their banners and gonfalons, their gay pennons unfolding their points along the breeze, the King-Emperor might look towards the wide lands sweeping to the sea and that jealously guarded strategic jewel, the Nenian Landbridge. And they would all await the coming of the Hordes of Namarre.

Long ago in Tiriendor, in what now seemed happier days, Thorn had spoken of Namarre.

'The Dainnan are everywhere at this time—even scouting in Namarre to pick up what information they can regarding this Namarran brigand Chieftain who is said to have arisen, who seems to have the power to unite the disparate factions of outlaws and outcasts—indeed, it is thought that he must be a wizard of great power, to draw even the fell creatures of eldritch to his aid—that, or he promises them great reward, such as the sacking of all humanity, save only his own supporters. If so, he is sadly deluded, for unseelie wights would as soon turn on him as on the rest of humankind.'

Diarmid had said, *'Never before in history has man been allied with the unseelie.'*

Thorn's reply: *'Never.'*

As she recalled these words, a cold dread clutched Tahquil-Ashalind.

'It is he,' she whispered to herself. 'It must be Morragan who allies unseelie and seditionist brigands against us in Namarre. What hope have all our armies against the terrible power of a Faêran Prince? Cry mercy! Only I can rid Erith of the Raven.'

And she wondered how many of his spies walked among mortals, and whether any lodged at Appleton Thorn. Then she wanted to leave immediately, but she had already given her word that they would tarry.

On that day, the last of Spring, she and her companions were taken to visit every corner of the village on its perch high above the sea-arm of long, cold pewter.

Past the heather-thatched cottages they wandered, where gardens burgeoned with the season's adornments of foxgloves, pansies and marigolds, and honeysuckle twined the walls with sweet-scented prettiness. Children whistled tunes on white deadnettle stalks or willow stems, and sucked the nectar out of flowers, and played Fighting Cocks with the stems of ribwort plantain. On porches washed with saffron sunlight, elderly women sat weaving withy-baskets, while old men fashioned ropes from marram grass.

By the duck pond to the Errechd the visitors walked. The Errechd was the Assembly Place in the village square where, all alone, grew the Noble Thorn with its lichen-covered boughs. The ancient tree seemed to bow down beneath the weight of accumulated knowledge, the tips of its twigs almost touching the lawn. Now they were misted with new, green leaves.

Later, down the precipitous stair cut zigzag into the living cliffs the three damsels were guided, to where small boats lay at anchor in the scoop of a bay. Waves surged up and down, hanging pale waterfalls all along the lower rocks. Wavelets made white frills on leaden water and frilled gulls chalked white waves on a sky of slate.

Nine canoes floated out on the firth, fragile vessels made of untanned animal skins stretched over a framework of hazel or willow withies. In each boat a man was standing, holding a short-bladed scythe with a handle twelve feet long. The men dipped the scythes under the water and severed the ribbons of seaweed, then with a rack they gathered it out of the water into the boat. Others on the shore were cutting rock seaweed that grew at the base of the cliffs, where it was exposed at low tide. Nodding donkeys walked up the cliff stair carrying panniers filled with kelp and dulse, wrack, oar weed and laver. Far away, out in the deep channels, fishing boats rocked like curled leaves on the grey water.

'The firth is calm, most days,' said the water bailiff, one of the guests' guides, 'but Gentle Annie haunts these parts and she can be treacherous. We are well protected from the north and the east but Annie is apt to blow unexpected squalls through a gap in the hills. Many's the time on a fine, calm morning the fishermen have been tempted out on the water, only to encounter a sudden violent gale, sweeping in and endangering the boats. Annie's sister Black Annis lurks beyond Creech Hill, deep in the heart of Khazathdaur, but she raids us when her hunger grows.'

'Do you have a protector, a wizard?' asked Viviana.

'We have a dyn-cynnil who is learned in wight-lore. Webweaver is his name—we call him Spider.'

Up to the sheep-pricked meadows they rode on horseback, to

survey Finoderee's work of the previous night. The steward, reeve and bailiff accompanied Arrowsmith, as was their wont. Along the wayside, buttercups and daisies, late harebells and amethyst clusters of grape hyacinth were still springing in the grass. Cows grazed beneath blowing showers of peppercorn trees with pale green leaves. Some stared over stone walls with the eyes of bold lasses. Wind-grazed cirrus feathered the sky with ibis' wings and five herons took startled flight from the water-meadows.

Sprouts of barley dusted the furrowed fields with powdered emeralds. A water-driven gorse mill was grinding away on the banks of the rollicking Churrachan, its heavy metal spikes crushing and bruising the boughs of whin to make feed for the horses. Further upstream squatted a fenced grain mill flanked by its stone storehouses. From the nearby steamy curraghs leaped the cool song of frogs and the hot trill of insects. Women were gathering rushes there, for making candles.

A long meadow had been scythed flat. The cut grasses lay flat in the sun, drying.

'He's too hasty,' objected Cooper, the bailiff. 'He does not cut close enough to the ground. There's a great deal of waste.'

'Nay,' laughed Arrowsmith. 'You quibble, man. 'Tis right enough in my eyes.'

'Right enough? See how long the stubble stands, Arrowsmith. You favour the wight as no other man would.'

Arrowsmith bristled. 'I favour him no more than would any other mortal man.'

It was then that Tahquil fancied she caught, in the flash of Arrowsmith's eyes, a fleeting fey quality.

'Did Finoderee in sooth mow this meadow single-handed in one night?' she digressed, to temper the strange antagonism that seemed to have arisen between Master and bailiff.

'Aye that he did,' lazily said Cooper. 'He's a good worker, if he can be kept under the thumb.'

The steward rejoined, 'The vigour of his mowing is like a whirlwind! His scythe thrashes too fast for the human eye to perceive, and the grass flies up so thick it blocks out the sun! You ought to see his threshing!'

'He whisks horseloads of stone and wrack about the country-side like a little giant,' elaborated the reeve, 'and when he shepherds, sometimes in his enthusiasm he folds in wild goats, purrs and hares along with the sheep.'

''Tis a pity about Dan Broome's red cow,' remarked Caitri.

'Dan Broome? Who is he?' the men wondered.

'There haven't been Broomes in Appleton Thorn for nigh on eighty years,' said the reeve.

At all times, Arrowsmith poured libations of hospitality upon his guests. Wherever they went they were greeted with friendly smiles and small gifts of local wares until they thought that Appleton Thorn must be one of the best places in Erith, but Tahquil's heart never ceased to ache. Ever and anon she would lift her head and glance to the north, and Arrowsmith did not fail to mark this.

On the way back from the fields, he let his horse drop back beside Tahquil's.

'You and your ladies cannot stay in my house tonight,' he said quietly. 'My house has been troubled by a certain presence every Flench Ridings Night for years. I have vowed that I am going to wait up for it tonight with a wizard-wrought tilhal and an axe, to get rid of it once and for all.'

'What manner of wight is it?'

''Tis a master of glamour. No two people looking at it see the same thing. One man might see a big lump of slub like a jellyfish, another might see a manlike form with no head. To me, it appears like a beast lacking legs.'

'Is it dangerous?'

He shrugged. 'Best to be sure. I have made arrangements for you and my sisters and the servant to lodge at my neighbour's house. I shall wait alone tonight.'

That evening, the Village Hornblower lifted up the great sickle-shaped, gold-clasped Forest Horn like a moon on its ornate baldric and sounded it three times, as he always did, as it had been sounded in Appleton Thorn every evening since antiquity.

''Tis to direct folk lost in the forest,' the inhabitants explained, 'a custom from olden times when folk used to walk among the trees, before the place turned wightish and unseelie. Nobody goes in there now. No need to keep Forest Horn going really, but 'tis one of the old village laws we've never bothered to revoke. If all is going well, why change things?'

After the sun had gone under the hills, Finoderee came to the East Gate.

'Let him in,' said Arrowsmith, hard at work in the midst of preparations for the customary ritual. Garlands of marsh marigolds and birch were being laid around the village well, and massed white hawthorn blossoms hung above every door, mingled with the goosey gullies, the catkins of sallow—none of which were allowed to be brought into the houses, for to do so ostensibly attracted bad luck.

Cooper brought Finoderee before the Master of the Village and Lord of the Hundred.

'More mowing tonight?' asked Finoderee. 'The round-field, under Bonfire Hill?'

'Aye, but let the work be better carried out this time,' said Arrowsmith testily. 'If you're going to do it, do it well. You're not cutting the stalks close enough to the ground.'

'Not close enough?' echoed the wight.

'Aye. The stubble is too long.'

'Too long?' repeated the wight again. 'Galan Arrowsmith, 'tis the mortal blood that's singing in yer ears. Is Sule Skerry so far away?'

'Go on with you. I am busy this night and have no time for idle chatter.'

Finoderee wandered off a short way then stopped. His shoulders seemed to swell.

'Too long? I'll give ye too long!' he shouted. 'Finoderee is a good mower. I plough, I sow, I reap, I mow. I herd cattle and sheep, I thresh and rake and carry, I build stacks. I can clear a daymath in an hour and want nothing better than a crockful of bithag afterwards. I'll not mow an inch without you mowing alongside o' me, Arrowsmith. I'll outswathe ye ten to one and I'll show you *too long.*'

'I need that meadow mowed, and tonight I am busy!'

Finoderee was unmoved.

'Very well,' exasperatedly said Arrowsmith. 'Meet me at the round-field at *uhta*. Will that give us enough time?'

'Enough time for Finoderee.'

'Good. Now go.'

'And by the by, Arrowsmith, where's me crock of bithag from yesternight?'

'Wainwright will give it you on the way out.'

'I've never heard of a village that makes so free with wights,' marvelled Caitri as Finoderee lumbered away to the inn, escorted by Fletcher. 'Talking to them and treating them like *lorraly* folk!'

'Appleton Thorn is different,' said Arrowsmith curtly.

A faceless figure rode around the village on a flench, a wide plank carried along by two burly flench-bearers. He stopped at all the houses to collect small coins, flowers and food, after which he returned to the inn, where the collected gifts were divided between him and his helpers. A crowd of children followed him, singing songs.

The enigmatic Flench Ridings was another seemingly redundant custom. Its origin had long ago passed into obscurity. The chosen villager dressed himself in old clothes stuck all over with burdock burrs so that not a particle of fabric showed. He put on a burry mask and a flower-covered hat, and took up two staves, one in each hand. On these staves were tied two flags, the Royal Standard of Eldaraigne and the Empire Jack, and the handles were decorated with spring flowers.

This event having taken place, to the great amusement of Caitri and Viviana who thought it ought to be introduced at Court, time came to retire for the evening. Most of the men went to the inn to carry on the celebrations. Arrowsmith was not amongst them. He sat alone in his house, waiting.

The village resonated soundlessly.

It was an eldritch outpouring of silence, below the reaches of hearing.

In the next-door house of an elderly neighbour, Tahquil toyed with a twisted hazel baton which Arrowsmith had given her on bidding them goodnight. She had noticed his hands then; the skin was rough. Between the fingers stretched a fine, translucent membrane.

The sisters, Betony and Sorrel, had eaten no supper. They feigned tranquillity as they sat with the spinster neighbour, teaching plant lore to Tahquil's companions.

'Yes, of course you know that you must not pick red campion,' said Sorrel sagely. 'If you do, 'twill bring thunder.'

'There are others that will bring thunder,' interjected old Hazel the neighbour, her gnarled fingers busy at lace-making. 'Thunderflowers and wood anemone and thunderbolts, which some call speedwell.'

'Nonetheless,' added Sorrel, 'you can protect against lightning with elder, house leek and biting stonecrop.'

'And hypericum,' said her sister. She bit her lip and looked towards the curtained window.

'What is the purpose of this?' asked Tahquil, holding up the hazel baton.

The sisters exchanged shy glances.

'That's a honeysuckle stick,' said Sorrel. 'Honeysuckle has entwined itself around that stem when it was green. Now that the woodbine has been removed, the hazel is twisted.'

'But for what purpose?'

''Tis just a good-luck charm.'

'A love charm,' breathed Caitri.

A wind came up. Something fell with a crash, or a door slammed. In the stables, a horse shrilled and kicked at the walls.

The sisters stiffened, turning their heads towards their house where their brother waited.

'What is this entity that troubles you every year?' asked Caitri. 'How does it get inside the Fence?'

'Alas, we know not,' answered Sorrel. 'Galan thinks it flies through the air and down the chimney, or maybe comes up under the hearthstone, using it like a trapdoor. It has been seen to run fleeter than a hound and fly swifter than an eagle.'

'What is your brother going to do?'

'Again, we know not. He has forbidden us to keep vigil with him. I cannot bear to contemplate what might happen—oh, let us converse again, that our thoughts might be distracted!'

In his empty house, Galan Arrowsmith sat in a chair with his axe resting across his knee and a carved ashen tilhal in his hand. On the table, rush-candles burned, each with its gorse-yellow bud at the tip. In the fireplace a gorse-wood fire leaped with a bright, clear flame, and the wind came invading down the chimney like Namarran raiders. Sparks went up in evanescent flowers.

The hour was getting late when there came a sound like dead meat slammed down, as if someone had flung a carcass on the floor. Arrowsmith looked up.

'Myrtle is lovely,' said Betony next door, speaking a little too loudly, 'but of all the plants not cultivated in gardens the hawthorn is my favourite, for it is both fair and strong. Its blossoms are as white as purity, its berries as red as passion, its leaves are painted with the green of youthful Springtime. Its thorny branches are kind to small birds of all descriptions, giving them shelter, so that hawthorn hedgerows ring with song. Even its Winter starkness has a wild sort of beauty, etched in black lines against grey skies.'

'Yet those thorns can be cruel,' Sorrel pointed out, after a quick glance at the window. 'And of course bringing the flowers of the may into the house invites ill fortune.'

''Tis the same with lily-of-the-valley and all white flowers,' averred Betony.

'Ah, but 'tis not as dangerous as bringing in lilac,' interjected Hazel.

'I'll not disagree that thorns can be harsh and fierce,' Betony said, 'yet only towards the foolish, or to the ignorant who approach them without due caution. And as for bringing the blossoms indoors—why would one wish to pluck such beauty and watch it wither, when it might display its loveliness for so much longer, crisp and strong on the twig, kissed by sunshine and rain? It is said that of all white flowers, the may was most beloved by the Faêran, and that is why they cursed those who would break its boughs, and hide it away within walls.'

'It is reputed that thorn bushes were under the protection of the Fair Ones,' said Hazel. 'Some say the protection lingers yet. When I was a girl, any thorn which grew alone in a field was called a Faêrie Thorn. To this day, people say it is not right to cut such a bush. Cutting down a Faêrie tree brings death and madness—' She broke off.

Outside, a commotion had erupted. The five damsels and the elderly neighbour hastened from the house. A man ran through the Errechd, shouting, 'Come and see! Come and see! Out along the West Road, at the top of the cliffs!'

A knot of villagers was heading out of the West Gate where the guards were still talking excitedly about what the Master of the Village had been hunting when he passed through it last.

Grabbing their cloaks, the girls followed. Out along the cliff tops they went, and the salt gale rode up over the side, out of the firth to meet them. Spray blew upward in jets spouting over the top of the cliff. Violent, the sea below churned where it met the rocks, like boiling cream. Away on the far bank the cliffs gleamed like chiselled stone doves in the starlight. Crystal halls of water smashed there, gauzed by the mist of their own vapourisation. Their thundering was blown ragged by the gale.

At the top of the cliffs, It was pinned, with Arrowsmith's axe sticking out of It. To Tahquil, It looked like a sack of white wool.

'Don't be afeard,' said Arrowsmith, his rough hand warm around hers. 'It came to the house. I chased It, with the tilhal in one hand and the axe in the other. It took the road to the cliffs and I followed hard after. Just as It was going to slide over the cliffs and into the sea, I said a Word and slung the axe, which stuck fast in It.'

'Where's Spider?' the villagers were shouting. 'Fetch Spider!'

However, Spider, it seemed, had made overly merry on Flench Ridings Night and still slept the sticky apple-wine slumber.

Gathered together at a distance they considered safe, the audience scrutinised the strange thing pinned to the cliff top. It did not move. There was no way of knowing whether It was alive or dead. Indeed, there was no way of knowing Its true appearance, if It had one, because each person saw something different.

'We'd better cover It over,' someone suggested, so a few young men ran to fetch shovels. They scooped up soil and flung it over the entity, until It was buried under a thick layer of dirt. Then they dug a deep, wide trench around It, so that neither man nor beast might approach the dangerous object and possibly disturb It.

In fact, none of the villagers dared go near It. They stood around with the wind whipping and harrying at their cloaks, like a flock of strange birds flapping.

Now that the agitation was over and they discovered that they were in the perilous position of being outside the Fence at night, folk began to hasten homewards, clapping Arrowsmith on the back and congratulating him on a fine night's work.

'I shall stay alone in the house for the rest of the night,' he said, 'in case.' He turned to Tahquil. 'Do you hear the wet wind off the water, Mistress Mellyn? A sound like the calling of a name.'

'I hear the wind, sir,' called Tahquil, drifting away in a bouquet of maidens.

'Good night,' he said.

'Good night.'

Uhta woke Tahquil from tortured dreams with a sudden tightening as of a coiled spring—the imminence of the day. Something was about to happen at this early hour.

The wind had dropped. All was still. The clatter of hooves on cobblestones alerted her—looking out of the window she saw Arrowsmith mounted on his horse, leaving the stable. Finoderee was going to mow the round-field with him and Finoderee was angry. The urisk had warned, '. . . *he can be spiteful.*'

Betony and Sorrel were stirring too.

'Will you venture out?' they said. 'The men are taking Spider to see where It is pinned on the cliffs. He will know what to do. And on the way we shall bathe our faces in the early dew. If 'tis done before dawn on the first of Uainemis, one is assured of an improved complexion. It cures freckles.'

'We shall come.' Tahquil and her friends dressed hastily, tugging cloaks around their shoulders. Already, out on the Errechd, many grey figures were assembling in the almost-darkness. The flames of their torches wove in a dance but their faces were morose. This was the hour that made any festive atmosphere impossible. There was something about the chill, the stillness, the tense and expectant obscurity and the bleak blue tinge of pre-dawn air that would unfailingly bring melancholy to even the highest-spirited reveller wending home from a merry night at the inn.

Of which there were none this *uhta*—carousing throughout the entire night was a luxury the folk of Appleton Thorn only permitted themselves at Midsummer's. Rest was a necessity; they had to work hard for a living, although not as hard as they would have had to work without the help of a certain brawny wight.

Spider was late, it having been difficult to rouse him. The village girls used this spare time to splash their faces with dew from the leaves of hawthorn and ivy, which were said to be most powerful.

'Dew of ivy can bring ye a husband within the year,' they whispered, giggling.

The wiry old dyn-cynnil arrived, yawning, and the three visitors joined the torchlit throng as it moved off towards the gate in the glimmering darkness. Along the cliff-top road the procession walked, its members conversing in muted tones, until they arrived at the place; the wide, deep trench and the mound in the middle. The tip of the axe-handle stuck out of the top. Here, the procession halted and gathered expectantly around Spider.

Spider looked solemn. He gazed at the blank dirt. Beyond it, the sea glimmered with a satin lustre. Gentle draughts blowing up the land's wall stole under the onlookers' cloaks and flared them wide and hollow, spreading them out like war-banners.

'Got to have a look at It,' said Spider.

Someone handed him a shovel. He jumped over the trench and began to raise the soil. As he lifted the seventh spadeful, a lurid light glowed up at him and the spectators drew back with gasps and muted cries. Then a dense mist steamed out of nowhere, wrapping Spider in a nebulous smear. Through the blur, the onlookers could dimly discern something rising out of the hole. Next moment it rolled down the cliff and into the sea.

Startled shouts jumped from many throats, but It was gone.

The mist tore into tattered strips and blew away. Spider stood leaning on the shovel, looking out across the firth.

'It might have been a seal, or maybe an otter!' proposed a voice.

Gravely, the dyn-cynnil shook his head.

'Eldritch wights that dwell in the air, in the ground and water are more numerous and various than we can ever know. What chance have such as we of understanding them, or even seeing them aright?' he said. 'Better to leave that to the mighty wizards, and those that have the Sight.'

They all made their way home, shaking their heads at the strangeness of it all, and the sun ran the gilded line of its upper edge along the horizon's maiden blush.

As the damsels reached the house three horses came cantering up, wheeling to a halt. Arrowsmith and his reeve and steward dismounted. Crimson rivulets, as dark as wine, soaked through the fabric of Arrowsmith's breeches. One leg was drenched with blood from the thigh down. Wincing, he limped to the door, shrugging off help from his friends. The sisters flew to him like wrens, uttering soft cries of distress.

Once indoors, they made him rest his leg on a stool while they tended it.

'The wretch most unworthy!' Arrowsmith expostulated. 'As I mowed he followed me, grubbing up the roots so ferociously that at one time his pickaxe grazed my hamstrings. Indeed, my legs were in grave danger of being cut to the bone, had I not moved nimbly. I told him that he will never work for me again, now that he has so offended me, but he said he will continue to do so, and went off to drive my sheep up to pasture on Bonfire Hill. We went after him but already in his vengeful zeal he had driven them too close to the cliffs and some of them had fallen over. I shall call all the men together to drive him out!'

'I fear you will not be able to rid yourselves of him by force,' said Tahquil.

'That's as may be,' said Arrowsmith grimly.

In the mellow morning the village turned out to pay respects to the Noble Thorn. They bawmed and adorned it with flowers and ribbons. Six village girls came riding on black rams to dance in a ring about the tree while the traditional Bawming Song was sung. This was followed by a festive picnic on the green lawns of the Errechd, and various rowdy sports.

Then horsemen in splendid costume trotted forth from the gates to perform the annual Riding of the Marches. The inspection of the boundaries of the common land outside the village was a dangerous mission, since it must pass under the eaves of the Khazathdaur. The cavalcade was headed by a young man chosen to be the Cornet, who bore the village banner and who led the Cornet's Gallop at the end of the Ride.

The Summer ceremonies did not cease there. When the light lengthened in the afternoon, those responsible for keeping watch and ward over Appleton Thorn set out to collect their head-penny from every householder and, by an old statute both bawdy and chaste, a kiss from every woman they met. The reeve, the bailiff, the steward, the Keeper of the Keys of the Common Coffer, the water bailiff, the constable and the Village Master had a merry duty as, armed with their ribbon-decked tithing pole, they toured the cottages. They were accompanied by a Pumpkin Scrambler in extraordinary raiment, who tossed to the children miniature pumpkins hollowed out and filled with honey cake and spiced fruits, and who offered these dainty victuals to each woman kissed.

'Fie! 'Tis a silly game,' said Caitri, watching the shrieking good-wives pretending to avoid the tithingmen's jocular advances.

'You are too young for it anyway,' said Viviana, glancing in the tiny looking-glass chained to her chatelaine, and pinching her cheeks to redden them.

'I wouldn't wish to be kissed by those churls!'

'I would not scorn a kiss from Master Arrowsmith,' said Viviana, who relished any sort of merrymaking. 'And that young water bailiff—the set of his shoulders is not entirely odious.'

'I shall shut myself in the house,' decided Caitri, 'and they will never find me.'

'I too,' said Tahquil, 'am surfeited with celebration.'

The Langothe worked its claws deeper in her, with every hour.

The distant sounds of laughing and cheering scratched at the upstairs shutters while the day faded. The Forest Horn sounded from the now deserted Errechd, and the shutters flew open. Favouring his injured leg, Arrowsmith climbed in.

'I'll not let the men trouble you,' he said. 'My sisters locked the house and kept the key. The village ladder is mine.' Looking at Tahquil, who sat calmly by Caitri, he faltered.

'Are you come to claim the kiss,' said Tahquil, 'which lawfully is yours? I cannot stop you.'

For a time he did not reply. Then he proffered a honey-coloured globe dripping with ribbons.

'No,' he said. 'You are not of the village, Mistress Mellyn. You owe naught.'

Tahquil accepted the gift. As Arrowsmith turned to leave, Caitri rose, stood on tiptoe and kissed him on the side of his stubbly jaw. He muttered something, then awkwardly flung a leg over the windowsill. Before he descended out of view he hesitated once more. Turning his eyes upon Tahquil he said, 'Will you stay till Meathensun? You will be Queen of the Garlands.'

'No,' said Tahquil, 'I cannot stay.'

She gazed past him, over his shoulder, as though focused on some distance he could not see.

'Aye,' said Arrowsmith.

He climbed down, disappearing from view.

Handbells were ringing throughout Appleton Thorn, ringing like cup-lilies on the brink of clear pools. Night stalked through narrow streets.

A horse's skull with snapping jaws came roaming in the dark from house to house, seeking admittance. Terrifyingly it pranced; the jaws flapped and clicked. Youths swaggered at a safe distance, but immune at the side of this equine spectre sauntered a huge man dressed as a woman and brandishing a besom.

'Hey, Sally!' called the youths, and the man-woman roared. He shook the broom and chased them, and the horse-impersonator hidden under a sheet of linen, and bearing the skull on a pole, chased them too, pulling the strings to make the jaws snap. Tonight was for Burning the Boatman, so the Hooden Horse was abroad.

At the other end of the village an effigy issued from a cottage, its arms hanging limply across the shoulders of two men. His body, larger than a man's, was crammed with old rags and shabby fleeces, saturated with turpentine and whale oil. The amorphous head was eerily and somewhat riskily lit by two candle-lamps for eyes. A crowd assembled, marching in his wake. As he travelled down the main street he stopped at the doors of the oldest and the most esteemed villagers, whereupon one of his attendants would sing loudly, on a single note:

'At Pikehall Crags he tore his rags
At Appleton Thorn he blew his horn
At Churrachan Stee he broke his knee
At Grassrill Beck he broke his neck
At Cliffroad's bend we'll make his end
Shout boys, shout!'

After which the members of the crowd would give three cheers, take another swig from their spilling jugs and continue on their way. The Hooden Horse and facetious 'Sally', meanwhile, jumped unexpectedly out from corners at anyone straying on the fringe of the mob. Carrying flaming brands, Tahquil and Viviana found themselves in the centre of the press, borne along with the tide. Still ringing the handbells, the villagers exited from the West Gate and continued out along the cliff road, past the excavated spot where It had rolled into the sea the night before. Down the rough-hewn wall stair went the Boatman and the crowd, with the Hooden Horse's jaws snapping at their heels and enormous Sally sweeping. There at the bend where the stair terminated on a level platform just above the high tide mark, all torches save one were extinguished and the Boatman met his end.

They stabbed him with a knife and laid him in a canoe, then

set him on fire. The canoe was pushed out onto the black waters of the firth. As the Boatman burned, the villagers sang—not any traditional verse, but whatever songs came into their heads. He blazed up with a popping and a crackling and the orange flames, moving away, cast their dazzling reflections way down into the obsidian depths. The current and the tide caught hold and bore the boat from shore. It dwindled as it departed, but the fire leaped higher until it became a splendid blossom of pure, radiant energy suspended in total darkness, its light eclipsing, for the moment, all others—a blend of dazzling ruby, topaz, citrine. For a long time the audience stood, and the choruses from their combined throats, bass and alto, tenor and soprano, sobered now. Far out across the water the flames began to die and soon the burning Boatman was only a glowing speck, a hot coal in a black pit. Then the boat sank—they heard the hiss of steam, and all was over.

The reason for it all had long ago been forgotten.

The single torch gave life to the others, and led by the Hooden Horse, the procession wound its way back up the cliffs and into the village. The bells were silent now. Some folk dawdled—Cooper was the last man in tow. The rest had just passed inside the gate when they heard him shout and turned to see him pointing to a figure lying beside the road.

He cupped his hands around his mouth. 'Someone's hurt!' he yelled. 'Come and help!'

Before anyone else had time to move in its direction the figure abruptly grew to the supernatural stature of thirteen feet. Like a tower on legs, it began chasing Cooper towards the gate. Shrieking madly, the man came bolting along, his cloak flying. With one last despairing effort he hurled himself sprawling on village ground and the guards slammed the gate. The figure, which had now shrunk to a respectable height, bounded away laughing wildly.

'The Bullbeggar!' wailed the crowd. 'The Bullbeggar of Creech Hill!'

Cooper lay gasping, moaning.

His friends hauled him to his feet.

'Come on, Cooper,' they said philosophically. 'There's naught wrong with ye that a pint of best beer wouldn't set to rights.'

They repaired to the Thorn Tree, but an uneasiness had crept amongst them.

'Bullbeggars one night, It another,' some muttered, 'not to mention Shocks. Black Annis will be next no doubt, we shall hear the gnashing of her teeth and she'll be reaching her metal claws in our windows to steal our babes and how shall we defend them?'

Some began again to look askance at the newcomers.

Despite these undertones their stay at Appleton Thorn lengthened. Each day brought a new excuse as to why they should not yet depart. However, while most of the inhabitants tempted them to tarry and argued that to leave now would be to travel at a perfidious season, there were those who whispered to each other that these three damsels on their untoward, unaccompanied journey had drawn after them unwholesome things, that an extended visit might bring down some eldritch threat upon the hamlet.

There were questions, too, as to where they must go, and why, and by what means they would travel. Unwilling to divulge anything which might provide a clue to spies, the travellers gave out the only story they could fabricate—that they had disembarked from a merchantman at the firth's mouth and walked up the coast road to see the famous Summer celebrations of Appleton Thorn. They would rendezvous with friends at a specified location to the north, and they must meet them there early in Grianmis.

'Why did they not accompany you?' persisted their inquisitors. 'Three young damsels, all alone, 'tis not right. Or do you have some manner of special protection?'

'We do,' they said, but they would not disclose its nature.

'And why north? And where?'

Arrowsmith defended them against such inquisitions, saying, 'Pry not into the affairs of our guests. You would have them believe us discourteous rustics.'

But this only had the effect of whetting the curiosity of the villagers and, deprived of facts, they began to hypothesise their own.

Since his altercation with Arrowsmith, Finoderee was proving more and more troublesome. He used his hideous strength to extremes with every task he undertook, resulting in the loss of livestock, damage to ploughs and other equipment, and the spoiling of cartloads of produce. Constantly he oppressed Arrowsmith with his excess of zeal.

'He's turning unseelie,' lamented the men and wives of Appleton Thorn. 'He is corrupted. Something must be done.'

One evening in the middle of Uainemis, Greenmonth, after Finoderee had thrown all the cut hay over Bonfire Hill, scattering it far and wide, Tahquil said, 'Master Arrowsmith, how shall you deal with Finoderee?'

'This very night,' he replied quietly, glancing to right and left in case of eavesdroppers, 'we assemble. The wight turns unseelie. He runs awry and must not be permitted to remain in these parts any longer. Who can tell what damage he might be doing at this moment?'

'He has haunted around here for many years, has he not? Is he not as old as your customs, or older?'

'We shall take iron,' the headman continued without heeding her, 'scythes and pitchforks, halberds and good Eldaraigne broadswords. Spider shall stand alongside us. And I have a Word, a Word of Gramarye.'

'Your men will suffer sorely. He is strong, Finoderee. I have heard it said that he once lifted a block of stone that all the men of the village together could not budge. Are you wanting to be revenged on him or do you truly wish only to protect the village?'

'The desire for vengeance is strong. But the village comes first, while I am at its head.'

'Then I beg you to do one thing.'

'Aye, and what might that be, Mistress Mellyn?'

'Once—how long ago it seems—I offered to pay him, and he said, *"Alas, poor Finoderee, don't send him away, he only wants to help."* Give him a suit of clothes, good clothes made to fit. He is dressed in rags like a household bruney, and he might depart if rewarded. Besides, after he has laboured so diligently for the village, would you not agree that he deserves proper remuneration?'

Arrowsmith looked up at the stars. The sound of the sea booming in the firth came down the wind and, as many times before, he seemed to be hearkening to it.

He looked down and said, 'There might be sense in what you say. I will not be forsworn—aye, it will be done, but if he does not depart we shall drive him forth or vanquish him.'

Men stood inside the East Gate at *uhta*. Helmed they were, and clad in a motley assortment of half-armour and brigandines. Their pikes and halberds and common farming implements stood up like a thicket.

'Open the gate,' commanded Arrowsmith.

'Aye.' A throaty grunt. 'Open the gate, boys, that Arrowsmith might come a-mowing the meadows with Finoderee. We shall raze the tares and marram alike to the naked ground.'

The gate swung wide. Finoderee stood grinning.

'There are no meadows in need of mowing,' said Arrowsmith, 'or reaping.'

'But there's a field of barley,' grimaced Finoderee.

'The barley's only new-sprung.'

'Better early than late,' said the wight, having the last word.

Arrowsmith stepped forward and held out a bundle.

'Take these clouts, Finoderee. You have worked long and hard for Appleton Thorn. Here is your reward.'

Finoderee's face metamorphosed into a cameo of surprise and dismay. Tenderly, almost fearfully, he took the bundle and opened it. He shook out every article as it came to hand and held each one aloft.

'Cap for the head,' he said, 'alas poor head! Coat for the back, alas poor back! Breeches for the bum, alas poor bum! If these be all thine, thine cannot be Ishkiliath.'

The burly old wight threw off his old rags then and there before the gate. He donned the new clothes, then turned and walked away towards the forest, singing as he strode:

'It's not well mowed! It's not well mowed!
Then 'tis never to be mowed by me again.
I've scattered it all to the east and west—
They'll have some work ere they get their rest!'

But when he had passed out of sight his voice could still be heard, and his plaint—faint . . .

'Far from me is the fen of weeping,
Far from me is the glen of sleeping,
Far from me is the field of reaping.
No more the watch-hours I'll be keeping
When the yellow moon comes creeping.'

Finoderee never returned to Grey Glass Firth. The men went back to their homes and took off their armour and laid down their weapons. When the sun rose that day, there would be many heavy tasks awaiting.

On the land, they had to work hard for a living.

Tahquil and the sisters were still wakeful when Arrowsmith came limping back to the stable to throw himself on the fragrant hay and find repose. They came away from the window after they saw him go in.

'Will you not stay for Weighing the Lord of the Hundred and Hare Pie Scramble next moon?' asked Betony. 'Will you not remain and dwell with us?

Tahquil shook her head.

'The Lord of the Hundred and Master of the Village has always been an Arrowsmith,' Sorrel said. 'It is not a hereditary title, but an elected one, by secret ballot. Appleton Thorn has thrived under the watch and ward of our forefathers' line. The Noble Thorn itself has thrived, living far beyond the years of any other tree. We dwell so remote here, beyond the aid of the greater world. They say that if ever the Arrowsmiths leave the village then the luck will go and the Noble Thorn will perish.'

'A mere superstition, surely.'

'They say in the village that you have spelled our brother,' said Betony. 'And in sooth, he was a merrier man ere he set eyes on you.'

'That is hardly my fault.'

'He might be married now, if he had wanted. Every maid

wants to marry a silkie's son. Have you seen him, swimming in the firth, quick and sleek as a seal? No man has dived so deep and so long. No man can catch fish with his hands and swim so fast, swim down to the ocean and the skerries out beyond the firth's mouth, where the seals play.'

'There is a power of him,' said Sorrel. 'And he has the Word. His mother taught it him, but she was not our mother—two marriages had our father. Sometimes at nights Galan stands at the window and listens to the water mulling and brewing in the firth.

'He longs for the open ocean, but he has said he will stay if he takes a landwife. If not, then the land cannot bind him much longer. None here please him enough, not that he is hard to please, but being of the blood that he is, he looks for different qualities in a wife than most men.'

'Would you have me bear the doom of the village upon my shoulders?' cried Tahquil angrily. 'I have never given any sign of love. I do not play with men's affections.'

'You kept the honeysuckle stick—'

'Was that some meaningful gesture? I know naught of your customs. Here it is. Take it back now.'

The sisters gazed upon her sorrowfully.

'Pray do not reproach me!' Tahquil said. 'Three reasons I will give to you. The first is this—as has been proved time and over in every tale of yore, all liaison between mortal and immortal is doomed to tragedy. Where is his silkie mother now? And where your mortal father? I would hazard that the one swims far out in the cold ocean while the other lies deep beneath the cold stone.'

'Ah, but that brings a question. Does our brother's blood run with the sealkind or with humankind? Is he mortal or no? But tell on, if so 'tis your will.'

'The second is that my heart is already given. I love another, and it will be so while I have life. 'Twas he who gave me the ring on my finger. Thirdly, if this were not so, yet could I not marry Galan, for there is no real love between us. I honour and admire him. Perhaps he thinks me comely—that is all.'

Sorrel turned the honeysuckle stick over in her hands.

'Then you will depart.'

'This very day.'

Sorrel threw the stick into the gorse fire where it burst into yellow buds like a sudden, brief Spring.

Tahquil and her companions rode out of the East Gate with Arrowsmith. His sisters and most of the villagers followed at their backs, some mounted, some on foot. Slowly they rode up to the barleymow and the meadows where Finoderee used to wield the scythe, and around past the rushy curraghs and the glen where he no longer slept the days. They splashed through Grassrill Beck and clattered across the stone bridge by the gorse mill. They passed across the open downlands while away to their left the firth boomed and rolled with a grey swell like sounding whales, and white stitchery seabirds braced themselves against the salt wind out of the west.

At the northern marches of the common lands, Arrowsmith and the three travellers detached themselves from the concourse and took their leave. For he had sworn that he would ride with them and deliver them safely into the care of their friends and nothing would dissuade him from this resolve. In tears, his sisters fell upon his neck and clung to him. The men saluted and the women curtsied. One would have thought they were losing their headman forever.

Leaving the villagers, the three companions and their defender turned their horses' heads to the north. As they rode away they heard the voices—bass, alto, tenor, soprano, raised again in song:

'The wind whistles wild in the withies of willows,
The magpie is calling to welcome the dawn.
The Churrachan sings to the wheel of the mill-o,
Where green are the hillsides and golden the corn.

In rushen-grown curraghs where water is shallow,
The herons are wading, the frogs are a-spawn.
Bright marigold, bog-bean, flag-lily and mallow
Spring under the leaves of the old peppercorn.

The wind from the Firth lifts the hulls at the winnow,
The waves on the Firth lift the hulls in the morn.
The fishing boats sail for the sturgeon and minnow
So pearly. So early, the fishermen yawn.

Beyond the curs'd reach of the forest's dark shadow
Where loiter foul wretches that make us to mourn,
We bide at the edge of the wide, open meadow.
Unseelie we banish, malign wights we scorn.

So if you'll but lend me the wings of a swallow,
No more shall I linger bereft and forlorn—
I'll fly on the path that my heart yearns to follow,
Back to the Grey Firth and the place I was born.

Where applejack cider's abundant and mellow
And we'll sit 'round a pint when the sheep have been shorn.
Where the gorse on the Creech is a buttery yellow,
We'll raise up our jugs. Drink to Appleton Thorn!'

Just before they reached the shoulder of the hill, the four riders turned and looked back. Small against the wide, green land looked the knot of villagers, insignificant against the sky's dizzying heights. Their song came lilting clearly on the breeze and every hand lifted in a flourish of farewell.

3
LALLILLIR
The Veiled Vale

In Lallillir I heard the water falling
Through secret places hung with dripping ferns.
And, as it fell, the water-voices calling
From rushing gills, and mossy becks and burns.

FROM THE CHAP-BOOK: 'POEMS OF THE NORTH COUNTRY'

Tahquil tied a scarf over the lower part of her face as soon as they had passed out of sight. On leaving the village she had drawn on a pair of gloves, lest the leaf-ring should betray her identity to questing wights. Her garments, the travel-worn garb from the fisher-cot, were drenched in oil of lavender—a gift from Betony and Sorrel. Her head swam with the intensity of its fumes. Surely no unfriendly wight could penetrate that smothering fragrance . . . or was it already too late for disguise? During their sojourn in the village she had unwittingly relaxed her vigilance. Reconsidering, she pulled off the scarf. To go about masked would surely attract more interest than not. The inevitable dirt of travel would conceal her features less conspicuously.

Their borrowed steeds were a welcome means of travel. Three of the horses belonged to Arrowsmith and his sisters, the fourth had been lent by the water bailiff. To lend a horse was a generous gesture indeed, for which Tahquil and her friends were deeply grateful. It had been arranged that Arrowsmith would bring the beasts back with him after he saw the travellers safe to their destination.

The Master of the Village might have been a welcome addition to their band, except that he was a well-known figure in these parts. The news that he had ridden off with a trio of young women could not fail to attract the attention of inquisitive wights. His presence could only make them more obvious.

'Your sisters' tears threatened to drown you,' Tahquil said to him as they cantered on. 'You will return soon, within a day or two surely—not long enough to warrant such distress. They love you dearly.'

But will he turn back when he finds out we have no protectors to guard us along our further journey?

'This I have said to my sisters and to all the rest,' replied Arrowsmith, 'that either I will return in two days or my horse will return without me. And if they find tied to the saddle a strand of kelp, then they will know where I have gone.'

Then he rode his horse close up beside her and looked her in the eyes.

'Fear not,' he said. 'My sisters have spoken to me. By the ring on your finger I now know you to be pledged. I force no suit.'

He flicked the reins and cantered ahead.

She had seen what it cost him and her heart quickened with compassion. For that alone, she might have loved him, almost.

The northerly way they followed was an old road, a faint path cut into the hillsides, called the Long Lane. Rising gradually all the time it crossed a land of dales not rugged, grand or majestic but rounded and gentle, with no peak rising more than two thousand feet. So vast and open was the sky that the land seemed no more than a rim pressed against it, the horizon framing the surging clouds and sun-rinsed blue of the heavens.

Thickly wooded hills stood above beck-threaded valley floors where bird's-eye primula, hart's tongue fern and pink foxglove peeped from stony crevices. An ancient rune-carved monolith, its edges softened and worn by the loving, ruthless caresses of wind and water, stood by itself—a lonely sentinel rooted in the turf of a distant slope. A windhover falcon gracefully rode a thermal, hanging in the lucid air.

'By Kingsdale Beck we go,' said Arrowsmith, 'and past Churnmilk Hole. By Frostrow and Shaking Moss, and Hollybush Spout.'

The Long Lane entered woodlands of wych elm and aspen. Spindly trunks like painted streaks, gold-flecked with sunlight, supported a misty tracery of leaves. Epiphytic lichens, ferns and mosses lived firm-footed on the organic debris which, for centuries undisturbed, had built up in clefts and hollows in the boughs. The undergrowth was rich with pink valerian, woodsage and early purple orchid. Red deer raised their heads at the sound of hoofbeats and darted into thickets. Grouse flew up in fright from wild shaws and bosky braes.

The horses splashed through shallow stony fords across fair streams of silver which cut through overhanging woods. Droplets flew from their hooves, as bright as polished threepences. Fish leaped like silver-plated leaves. Towering trees leaned their long boughs over the water and the banks were in flower with primroses and celandine, marsh marigold and herb robert.

Into open country they passed again, still climbing. From the peaks to the east, gills hung long and glittering like strands of Icemen's hair.

'Over there to the east,' said Arrowsmith, 'Ashgill Waterfall goes tumbling down the scar by Crooked Oak. In Autumn after rain the falls are thundering and the trees seem to have been wrought of copper. Look to the northeast—Rookhope Chimney rises beyond Briarwood Bank. The dales have names, though Men have never dwelt here. Only the road and the Runestone have been wrought by the hand of man, long ago, but the Long Lane ends at the foot of Mallorstang Edge.'

The late sun was turning towards dusk and mauve vapours coagulated in the still air. The distant hills took on shades of lilac and purple. Clouds kissed their tops. A small owl out hunting early was perched in the fork of a silver birch looking for mice and shrews in the long grass. It flew away as the riders disturbed it.

Tortuously the path began to wind, ascending a long fell-side out of the dales. Here the trees crouched, stunted. Higher up, they disappeared altogether. Wildflowers were overtaken by thick, tufted grasses. Swift, wild gills tumbled recklessly down narrow sluices.

By evenfall they had almost reached the top of Mallorstang Edge on the outer marches of Lallillir. Rising from the hill's brow, a twisted tree leaned stark against an arch of pale cloud flaring across deepening twilight. Beneath its roots a couple of shallow cave-openings bored into the rock face, overhung with ivy and ferns. Nearby, white-flowered enchanter's nightshade sprang in the grasses. A black fox loped past and uttered its rusty bark, so unlike a dog's, so strange it seemed more like the cry the moon would make, had it a voice.

There they halted to rest, kindling their fire just inside one of the caves in case it rained. They sat around its glassy blaze and ate some of their provisions: bannocks and dried fish, cheese, salty dulse and red carrageen from the firth. The treble *pip* of an insect chipped away at the upper edges of hearing. Caitri idly piped a few notes on Viviana's whistle of white deadnettle, until Arrowsmith hushed her with a wave of his hand.

'Soft,' he advised. 'Wights may be moving up there on the edge-top, on the high land above the rising of the rills.'

The horses at their pickets seemed to sense the whiff of danger. They pricked up their ears but remained quiet. Only an occasional shuffling in the grasses indicated their presence.

Overhead, the sky deepened. The stars appeared, so huge and close that Tahquil fancied she might reach out and touch them. Disrupted from its swarm by a passing star, a frozen nucleus of ice in a coma of nebulous gases hurtled along its sky track. Pushed by the sun's wind the comet's tail streamed out a hundred million miles long.

'Turn back,' said Arrowsmith. Perhaps he said it to the comet. If so, futilely.

Tahquil shook her head.

'A war is brewing,' she said. 'I can stop it.'

She thought he might laugh, but he did not. He merely looked down at his elbows, which rested on his knees.

'A young lad was lost out towards Mallorstang not two weeks ago,' he said. 'Seven rode out, six returned. Lallillir is a mighty perilous land. You will not survive there without aid, clever though you are, possessed of a ring of gramarye though you may be. You would not have made it as far as you have, except that many wights have departed from hereabouts and vanished eastwards. For good or ill, fewer remain here now than ever in living memory.'

Said Tahquil, 'As you have suspected, we make our journey alone. The ring I wear is protection enough.'

Arrowsmith stilled then, suddenly; every line of his body was taut.

Without glancing around he took the last bannock from the stone on which it had been warming beside the fire, and placed it beyond the circle of light. Then he resumed his position. Taking their cue from him, Tahquil and her companions continued as though nothing were afoot.

'Not enough,' Arrowsmith went on, 'for you were all tired and hungry and ragged when you came to Appleton Thorn. Why so unguarded on an enterprise which you say is of gravest importance to every kingdom?'

'For secrecy.'

'From whom?'

'Galan,' she said, 'only three people know the truth—myself and these two with me. Too many know already. The knowledge in itself may be dangerous to the bearer of it.'

He laughed softly. 'Think you that I cannot withstand a peril flouted by three girls? Very well, if you will not tell me, so be it. I will accompany you nonetheless. In Lallillir you will be in need of more than mortal strength.'

'Aye, and that is the truth,' hooted a voice. 'That is the truth indeed, Galan Siune's son.'

Beyond the globe of firelight the speaker propped himself against the twisted tree, flicking bannock crumbs from his hairy flanks. His deft hooves balanced on roots which were tangled like skeins of hair, caging the ground with an intricate, interlocking design like the embellished borders of manuscripts.

'Urisk,' said Arrowsmith, 'have you come back, then?'

'Och,' said the urisk drily. 'Ye mun be dreaming.'

'A welcome sight you are, sir,' chimed Viviana.

'Friend urisk!' exclaimed Caitri.

'Will you sit with us?' Tahquil asked. 'By the fire?'

'Dinnae mind if I do.'

Graciously the wight squatted down on his haunches. The ruddy glow played across his features: the pointed ears, the snub nose, the slanted eyes with vertical slits of pupils narrowing in the firelight. Neat, he looked, and dignified—artistic in the way that an agile woodland creature or a gnarled, wind-wrung tree is a work of art. It seemed he remained part of the landscape against which their group huddled. Although he was inside the circle of light, he belonged outside it.

'You have been long away,' said Arrowsmith.

'Aye. Syne the sons o' the Arbalisters left their hame on the Churrachan and sailed across the Great Salt where sich as I could-nae follow.'

'The old cot is naught but broken stones now, and bindweed clambers over the remains of the walls.'

'The hame I used tae keep fine for them, and all. Still, that's the way o't. The forest reaches oot, the village dwindles, folk take their leave.'

'You would have been welcome at any house in Appleton Thorn.'

'Now dinna be tellin' me ye don't understand the way of it, Galan Siune's son,' chided the wight. ''Tis the *place* that's the thing. The Churrachan's my ain stream o' water. 'Tis in me bluid and 'tis mighty hard tae leave it.'

'But you cannot cross it, can you?' asked Caitri. 'A running stream? How did you reach this side?'

'Lassie, there be a mindful o' matters ye ken nowt of, I see!' chuckled the urisk. 'There be more than one way tae get tae t'ither side o' a running water. I went around by the springhead, up where the stream rises out o' the hills. The mightiest barrier agin our crossing be the *south*-running water. Churrachan flows tae the west, otherwise Siune's son wouldnae be here the noo. Saw ye how his horse fashed itsel' against crossing the Grassrill, and baulked at goin' over the Churrachan Bridge? It felt the current flowin' aslant its rider. But there be an affinity there too, with the water, and the bluid that's half mortal is insensitive. So you ride over it, Siune's son, but ye feel it sorely, do ye no'?'

''Tis naught,' said Arrowsmith curtly.

'Oh aye, 'tis naught by comparison tae Lallillir,' said the urisk. 'Lallillir be the Land of Running Waters.'

'What can you tell us of this land?' asked Tahquil.

'Much,' said the urisk, and he proceeded to do so.

He told them about the four long ridges running parallel, south to north. Swarth Fell, the highest, bordered the coast and attracted rain to the three sharp valleys: the Vales of Wood, Water and Stone. Elfinwoodsdale was the westernmost, Blackwatervale lay in the centre, and to the east delved Ravenstonedale. The early tributaries of the river Elfinwater rose on Mallorstang Ridge and rushed away down between Swarth Fell and Bleak Fell, until at the northern marches of Lallillir the river turned west through the last foothills of Swarth Fell and ran to the sea. The middle waterway, the Blackwater, began in the same heights and was fed by the thousands of springs on the eastern side of Bleak Fell and the western slopes of Wold Fell. Where Bleak Fell sank in the north, the Blackwater curved to meet the Elfinwater on its journey oceanwards and at that point the names of both the rivers changed, for though mighty, they became but feudatories to the thundering Ravenswater gushing down from the east.

The Ravenswater flowed furthest inland. Its valley clove between Wold Fell and Scarrow Fell. Like its siblings it received tribute from the myriad brooks, streams, waterfalls and fountains gushing from the hillsides and cliffs. The entire rain-drenched landscape of Lallillir was threaded with silver and electrum and faceted with sheets of platinum where water curtained down great rock shields. It was diamonded with the brilliant necklaces of sudden jets spurting from subterranean chambers. Bleak and gaunt were the heights of the Fells, but the vales were rich with ferns, thick with moss-crusted trees dripping with epiphytes, hung with permanent rainbows in a crystal mist.

Wights of water haunted Lallillir, but it was a land to dwell in for aeons, not to roam, for they could not leave their rivers or streams for long without fading. And wights of land could not traverse Lallillir's surging currents, the flowing waters inimical to the eldritch of their gramarye. They must keep to the ridge tops, to the roofs of the fells, and so they did. Yet, while it was possible to reach the fell-tops from the south without crossing running water, it was also impossible to leave them in the north without crossing the Ravenswater—except in the eastern foothills of Scarrow Fell. For this reason, wights must traverse Lallillir along the top of Scarrow Fell. Ever since the land was formed, they had done so. The path they travelled came to be known as Wight's Way.

'No mortal walks Wight's Way and survives,' said the urisk sombrely. 'Ye canna go that way. Ye mun go by the western slopes o' Wold Fell, in the upper reaches o' Blackwatervale. 'Tis directly to the north o' us noo, if ye could but see it o'er the top o' Mallorstang. Ye'll hae many's the brook tae cross, but each one shall put a fence atween ye and whatever's got on yer tracks.'

'Wights might still come on us from the fell-top above,' said Viviana.

'The trick be tae get between a stream's fork, then. If any should lay siege tae ye, then move downhill till ye've crossed some more water and put yerselves beyond reach. But mind, the further down ye go towards the brae's floor, the broader the streams, the swifter, the harder tae ford.'

'And what shall we do,' said Tahquil, 'when we come to valley's end, with the Ravenswater turning its elbow to bar our path? For surely a spate so immense might not be forded.'

'Black Bridge,' said Arrowsmith. 'Black Bridge spans the Ravenswater at that point. 'Tis the only bridge across it, since the old Wynch Bridge fell into the torrent downstream. The Wynch used to be part of the King's High Way, but in these regions that road has fallen into disrepair.'

'One bridge?' said Tahquil. 'I mislike this. One bridge is dangerous, for, knowing that we have no choice but to cross it, that is where our enemies would look for us, and perhaps lay ambush.'

'In sooth,' said Arrowsmith. 'And that is why you need a man's strong arm to smite those enemies.'

'Sealman!' the urisk said sharply, his ears flattened to his curly hair. ''Tis the salt water that loves ye, not the fresh! These fells and vales sit well above the high tide mark! How far d'ye think ye'll get in Lallillir before the currents pull the marrow out o' ye and weaken ye like a babe? Then ye'll be naught but a burden to these lasses.'

'Who's to go with them then?' Arrowsmith snapped. 'You? You'd be worse off than I, goatfellow. You cannot even cross the Churrachan. Besides, you know nothing more than farming and housekeeping. You are no fighter.'

'No fighter, aye, but is it a fighter that's needed? 'Tis cunning that's needed, and knowledge and maybe gramarye tae boot, if mortals are tae conquer Lallillir.'

'What is your suggestion, urisk?' asked Tahquil.

Flames swayed like Autumn forests, bronze and cinnabar in the urisk's peculiar eyes.

'I have none.'

Viviana broke in unexpectedly, 'Mistress, do you not recall the article which Dain Pennyrigg found in his saddlebags when we returned from the Storm Tower to the City?'

Tahquil shook her head, wrinkling her brows in puzzlement.

'The feather of the swan, mistress,' Viviana went on. 'You said it was a powerful talisman. Mayhap it will prove useful now.'

Slowly, Tahquil nodded.

'If ye have a Summoner on ye,' the wight said eagerly, 'use it.'

Tahquil drew out the tattered aulmoniere, one of the few keepsakes she had salvaged from Tamhania. Within, the black feather nestled beside the vial of *nathrach deirge*. It looked even more dilapidated, bedraggled and bent than ever. Indeed, events had battered it into such insignificance that she had overlooked its very existence.

'Och, 'tis braw and blythe, true!' exclaimed the urisk upon beholding the plume. 'There's more than one way tae cross running water! Use it, lass!'

'Now?' Tahquil asked. Arrowsmith smiled. The urisk inclined his curly head in assent. 'How?' she inquired.

'Give it your message,' said Arrowsmith. 'Cast it high.'

Tahquil stood up. Recalling the words Maeve One-Eye had told her, she whispered to the swan's feather, 'Come, Whithiue. Aid us.'

Lifting her arm she flicked the pinion up, expecting it to drift down immediately in the windless night. A cold-blooded draught entered from nowhere, snatched it and twirled it away out of sight. The gust swirled Tahquil's cinnamon-dyed hair, rushing the tresses up around her face in a flare of singed fleece.

'And now?' she asked.

'Wait.'

That night the three mortals lay down to sleep with the tension of excitement stretched like a cord between them. Their two self-appointed guardians did not close their eyes.

Towards *uhta* she came, in those ephemeral pre-dawn moments on the borders of day and night when the world swings around and odd things may easily occur. They knew her first by a clap of wings and a rush of air. Presently a feminine manifestation emerged out of grey dewdrop stillness, forming as though she gathered shape to herself from the sky, the clouds, the last fading star. A startlingly scarlet band glimmered like a crescent of roses across her brow. The black cloak of feathers dripped from delicate shoulders to her bare feet. Coral-red bangles encircled the narrow ankles, matching the poppy-petal nails on the tips of her webbed toes. Like a wondrous girl she appeared, yet imbued with an inhuman wildness and a strangeness that evoked glimmering meres glimpsed through rising mist. Afar off she stood—unspeaking, remote.

Tahquil was already awake, smudge-faced and gloved to conceal identifying features.

'I called you,' she said. 'I need your help.'

The swanmaiden uttered a soft, hissing whistle. Stirring restively, the horses whickered.

The urisk trotted over to the wight-girl. He spoke in a low, soothing undertone and returned to Tahquil's side.

'I hae informed her of your need,' he fluted. 'She'll aid ye in your journey across Lallillir. She'll see ye safe—gin 'tis possible—tae Black Bridge, nae further. She'd nae do that much, were it no' tae honour the geas o' the feather.'

'I see,' said Tahquil. The swanmaiden's chill gaze struck through her like a sharpened icicle, or like a quill pen writing *aversion* on the air in frozen characters.

'Tell her she must help us get across the river to Cinnarine, at the least, at the very least.'

The two wights conversed again.

'Ye hold the feather. She must obey ye tae the word,' said the urisk. 'But the swans dinnae favour mortalkind—they opine ye're all thieves and hunters.'

'And not far from the truth, I suppose,' said Tahquil.

'The sun's about to lift his head,' said the urisk. 'I'll toddle along, and swans must fly. As ye make your journey she'll patrol the skies. She'll come down and tell ye if peril approaches. She'll point out the best ways to go. Mind, she doesnae love shifting tae her woman's form under the sun's eye—'tis not the wont o' her folk. She mun do it, if she be forced tae speak wi' ye, but she'll nae stay in that shape for lang.'

Already the swanmaiden's pale face was turning away, hidden by the long fall of ebony hair. Her slender form glided out of sight behind a rocky outcrop. A swan flew up with an elegant down-sweep of wide wings, the serpentine neck outstretched, the red feet tucked up underneath. Wings beat hard, like sail canvas snatching at the wind. Soon she was no more than a pinprick on the sky.

The sun opened its eye over Scarrow Fell.

The paling of the dawn revealed a lack of urisks. In the little caves beneath the tree roots, Viviana and Caitri slept with their arms loosely woven about each other, their peaceful faces as soft and guileless as two pastel-hued peaches. Tahquil sat beside the cold embers of the fire, her hands clasped about her knees. Adrift in some sorrowful reverie, she gazed sightlessly at the ashes. The enchanter's nightshade had closed its blooms. It hung its many-hooded heads, eschewing the day. Only Arrowsmith stood under the twisted tree that canted its limbs over the rocks and the dew-limned ferns.

As so often, he looked to the west. A mauve breeze blew up over a powdered violet horizon, bearing with it the spine-raking whistles, the descending, burred notes and boy's-throat calls of magpies. Arrowsmith turned his silver-grey head. He directed at Tahquil-Ashalind a gaze of burning intensity.

That was all.

Up and over Mallorstang Edge the travellers climbed that morning, leading their horses. At the summit a wide vista lay spread above and below them.

Overhead, the sky was a drama of clouds, dark thunder-grey in the centres. The sun behind them made a dazzling white-goldness of teased wool around the edges. Fraying spaces revealed the azure layers deepening to infinity behind the clouds.

Out away towards a distant haze stretched Blackwatervale, a deep valley embowered in wild and lovely woods, filled with gauzy veils of vapours. The river's snail-track spurled down the centre, but only an aqueous glint appeared here and there through the trees. Close together clustered those trees, but as the slopes of the land rose up on either side, so the stature of the trees dwindled. Like sleeping giants the high, grassy fell-tops loured bare and windswept against the horizon—the domain of grey stones and vacuous bights of space, the haunt of cool barrenness and avenging winds to catch the traveller unawares and whisk him off the brink. Yet down their sides plashed their tinsel hair, skein on skein, strand on strand. Thickly wooded, the gills tumbled from the very edges of the fells to the valley floor. Sometimes they vanished, falling into sinkholes and coursing through underground caverns until, driven against a bed of solid sandstone, they were forced out as springs or founts upon the hillside. Larger becks toppled through the mist on the high crags and down their own little valleys in chains of falls.

Beyond the western wall of Blackwatervale a tenebrous line indicated the serrations of Bleak Fell's spine. To the east, the high route of Wight's Way pressed against the sky. But it was lost from view in the mists.

Keeping to high ground the riders picked their way to the right. Cotton grass and heather rolled green, brown and purple at their feet. Curlew and snipe flew up into the crisp air and grouse broke cover chattering a warning: 'Go-bak, go-bak.'

Noon saw the travellers reaching the southern limit of Wold Fell. This formidable ridge dividing two river valleys culminated in a flat top, as narrow and tortuous as a crumpled ribbon. Here and there, its width contracted to no more than two feet. A few steps further on, it would broaden to seven feet or more, only to narrow again within a furlong. In places, thrusting crags flanked this high way, but in the greater part the ground fell steeply away on both sides. Those who would walk this open, windswept path might obtain a view of both valleys, Blackwatervale on the one hand and Ravenstonedale on the other. Out of the fell-sides, sometimes only yards below its crest, rivers were born. The walker might perceive the slender beginnings of the Blackwater spouting forth beneath his left heel, while the many sources of the Ravenswater trickled below his right.

Because it hung above these stony gushings and spoutings and did not cross them, this was a road favourable to creatures of eldritch. At noon it might appear quiet and inviting. Later it would not be so.

'We ought to turn now down to the slopes of Blackwatervale,' said Tahquil, 'to put some distance between ourselves and these heights before nightfall. Here, where the incline to the left is gentler, we might find our way. And here, by rights, we ought to part company.'

'Nay, do not leave us, Master Arrowsmith,' cried Viviana before he could make reply. 'Do not heed the urisk's words. I am certain you may cross these tiny waterways without trouble—why, up here they are a mere finger's width and nothing at all compared to the Churrachan.'

'Yet so many,' said Tahquil. 'And there may be a need to find a route lower along the hillsides for safety, where flow many streams like the Churrachan. Your bravery, sir, is not at question. But freshwater, running, must be like poison to you.'

'Its force pulls and tears,' he confessed. 'It cruelly disrupts the eldritch patterns of gramarye woven into the fibres of half my being. Yet only half—the other half can master it.'

Tahquil remonstrated, 'To ride or walk the lower slopes of Lallillir would drain your strength. She will be our watcher, the swanmaiden, according to her geas. You can leave us in no better care.'

The man shook his head. 'Come. It is dangerous to tarry here,' he said. Loosening his reins he moved on.

Flower heads of hard rush poked up out of the middle of the plant's round rosettes. The one-sided blooms of mat grasses thrust forth like tiny hay rakes. Among this low vegetation the horses' hooves slipped and slid on the steep ground. Soon their riders dismounted and led them by the reins, in single file, with Arrowsmith in the lead. It was not long before they must cross a chattering cascade no bigger than the dribble poured from the spout of a pitcher—then another, and another. Tahquil watched Arrowsmith's back. He did not falter. The fell rose high to their right, blocking out all view of Ravenstonedale. Below, a sea of trees engulfed the valley sides and floor. From all around echoed the sounds of water babbling, chuckling, clattering, arguing vociferously, gossiping, laughing; the rich warm roar of a far-off river behind the high crystal chimes of droplets striking clear liquid, flung from a great height.

The cataracts matured as the travellers descended.

'We shall not own a dry boot between us before long, if I am not mistaken,' predicted Viviana, sloshing through the most recent rill. She spoke loudly, to be heard above the white noise.

Keeping above the tall trees clustered on the lower slopes, they levelled out their course. Open country provided a better vantage from which to scan for danger. Here, brakes of low bushes squatted, well spaced and no more than waist-high.

Horizontal surfaces were a rarity on the fell-side. Caitri laughingly declared that her right leg must be growing shorter, her left longer. As night approached, Arrowsmith seemed weary. On reaching a spot where the incline flattened out to form a semicircular apron ringed with low scrub, they halted to make camp. The Summer evening drew in, damp and mellow. Lily-of-the-valley sprang in crevices, its racemes of tiny snow-bells sweetly perfumed. A rush-fringed pool had collected in the hollow at the centre of this grassy ring. On the utterly black surface of the water the campfire mirrored itself.

Having helped to construct the fire, Arrowsmith lay back on the ground, breathing heavily. He refused to take food. Constellations of sweat bestarred his brow. His face was dark, as if congested.

Tahquil offered him water. 'You are ill. Turn back,' she said, unintentionally echoing his earlier words.

'No,' he muttered. 'I will heal.'

Caitri rinsed a strip of cloth in the opacity of the pool. She shrieked. Clumsily, Arrowsmith jumped to his feet, knife in hand.

'I thought I saw something,' said the little girl, between fear and doubt, 'something in the water.'

There was nothing to be seen now, not even a ripple.

Arrowsmith sank down, his knees buckling beneath him. Caitri laid the damp cloth across his forehead while Viviana arranged his cloak in folds across his body.

'Don't fuss,' he rasped. ''Tis hale I am. I shall keep watch.'

A moment later his lids were shuttering his eyes. His jaw sagged. Starlight silvered his face to match his arctic hair, and pooled blue shadows under his cheekbones. Save for the slight rise and fall of his chest he might have been unliving. Water hurdled and gurgled, bubbled and burbled and snickered like a chorus of eldritch voices. Osmosis seeped.

Tahquil took first watch. She sat with her mud-smeared face turned to the pool, which remained profoundly calm, profoundly black.

How secretive is water, and how deceptive! It can act as a shield to throw off sheets of light, or as a sucking void like this well, to absorb light, or as a kind of passive nothingness to let light down through sheer translucency. But even when it allows radiance to penetrate, water bends and magnifies—distorts and plays tricks on the eye. An arm inserted partway appears disjointed, severed at the point of entry. Reflected in the convex surface of a drop, a face bulges at the brow and the eyes slide outward like a fish's.

Little wonder that so many wights are attached to water.

This pool, now. So dark is it, so absolutely blank-faced, that its depth is a mystery. It might be a mere scum of water skimming a flat bowl—no more than a puddle. Yet again that inkiness might extend far below us, deep into the fell-side, a hundred feet, two hundred feet—even as far as some subterranean river system below the valley floor . . .

Lallillir crooned soothing lullabies close to Tahquil's ears, singing songs of the susurrating sea and a synthesis of shadows sliding stealthily shorewards, soon to subsume . . .

The leaf-ring clenched. With a sick spasm, its wearer's head jerked up.

Have I dozed?

Something had broken through the pool's surface from below. It poised there regarding her, unblinking. What it was, she could not be certain, but it looked like the staring head of a debauched sheep or goat. As she watched, the apparition sank without haste. Seven ripples opened in ever-widening circles from its absence.

Viviana and Caitri slept consummately. Arrowsmith muttered thickly in his sleep. He had rolled against a prickly bush and flung out his arm. Thin runnels of blood flamboyantly striped the back of his hand but he had not woken. She rose to attend him and throw more wood on the fire.

At the same moment the dark water coalesced, clothing itself with a shape. The shape ascended as smoothly as oiled machinery.

Dripping, a large goat emerged.

The goat's eyes were two wells of darkness. Water streamed from its greenish hide.

Tahquil stared at the fuath, not daring to move. She remained this way, motionless, on and on into the atrophying night. Her heart threw itself urgently against her side as though trying to escape. A desert had invaded her mouth. At length, with utmost care and deliberation, Tahquil began to move her hand towards the dagger strapped at her side. Closer her gloved fingers crept, while her eyes never left the goat-thing, yet never locked with its gaze.

The goat grinned.

Rather, it drew back its caprian lips and bared its fence of teeth. Bedded in bloodless gums, the teeth were long and pointed as stakes, yellow as old parchment, stained slime-green.

The fire went out with a hiss of steam.

Tahquil jerked her head towards the sound. When she looked back the entity no longer stood before her. Footprints led away from the pool, impressed into the mosses; the prints of cloven hooves.

Over at the pickets the horses began to stamp and whinny. Tahquil snatched the last burning brand out of the fire. Its uncertain glare described a form moving amongst the tethered animals—not that of a beast, but a woman. The figure stooped. A horse screamed, that unmistakable scream of mortal terror. The others instantly caracoled into a frenzy, pulling at their pickets. One mare uprooted her stake, another broke her rope. White-eyed, neighing shrilly, they fled. Tahquil ran towards the two horses which remained. One lay stretched on the ground, a terrible rose blooming under the arch of its neck where the throat had been torn out. The other struggled still to break free. Something was standing over the prone form—not a woman but a four-legged beast, as before. It raised its head as Tahquil approached.

The hairs of its chin-beard dripped crimson. It had been feeding.

The dagger dropped from Tahquil's nerveless fingers. An extraordinary stench of rotting vegetation surged over everything, so powerful that she retched. It was that same nauseating odour of decay given off by deep vases in which flowers have long since died, their immersed stalks putrefying to mush in the dregs. A spatter of spray assaulted her. Hooves plunged, long teeth snapped. Outlined against the sky she beheld an appalling shape—not a goat nor yet a woman or a man, but a man and a beast locked together in combat. In the thicket of their belligerence, Arrowsmith's blade glittered. Viviana was screaming, Caitri shouting, 'Avaunt! Avaunt!' Tahquil regained her feet and darted out of the way as Arrowsmith and the fuath came crashing down. Teeth snipped and snapped. Flames burst from the firebrand as she whirled it, ready to strike. Then came a rush of air and a beating of great wings.

With a snarl the fuath sprang sideways. It swung its wicked head. Five antagonists faced it, four armed with iron and fire, the fifth—for an instant a winged woman seemed to be rising there, but in the next instant it was clearly a swan, neck arched, head stretched forward like a serpent's, wings at full span as they stirred the air to a storm. Wind roared and clapped, mingled with the fierce sibilation of the bird.

Coldly, clear as ice through the tumult, the goat spoke with a woman's voice:

'*Raggid forrn,*' it pronounced, oddly.

The fuath jumped into the pool, which sealed itself seamlessly.

'Viviana, saddle the horse,' Tahquil cried. 'Caitri, watch the water. Encourage the fire.'

Arrowsmith swayed and tottered.

'Are you wounded?'

'Nay,' he gasped. 'The hooves gave my ribs a drubbing but the teeth did not meet in my flesh. And you? The damsels—'

Pushing herself under his arm, Tahquil manoeuvred him to the remaining horse, which stood trembling as Viviana tightened its girth. Arrowsmith's eyes rolled in his head. It appeared that he was not fully cognisant of his surroundings, nor of what had occurred. Weakened as he was by many crossings of running water, the act of repulsing this unseelie attack had driven him to the verge of death. His existence hung in the balance.

'Get up in the saddle. We will follow after,' Tahquil said, forcing ardent conviction into the lie.

'The horses . . .'

'They are nearby.'

'The world tilts. Weary. So weary—'

'Get on your horse, Galan, in the name of reason. Only death waits for you in Lallillir.'

'You *will* follow.'

Calling on the last of his strength, Arrowsmith heaved his frame up and flung his leg over the horse's back. Losing consciousness, he gradually fell forward onto his mount's neck.

They roped him securely to the animal, placing the knots beside his dangling hands so that he might reach them when he revived. Turning the horse to face south, Tahquil sent it on its way with a slap on the rump. Glad to be granted freedom, the gelding leaped forward, moving swiftly along the treacherous incline in the wake of its comrades.

Now they looked for the swanmaiden, but in the elusive manner of wights, she had vanished.

'No time to lose,' said Tahquil, gathering up a bundle. 'We must away from this place, ere the fuath returns to finish this night's work.'

She wept, and the others wept also, as they abandoned the carcass of the poor faithful beast that had stood no chance against the eldritch slaughterer. When they looked back they saw the seashell curve, the hull of its flank pale under the starlight, while from the ominous pool a shape arose once more, with the smooth precision of oiled machinery.

Through the night they walked, afraid to stop, afraid to cease the crossings of running water. When they had put a goodly number of falling streamlets between themselves and the fuath's pond, they dared to speak.

'Galan was kind and generous,' said Caitri with swimming eyes. 'I shall never forget him, or his sisters. I hope we shall meet again.'

'Perhaps we shall, one day, out upon the waves,' Tahquil said. A breeze from the west breathed coolly upon her cheek.

'He shared hearth and board with us,' added Viviana. 'We are in his debt.'

'We must travel by night from now on,' said Tahquil briskly, 'and use the days for sleeping. Our senses must be sharp and wakeful during the wighting hours.'

'The swanmaiden ought to have warned us not to camp by that fuath-haunted sink!' fumed Viviana aggrievedly. 'That is her duty! A poor sentry she has shown herself.'

At *uhta*, they halted from sheer exhaustion, throwing themselves down in a gully, narrow and rugged, near the confluence of two streams. Spikes of frog-orchids grew amongst the upland grasses. Hooded, toothed and spurred, their yellow-green flowers were tinged with russet. Below, the valley lay lead-grey in the half-light, the ancient furrows and folds of the land flowing down with unhurried grace to meet the riverbanks.

'I shall call the swanmaiden,' said Tahquil. 'Wights are unable to dishonour their word. She has vowed to oblige herself to whosoever should summon her with that feather.'

'How shall you call her now?' asked Caitri. 'The feather is gone.'

'I know her calling-name.'

With that, heedless of invisible eavesdroppers, Tahquil cupped her hands around her mouth and called, 'Whithiue!' into the echoes of the valley. Thrice she called the name—to the north, to the south and skywards. Thrice the walls of the fells tossed the syllables from one incline to the other.

The swan answered; a dark rune scribed on a grey slate sky, a swart and swooping serenity of flight, falling behind an outflung arm of the fell.

With the demure protocol habitually practised by shape-shifters, the swanmaiden made her transformation beyond the view of mortal observers. Then she was standing amid the angular rocks edging the gully's head, her pale face like a flower on a dark stem.

'Welcome,' said Tahquil. 'Pray sit with us.'

A low '*Whaiho*'; perhaps a symbol of derision. A soft pre-dawn breeze stirred the feathers of her cloak, but the preternaturally lovely maiden remained as poised as a bird stalking fish, and did not step forth.

'Well, then,' said Tahquil, 'explain yourself from your exalted position. Why did you not warn us as promised? Our lives were endangered by a fuath. Had you informed us of its presence we would never have bided by its pool.'

The swans have their own language. Can she understand my words? Is it possible for her to reply?

'*Whaiho*,' presently the swanmaiden deigned to say in a low, mellow voice. 'Sedulous stealers are squeamish.'

She understands very well. Her command of the Common Tongue is estimable—at any rate, it appears she is adept at alliteration.

'We are not thieves,' Tahquil said aloud, 'nor are we squeamish. Mayhap it is hard for you to comprehend, but we do not wish to be slain. You have promised to do your best to prevent this occurrence, have you not?'

'Said so,' replied the swanmaiden. 'Handsome humans not harmed, ho?'

'Do not congratulate yourself.'

'Furtive fuath hungers for horses' hide.'

'And would fain feed on further flesh, I fear,' retorted Tahquil angrily, seizing inspiration.

'*Whiath!* The eldritch maiden tossed her head. At her back, two wide ribbons bordered the length of the eastern horizon. One, of pastel blue, was dry-brushed with white-of-blue cloud puffs. Above it, a delicate lilac-pink band faded up to a dove-grey dome.

'In the future you must warn us of any imminent danger,' said Tahquil. 'You must tell us of the safe paths, the negotiable paths. Inform us of the secure resting places.'

'Weary wanderers wish for haven.'

'Aye, we do.'

'Sentinel shift-swan succours woeful wold-walkers.' The swanmaiden's demeanour remained wary, aloof, cold.

'Precisely. You must help us until we safely cross the northern border of Lallillir. After that, I will set you free from the geas. If we are now agreed, you may depart, but do not go too far away. I might summon you at any time.'

'Sorrowing shift-swan stays steadfast.'

'My heart breaks,' commented Viviana sourly, aside.

'Your command of the Common Tongue is excellent,' Tahquil said to the swan-girl. 'You have the ability to form all sounds. Why speak thus?'

'Swans speak smoothly. Humans have harsh sounds. Harrowing words wound,' the marvellous bird-girl said contemptuously, stretching her long neck.

First I am reviled for my ugliness, then for my beauty. Now I am despised for being born into the human race. Ah, but I must recollect—prejudice is merely the shield of the self-loving.

'If you mislike our speech,' said Tahquil, 'teach us yours.'

But she was speaking to emptiness.

The swan took flight against the dawn that blazed over Wold Fell.

The companions ate from the provisions brought from Appleton Thorn—hard black rye bread and dried seaweeds. Through the day they slept, taking turns to watch towards the fell-top, the unprotected side of their nook.

The western sky was glimmering with swirling colours, like the melting of a long spray of red wax roses dipped in gilt, when the travellers rose, stiff and craving more rest, from the stony ground. To rouse their blood they sipped *nathrach deirge*.

'We are become nocturnal,' declared Caitri.

The moon was just past the full; a silver mushroom grown lop-sided. Under its umbrella the mortals wended their way again. That night they saw no living thing save hunting owls and other *lorraly* creatures of the dark hours, yet their scalps prickled con-tinually and they could not shake off the impression that unseen figures were walking near them, keeping pace. Morning unfolded like silk, with no mishap, and they lay down as before. The day brought a light spangle of rain. Sheltered under an overhang, wrapped in their fishermen's oilskins, the three damsels remained dry.

A shang storm drove through in the evening, and Lallillir dehisced in glitter like a burning palace, so eerie and awful, so splendid that the travellers must halt and behold it. They looked out, narrow-eyed against the dazzle, at rocks of crystal, fern leaves black as jet and powdered with bright sparks, solid silver water, pale golden grass dappled with shifting colours, reeds of gold or silver or tinkling glass. Lighted lamps bestarred thorn bushes. The skies were meadows on fire with flowers.

The display passed away to the west, allowing the travellers to go on their way. Bats, or perhaps night birds, swooped low out of the firmament. The damsels were forced to duck to avoid colli-sion. Viviana, chewing dulse, passed the time voicing nostalgic reflections about dinners at Court.

Down through the summer night harp-strung with stars, cool as silver in these inland uplands, swept the maiden of the swans. Advice she bestowed: 'Steer for strong-stream. Shadow fliers harry the heights. Seek shelter. Stay far from standing streams, from foggy fens. Singing suck-spirit sirens sojourn. She scents. She steals. Her hunger's high-honed hum stabs so shrill. Thus, seeking sip-straws hunt hidden succulence.'

Which the listeners translated as: 'Turn downhill towards the river. Strange dark birds patrol the ridges. Seek cover. Yet keep away from the backwaters—culicidae haunt there, and the whine of hungry Vectors is as thin and piercing as their poisonous tongues.'

They descended to the lower slopes where the trees stood taller, affording cover. As they walked between the boles, sounds began to bubble from somewhere ahead; a hubbub of queer voices. Cautiously the three turned aside. Presently the clamour arose again, in front of them. They altered their course again, but to no avail—soon the cries broke out almost at their feet and unavoidably they stepped out into a market scene.

'Siofra?' whispered Viviana.

'No,' said Tahquil, although the scene looked almost familiar.

It was a marketplace indeed, but a travelling market, and the vendors differed from the siofra of the mountain forests as scimitars vary from penknives.

So did the wares. At first sight the goods displayed for sale seemed sweeter, the purveyors of those goods fouler, than at any market of the diminutive siofra with their glamoured slugs and withered acorns disguised as meats and cakes. Odd little 'men' were these, some with the faces of cats, some with long, skinny tails tufted at the tips, some bent double into a crawling gait, as hunchbacked as snails—or hobbling bug-eyed, like fish or insects, some sprouting absurdly small bat wings from bony shoulders. Several crouched, thick and furry like giant mice, or leaped like sharp-eared, buck-toothed rats. Others came hopping in the manner of toads. Their voices whistled as scavenger birds whistle, were hoarse as parrots, soft as the cooing of doves. They chattered like mynahs, clucked and crowed like barnyard fowls, purred like cats. Winged and tailed, hunched and hairy, toothed and taloned, these wood-goblins—for such they were—lugged between them a wicker basket, an oaken platter and a dish of gold.

The fruits arrayed thereon gleamed. Marvels of perfection, they glistened as though glazed with Sugar-syrup, their colours as vibrant as Autumn, as rich as a treasury. They bloomed with the softness of velvet, or the smooth sheen of silk and samite, glass-glossy, fresh as the breath of mountain mornings, and still with their mint-green leaves attached. Each pericarp and drupe, each ovary and swollen stem plumped full-fleshed and flawless, ripe as wine. There were garnet-red cherries, peridot grapes, apples like great rubies streaked with gold and amber, amethyst blueberries, strawberries glowing like pink charcoal, yellow pears of topaz, lucid gooseberries of translucent green quartz, quinces still on their twigs, melons, pomegranates, polished damsons, figs like blushing drops of jade. Luscious, they promised to fill the mouth with a sweetness, a flavour, a succulence unsurpassable.

Without thinking twice the companions advanced, fastening passionate eyes on these magical treats. In their uncanny voices, the merchants were loudly hawking their wares. Viviana and Caitri heard them cry, 'Come and buy, come and buy!', but to Tahquil's ears the summons sounded like *'Come and die, come and die.'* Leering, the little mannish creatures crowded around the three damsels, pushing their basket and plate and dish aloft, holding them high, the better to display the delectable delights heaped there. Juicy clusters of grapes overspilled the sides of the dishes, hanging pendants like chandeliers of lapis lazuli, lit softly from within.

'Don't touch them!' cautioned Tahquil, and as her lips formed the words, it seemed a veil was peeled from her eyes. The red of the pomegranates now appeared overhectic, the purple of the blackberries was an angry lividness, and the strawberries resembled nothing more than gobbets of par-boiled flesh. Bilious pears wallowed alongside gelid grapes. On envious leaves, apples rolled like fibroid tumours. Plums winked like giants' eyeballs, flayed and bleeding.

A nursery tale of wood-goblins returned to Tahquil. She recollected that their wares were far more deadly than those of the

pretentious siofra. Once, Sianadh had eaten glamoured victuals at
a siofran fair and suffered nothing worse than a bellyache. The
fruits sold by wood-goblins, however, were *very* different.

'Come and buy!'

Encouraged by the cries of the hawkers, Viviana and Caitri
reached out. Tahquil pulled their elbows back.

'Do not eat!' she warned urgently.

The cat-faced, rat-eared wood-goblins laughed and jeered
while Tahquil's companions slapped her, wrenched their arms
from her grasp, scuffled, quarrelled.

'No, no!' Tahquil cried. 'The ring lets me see the truth. This display is all glamour. Look through the crook of my arm and you shall
pierce these mockeries. These are the fruits of death! Come away,
do not look, do not hearken, do not touch!' The squeakings and
howlings of the guileful merchants proved louder and shriller than
her voice, as they exhorted the mortals to taste. Yet, when Viviana's
fingers almost alighted on a distended plum the hue of a bruised
bladder, the wood-goblins whipped away both dish and plum.

'Come and buy!'

'We have no coin!' despaired Caitri. 'No gold or silver, nor
even bronze.'

'Will you take my chatelaine as payment?' beseeched Viviana.

'Or my silver locket!' entreated Caitri.

'You fools!' Tahquil cried in consternation, dragging them back
with strength born of desperation. Again, they thrust her aside.
The sly wood-goblins, cajoling, joined their various voices in a
chorus:

'The older girl shall give a curl as bright as precious gold.
The younger dear, a silver tear, as pure as ice is cold.'

With alacrity, Viviana took her scissors from her chatelaine and
snipped off a lock of her bleached hair. Tahquil knocked it from
her hand—the goblins snatched it up. They took hold of Tahquil
by the hair and clothes. Laughing, screeching, fleering, they
leaped to her shoulders and head, restraining her. They kicked,
pinched and pummelled.

'Give me my fruit!' screamed Viviana. Caitri wept. Then apples and pears and grapes and plums spilled into the hands of the courtier. She sat down while the wood-goblins poured them into her lap. Tahquil, her hair and clothes caught in wicked hands, must watch helplessly as Viviana took up a seductive plum, parted her lips on her white teeth, opened her mouth—

A wind like a cold current forced between rocks came blasting. In the heart of that wind was a clapping and a heartbeat of thunder, and a tremendous rustling as of a forest in a gale. Three black snowflakes whirled, and the blast blew away the insidious fruit. It went rolling helter-skelter through the trees, with the wood-goblins at full pelt after it, scampering, scuttling, prancing, shrieking, their empty dishes and basket bowling over and over.

The swan's black wings continued to beat out their fury until all the wood-goblins had fled. Not a trace of them was left, save their cries, fainter and smaller, fading through the wood. And the swan folded her wings.

Tahquil bowed. The bird, larger than *lorraly* swans, extended her sinuous neck and hissed savagely. Gathering herself, she launched upwards into flight. In the backwash of her departure, yellow filaments eddied. Tahquil caught one between finger and thumb.

'I wonder how the wights would have served you, Via, had they discovered your gold is counterfeit.'

Viviana's gaze was as cold as the pallid oculars of a deep-sea fish.

'You took it all from me,' she said.

'I shall find you fairer food—Fairbread, indeed.'

'No. No friend are you.'

Caitri dried her tears but said nothing.

As the hunger of the Langothe increased day by day it wore away Tahquil's appetite, sleep, strength, joy. Eventually it would wear away life itself. Coupled with this, another unfulfilled longing inexorably drove her towards madness—the hurt that is born of profound passion. Thoughts of one who was all the enchantment of the night and more beautiful than truth were with her always, along with the appalling, intolerable possibility that he might not be living still.

Now it seemed that she had lost also the loyalty of a cherished friend.

Food supplies were running low. Thorn had told her: *'Fairbread is the fruit of a mistletoe which loves only certain trees— apple, alder, hazel, holly and willow, elder, oak, banksia and elm, birch and blackthorn. It will never grow on other trees, and not always on those I have catalogued.'*

But where were such trees? None grew here, on the misted heights of Blackwatervale. Maybe willows leaned down by the river itself, down where wights lingered and perhaps mosquito-girls hovered on gauzy wings of spun moonlight.

They foraged as they journeyed, but Lallillir in Summer was not as generous as Tiriendor in Autumn—the lessons learned in one region and season were barely relevant to another. Once, the swanmaiden brought three small fishes, green-silver as winking waves, to be roasted in the crimson coals of the travellers' camp-fire. Tahquil gave her share to the others. Ever since breathing the air of the Fair Realm she had not been able to endure the taste of flesh.

It was not always easy to cross the volatile waters of Lallillir. In some places the gills plashed down vertical drops. In others they split into many channels, as wide networks, or they chiselled deep and narrow clefts to trap clumsy feet, or rushed so quickly that to dare a step in the current was to be swept from one's footing. In seemingly innocent banks sudden jets squirted where none had been evident. Rocky margins and boggy soaks barred the way. From time to time the travellers must retrace their steps and locate an alternative path, which in turn might prove inconclusive.

The ground, the rocks and water, the green places and the flowers of verge and slope passed arduously or easily beneath the feet of the three companions; however, Viviana remained taciturn and dour of countenance. Caitri overcame her own silence— unlike the courtier, she had not touched the fruits.

'I have heard of the Wood-Goblins' Market,' she murmured at last. 'Those who taste of the juicy wares cannot help but gorge and glut themselves, so delicious are those fruits of gramarye. To taste once instantly outlaws them from ever tasting the goblin fruits again—nor shall their eyes ever again behold the insidious wood-goblins or their wares, nor shall their ears catch the beckoning call to buy. All else becomes as nothing. Longing to taste again, they pine and wither, caring naught for food or sleep, dwelling only on this obsession—to find once more the Wood-Goblins' Market that they shall never find, and suck the fruits they shall never suck.'

'The fruits induce a kind of Langothe,' said Tahquil. 'A wicked kind, swifter to act but more cruel.'

'So you say,' responded Viviana, walking on ahead.

Dawn diluted the sky between the willows that leaned out over a stream. The breeze was in the west. Beneath a green-haired tree, Tahquil stood. She looked to the left and upwards. In the dim light she glimpsed, at the edges of sight, leafy sprouts and amongst them small soft spheres like softly glowing lamps. Reaching up, she plucked them.

'Fairbread of Willow for our supper.'

The taste was a cream of confectionery with an after-effect similar to mild intoxication. Fairbread stimulated strength, well-being and serenity, energising the heart, firming the sinews, refreshing the blood, sending the very roots of the hair thrusting more vigorously up through the scalp. But it did not cure Viviana of her wood-goblin-induced gall.

Several nights after entering Lallillir, they came to a gorge cut out of the fell-side, between two ferny shoulders. Along its nadir gushed a loud, broad stair of water, so dark and swift in the moon-light that the companions gave it a name—'Black Force'. This watercourse was too wide and swift to cross on foot, and the swan-girl, during one of her brief visits, had advised the travellers to divert to lower levels. She told them stepping stones crossed the Force where, silted and shallow, it entered the Blackwater.

The deeply cloven rift that birthed Black Force was too stark and precipitous to allow anyone to cross, except goats and other sure-footed beasts. The travellers began to search for another route. Above the cleft, the fell-top hung like a curtain against the hyacinthine storm-roil. Tahquil tilted her head back and regarded it measuringly.

'I would like to go that way,' she said at last, 'but 'tis more than likely the fell-tops are rife with creatures of eldritch, despite the growing light of day, such as it is. Indeed, here we are too close to their roads for comfort. Reluctant am I to say this, but we must go all the way down to the ford of stones.'

'Let us sleep first,' said Caitri. Her young face was drawn and haggard, grey as a crone's. At her side Viviana sat, hollow-eyed.

'Sleep,' said Tahquil gently. 'I shall keep watch.'

Her two companions lay down in the dawn, beneath the meagre shelter of a jutting rock. New light brushed the ancient, cracked stone, burnishing it with nacre. Dew twinked gold, ruby and sapphire on the beards of grasses.

At dusk, the eerily gorgeous shape-shifter came.

'Windwater soon shall skim, sheeting, from far westaway sea,' she declared. Her flawless alabaster face peered obliquely from the long flowering of black hair. On her brow was bound a head-band woven of scarlet geraniums. The white feathers edging the cloak's front opening glowed palely.

'From salt-stream steams, water-hoisting winds scull, shimmer-ing,' she proclaimed, 'funnelled forcibly high where sharp horns of first fell scrape skies. Soon waterclouds shall shed windwater, wetting Elfinwoodsdale and, hastening for hinterlands, shall shower wild wolds, steeps and summits, hills and heights, hollows and holms, fissures, fosses and furrows. Streams, waters, forces of Blackwatervale shall swell, shape-shifting, forming formidable sluices. Hurry! Hasten! Slow wingless ones ford Swarth Force soon, soon since she's still small. When windwater falls, fierce, foaming, fulminating waters will forbid further wayfaring.'

'Your warning is well received. I presume by "Swarth Force" you mean "Black Force",' said Tahquil coolly. 'Yet you did not warn us earlier of the approach of wood-goblins.'

'Ho-iss!' The bird-girl raised her narrow arms, the feather cloak fanning from them in jagged folds like wings. 'Shift-swan slave hoped wingless ones were wiser.'

'In unfamiliar waters even *fowl queens* may become ensnared,' said Tahquil, unable to resist a hint of sarcasm. 'Warn us of everything. Do not fail us another time.'

'Hearken,' hissed the swanmaiden, leaning one degree closer. 'Sweet-speaking handsome one woos where sprigs hang heavy with fruit. Fair face, fair words, sinister intent. She who falls for shadows shall soon weave her shroud.'

'You speak of dangers in Cinnarine, which lies far ahead, if we ever reach it. But more immediately, what awaits us in Lallillir?'

'Water wights haunt shores of Swarth Force—seelie, harmless. Fair or foul, sweet wench of shining hair or wizened hag, slender, well-favoured stalwart or strange, hairy fellow. Speak well. Wet wights wish for fire's heat. Show hospitality. Say "welcome".'

'Gruagachs? You speak of gruagachs?'

'Sooth,' said the swanmaiden, or perhaps it was the wind that spoke, for she was no longer there.

Out of sight to the west, far beyond Swarth Fell and Bleak Fell, several thousand tons of water approached rapidly. High above the sea they rolled, driven by powerful atmospheric pressures. Part of the ocean had once again risen, distilled, into the welkin; another quarter-turn of the wheel that forever rotated, pumping the pure and colourless heart's blood of Aia.

On the fell-sides of Lallillir a poignant wail drew itself out like spun flax and wound itself on night's spindle—an eldritch storm-harbinger's alert. The moon like a thin smile stretched itself behind the imminence of rain and was intermittently obscured. Sporadically moonless and starless, the night concealed stumbling blocks, rude fountains and other obstacles. The three who endeavoured to hasten downhill on the southern shore of Black Force had only the tilt of the land to guide them, and brief glimmers of nocturnal radiance, and the shouting waters and a sense of the cold stream-bed at their right hands, steep deep, rugged as broken teeth. Soon this wicked, chuckling, innocent gush would be fed from the skies. The fell-tops, the fell-sides would deliver to it the excess of the saturated air's bounty in long strands, in shallow blowing sheets, in beaded chains and spatters of glassy globules mirroring the night. Then, Black Force would transform. A brimming, thundering engine, it would grow mighty enough to bruise the bones of Erith, to break trees, to crush those who dared to step across the stones strewn across its terminus.

Before then, would-be traversers must reach the crossing place.

Down alongside Black Force they clambered. Fallen logs lay across their way, bright with dinner plates of orange fungus. Here, tiny siofra frolicked. The wights themselves were reminiscent of red-capped mushrooms. They swaggered, slyly peeping and snickering—until Viviana, in a temper, cast a stone at them and they seemed to go up in smoke, leaving only a hollow, heartless emptiness of roaring water that was somehow worse than the petty harassment, and accompanied by the awareness of being studied by antipathetic eyes.

Again, clouds shrouded the stars.

Slipping, staggering, they went blindly in the darkness, crawling sometimes, feeling with their hands for purchase. In this domain of unseelie watchers, Tahquil had no inclination to remove her glove to exploit the ring's illuminative qualities. Hampered by obstacles of rocky outcroppings, cliffs, thickset rearing tree-roots whose soil had been washed from their arches in past times of spate, and deep brakes of fern across their route, the travellers wondered if it would take the entire night to reach the river.

Thunder gonged the sky in the distance, pushing Tahquil and her companions forward with greater urgency, yet progress was protracted, for while speed was paramount, care must be exercised. A turned ankle, a fractured limb would ultimately prove fatal.

Above the dinning of approaching thunder and the cacophony of water could be heard a rattling of shells, a chorus of shrill laughter, an argument of nasty tongues in some unfamiliar patois—yet this might have been imaginary, a hallucination of hearing, brought about by continual high-level noise. Tahquil even considered she could hear an orchestra of violins. The uncanny melody revolved continuously in her head, playing throughout the inmost halls of her brain.

There was no stopping for rest or refreshment. Fat raindrops began to fall desultorily, patting the cheeks of the travellers like fond mothers. The damsels licked their moisture from their lips. No one spoke. No one emitted any sound save an indrawn breath when balance was momentarily forfeited, an involuntary yelp when an unseen rock or twig scored flesh, a muffled exclamation at unexpected eccentricities of the terrain. All night they battled on, the gravid rainclouds pressing lower over their heads, the thunder pounding its premonitory drums ever closer. Static charges were building in the ether. Towards the bleak morning, an eldritch singing started up from all directions—a joining of reedy and croaking and pure, high voices structured in a weird progression and relationship of chords, raising the hair of the listeners.

At *uhta*, they reached the ford.

For a moment, a rift in the clouds allowed a sidereal gleam to splinter down. The mouth of Black Force smiled wide and shallow. Flat stones spanned it, as promised by the swanmaiden. Dark as polished jet, the torrent ran rapidly between these spray-spattered slabs. The opposite bank of the Force was hidden in an undergrowth of umbellifers—wild angelica, lesser water parsnip, hemlock—their flat-topped blossoms nodding like meringues of white lace.

In that very pre-dawn hour, the heavens unleashed their pent-up tears. Rain sprang down in diagonal spars. As though they were aware of the impending increase in their strength, the waters of Black Force noisily poured themselves with greater exuberance around the flat, irregular stones. They spurled in cascades of black sheened with silver, in whirlpools like spiral nebulae, in whale spouts and tiny fountains, all dimpled by the impact of raindrops whose craters were ringed with leaping droplets of displaced water like tiny, split-second coronets. Wet and shiny the flagstones lay, in a lengthy disjointed line. Some low-lying ones were already water-filmed.

'Too soon the waters rise!' Caitri's shouts filtered through the tumult of rain, through the crashing and booming of air rapidly expanding along the paths of lightning. 'Sorrow take the swan's foul and paltry advice—we are too late!'

Tahquil turned a rain-lashed face towards the little girl.

'No. If we do not cross now it might be many days before the Force subsides enough. It is perilous to wait for long in one place—because of what lies ahead, no less than what comes from behind. I dare not waste any more time.'

She pulled a rope from her pack and tied one end about her waist. After paying out a few lengths, she attached Caitri similarly. The other end of the rope she offered to Viviana.

'Crossing now is folly,' shrieked the courtier. 'I remain here.'

'Solitude in Lallillir is a worse folly,' bawled Tahquil, securing the straps on her pack. 'And each moment we stand here in argument, the waters rise a little further. Come!'

She strode to the stony verge of the watercourse. From this point, the distance to the nearest stepping stone was a daunting five feet or more across boiling glass. Stepping back a couple of yards, she ran up and launched herself out over the water, landing jarringly on the barren islet. From there she leaped to the second step.

'Caitri?'

Presently, the young girl followed. Looking back, Tahquil saw Viviana gaining the first stepping stone. Rain sluiced down in blinding sheets, in drowning torrents, in liquid walls. The air was solid rain. It hammered on their heads, their shoulders and packs. It dragged down their clothing, filled their boots, their eyes, their mouths and ears and overbrimmed the cups of their skulls. *Down, down, down,* it sang, and *down, down, down* sang the surging Force meeting the swarming river. Another quarter-turn of the wheel—what rises must fall.

Like improbable frogs, the travellers bounded from one stone to another, and now each landing place was skimmed with the newborn flood. The water was a silver dragon, its surface laminated with scales formed by pelting raindrops. The dragon clashed and steamed.

There was no turning back—the ford's centre point had been achieved. Now, as much distance divided them from the northern shore as from the southern, and both were invisible. They imagined themselves marooned in a vitreous chamber, close-walled.

Tahquil leaped to the next islet. Her foot splashed into the two inches of water racing over it. The vigorous current tugged and she leaned against its drag, leaned on billowing robes of fluidity.

The rope cinching her waist jerked her painfully to her knees. Taut as a gittern-string it dragged at her, stretching like a rod away into the massed armies of rain lances. Caitri, one moment ago a shadowy figure melting through layers of water, had vanished. She had been taken by the waters, and Black Force was rising.

Tilting back, Tahquil braced herself against the submerged rock, contrary to the determined pressure of this tide. She drew hard on the rope. Her sinews cracked. At vision's edge, the form of Viviana crouched and did the same. The river boiled. Its flow banked up powerfully against the form of Caitri downstream, held against it by the ropes. The driving waters curled like surf over the little girl's head. When they dragged her in she was conscious, but Black Force had whisked her pack away and the waters were still rising.

Tahquil held Caitri in her arms, putting her mouth to the child's ear.

'I have not the strength to support you. Should we jump together and our timing fail, we should both fall. You must do it alone.'

'Cut the rope,' gasped Caitri. 'I cannot.'

'No.'

Tahquil left her, then, and sprang away through dark curtains. Her only hope lay in desperation. She willed Caitri to follow, and in a moment the antics of the rope indicated hope fulfilled.

The current's pressure grew. Soon the rising tide would become irresistible and sweep the feet of the travellers from under them, tossing them into the flood like dolls, filling not only their eyes but their lungs, their stomachs, the last moments of their awareness. Squinting through the vertical gloom, Tahquil perceived a ragged, linear darkness—the opposite shore. Breathing water, choking on fire, sometimes gasping a breath, they gained it at last.

There in drenched debilitation they lay and allowed panic to drain from them in pools on the ground, letting the rain rinse it from them and course down to suffuse the Blackwater along with the raging waters that had induced that terror.

Fear ebbed and light waxed, but the silver flails of the rain did not let up their scourging. The pewter and grisaille radiance of the day revealed drowning forests on the northern shore of Black Force, and now the travellers were shivering. Beneath a half-fallen tree they sipped the glistening red syrup of *nathrach deirge*. Somewhat revived, they struggled to their feet and tramped off in search of a dry place to eke out the day in repose.

Nothing remained unwet. Not a leaf, not a sprig nor raceme nor shard did not drip and run with moisture. Not a stick touted itself as fit for kindling.

It rained all day, a shimmering rain. The black bread which was all that remained of their provisions had softened in their packs and become black mud. Kept warm by dragon's blood, the travellers tried futilely to shelter in the lee of fallen logs. Sleep was impossible. The heavy sounds of pouring gallons thundered blankly in the skulls of the three companions. When taking their turn at the watch, they instinctively listened for untoward resonances, notes out of key, any signal of peril approaching. But the water's roar rose up like a wall all around and would allow no other sound to penetrate. They were forcibly deaf to all save the water's utterance.

That evening the deluge petered out. In the last light of the day Tahquil haunted the willows, watching for more spheres of Fairbread. Perhaps her eyes were obfuscated with the sands of sleep deprivation. Perhaps the elusive mistletoe did not grow on the sallies to the north of Black Force. In any event, she discovered none.

Caitri found a tree trunk which had fallen across another. So rotten was its underside that she was able to punch right through the cortex. Inside was a mass of fibrous debris, the desiccated pith of the tree, still arid within its rind. Soon the travellers had it piled up and burning. Their clothes began to dry.

As night endured, Tahquil stared deeply into the fire. The flames burned themselves into the backs of her eyes. When the ring unexpectedly constricted her finger she looked away, accustoming her vision to the shadows, murmuring a warning to her friends: 'Wights are nearby.'

A swatch of bullion gleamed. Some marsh flower—a tall, luteous lily perhaps—stood at the brink of darkness. Tahquil's eyes widened. She held her breath.

Could this be a Talith woman?

The lady in green glided forward. Her hair was the yellow of daffodils, marsh marigolds and buttercups. It draped in silken folds over her shoulders and down past her slight waist, which was girdled with waterlilies. Small green-white blossoms entwined themselves, or conceivably were *rooted* in that hair. Strikingly attractive was the face, and clearly not human. Sparkles of reflected firelight ran up and down the filaments of her butter-lemon hair. They coursed along the water runnels which streamed from it, and from the leaf-green gown with the dagged sleeves flowing to the ground where her two bare feet stood in a puddle, like twin fishes.

Comparably with fuaths and the hair of sea-folk, gruagachs could never get dry.

The gruagach parted the petals of her river-rose mouth.

'May I dry myself at your fire?'

A husky tone, sumptuous, rich with verdancy and fruitfulness. Tahquil recalled the swanmaiden's rede—'*Speak well.*'

'You are welcome,' she said formally, concealing her apprehension.

Viviana and Caitri edged nervously away from the eldritch visitor, who regarded them from beneath heavy lids and stretched out long-fingered hands towards the blaze. Water trickled down the slim arms and dripped from the wrists.

'Star save me,' whispered Caitri, round-eyed. She clutched at the ragged folds of her garments as a drowning mortal might clutch at floating twigs.

Viviana fingered the knife at her belt. Catching her eye, Tahquil shook her head.

Through the night other gruagachs came. They asked the same question, receiving the same answer. The second to come out of the darkness was a manlike wight, naked and shaggy. The third was a comely, slender youth clad in lettuce-green and poppy-red.

'We ought to be on our way by now,' Viviana muttered to Tahquil behind her hand. 'You said we must not tarry.'

'Do you suggest that we turn our backs on our visitors and walk away?' asked Tahquil in a low tone. 'That we take our eyes off them and simultaneously give them offence? Nay. While they remain, we must remain also. Take advantage of this lull. Sleep.'

Ignoring the intriguing phenomenon of wightish masculinity uncovered, Caitri was already slumbering, curled up like a kitten. When Tahquil glanced again at the girl-gruagach she saw a crone, wan and haggard, stretching out bony fingers towards the blaze. Water flowed down her skinny arms and dripped off her wrists. Shuddering, Viviana made as if to rise.

'Bide!' Tahquil pleaded, clutching Viviana by the elbow. It was curiously easy to restrain the courtier. Perhaps she had not been so keen to depart after all, or else she could not resist the grip of the ring-hand.

'Since your hands touched the goblin fruit you have not been the same,' said Tahquil.

'It is you who has altered,' sneered Viviana, yet she made no further move.

Tahquil looked at the crone. She was a fair damsel again, with long, golden hair like Summer sunlight on water. A frog of jade perched on her shoulder.

'Cows' milk is sweet,' suddenly stated the naked, hairy fellow. His skin was slick, his curly brown hair and beard wringing wet as though he had just that instant climbed from a bath. Hirsute mats covered his chest and back. Nests of it clustered under his armpits and at his groin. Hair thickly thatched his arms and sprouted on the backs of his hands.

'If we had any milk we would share it gladly,' said Tahquil. 'Alas, we have none.'

Under bushy brows the gruagach's eyes scintillated; chips of emerald, like the eyes of drowners. He turned that green regard back to the fire, stretching out his big, rough hands. Water sputtered and sizzled, going up in tendrils of steam.

The ground canted slightly towards the gruagachs, otherwise the mortals would presently have found themselves sitting in an expanding pool upon which tiny green-white blossoms floated.

'Shillava shillava, sonsirrilon delahirrina.' The voice of the handsome youth in grass-green and holly-berry red was a rippling of water over stones, a sighing of shaken reeds.

'Immerse,' enigmatically responded the golden maiden.

That was all the conversation there was to be had with the gruagachs pointlessly drying themselves at the fire, and of that fact Tahquil was glad. Seduced, sedated by warmth, it was all she could do to remain vigilant. She noticed that the belle again appeared as a hag, and a most decrepit one.

Make up your mind . . .

By dawn the water wights had, inevitably, disappeared.

A trail of water and miniature green-white flowers led to a backwater down by a loop in the river. The companions followed it to the water's marge and stood beneath the willows, looking out across the glimmering surface. On slim green stalks, the dart-shaped leaves of arrowhead poked up from the shallows. The plant bore three-petalled blooms, white with a purple blotch at the centre, short-stemmed whorls on long fingers.

'The tubers of arrowhead are starchy. They are edible,' said Tahquil.

'But are not gruagachs dwelling down there?' asked Caitri, gazing at the black water.

'I doubt it. I consider that leading us here was their way of rewarding us for our rather useless hospitality.'

Tahquil stripped off her damp clothes and slipped between the greenish water-panes of the billabong. The chill was a sudden violation, like a slap in the face. Mud oozed between her toes. She felt the swollen tubers beneath the mire, dug around them with her feet, gulped air, ducked underwater and pulled them up. Waist-deep she waded among flat discs of pondweed, her hair streaming like wet leaves over the waxy contours of her body. Returning to the banks she reached up and offered the produce to her friends. They took the dripping food from her hands, momentarily in awe of her.

Carefully, Caitri said, 'My eyes deceive me. You are a semblance of—'

Tahquil flicked water in her face. 'I am no water wight! In good sooth, I am weary of wetness and long to be dry. I should not be surprised if my ears soon begin to sprout watercress.' She dived a second time.

By the time the succulent tubers had been harvested, cooked and consumed, the sun behind the roiling clouds still roofing Lallillir had reached its zenith. Having fed themselves, the travellers fed the fire with the last of the arid fuel and slept until dusk.

'According to the urisk, Black Bridge crosses the Ravenswater upstream of its conjunction with our friend the Blackwater,' said Tahquil, stuffing her pack with cooked arrowhead tubers. 'We must direct our steps uphill again from here, away from the river.'

'Besides, the swan told us culicidae lurk down here in the sheltered deeps of the valley,' said Caitri.

'The rain will have driven them away,' responded Tahquil, 'for the nonce. Though, doubtless they will soon return.'

Uphill they went, veering northeast to where they reckoned Black Bridge must lie.

More rain fell throughout that night, in listless curtains of monotony. The fishers' oilskins by now were too ragged to be waterproof. The travellers' garments again became waterlogged. Mud sucked at their boots. From beyond the rain curtains came the percussive *plink* of droplets like glass chimes, and sometimes a light patter as of fingertips drumming on a tabletop. Freshets chortled in channels. Of wind there was no breath. Between showers all was silent, save for the chuckle and tinkle of condensing vapour rolling off leaves. Lallillir loomed pearl-grey, her dripping trees swathed in mist, the nearer trunks glistening dark and wet, the further ones fading as they marched into obscurity.

'And my hair to grow toadstools,' said Tahquil to herself, wiping rain out of her eyes and contemplating the advantages of an afternoon in the desert.

On the twenty-fifth day of Uianemis the rain contracted to the east. While the travellers slept, or drowsily kept watch, the sky cleared. The primrose sun of Summer bloomed through skies of raucous blue and Lallillir smoked like a flagon of mulled wine in a nightwatchman's chilblained hands. The travellers stowed their tattered oilskins in their packs.

'No need to smear my face with mud for disguise,' said Tahquil. 'It has occurred naturally.'

The top of Wold Fell was running down to meet them now, descending towards the east-west arm of Ravenstonedale. Sharply it dropped, and by the closing of the following night the travellers had reached its furthest point.

They stood at the lip of a steep and narrow dene, congested with shadows. Steaming mountain ash trees clad its walls, soaring above tree ferns and low-growing fronds. Tier below hazy tier dropped to the broad band of a river as black as schorl: the Ravenswater.

Further to the right, a high and windy shape could be discerned. Tall, pointed arches grew out of spindly pillars of black stone. Black Bridge was narrow; it seemed to have been drafted and embellished by a fine-pointed pen.

Moving down into the shelter of the mountain ashes, the travellers nestled uncomfortably between their massive roots, and there passed the day in vaporous black-green shade.

Towards nightfall a breeze stirred.

The howl that tore the mantle of evening was like no vocalisation Tahquil had ever heard. No storm-warner, no Boubrie-bird made such a sound. It was a round, melodious, chilling summons that began with a bass yodel, soared suddenly to a high pitch and finished on a descending note—imperative and primitive as instinct, savage as hunger, wild as wind, remote and solitary as the moon. At the noise, Viviana cursed in courtingle and jumped up, tilting her head back to look up into the tree beneath which they sheltered.

'What yowls?' cried Caitri, following her gaze as though she expected something deadly to immediately drop out on their heads.

'How swiftly can you climb a tree?' cried the courtier. 'That was the howl of the morthadu!' She reached for a low branch.

'Wait,' said Tahquil. 'What's the use of trapping ourselves in a tree? The morthadu might not be able to climb but they will only scent us, and lay siege until we drop down with weakness like starved possums. We are downwind of them—I am certain they have not detected us. See—the breeze that stirs the ash leaves blows from the northeast and that, I suspect, is where the call issued from.'

'How agreeable,' said Viviana. 'That is also the direction of the bridge.'

'I'd rather,' said Caitri, 'cross the bridge and be stuck in a tree in Cinnarine eating apples than stuck in an ash tree gnawing on my knuckles.'

'Either way you would end up as wight-fodder,' said Viviana pessimistically.

The howl came rolling again, wheeling vertiginously across the sky and through the trees.

'We cannot go back,' reasoned Tahquil, her voice rising with urgency, 'nor is there any purpose in turning east or west and remaining in Lallillir. We must depart from this soggy land and the only way is by crossing the Ravenswater. While the wind continues to blow from the northeast we shall be safe—'

'Oh yes, and the morthadu shall sit back on their haunches and stay exactly where they are to enable us to avoid them,' said Viviana.

'They will roam,' answered Tahquil. 'But with luck they will roam upwind. At any rate—'

'We have no choice,' Caitri completed the sentence.

As noiselessly as possible, they set off towards the bridge.

Hours later, the sun rose, like a rose.

No light penetrated Ravenstonedale. The high walls of the valley blocked it out. Dark birds floated in circles over the fell-tops.

'Listen,' said Tahquil. Her face closed in concentration.

Zephyrs streamed like gauze scarves stitched with the chirruping of birds, the hum and scratch of sequined arthropods, the satiny chains of running water.

At length Caitri said, 'To what?'

'The howling. It has ceased.'

'They are nocturnal, the morthadu,' said Viviana caustically. 'I thought it common knowledge.'

'Perhaps they sleep,' said Tahquil. 'But while they sleep we do not. Beneath the day's eye we shall continue to make our way to Black Bridge and across it.'

None argued, but tiredness bullied them for they had trudged all night. Foodless, fireless, sleepless, they had plodded on like three ragged, filthy beggars. Their fisherfolks' garb hung in unidentifiable tatters. Their boots, softened by water and minced by uneven ground, were coming apart. Mud sullied them in patches from head to foot. Their hair appeared to be all of the same drab shade—a mousy brownish-grey. In matted hanks it tangled about their shoulders, interwoven with small twigs and leaves. Even their eyes, peering dispiritedly from pinched and grimy faces, were not unblemished. Fine blood-threads knitted across their white ground.

'What has she put on today, the queen, the queen? What has she put on today, the comely queen?' sang Viviana. 'Is it crimson is it yellow, is it purple is it blue? Are there diamonds on her collar, are there rubies on her shoe?'

'Hold your noise!' Caitri flared.

Viviana laughed. 'No, her gown is dirty brown and her hair is falling down, and they'll run her out of town, the comely queen!'

'What are you playing at?' Tahquil demanded. 'Are you deliberately trying to make our position known? To identify me?'

Viviana shrugged. 'My singing shall make no difference. What might be aware of our presence is aware already and the morthadu are, presumably, asleep.' She began to hum.

'Please, Via.'

The courtier smiled, though not with her eyes, and the humming evolved into something more tuneless.

Caitri said, 'Via, if you do not stop that, Tahquil and I shall knock you down and stuff rags in your mouth.'

The humming ceased.

''Tis a pity the rain could not wash off the taint of goblin fruit,' sighed Tahquil.

Two pearls crystallised in Viviana's eyes.

'I cannot help it,' she said. Then she blinked, the tears fell and in their dry sources a cold, remote expression returned.

Halfway down the slope the ring bit into Tahquil's finger. She raised her hand in mute signal and the three of them fluttered like bedraggled thrushes into concealment beneath the shadows of a linden tree. Tahquil extended her senses, probing out into the far reaches of hearing, taste, scent, sight.

Presently she said, 'I can detect no danger.'

'Where is the swanmaiden,' sighed Caitri, 'when we need her?'

Tahquil's finger hurt where the ring stung it. She slipped off both glove and ring, weighing the starry gold circle in her palm. No ridged band of reddened flesh marked its erstwhile abode— her finger remained unmarred. Caitri was shading her eyes with her hand, gazing down towards Black Bridge.

'I am not certain of it,' the little girl said, 'but I think I see things moving down there.'

Tahquil looked again. 'You may be right.'

With a flash of inspiration she held the ring to her eye like a spyglass. All at once the world expanded, clarified. Every detail appeared intensified, sharp-cut. There, seemingly close enough to touch, was Black Bridge. It stalked across the deep gorge, over waters as smooth and dark as oil. The stone of the bridge was rotten, necrotic. Mosses crawled in the jointed apexes of each arch. Grotesqueries were carved into its stanchions and its ribbed vaulting. This was an ancient structure, mysterious, and desolate, falling into ruin.

At the near end of the bridge and almost out on the span between its low walls, prowled long, lean coagulations of twilight, each one pierced with a double-pronged fork to reveal the red fires smouldering within the black hide. On the river's opposite bank the long grasses stirred, but there was no breeze.

'Five walk on this shore, two wait at the near edge of the bridge,' Tahquil said wonderingly. 'Wolf-seemings. The morthadu. I suspect that more of their kind prowl on the far side of the bridge.' Slowly, she moved her spy-ring to the right, scanning the rest of the landscape. Two long, feline shapes disconnected themselves from the arch of a fallen tree trunk, then melted elegantly into a fern brake. 'And that is not the worst of our troubles,' Tahquil added. 'A pair of grey malkins lurks nigh. Being *lorraly* beasts, mortal to the bone, they will have no qualms about crossing the Ravenswater.'

A strand of unkempt hair whipped across her face. '*Obban tesh!* The wind—'tis veering to the east. Should it swing further about they will catch our scent for sure.'

'What now?' asked Caitri.

'What now indeed! Stalemate, for the moment. We have not the power to fight malkins or the morthadu—neither can the swanmaiden drive them off. The great cats would rend a bird to shreds and devour her, eldritch or not—and treat us the same way.'

'Methinks they fear fire,' suggested Caitri, hesitantly.

'And where's a dry twig to be had,' interjected Viviana, 'let alone enough material to make brands to bear with us? And what if it rained and our torches were extinguished? The trees are still laden with water enough to provide their own rainstorms. See?'

Perversely she shook a tree fern, kicked its fibrous stem. Glassy beads came rolling off its fronds and showered down on her. She laughed and shook back her wet hair.

'Hush!' said Tahquil. 'Sound carries on the wind. The beasts of the pack have sharp ears.'

''Zooks, that precludes your calling the Bird I suppose,' said Viviana carelessly. 'Not that she is much help.'

As if on cue, a shadow passed briefly overhead. The swan sank behind the trees, instantly reappearing in her *alter-native* shape, pushing through malachite frondery. The feathers of her cloak were ruffled, as was her previous cool aloofness. Birdlike, her head jerked abruptly. She kept glancing nervously over her shoulder. The pupils of her strange, avian eyes had dilated like black suns—her kind detested taking their humanlike shape during the day. Only dire circumstances would have driven her to such desperate measures.

'Hazard!' she hissed, without preamble. 'Unwholesome wolverhounds hold the span. Sly, sneaking malkins hunt hither. The wind wavers and soon sniffing spiracles shall scent humans.

Unseelie hounds and feral felines wait, with hidden hopes. Hazard follows subsequently in Lallillir. Foul water wights wander, singing suck-spirits set forth. Three on foot should swiftly surmount strong-streaming watercourse.'

'How shall we elude the cats and the lupine guardians of the bridge?' demanded Tahquil eloquently. 'Surely you cannot lift us and fly us across the Ravenswater?'

'Several ways suffice to straddle flowing waters. Follow. Follow.'

Down the dene's sheer sides the travellers plunged in the swanmaiden's wake, slipping beneath the emerald lattices of tree ferns. Embroideries of spaghnum moss squelched underfoot. Whithiue was leading them towards the left, downstream of the bridge. What her purpose was they could not guess.

'Is there a second bridge?' panted Caitri.

'I saw only one,' returned Tahquil.

The breeze swung gently to the south. A ululation, pure and sombre, echoed down the valley. The travellers thrust words aside and hastened on. After an hour, or maybe two or three, it came to Tahquil that the thunder of a mighty river rumbled more loudly through her consciousness. By now they must be almost level with the Ravenswater's swift and terrible tide. Ahead, the tall stalks of tree ferns parted to reveal the gloss of the sombre river only some ten yards below. Although no rocks tore the surface of the Ravenswater and no snags interrupted the smooth race, foam and bubbles whipping past indicated a flood moving at incalculable speeds.

'I do not care what sort of boat she has waiting!' declared Caitri. 'No vessel could navigate *that* current safely. Even if it with-stood the battering, we should be swept down to the sea, for how could we hope to achieve landfall?'

The swanmaiden beckoned. Glistering droplets on her feather cloak imprisoned images of leaves, distorting them to a semblance of dark green lace.

She stood beside a low stonework thrusting up out of the hill-side, as crumbling and corrupt as Black Bridge itself. Leaf mould and detritus had built up against its buttresses, partially submerging them. Moss and lichens velveted the massive blocks so that only their shape betrayed their mortal-sculpted origins.

The swanmaiden pointed with a bird-bone finger.

Deep in the stonework loomed an arched void—an entrance screened with leaves.

'Here stair starts,' their guide said. 'Step within. Stair sinks sub-terraneously. Stone-hewn warren sub-fathoms foundations of watercourse. Here's a historic subway, the hour-honoured under-mine. Wights fail to follow here, for water flows circumjacently, squarely sideways, flawing and fracturing. Finite-span felines fear to stray in such a worm's warren. Hasten. Sooth, wild ones scent sweet flesh and hunt.'

As she and her companions fumbled through the archway, extending their toes to feel for the stair, Tahquil briefly thought, *Why should malkins fear to walk down there?*

But it was too late to reconsider. Fiendish howls came scream-ing from every direction. Incandescent-eyed bolts of black energy burst out of the foliage. Instantaneously, a wraithlike darkness shot up and arrowed away into the sky: the swan taking flight. Scissoring jaws followed Tahquil into the orifice of stone, snap-ping shut on her sleeve, tearing it away. Still ungloved, the ring flashed with the brilliance of magnified stars. The scarlet eyes siz-zled and disappeared. The stair treads pushed themselves at the soles of her feet, and with a crunching patter of boots, the refugees passed rapidly underground.

By the saffron effulgence of the ring they descended five hun-dred and eighty-eight corkscrewed steps that plumbed the ground like a vertical drill. Sometimes the walls pressed close, and the stair bored tightly through. At other times they opened out and the stair hung in emptiness from thin stalks of pillars, with no appar-ent means of support from beneath. As they went down, a dreadful certitude developed in Tahquil's thoughts—the vial of *nathrach deirge* was missing. During that last flight down the val-ley-side the neck-chain had snagged on something—a twig, perhaps. Momentarily trapped, Tahquil had wrenched free, plunged on heedlessly, dwelling only on escape. Her right hand now sought her throat. Uncluttered, the tender expanse of skin stretched over the slender collarbones, the throbbing carotid. Her throat was indeed bereft of its precious ornament.

The vial shall be sorely missed. Down here, cold reigns.

Yet this stairwell felt different from the under-roads of Doundelding and the Beithir's lair. In the first place, no friendly wall-fungi conveniently illuminated it, no ionised taste embittered the air. Dead was the air but not entirely, not as air would be that for aeons had failed to circulate through living tissue, nor been stirred through by the passage of living things. It smelled like air that occasionally escaped to be sweetened with sunlight and leaves, before re-entering refreshed. Ventilation must exist, hereabouts. Possibly also, lungs which required it.

Thoughts berated Tahquil.

Why should malkins fear to walk beneath the Ravenswater? Has she stooped to perfidy at last, the swanmaiden? But no. It is impossible for creatures of eldritch to break their word—she promised to see us safe to Cinnarine. Yet perhaps she considers this under-mine to be part of Cinnarine . . .

After treading upon the five hundred and eighty-eighth step, the companions reached a level place. Many gnawings ate at them, not least hunger. But no food was to be obtained, no heartening dragon's blood was there to be sipped, only water filming the sandstone substrata in random patches. Of course—the stair ended below the uttermost dregs of the minacious Ravenswater.

Caitri collapsed.

How long is it since we slept? Tahquil's rationality was hampered by a melange of weariness, hunger and longing. *My wits are fuddled. I cannot reason aright. We must keep moving.*

'Caitri has never entirely recovered her strength since being struck by ælf-shot,' she said aloud to Viviana. 'A stroke's effects can linger. By rights, we ought to have left her safe in Appleton Thorn. We must keep moving, for warmth.'

Viviana stated, 'There's dragon's blood.'

'I do not wish to use it all up,' Tahquil quickly replied. She had no desire to reveal the truth at this time, thus paving the path to despair.

'Tis inexhaustible,' countered Viviana.

'Not necessarily. Let us hoard it for more dire circumstances.'

'What could be more urgent?'

Caitri made a small sound like a sick bird.

'Lean on me,' said Tahquil to the little girl. 'I am no stalwart to bear you on my shoulders, but I can lend you strength.'

For what it is worth.

'Come, Caitri,' she urged, 'think what awaits us at the end of this under-mine—the fair, green orchards of Cinnarine blowing in sunny breezes at the height of Summer.'

Caitri stood up. She hooked her arm around Tahquil's shoulders. Viviana took hold of her other arm.

'And fruit,' the courtier said indistinctly, as though the juices already ran voluptuously in her mouth. 'Ripe fruit in bunches, waiting to be plucked and slurped.'

They walked on, side by side. Moisture trickled down Tahquil's face. Unlike the moisture behaving similarly on the walls, it was briny.

The under-mine was decorated with eroded carvings and cracked stone furniture. Pointed arches and ribbings had been incised into the natural sandstone. A gargoyle fountainhead jutted from the wall, spouting a thin jet of water into a worn basin. Further on, other fountains protruded, dry and clogged. The tunnel roared softly, like a predator; the resonance of the overhead current. Close, so close over their heads, the entire mass of the Ravenswater oppressed. Tahquil wondered—*How many tons of water? A million? Partitioned only by a layer of rock how thick? Fifty yards, thirty, perhaps in places only ten? That power, generated by water's flow but unable to be sensed by humankind, would here hold ultimate authority. To pass so close beneath the river would be anathema to wights. No cause for human alarm would emanate from eldritch quarters.*

'Hour-honoured', *and* 'historic' *were the words Whithiue had used to describe this under-mine. Ancient were its supports, old and neglected its rising vaults. What rises must fall. One day, or one night, the river would come crashing down through this roof. Would it be this moment?*

Fie! Tahquil chided herself. *Light-loving above-ground dwellers*

*typically turn to morbid musings when forced down to the world
below, with its connotations of graves and decay. If this secret way
has held back the Ravenswater for centuries, there is no reason
why it should choose this particular moment to surrender.*

The tunnel passed through an archway endowed with carvings
of harvest-laden wains, and widened out into a rectangular cavern, high-vaulted. The leaf-ring's dandelion radiance extended to
the walls. Tahquil looked for the evidence of other entrances and
exits.

What if this were a maze, like the diggings of Doundelding—
a labyrinth to lose, abuse and confuse them? No openings showed
themselves, save one archway directly ahead. As they made for it,
part of the cavern wall gave a heave.

In Tahquil's chest, wings of fear clapped frenetically, like an
arrow-impaled bird.

'Keep moving!' she cried.

But it seemed as though she and her companions swam
through honey. Their limbs, overtaxed, were loath to obey.

A lustre awoke and ran along a flexuosity. A dorsal wing partially erected itself, brazen, like a half-opened fan. A spangle
disclosed then reshuttered its eye. The cavern's exit dwindled until
it was a hundred miles away, unreachable.

'Keep moving!'

Rustlings and scrapings issued from the margins of the chamber. A stone mouth gaped in front of them. Swallowed, the
travellers fled the place with many a backward glance.

A sere slithering sounded.

'What was that?'

'I know not.'

'Can it follow us? Is it following?'

Tahquil gave no answer. Caitri's arm across her shoulders
weighed like a collar of iron. Presently, Viviana said, 'It comes
after.'

'I know,' said Tahquil.

That which trailed them equalled their pace, while the river's
ear-numbing roar crescendoed. Onward they hastened. Against
the tunnel's wall, a high-backed chair stood like an empty throne,

crudely engraved with motifs of candles and swords. A scrolled pedestal upheld a stone cup. The flesh of the travellers crawled like corpse-maggots.

It was not until the passageway flared to a second chamber and they had crossed the greater part of it, that a disturbance forced them to halt, whirling to face their pursuer. The sidings of this subsequent dungeon roused now, shimmering from bland stone-grey to coils of iridescence. Fugacious rainbows rippled along reptilian convolutions like oil spilled on water; rubious, rubicelle, aureate, viridescent, argent, cerulean. A fork, nigrescent, flicked out and tasted the air.

'Fare thee well, dear friends,' said Viviana sardonically.

Caitri clung to her in unspeaking horror.

'I never thought to be worm's food *before* I met the grave,' said the courtier, with a bitter smile.

Tahquil held up the ringed hand. The watch-worms, their colours cycling, did not flinch or draw back.

'They do not fear the ring. But I have met such a worm before,' said Tahquil, 'in Gilvaris Tarv.'

'Tell it your name, then,' sneered Viviana. 'Maybe 'twill remember you and smile as it bites.'

'I wonder, could this be the same one? There's no way of telling.'

'Do they eat humankind?'

'Yes. Perhaps discerningly.'

'If discerningly, then you are done for, sweet my lady.'

'The worm I saw slew only one who had tormented it.'

'Tell it we adore it, since you two are on such good terms.'

'Viviana, you *are* amusing when spiteful.'

'Die laughing,' carelessly said Mistress Wellesley, goblin-corrupted.

Thrice the monstrous beasts circumnavigated the cavern, aiming their crystal eyes from all angles. One, perhaps the one which had followed the travellers, unclosed its maw, unhinging its dislocatable lower mandible to reveal a second set of jaws nestled within. These opened, shut and were closed upon. With a flutter of its dorsal spines and vestigial gill-wings, the oscillating worm recoiled on itself, retracting through the archway. The others sub-sided against the wall carvings, dulling to an emberous glow as of moonlight seen through stained glass or candlelight shining behind jewels.

'Reprieved,' said Tahquil, wiping the sweat from her brow.

'My life I'd not wager on it,' said Viviana as they vacated the precincts through a patterned archway, dragging Caitri, half-insensible, between them.

The throaty call of the river drew away and upward. Their way passed through a third worms' nest in the rock, another stretch of passageway and then a cul-de-sac footing a spiral stair. There, at the limit of endurance, on the naked floor they prostrated them-selves and let insentience claim them.

When they awoke after their vulnerable hours, aching and stiff, thin grey scales lay scattered about like coins. Watch-worms had been moving, close by.

Unmolested, the travellers drank from a gargoyle wall-fount. Afterwards they climbed the stair.

This stair seemed endless. The climbers, crawling on hands and knees, eventually resigned from craning their necks in search of a hint of light to indicate that they were approaching the north-ern exit. Then Tahquil, in the lead, put out her hand to reach the next step and yelped with surprise.

She had encountered a drapery of leaves.

No light gleamed through the interstices of this curtain.

'It is night outside,' whispered Tahquil.

'Have we reached the orchards of Cinnarine? Do you smell the fruit? Do you?' demanded Viviana, sniffing the air like a dog.

'No. But grey malkins may be lurking out there. They saw us enter the under-mine, and surely they know the location of this exit. They only have to run across the bridge, surround us and wait for the flies to embrace the web.'

'Thank you, O swanmaiden,' Viviana said, rolling her eyes heavenward.

Tahquil took off her pack. With all her might she flung it through the leaves. It landed with a thud, followed by silence. No sound of snarling or rending of fabric by sharp fangs disturbed the quietude.

'No malkins,' said Tahquil, and she heaved herself out of the hole, through the foliate curtain, before Viviana could append, *'At least, none foolish enough to dine upon a hempen pack.'*

On a rising slope of darkness she lay. Of fruit-glutted orchards there was no sign. At the top of the slope there was a row of pointing pines chiselled in black up a sky heavily sugared with stars. Far below and behind ran a river as heavy and lustrous as polished antimony—the Ravenswater, bisected by the swooping birds'-wing arches of Black Bridge.

They had emerged once more in Ravenstonedale, but on the other side of the bridge.

'It is perilous to remain here,' said Tahquil to Viviana as they seized Caitri by the arms and hauled her out of the crypt-like masonry. 'We must make for the heights. That way lies Cinnarine, for sure.'

The memory of a long, dark cry scoured through her head like lonely winds.

'Easier to utter than to execute,' said Viviana. 'I cannot go much further without nourishment. Fruit is what I need. Just a plum, or a small grape . . .'

Caitri groaned.

'Take her ankles,' said Tahquil, hoisting the recumbent form by the shoulders. They began to carry Caitri up the side of the valley, which the night had burned as black as cinders.

The wind remained in the south.

Awkwardly, with their burden, Tahquil and Viviana climbed the slope towards the pines lining the ridge top. Immediately behind the trees, immersed in their witchy shadows, a hedge grew high, untame and recklessly burgeoning. Formed of interlocking hawthorn bushes, this antique row of shrubbery stretched far in both directions. Small birds nested in it, tiny creatures of eldritch scampered in it, but large wights or *lorraly* beasts could never penetrate its dense and overgrown pleachings or brave its countless cusps. In days of yore the now vanished orchardists of

Cinnarine had planted this hedge-barrier along the outer perimeter of the sandstone windwall.

The windwall deflected the south wind and kept out the morthadu roaming in the vale of the sinister river. Those same orchardists had also constructed the under-mine, and a door was set in the windwall above the place where the under-mine emerged, but the iron-studded oaken beams of that door had long ago been penetrated and sundered and replaced by a weaving of living thorns, so that now no sign of its erstwhile existence remained.

Tahquil and Viviana studied the hedge behind the pines and guessed its purpose.

'I would rather be on the other side of that,' stated Viviana.

The two of them paced it for several yards in opposite directions, searching for a chink, an opening, a gap, knowing in their hearts there was no hope of this and being proved accurate.

They met together beside Caitri. She had dragged herself into a sitting position, resting her back against the rugose flank of a pine tree, her eyes as blank as two extinguished lamps.

'I expect to hear at any time the hunting notes of the morthadu,' said Tahquil, 'or see the baleful eyes of a malkin. Viviana, have you any rope in your pack? I have left mine down by the under-mine and am loath to retrace and retrieve.'

Without a word Viviana pulled out the vortex of hempen rope she had carried all the way from the abandoned cottage of Tavron Caiden near Huntingtowers. Sullenly she watched Tahquil select a pine and hoist herself up into the lower branches, the rope coiled about her shoulder.

The bark of the pines was deeply scored, harsh and unforgiving, like a clay surface baked in a desert sun. It tore at unprotected flesh. The rough lips of each crevice curled back on themselves in a grating snarl. Yet in all other affairs the pines showed benevolence. Their fallen needles mantled the ground with fragrant layers which allowed no growth of nettles or poisonous weeds or throttling undergrowth. Their arms were conveniently spaced and positioned for easy attainment, sprouting low on the trunk, sweeping the ground, offering a facile stair. The trees themselves stood vigorous, strong, noble. Higher up, dark green cone-laden boughs reached right across the top of the hedge of the windwall.

Blood oozed, stinging, from Tahquil's shins. It gathered in drops on her scraped elbows as she pulled herself up to the next branch and peered over the topmost sprigs of the green-berried hedge.

Almost imperceptibly, the air lightened by one shade. Far, far away—or maybe it was only a fancy—a cock crowed. And there beyond the hedge she beheld a sea of leaves stretching away to the north. It was gently tossed by tendrils of the south wind which flicked lasciviously at the skirts of the orchard trees to reveal, here and there, catching the waning starlight, clusters of hard orbs on their stems.

Tahquil secured the rope around a branch, close to the trunk.

'Caitri,' she called down softly, 'we are come to Cinnarine. Take hold of the rope. We will help you. One last effort and then you may rest.'

'I cannot do it,' said Caitri, but the warble of one of the morthadu came wavering from the direction of the river, and she struggled to her feet, stepping on the primary branches, hanging onto the rope. The branches bounced, swishing their tufts of clean, green pins beneath their new burden. Along an extended, horizontal limb she crawled on her belly, inch by inch, the cruel bark abrading. Just underneath the limb, the spikes of the hedge stuck up. They looked harsher than the pine bark, even in their pretty dresses and bunches of jade beads. The long bough dipped flexibly, even under Caitri's slight weight, as she edged further from the trunk. Down it bent, but she had moved past the hedge and with a cry of relief and despair she fell off, disappearing with a crash on the northern side of the windwall.

Her companions called her name and received an answer— not the answer they had expected, but the cries of many of the morthadu, almost upon them. Viviana shinnied up the tree like a squirrel. She and Tahquil pulled up the rope, as a cock crowed again, far off in some very distant remoteness. The unseelie dog-wolf-simulacra loped into the half-light of *uhta* and gathered about the foot of the tree, rearing up to put their front paws on the lower branches, gazing up out of furnace eyes and raising the great ruffs on their shoulders like black manes.

These were not mortal creatures, there was no doubting it. Long ago, the child Ashalind had seen some wolves of Erith. The pups tumbled playfully as their parents licked them with long, lolling tongues as pink as newborn voles. Like the pines, erect and graceful, strong and untame, the wolves had possessed a vigour and a nobility unknown by wights of unseelie.

The morthadu, the colour of bereavement, were incarnations of malignance. They and the shadows seemed to belong together, to slide in and out of one another. Fascinated, Viviana and Tahquil stared down at the milling mass.

'Go, Via,' urged Tahquil. 'Cross the wall. Caitri needs us.'

In her turn, Viviana crawled out along the bough. Tahquil, overly conscious of the steady regard of the attentive crowd below, watched the courtier instead. Viviana went as far as she could. When the branch narrowed enough that it was impossible to keep balance, she swung herself down, hung by her hands for an instant and dropped. The morthadu began a terrible chorus as Tahquil also left their scope, but the sky was brightening swiftly now. A blinding ray punctured the east and the treetops of Cinnarine were suddenly turned to flying green-gold. The sun rose over the wild orchards almost as rapidly as Tahquil fell into them.

Now the morthadu fell silent and fled, coursing away in a fleet pack like lean, black waves down the valley. On the other side of the windwall, the warm winds of Summer were tossing hot motes of sunlight like crushed gilt through the trees, and caressing the sweet grasses of Cinnarine.

It was Midsummer's Day.

4
CINNARINE
Forbidden Fruit

Cinnarine—orchard green, in Summer's listless noon,
Tourmaline, tangerine, when winds of Autumn croon.
Leafless treen, gnarled and lean when frost bestows its sting—
Cinnarine, Blossom Queen in heady days of Spring.

FROM THE CHAP-BOOK: 'POEMS OF THE NORTH COUNTRY'

Gentle brooks flowed in the folds and pooled in the hollows of this land. The orchards, for centuries untended, had spread wide and far. Wind and water and birds had borne their seeds away, broadcasting them over acres far beyond the borders of the original plantations, whose ancient moss-bearded trees, or the descendants of them, remained hidden in the secret cores of Cinnarine. Stretching one hundred and seventy miles from south to north, a wild tangle of fruit trees had grown up. They had aged, toppled and decayed in the grassy mould to give nourishment to rank upon rank of succeeding generations.

At this warm season and latitude, early fruit, peeping from beneath chaste leaves, ripened to shades of maroon, jacinth and passion-red, rosamber and cochineal. Already the first astringent apples, cherries, peaches, pears, yellow and red plums were ready to be gathered. Apricot and orange trees, figs and mulberries grew in their midst, fruited with bitter green jewels, for the season was too young for their bounty.

The wild harvest was abundant. Rich-hued raspberries, black-berries and wild strawberries peeped from their luscious bowers; honey dripped down from hollow trees where hives hummed; grasses waved feathery seed-heads; watercress dappled the frequent ponds; daisies rioted and dandelions spattered the ground with splashes of bright yellow.

'Here is a place to be drunk on sweet nectars,' sighed Caitri, 'to gluttonise on ripe flesh until the juices run down one's chin and one's belly sticks forth like a sail in the wind.'

'Pah. These fruits are plaster imitations,' contested Viviana. 'Where are the goblin trees?'

'Where wood-goblins can find them,' answered Tahquil, measuring a length of rope to use as a belt. Her leather belt had broken as she fell into Cinnarine. Wishing to save the metal against some future need, while leaving no trace of their presence, she strung the iron buckle from the chain of her jade tilhal and buried the severed strap in the loam.

It was now three days since the companions had entered Cinnarine—pleasant days of drowsy sunshine, spent sleeping in mansions of foliage; nights spent wandering northwards, gorging on succulence. Peril seemed far away, allowing Tahquil leisure to dwell only on Thorn—yearning, constantly, to be back at his side. Sometimes she expected to see him come walking through the trees, emerging from the shadows with that graceful, easy stride.

Viviana remained enclosed in her dark prison of enchanted longing, and only Caitri was free to enjoy fully the bounty of this silvan land.

Embowered, the little girl reached up her hand. A peach filled it, flecked and striped as though spattered with multicoloured wax. Next, it filled her mouth with juices melliferous and tart. As she sat in the bower with late sunshine showering flakes of lime and gold on her skin and hair, she began to notice movements throughout the woods. About forty feet above the ground, it seemed as though the sunlight itself had condensed its rainbow colours to form living things.

Numbers of flimsy creatures were busy at the leaves and branches. Initially, the human watcher believed the quick movements belonged to birds or butterflies, but they proved to be neither. They were intent only on the trees. For this reason, in addition to their diurnal manifestation and benign appearance, Caitri viewed them without trepidation.

Indeed, the tree-beings displayed a preternatural loveliness. Of human height and form they were, but they appeared to be neither male nor female, possessing the genderless look of prepubescent youths or maidens. Although their faces were flesh-coloured, the hue of their skin altered at the shoulders to pale apple-green, deepening to become raiment of dazzling jade which flowed far below their bare toes in long trails like translucent mother-of-pearl.

They glided up and down the arbours, reflecting glints of light like shoals of fish in the sea, rising and falling swiftly as they flew back and forth. The undulations of their diaphanous trains created incessant pleats and flutings of pale rose, saffron, silver and hazy emerald-green. Yet they were not garments at all, these glistening trains, but veils of light or some other form of energy stream descending and spreading from the shoulders. As Caitri watched, the beings faded into the trees.

From time to time in their travels through Cinnarine, the wanderers would spy these and other elementals of the trees flitting rapidly in and out among the trunks or at the height of the topmost boughs. At whiles they floated higher, but they never descended to the ground as they occupied themselves ceaselessly with their esoteric tasks.

'These nebulous sylphs,' said Tahquil. 'Meganwy taught me of such as they—the *coillduine*, wights of the trees, who dwell in the sun. Lovely they are, but their thought is closed to us. Some say they are almost mindless, like the plants they inhabit.'

Viviana cared nothing for the habits of the coillduine. Perversely, she searched for goblin fruits. The restlessness in her would not die—never was she satisfied, despite that her friends gave her the best of everything.

Would that I knew how to cure this affliction, thought Tahquil despairingly. *Now two of us are infected with Yearning.* She touched the ring on her finger, wondering how long its power would keep her from the pining-death.

But Tahquil bore her suffering with better grace than the courtier. When Viviana's frustration overbrimmed its well, she would rail at the trees and kick them, or tear off their brittle boughs and use them to beat the boles.

Towards the close of the third day, the companions rested on a slope of springy turf beneath peach and pear trees. At the foot of the incline, reflections glimmered between the leaves. A pool lay in a depression there, like a dark green eye. They had been wary of pools since encountering the carnivorous fuath in Lallillir, but in this peaceful, wooded region the edge had worn off their apprehension. They had seen no wights save for the harmless tree-sylphs who were neither malign nor benign to mortals, and oblivious of the human race. Relaxed, filled with a drowsiness born of satiation, lulled by a ferment of perfumes and warmth, the maidens dozed late. Each vaguely hoped that another was keeping watch. To inquire who was on guard duty seemed bothersome and would possibly lead to shouldering that responsibility oneself. It was easier to let it be.

And what danger could await in these innocent orchards, here behind the protective sandstone windwall with its thorny hedge? The swanmaiden had warned of a ganconer, an unseelie wight whose honeyed words were poison: *'Sweet-speaking handsome one woos,'* she had said, *'where sprigs hang heavy with fruit. Fair face, fair words, sinister intent. She who falls for shadows shall soon weave her shroud.'*

Yet there had been no sign of wicked things. Conceivably, the ganconer had long since followed eastwards to the musterings in Namarre.

So the travellers dozed. They did not notice this: that some boughs dipped and swayed, though no wind blew, or that the waters of the green pool stirred.

Evening came with beauty to Cinnarine. The richness of it, the deep mazarine blue of the northern horizon, the lather of sombre,

white-tipped clouds lavishing the sky-ceiling, the boughs luxuriantly festooned in every shade of green, the layered wall-hangings
of leaves—all made it a time for slow and tranquil awakenings.
The orchards were tinged with an ambient light which might have
been filtered through panes of antique amber glass, or through
tannin-rich waters of a mountain stream—mellow, yellow light
tinged with bottle-brown.

The leaf-ring quivered. Tahquil's lids snapped open like two
leaden hatches which had been fastening down her eyes.

A man—maybe—came out of the shadows. Roughly, Tahquil
seized her companions by the shoulders and shook them out of
their lethargy.

'Awake!' she said. 'It is he, the Ganconer of Cinnarine. Stopper
your ears and avert your gaze. His words and looks ensnare . . .'

Like some wild creature he walked, easy, graceful, long of
stride. Spying this unexpected manifestation, Caitri, half awake and
not yet free from the adhesive webs of dream-illusion, wailed and
fled. Tahquil sped after her, lest they should lose her in the
wooden maze, and Viviana, not to be abandoned, came in pursuit.

But as they ran on they heard the pounding of hooves in muffled thuds on the grass. A grey horse raced up beside them, yet it
was riderless. Sharply it veered sideways to head them off in a
small glade where moonlight fell like silver snow, and as the horse
crossed their path they flung themselves backwards. The beast
reared, its forelegs flailing. It swung its head towards the mortals
as it came down, and its eyes looked through them, *knowing*. In
terror they retreated, turned in the opposite direction to flee
afresh. A shaft of moonlight pierced between leaves and illumined
a pair of horns sprouting from a moving skull—the head of a second manifestation which barred their path of flight. They stumbled
to a halt.

At Tahquil's back, Viviana and Caitri clung to each other,
pressed hard against the knobbed bole of a hoary plum tree.
Under the glove, the ring zapped warning tingles up and down
Tahquil's arm.

'Rest easy lasses,' fluted the horned one. 'Och, there's no call
tae be afeard. 'Tis seelie we both be and wishin' ye no harm.'

It was only an urisk.

'No, I'll not rest easy,' cried Tahquil holding up her ringed hand in an effort to ward off wickedness. 'There is a ganconer here, and that's as unseelie as ever was.'

The grey horse was no longer in the glade. Instead, there emerged once more the man with the walk of a beast. He went down on one knee and bowed his head. Long, coarse hair slid off his powerful shoulders and hung in curtains as straight as weighted strings. In its glossiness, fluted water-leaves were twined like thin, green ribbons. He was naked from head to middle, clad only in leggings of some rough weave. The long nose drooped, the face too was elongated—strong-boned but not handsome. So pale was his skin that it seemed formed of cloud, and sheened with the polish of water seen by starlight. Smooth slate-grey hair grew thickly along sculpted forearms.

'I am at yarr sarrvice, maiden,' he said in strange accents.

'A waterhorse indeed!' Tahquil exclaimed. 'Or is this some glamour?'

'Nay, maiden,' said the man-creature. 'I am av the nygels as ye see me and I have sarrt after ye farr many a night, since ye bart me freeness.'

'I manumitted you? How can this be?'

He raised his head, his lips drawn back in a smile. There was no white to his eyes. They were the eyes of a horse, the centres huge discs of jet set in liquid malt.

'De ye nat ken me?'

Tahquil's mind jumped back to the day in the marketplace at Gilvaris Tarv, when her name had been Imrhien and she had possessed a purse filled with gold.

'A pony for the pony!' called Roisin.

There was general laughter, but the miller who held the rope said, 'Is that a genuine offer?'

'It is.'

Imrhien began rummaging in her purse.

'What? Be ye turning scothy?' hissed Muirne.

<<No. Please, show him the money.>>

Nobody outdid the offer. People stepped back, gawping in

*amazement—few had ever seen a coin of as high value as an
angel. The Picktree miller made sure they didn't get much of a look
at it. As soon as he had bitten the heavy golden disc to test its
authenticity, he pocketed it, handed the rope halter to Roisin, and
disappeared swiftly into the crowd, doubtless afraid he might have
become a target for cut-purses or less subtle robbers.*

*The transaction completed, the bystanders now focused their
attention on the new owners, calling out advice and questions.
Imrhien stepped up to the terrified wight and slipped off the rope.
Instantly the crowd scattered.*

'Oh yes,' breathed Tahquil, 'I ken you now.'

'Then ye'll ken I credit ye with a favarr,' said the nygel. 'Ye
served me well.'

'You owe me nothing, sir.'

Then spoke the urisk: 'Dinnae be sae swift tae dismiss your
debtors, mistress. The favours of the eldritch are not tae be taken
lightly.'

'Nygels are the most seelie of all waterhorses, but they are
practical jokers,' she responded.

'Aye,' averred the urisk, 'yet they can be stark and brawly and
true.'

Beneath the plum tree, Viviana and Caitri shivered in each
other's arms. Unconvinced, Tahquil regarded the urisk. The night's
light sketched his strange form indistinctly.

*Might this be the same urisk who has helped us before? It is dif-
ficult to tell one from another.*

'Are you the urisk of the Churrachan?'

'Sure, ye've misca'ed me in the asking, madam.'

'If I have insulted you, I am sorry. My vision is not as clear as
yours, in the darkness. But are you?' she persisted.

'I am.'

'How came you here?'

'By Wight's Way, what ither? And maist deserted it was, for on
my journey I met wi' anly twa. The first was the Glashan itsel'.'

'The Glashan!' Tahquil thought she recalled the name. 'Is that
not the handsome waterhorse who is far more dangerous than any
nygel? I have met him—once,' she shuddered, recalling the cottage

at Rosedale. *Thanks be to fate, that at that meeting I hid the gold of my hair beneath my taltry.*

'Not the *Glastyn*, mistress, but the *Glashan*, a hobgoblin. He had words wi' me—words that might weel be o' interest tae ye.'

'What did he say?' Tahquil asked, momentarily forgetting her apprehension regarding the nygel.

'"I'm after a huzzie wi' yellow birss," quo' the Glashan uncouthly,' said the urisk somewhat unintelligibly.

'"For what purpose?" quo' I.

'"For taen her tae the Lord Huon," quo' the Glashan, "and the Lord Each Uisge."

'"Spier some ither birkie," quo' I, and I went on my way.

'Next, I happed tae meet wi' the nygel. Quo' he, couthly, "I'm after a lass wi' hair of yellow."

'"Wi' what purpose?" quo' I, for I's no be the agent of ane that delivers ye to the likes of Huon and his louns.'

Here the urisk bowed neatly to bleach-haired Viviana, who stared at him blank-faced.

'So the sonsy waterhorse here,' he continued, 'tell'd me about his debt. "Come alang wi' me," quo' I. "For gin the luck is wi' tham, bye and bye the yellow lass and her sisters will arrive in the *Talam Meith*, the koontrie men call Cinnarine."'

He paused, frowning.

'But I see the lass wi' yellow hair is not the yin ye sought, nygel, and 'tis the dark yin after a'!'

'How did you know me, sir?' Tahquil quickly asked the water wight.

'I did nat, at first,' he replied, 'because yarr hair is changed. Nearerr, I catched the tang av ye and the way in yarr standing. Lang back in the city I marked ye well, be sarrtain.'

Tahquil folded her arms and commenced pacing back and forth in agitation.

'This wight, the Glashan, told you that the Lords of Wickedness hunt after a yellow-haired girl,' she said abruptly. 'Tell me more, urisk, prithee. Tell me about Prince Morragan—all that you know.'

'I ken only what the nygel tell'd me. I've fared in faraway corners this many a lang year and hae not ventured into the heigh, broad world. A solitary I be, like all urisks. We only meet once every nine years, on the banks o' Loch Katrine, and I've missed the last couple o' gatherings.

'I hae heard no ither news, except that when the black wings o' the three Crows o' War unfolded tae darken Erith's skies and pass intae the west, there was naething o' eldritch, whether seelie or *unket*, domestic or wild, shape-shifter or shape-stayer, solitary or trooping, dwelling in high places or low, in water or woods, that did not alarum tae that sally-forth. What hae ye done, that they should hunt ye so?'

Tahquil shrugged and turned her face from the urisk, unwilling to reveal anything to any wight.

Moonlight blinked out in the small glade, blinked on again. A shadow had passed between the sky and the ground. A hooting cry sounded far overhead and the nygel craned his neck skywards. He snorted.

'What goes there?' demanded Tahquil, squinting at the sky. Stars sprinkled its dark dome.

'Ainly a birrid,' said the mane-haired nygel-man. 'Sit ye dane and I'll tell ye the tale ye've requested. I'll tell ye whay all acruss the land the hunt is an for a lass wi' hair of yellie.'

'Very well.' Tahquil nodded guardedly. 'I am eager to hear your story.'

They lowered themselves onto the grass, Caitri and Viviana at a short distance from Tahquil, wary of the two wights. The nygel began to speak.

He commenced with the story of Morragan, Crown Prince of the Faêran, who had been exiled with his elder brother the High King. For many years after the Closing of the Gates to the Fair Realm, the exiled Faêran had walked the known lands, and that period was known as the Era of Glory. Eventually tiring of Erith, however, these two Faêran lords had both chosen to lie locked in the Pendur Sleep for centuries, surrounded by those of their knights and other retinue who had been exiled with them. Under two hills had they slept—two hills many leagues apart, with the whole of Erith lying between, for the brothers' feud had waxed more bitter than ever since the Closing of the Gates to Faêrie.

In the Erithan year 1039, Morragan had woken under Raven's Howe. Perhaps, as the tales would have it, he had been awakened by some foolish shepherd wandering where he should never have ventured, or maybe something else had disturbed this mighty Prince of the Faêran. Some surmised that he had merely chosen to leave the stasis and the timelessness of the Pendur Sleep in order to experience a variation on eternity. Whatever the reason, out into the world, unlooked-for, he had gone. With him went the knights and ladies who had accompanied him, first in exile and then in sleep under Raven's Howe.

Meanwhile, under Eagle's Howe, Angavar High King and his retinue slept on.

Changes had occurred in Erith since the end of the Era of Glory, that early period when Angavar and his knights had imparted much knowledge to humankind, and mighty cities had been raised and great deeds performed, and splendid songs had been wrought. The Crown Prince and his Faêran entourage from Raven's Howe found a world much altered. Most of the cities lay abandoned and overgrown. Men had forgotten much that had once been known. While the Faêran slept, war had riven the lands. The dynasty of D'Armancourt had been cast down in the Dark Ages and had arisen again with James the Uniter. Stormriders now ruled the skies. Yet wights still roamed, haunting inglenooks and millponds, lurking beneath hearthstones, inhabiting wells. Those of unseelie ilk preyed, as ever, on humanity.

Morragan's contempt for the races of Men had not diminished. He did not mingle with mortalkind. Eldritch wights were drawn to him, attracted by his power, by the forces of gramarye that played about him like silent, invisible lightnings. Driven to frustration by ennui and hatred of exile, their company he tolerated. He was inclined to favour those of unseelie, whose antics and pranks at the expense of humans proved diverting.

'An attitude typical of the Faêran,' Tahquil interjected with bitterness. 'The deaths of mortals seem of little concern to them—they have no love in their hearts. Merciless are they, unjust and arrogant.'

'Ye ken not o' whom ye speak,' said the urisk, glancing over his shoulder as though fearful of listeners.

'Behold, I am confirmed. Even the gentlest of wights fears their wrath,' Tahquil said with a sigh. Shaking his head warningly, the nygel resumed his narrative.

Long ago the six greatest unseelie wights, sometimes called the Lords of Wickedness or the Nightmare Princes, had been deprived of their leader, the formidable Waelghast. In those earlier days of yore they had formed an Unseelie Attriod, with the Waelghast at its head. Without their leader the structure of their collective was rent asunder, and the Unseelie Attriod was dispersed.

Locked out of Faêrie at the Closing, these Nightmare Princes had scattered, to wander Erith through the long years, bereft of purpose. When the Raven Prince returned to wakefulness and emerged from Raven's Howe, the Unseelie Attriod reformed around him. The Lords of Wickedness claimed him as their leader, and while he hardly acknowledged their claim, neither did he gainsay it. Grouped in this structure, they once again became a powerful force in Erith. Whiling away their immortal spans, they amused themselves with many sports and depredations, including predatory forays against Men. Yet in these Hunts, the Faêran themselves did not take part, being more inclined to chase Faêran deer, a quarry more elusive and worthy of their prowess.

Then the nygel recounted how in Autumn of 1089, in the month of Gaothmis, an intruder had been detected in Huntingtowers, the stronghold of the Antlered One. The spy had escaped, been hunted down and, as it was believed, had perished beneath a cave-in of the old mines. In wrath, Morragan demanded to know how such a mortal intruder had penetrated Huon's fortress. This was not revealed, until months later a certain duergar was discovered furtively making his way towards the mountains. In his possession was a swatch of golden hair, which had been partially plaited into a whip. In his terror of Huon and hope of deflecting punishment, the hapless duergar loosened his tongue and told all, explaining that he had received the hair in exchange for a foolish mortal's clandestine entry to Huntingtowers. He had taken the precaution of rendering mute the potential spy, merely out of malice, but he had augured that the wench would not long remain undetected in the fortress of Huon.

Despite his confession, no mercy was shown him. His fate at the hands of Huon's servants had been most terrible, as was Huon's way with all those who angered him. Throughout the length and breadth of Erith the word went out from Prince Morragan and from the Unseelie Attriod to all creatures of eldritch—*find the yellow-haired spy.*

'Therefarr,' concluded the nygel, 'I'll warrant the Prince is after ye tae take reprisal because ye were eavesdrapping an him. That is a crime utterly candemned by the Faêran. He will nat farrget ye.'

At this point the nygel's story ended, for he had passed into remote regions and heard no further tidings. Having deserted Millbeck Tarn after his capture there, he had gone looking for another pool to inhabit. He found himself moving northward, impelled by the strange and continuous Call that made all things eldritch lift up their eyes and hearken, and one by one to leave their haunts and respond: the Summoning Call issued by the Raven Prince.

'Och, but we owe no allegiance tae the great lords,' interjected the urisk, 'and although I lo'e the Faêran weel, I'll not dance to Prince Morragan's tune gin he's hand in glove wi' those who would do ye harm, lass.'

'You are very kind,' said Tahquil.

'Ye're the make o' a lassie I once kenned. One o' the Arbalisters. I hav'nae dwelt wi' a family for some centuries.'

'Myself also.'

'Among them I kept an un-name, a kenning. "Tully" they ca'ed me.'

'May I address you by it?'

'Aye.' The urisk's eyes shone. He was, after all, a domestic wight and although a Solitary, he belonged at the fringes of company, the outer edges of firelit circles. The wilderness was not his preferred haunt.

Again, Tahquil raised her eyes to the sky, as though she feared a presence there.

'If Morragan is able to hold converse with the morthadu, which I doubt not, the beasts of Black Bridge might already have sped to him with tidings of three wandering damsels—a notable trio in the wilderness.'

'Even so,' agreed the urisk, nodding his cornuted head solemnly, 'even so.'

'There's one av the white kine as dwells in yon green tarrn,' interjected the nygel, changing the subject unexpectedly—it appeared his equine mind was erratic and seldom able to remain focused. 'She is av the *Gwartheg Illyn* and will allow harrself ta be milked, this night.'

'We have no pail.'

'Suck't fram her dugs.'

"Tis not our way.'

'Marr's the pity for ye.'

'For almost two years,' Tahquil resumed, directing her discourse at the urisk, 'Prince Morragan has been toying with the armies of Erith—why, I can only surmise. Possibly, his disdain of mortal men grows and he wishes to set us at each other's throats, leading to our eventual destruction. Or perhaps the Prince's brother, Angavar High King, has woken and these two Lords of Gramarye use us as pawns in their war games, to while away the tedious years of Erith.

'For, who would Morragan wish to harass, if not his brother who exiled him? Of course, one who sleeps dreamlessly beneath a hill is hardly a worthy adversary. I would warrant that, like the Raven Prince himself, Angavar High King of the Fair Realm is indeed awake and walks the lands of Erith or holds Faêran Court with his followers in some remote fastness—even in the leafy bowers of some light-dappled greenwood such as this!' She paused reflectively. 'Yet surely there would be some hint of his presence in Erith, some flavour? How could Aia's greatest potency of gramarye reawaken and it not be sensed in every blade of grass, known in every stone, sung in the wind, borne on the water, shouted in thunder, whispered in the leaves? Does he yet sleep, the High King of the Faêran, or has he woken?'

'To my knowing,' said the urisk with a shrug, 'the Righ Ard sleeps yet. But I ken little o' the ways o' the warld. I hae kept tae mesel' these past decades. Mickle a drap o' water has passed beneath mony a bridge since Tully last heard fresh tidings.'

There was a short silence, filled with apprehension.

'Via,' Tahquil turned to the courtier, 'it appears Morragan and the Unseelie Attriod and untold numbers of wights hunt yet for a *yellow*-haired girl wandering in the wilderness. With your bleached locks, in my company, you are in danger. Dark dye for your hair must be found!'

Viviana scowled. Her hair, unkempt, was a tangle of dry yellow straw. Close to the scalp it resembled brown silk threads.

'And for my own pale regrowth as well!' Tahquil added. 'We shall look out for dyestuffs as we travel,' she promised, rising to her feet. 'For the nonce, it is urgent that we continue on our way. Sir Waterhorse, if you truly mean to aid me, I shall not discharge you. Accompany us if you will. Your help may prove invaluable in our journey north.'

The nygel bared his square teeth in a horse-smile.

'I will join ye.'

'Och, and mesel' also,' said the urisk.

'Oh, fither,' snapped Viviana, recidivating into broken slingua. 'Now we must contend with yet another uncouthant half-beast that minces its vowels and otherwise butchers the Common Tongue. Storfable, Es raith-na?'

'Ignore her—she is half-spelled,' said Tahquil quietly.

'I am uneasy with this creature,' Caitri murmured in Tahquil's ear. 'It is one thing to travel in the company of an urisk, a domestic wight, but quite another to journey with a waterhorse.'

'A waterhorse indeed, but one of the most harmless type of all, and he says he owes me a favour.'

'Owes *you*, m'lady.'

'Depend on it, I shall ensure the favour extends to my friends.'

Faint and far off, a long, eerie stridor issued from the southeast, sliding down the night breeze and trailing into silence. It was not the voice of a howler predicting storms, nor yet a weeper grieving for a fatality to come, nor yet one of the morthadu yowling. It was a multiple baying and yelping, as from the throats of a pack of hounds.

'The Hunt is out somewhere tonight!' said the urisk, glancing up. 'They havnae been about these parts for many a lang nicht.'

'Might aerial riders see us through the trees?'

'Not unless they ride directly over us, or mighty close to't.'

'Maybe they have picked up a trail,' said Tahquil, shuddering in every limb, glad of the shelter of the trees. 'All the more reason for haste.'

The shadow of a bird fled again between the stars and the ground. Following it, clouds rubbed out the moon. The black ruby of night held all things captive within its prism. Through it, five travellers passed swiftly through the woodlands of Cinnarine until morning brushed the east with colours. At *uhta*, some boughs dipped and swayed though no wind blew, the waters of a lonely pool stirred and the mortals found themselves walking alone.

In the mornings, the world was the bowl of a crystal goblet, its rim the horizon, pinging with pure resonant notes as though struck by tiny hammers. Birds in their gorgeous livery ushered in the day.

The coillduine flitted through the orchards between sunrise and sunset, lightly clad in opalescent radiance, through which their pale forms were dimly discernible.

'Peacock feathers brush my eyes,' murmured Caitri, loath to close her lids against these sights and sleep each morning, but too weary to do otherwise. Despite and because of their seelie escort, the little band must continue its nocturnal existence, remaining alert in the most perilous hours, resting only under the sun.

Northward they traipsed through Cinnarine by night. The urisk Tully openly trotted by their sides, the nygel slithered, a vague shadow in the trees horsing around with things he met along his way, betrayed now and then by a splash, or a mischievous whicker of a laugh that the urisk called 'nichering'. When narrow brooks crossed their path, the urisk would disappear to skirt them by some mysterious means. After a night or two the mortals became less uncomfortable with the ways and manners of their eldritch companions.

And so it has come about, thought Tahquil, *that we three are now six. One escorts us by choice, one by design and,* she tilted her head to the dark skies, *perhaps another, by obligation . . .*

But it was all she could do to keep going, with the chains of desperate longing dragging behind.

Viviana raged alone among the trees at dusk, bitterness eating out the apple of her heart like codling larvae. A pear dangled like a drop of gilded jade. She plucked it. Could this be fruit of a goblin tree? Her teeth met in its flesh. She spat and flung the spoiled thing away. Thin fluids trickled from her snarling lips.

'Everything here is so fair and preciously ornamented,' she cried to no one but the trees, 'and as dependable as stairs of sand.' Tearing sprigs from the pear tree, she trampled them underfoot.

Alone she was, having left her companions in a grove of cherry trees, where they broke their fast on fruit and cold water. Unassuaged, stung by restlessness, the courtier had flounced away, as was her wont from time to time, to roam the woods in the lingering heat which was all that remained of the Summer's day, searching for wood-goblin fare. Hurtful as her wight-induced pining was, she could not guess at the depths of the greater anguish that was about to afflict her. Sometimes, moodily, she sang nonsensical ditties, spontaneously composed—for a kind of madness had taken root in her.

'Oh, the blue-faced cat is merry when she moos,
With wings of grass to fly on.
And the hog is shod with dainty little shoes
That I should like to try on.
And the fruit-bat spins a web of many grins
That men must hang and die on!'

A stranger's voice said—
'Might a nightingale endeavour to sing thus?'
The trees sighed beneath a sudden wind. A thrush ceased its singing and Viviana snapped her mouth shut on her own. The question had risen, with a tendril of mist, from a thicket of close-growing, antique apple trees, whose semirecumbent boughs had surrendered to weariness. It was not the abruptness of the sound nor the surprise at finding herself not alone as she had supposed,

nor yet the unmistakable masculinity of the tones which deprived her of movement and speech—it was the thrilling music of the voice, to which she leaned and hearkened without hearing the words.

'Might it dare, were it audience to superior accomplishment?' murmured the slender young knight who pushed aside foliage and stepped out of the thicket.

The blood pounded into Viviana's face.

'The King,' she gasped, stretching out a hand to steady herself against a mossy column. She flinched, once, then resumed her stillness. Only a slight quiver scurried back and forth through her, like ripples in a cup—only that. Beneath the apparent stasis, her blood had ignited. She was aflame, she was assailed by dizziness, she was drunk. Her eyes drank him in but already her fever burned unquenchable.

He was clad in bleached linen, buckled over with half-armour in the soft grey tones and pure white highlights of silver; chain mail and plate which lent him the air of a dire machine of metal, or a carapaced insect or a cold-blooded sea-creature, yet within this casing, his excellence was obviously superlative.

Darker than wickedness was his hair, falling unbound past his shoulders. As compelling as forbidden pleasure was his counte-nance, but 'Nay, I am mistaken . . .' she said, and now she saw clearly that surprise had confused her. This champion whose looks and voice stirred the very marrow of her bones was not the King-Emperor. Slighter of build and somewhat less in height, paler of skin was the one who stood looking down at her from eyes not the hue of storms but black as sloes, eyes as alight with passion as her own—a passion matching in intensity, but very different, had she but known it.

And to Viviana now, any man not possessed of this exact stature, this frame, this hair and skin and eyes, was insufficient. The attractiveness of all good-looking men she had known was like candles to the sun. Never had she beheld anything more desirable, and she willed the moment to last for all time, that he might never leave her sight.

'What maiden wanders here?' he said, or sang, and she did not think to ask his name, nor why he cast no shadow. He did not smile; his look was sorrowful, like that of a brilliant poet precociously doomed—a sadness which, if it affected his comeliness at all, enhanced it.

Then he began to speak again, this time in rhyme—rhyme and metre being as natural to the speech of wights as prose, or more so. In fact, 'ganconer' was a word the Common Tongue had derived from the original; '*gean-cannah*', which meant 'Love Talker'. The words of ganconers were enchantment in its true meaning: snares to the senses. A sonnet was the form his wooing took, that traditional pattern of love's eloquence. Hearkening to the puissance of his syllables, Viviana did not notice the skew of the narrative or its menace, its obscenity.

> 'What maiden wanders here? Whose locks of gold
> Frame youth's fresh looks? What mortal paradigm?
> Pulchritude sweet as this ought ne'er grow old
> And suffer from the ravages of time.
> With such hot passion do I burn for thee
> That I would ward thee from that odious fate.
> All other joys in life shall worthless be
> When once our union is consummate.
> The act of love reflects a violent death:
> The piercing of the sword, the gasping cry,
> Th'expense of spirit and th'expense of breath—
> Close, ecstasy and agony do lie.
> Now, hearken to the hungers of thine heart—
> Let's lovers be, whom death alone shall part.'

His tragic appearance was concupiscently romantic. Inside Viviana a bird sang shrilly, its beak perforating her heart.

'You shall find me,' added this vision of male allure, '*breathtaking.*'

He drew closer and she felt a chill like the utter coldness of a marble tombstone. A phantasmal mist rose out of the trees and twined about them, shutting out the world.

'Silken of flesh,' he said, provocatively brushing her cheek with a long finger, 'hazel of eye and rose of mouth.' His fingertip trailed across her lips. She trembled frenetically, distracted unbearably by his ardency, his nearness. The potent outline of his face was carved in alabaster against the spilled ink of his hair. Sloe eyes looked into her wide pupils, through her vulnerability to the wellspring of her psyche, and where they looked a wound opened and began to bleed.

'But why so thirsty,' he concluded softly, drawing away a finger on whose tip stood out a cloudy bead of pear juice, 'beloved?'

All senses abandoned Viviana, consumed by obsession. She reached out. His arms closed around her. He filled her embrace with his passion, her mouth with his kisses, her eyes with his blinding hair, her thoughts with chaos, her lungs with his breath.

And that breath was as icy as a comet's heart.

Tahquil sat with Caitri and the urisk in the grove of cherry trees while evening thickened. It was unspoken, but tension always eased with these brief absences of Viviana, who took her ill temper and sarcasm and fidgetiness away with her.

Tahquil's fingers twirled a closed daisy plucked from the long grasses. She had just seen the nygel in horse-form, kicking up his heels and chasing a bevy of small, white pigs. Now he was feeding down by the nearby brook. From his muzzle trailed long, green ribbons that might have been water-weed or the feathers of a parrot.

Are nygels herbivorous like lorraly *horses, or carnivorous like that prince of their breed, the cruel Each Uisge, devourer of mortalkind?*

Recollecting her meeting with the Each Uisge under Hob's Hill, she fell to brooding about her experiences at the Hall of Carnconnor, a thousand years since. 'Cochal-eater', the sadistic Yallery Brown had called her.

'What does it mean, the term "cochal"?' she idly asked the urisk.

'Cochal? 'Tis a husk—a glume or a shell, an outer structure.'

'Why should a wight accuse me of being a cochal-eater?'

'Only some windy-wa' blusterer wad scauld like that. Mortals a', and wights also when dining, eat baith the *toradh* o' the fairin', which is the essential guidness, and the *cochal* as weel. The *cochal* is only the appearance, the container, gin ye will, but the *toradh's* the prie and the smell and the life-giving powers.'

'Good sir—Tully—were you to be a little less, ah, parochial in your speech, I should understand you better.'

'Och, then I mun give feater currency tae my jandering, lass!'

'How is it possible to consume the one and not the other? To dine upon the taste and goodness of victuals, without eating the unnourishing substance?'

'It is not possible, for yoursel' or mysel'. Only the Lords of Gramarye, the Faêran, can take the *toradh* and not the *cochal*, leaving the fare to appear untouched.'

'But food left without *toradh* must look hollow within—'

'Not so. Ye mun understand the nature o' *toradh*. It cannae be seen, nor touched, but it imbues e'en a pickle o' wheat, a drap o' milk.'

'What would betide, were you or I to eat seemingly whole food from which the *toradh* had been stolen?'

'We wouldnae thrive on't. We might feast forever and niver gain an ounce o' flesh, a doit o' strength. In the transports of gluttony we would shrivel.'

'Would we not notice a difference in the food?'

'Nay. Though the true taste is removed with the *toradh*, a semblance remains—enough tae trick the palates o' sich as you and I. Only the Faêran could tell the difference, and that at the verra crack, at the instant.'

'Therefore the Faêran eat to live, in the same manner as mortals and wights, is it not so?'

A bird soared silently over the treetops: a swan. The urisk did not reply immediately. He seemed agitated, glancing about at the thick shadows woven by the trees, which his nocturnal eyes could pierce.

'Nay,' he said eventually. 'The Faêran dine for pleasure alone. They hae no need for meat or drink tae support them. Tae sich as they, food is not a source o' life but a source o' entertainment.

Often wad they come tae feast by night in Erith's groves before the Closing, but their feast tables were laid with *toradh* clothed in illusion, or else true fare which in the morning wad lie scattered on the ground.'

The leaves rustled. Drifting into a half-dream, Tahquil invented a scene in which Thorn was lounging idly on the grass close by, and she had only to reach out and she might touch him.

The urisk turned his curly head again, scanning the grove of cherries.

'I'm waur't Mistress Wellesley may be tint. She has been gane too lang,' he muttered, 'and something *unket* and kittle roams close by.'

The leaf-ring stung. Tahquil jumped up. Simultaneously, a willowy feminine form materialised out of the trees leading to the brook.

'Sweet-speaking handsome one haunts here,' hissed the swan-maiden urgently. 'Heedless hussie hearkens. She stumbles. She who falls for shadows shall soon weave her shroud!'

Sickness punched Tahquil in the stomach. Her blood drained to her feet.

'We must find her immediately!' she cried. 'Come, Cait! Ho, nygel, now's the time to render assistance! *Obban tesh*, I should have known better than to let her from my sight.' She grasped Caitri's hand. 'Stay with me, Caitri. Tully, prithee do not leave us. Against a ganconer we are as sparrows to a hawk.'

'This way, I ween,' honked the urisk, leading the way. Into the darkling woods they plunged.

A very faint, faraway music drifted through the arbours of Cinnarine, such tinkling music as might be produced by diminutive needles, delicately tuned, hung and struck with tiny drumsticks of iridium. A light breath of shang wind, only the edge of a greater unstorm rolling towards the east, briefly flicked over Cinnarine in passing. By its fires and velvet darknesses the companions made their way. They passed through colonnades of dark electrum, where silver branches dipped, picked out with mercurial leaves, along fructuous avenues arched over with trees of solid gold and then through silvan palaces upheld with pillars of diamond and emerald, coronalled with flickering lights. Hooded were the mortals—not so the wights. This was their element and would not mock them by replication. The thin sound of singing came threading through the trees. Following it, the searchers found Viviana.

Death by pining is a protracted affair. She was alive, although she had already begun to die, unaware of her condition. Untaltried, she sat alone at the edge of a glade, wearing a pair of long, red gloves. As Tahquil and Caitri approached it became apparent that Viviana's hands were, in fact, bare. Blood glistened all over them, coating her arms to the elbows. Between her fingers she held a green pulp of nettles, which she was kneading. The prickles tore her flesh but she worked on without a sound, without complaint. No tear blurred her lily cheek and a woven circlet of willow osiers crowned her sunflower head. In a sweet voice, she sang the old folk song:

'All around my hat I will wear the green willow,
And all around my hat, for a twelve-month and a day,
And if anyone should ask me the reason I'm wearing it,
It's all for my true-love who is far, far away.'

The courtier's shang image hovered around her like an aura. It must have been playing and replaying itself, but no change of expression flitted spectrally across the spectral copy of Viviana's features; her air-imprinted countenance, shadow-eyed and utterly without mirth, remained stagnant.

They tried to dash the weeds from her hands but she would not relinquish them. Neither would she speak, or look at her companions. Only she sighed deeply as though a wound bled inside her that could not heal.

Pliable she was, and acquiescent. The spirit had been drained out of her. They raised her to her feet and led her away. She complied without demur.

'She's fa'en,' mourned the urisk. 'The bairn's fa'en.'

The unstorm fled.

When they were far away from that place, Tahquil said gently, 'Viviana, give the nettles to me. They are hurting you.'

Viviana shook her head. 'When the flesh is parted from the fibres, then shall I take the fibres and weave them.'

'What will you weave, Via?'

'I will weave my shroud,' said the courtier, emotionlessly. 'For I have met the ganconer, in a bitter hour. I thought him a human sweetheart, but his lips were cold on mine and his breath as keen as death. Too late I knew. No longer can I joy in life. He has left me now, but for love of him I must pine to my grave.'

Then Tahquil knew the full meaning of powerlessness, futility and grief. Rage rose like magma to her eyes but streamed out as tears.

'Three guardians to guide us!' she railed loudly. 'Three we have to protect us and not one, not one of you has prevented this. Hundreds of leagues we travelled on our own. A thousand dangers we faced without assistance and we won through. Yet now, under your so-called patronage, one of us is doomed. Tully, you I cannot fault—you gave us life in Khazathdaur, and on the slopes of Creech Hill you succoured us. But what use are you, swan, if you always come too late? And you, horse, what use are you?'

The waterhorse bared his teeth, laying his ears flat. The swan-maiden uttered a sound like escaping steam and raised her arms wide so that her feather cloak spread out like a black-petalled flower.

'Feather-wielder forgets!' she hissed savagely. 'Swan's sworn fealty in Cinnarine is finished. Honour is fulfilled. Horse of Water has vowed to help freedom-spinner *singly*. Spelled wench, suffering, heartsick wench, she's no fret of horse or swan—no holder of wight-service.'

Caitri sobbed. Wringing her hands, Tahquil felt the hard lump of the ring beneath the glove. Somehow that pressure brought reassurance. *Thorn's ring.* She regained her composure.

'You are right,' she said, 'I am sorry. I spoke rashly and without thought. Forgive me.' Putting her arm about the little girl's shoulders she said in a low voice, 'Peace, Caitri, be comforted. Do not lose hope. Maybe we shall find a cure.' But even as the words left her lips, the forlornness of that hope made them clang as hollow as bells.

Both waterhorse and swan folded themselves into the pages of night.

'They are not far away,' said the urisk. 'Ye can be certain they'll not abandon ye.'

'The swan has fulfilled her bond. Why does she remain?'

'In your ain words, tae which she agreed, she mun see ye safe *at least* tae Cinnarine. Ye hae her at checkmate. There's a lingering effect o' such an indefinite phrase. Unwittingly ye might have bound her to ye forever.'

Taking Viviana between them, her bloody elbows hooked through theirs, Caitri and Tahquil resumed their northward journey.

At midnight, when they halted to rest, Viviana would not help them wash the blood from her hands. She would not look at the fruits they piled in her lap.

''Tis nae use tryin' tae reason wi' her,' compassionately explained the urisk. Despite his words, born of his ancient knowledge, Tahquil and Caitri tried to tempt their friend with the most succulent of fare. Of course, it availed them not.

At early morn, when the urisk had departed and the sun's newborn, age-old rays penetrated the canopy, making patterns through interlocking leaf ovoids, Tahquil drew off her gloves.

'It has dawned on me with the day,' she said to Caitri, 'that this ring may have the power to heal.'

She took it off her finger and placed it on Viviana's. The courtier remained passive, whey-faced, vacant-eyed.

'Gramercie,' she said, as automatically as a clockwork musical box might strike its notes.

'There let the ring remain,' said Tahquil, 'in the hope that it will do her some good.'

'And here let us rest,' said Caitri. 'Fain would I sleep now that the night's wickedness is behind us and the sun comes to drive away fear.'

As they made themselves comfortable in the waving grasses, the coillduines of the plum trees appeared, their auras fanning out in ellipses of coruscating colours, crimson and gold, that rose hundreds of feet into the air. The luminous streamers that swept down to swathe the trees were tinted cochineal, outlined with rarefied gossamers of golden spangles.

Sightless, Viviana's eyes stared through this glory.

At its going-down, the sun dragged night across the sky in its wake like a lambrequin stitched with baubles. As if caught up in the folds of this fandangled finery, the waterhorse and swan-maiden and urisk reappeared, an unobtrusive but persistent band of bodyguards. The swan flew or walked, scouting ahead; the urisk trotted alongside. In horse-form the nygel patrolled to the rear, irresponsibly playing leapfrog with water-leapers whenever he chanced upon a forest pool.

Two nights had passed since the encounter with the ganconer. Weariness had carved lines into the faces of the mortals, Tahquil and Caitri having alternately watched the unsleeping Viviana through the days. She would sit, her swollen hands trying to knit together the soggy sinews of bruised nettles. The courtier herself was so weak by now she could scarcely walk.

The urisk steered them a straight course by the stars—as straight as could be managed over the pathless, undulating country, so densely arrayed with timber. Up knoll and down brae they went, across brooks by fords or little stone bridges, through star-lit glades and around thickets of old wood too dense to penetrate. All the while, Tahquil searched for the stuffs with which to concoct black or brown dye.

'Look for iris or waterlily,' she told the waterhorse. 'Black walnut or sweet chestnut, bird-cherry or oak.'

But only tall reeds and straight-backed rushes grew in the pools of Cinnarine.

Soon after midnight, the nygel came bounding up in man-form, looking like a pleased puppy.

'Swun is thinking she has seen a stand of aiks dane by yander cleeve.'

'Not a coppice infested by unseelie wights, I trust.'

'Nay,' he neighed.

'Is it far?'

'Aye, she said it was, and aff yarr track.'

Tahquil looked at her companions. Viviana lay on the grass, motionless, her eyes open but blank. Caitri dozed beside her.

'They are not able to travel more than is necessary. Tully, will you stay here and watch over them while I go? Whithiue,' partially hidden in tree shadows, the lovely wight bridled as her name was spoken, 'will you guard them also?'

The swanmaiden gave a soft cry.

'She agrees,' the urisk translated.

'Guard them well,' admonished Tahquil warmly.

'As weel as we are able,' said the urisk. 'That is a promise, frae the baith o' us.'

Tahquil nodded, gripped by reluctance.

While she had been speaking the nygel had unexpectedly resumed his horse-shape behind her back. He trotted off and she followed after him.

If this is some practical joke, I'll cut off his curly tail.

Past the lattices of trees the stars rolled slowly by. The night was clear, so very clear it was extraordinary. Every leaf and blade stood out, articulated by celestial light. Even in the bosks and brakes and coverts the shadows seemed luminous.

'How much further?' panted Tahquil pushing through the trees, hot and scratched and hasty.

In answer, the waterhorse whickered. They emerged from an orangery to find themselves in a clearing ringed by grand oaks, just as the swanmaiden had affirmed. Tahquil began to strip bark from the nearest trunk.

'This must be soaked, preferably boiled,' she muttered, more to herself than to the waterhorse, who was nosing inquisitively in some undergrowth. 'How shall I boil it? And dye needs salt, and a mordant of rusty iron . . .'

The waterhorse neighed.

She followed the upward turn of his long head. Between the branches and far off in the starry southeastern skies, a swirl of darkness could be glimpsed, like ink stirred into clear water. Dimly echoed the baying of hounds.

The Wild Hunt approached.

'Will they be able to spy us beneath these oak leaves?' cried Tahquil, panic-stricken.

The horse-wight shook his head, spraying his mane like water. A seashell flew out.

The black swirl hammered through the air, resolving itself into riders and hounds. Excited by the proximity of other eldritch steeds, the nygel caracoled, curvetted.

'Do you see? Do you see where the Hunt is headed?' screamed Tahquil, scattering strips of oak bark as she let them fall. Above the orchards and out of them, a gaseous tower arose, a white feather of steam or mist, towards which the Hunt was making rapidly.

'That smoke!' she exclaimed. 'It is coming from precisely where we left the others. A signal! I must return to them. Hold still, if you honour me. Let me jump on your back, horse.'

A moment later, the waterhorse dashed into the trees with the girl clinging to his back. On her neck-chain, the iron buckle and the tilhal pounded against her breastbone.

Caitri had been sitting with willow-crowned Viviana on the grass, dozing in the warm and perfumed honey of the Summer's night. She was aware of the swanmaiden's vigilance in the trees and the urisk's watchfulness by her side as he sat hugging his hairy goat-knees to his chest. She was aware of Viviana's stillness, her pasty face, her slow, infrequent inhalations, as though she was forgetful of breathing and must try to remember, each time, just before she was about to asphyxiate.

'You are so cold, Via.' The little girl wrapped her arms around her friend. The fingers of the trees held stretched between them a starry canopy from which light trickled down. The sky was remarkably lucid, so fathomless and transparent that the world might fall, spinning, into its depths.

Three events then occurred simultaneously. The swan exclaimed, Viviana sat bolt upright and the urisk jumped to his hooves.

'What's amiss?' squeaked Caitri, for nothing else seemed to have altered and she could see no reason for such unnerving behaviour.

'Something *unket* this way comes,' the urisk whispered.

There was nowhere to hide.

Presently, he added, 'And has arrived. Stopper your lugs . . .'

Stuffing her fingers in her ears, Caitri swivelled her head. A slender young knight stood watching them, with long hair like waves of grief, and the face of a libidinous prince. His eyes were hungry—they were two black wolves. Viviana's gaze, fixed on him, poured adoration from her eyes like a libation.

'Ask me to tear out my heart, beloved,' she murmured, 'and I will.' But it seemed he was unaware of her existence.

'The wee lassies belang wi' mysel',' said the urisk, who looked small and feeble compared with the tall, elegant form of the ganconer. The eyes of the predatory knight flicked over Caitri. Meeting that ardent gaze, she wondered, with a rush, what it would be like to sample that finely made mouth, and surprised herself by starting up. The urisk pulled her back, clapping a hand across her eyes.

'Dinnae luik at him,' he said crossly. 'While I am here, he will-nae come near ye, gin ye dinnae go toddling tae him like a silly hawkie tae the slaughter.'

Obediently, Caitri looked away. The ganconer was speaking phrases of seduction to her, but she could not hear him. A tenu-ous mist was creeping along the ground, rising in wisps.

'A ganconer cloudie,' said the urisk, uneasily. 'What's he at?'

The mist thickened, floating in rings among the trees. Through its laminae, the swanmaiden came stepping lightly like a princess from legend. Her feather cloak lay in a heap at the foot of a mul-berry tree and she wore a gown of thin, snowy silk that clung to her lissom form like water.

'No!' shouted Caitri, starting up a second time, filled with con-cern. She whipped her fingers from her ears, gesturing wildly to emphasise her plea. 'You must not throw yourself away like this!'

It seemed now that the swan was not aware of Caitri's existence.

'But chiel, he cannae harm a down-feather o' her,' remon-strated the urisk, pulling her back again, 'nor could she cowe him, nae mair than twa trees in a forest wad blatter each other. Dinnae fash yoursel'.'

'What is she doing?'

From somewhere, or everywhere, a slow skirl of bagpipes began, dimly, as if muffled. The ganconer and the swanmaiden regarded one another. Mist unfurled in fans around them. Two long, white diamonds of vapour soared to pointed tips at the swanmaiden's back, like vast moth's wings hovering at her shoulder blades. The moon-pale chain mail of the ganconer remained undimmed, softly glimmering. Liquid star-shine ran up and down its sheen like quicksilver.

With her swathes of dark hair streaming through the translucent wings, and his shadowy locks cascading over the polished lames of his gorget and pauldrons, they made a breathtakingly striking couple. The eldritch loveliness of them was as poignant as a half-forgotten dream or a long-cherished vision never realised.

Caitri knew then that she was witnessing something of eldritch such as mortals were rarely privileged to behold. The plaint of bagpipes grew louder. It came from under the ground, from some subterranean road where, presumably, an eldritch piper or a long-enchanted mortal slave marched eternally in the darkness. The lonely piper halted directly beneath the spot where Caitri and Viviana sat. The ground stirred. The music's time signature changed, becoming three quarter notes to the bar and it was 'Sheemor' the piper was playing—'The High Sithean'. Caitri had heard Thomas Rhymer play the lilting melody once at Court, and it was said to have been taught to a Royal Harper of yore by the Faêran themselves. To its rhythm, the immortal couple now moved into a dance of exquisite grace.

'I trow she is trying tae draw him awa',' hoarsely whispered the urisk, but all the time the eldritch mist was pouring upwards, from eddies on the ground, filtering from the trees, rising ever higher between the branches, blotting out the stars.

Dancing, the swan and the seducer seemed to meet but not to touch. Their feet appeared to float just above the ground. Through the fingertips crammed into her ears, Caitri heard and felt the music, which itself played the strings of her nerves, jarred her bones with a kind of ecstasy, thrilling her in ways she had never thrilled before.

Then, through the plugs of flesh and bone, over the music, over the throbbing of her own tides, another sound entered. Long, low, bleak, ominous, dreadful it was—somehow Caitri knew it was coloured black, the instrument which disgorged that clangour—a hunting horn created from a void.

And a cacophony of hounds.

Caitri was dragging Viviana to her feet. The little girl was screeching against the lubricous cadences of the pipes and the tumult of whips and hooves, of savage baying and shrill war cries and deep voices shouting.

'Get up, get up!' she screamed, and Viviana was like a doll in her arms, a doll made of uncooked dough. The little urisk was trying to prop her up on the other side and failing, and shouting something Caitri could not make out. Branches were cracking, breaking. The mist was shredding, blown by the back-draughts of a swan's frantically beating wings, or by the massive displacement of air caused by huge horses dropping out of the sky with terrible riders on their backs.

Viviana was snatched from Caitri's arms. Her yellow hair went flying as she was thrown across a saddlebow. Caitri stood, dazed. A grinning horse loomed over her, disclosing pointed teeth. Boring into its muzzle were the most appalling gutters of nostrils she had ever seen, until she beheld the noxious cavities in the head of the apparition straddling its back.

That apparition leaned down. The last thing Caitri saw, looking back at the orchards dropping away as the Wild Hunt rose higher, was a tiny horse and rider wheeling to a halt between the trees on the ground below.

That rider was Tahquil.

Black against the night the trees reared their arms. Ragged ends of unnatural fog slipped between the leaves and dissipated among the stars. The hue and cry died away to the southeast. An owl flew by, hooting like a hollow pipe. A girl sat astride a horse, in Cinnarine. Zephyrs roused her tattered garments and draggled hair, but otherwise a vice of great stillness clamped around her.

She stared towards sunrise, where no sun was yet rising.

The horse beneath her shied. A horned and curly head peered around a cracked bole that oozed rows of resin like amber beads.

'Be still, Tighnacomaire. 'Tis only I!' reproached the urisk.

The cord suspending Tahquil's concentration snapped. She made as if to dismount, but was brought up short.

'Let me down, Tighnacomaire,' she lashed out, quick to learn a useful name at need. 'Have you forgotten who I am to you?'

Released from supernatural stickiness, her hands slipped down the glossy hide. She leaned forward, withdrew her leg over his croup and slid off.

'How dare you adhere me to your back!'

The waterhorse hung his head humbly.

'Yarr nat the best av riders. I had tae stick ye an.'

'The Hunt has ta'en the twa lassies,' said Tully heavily. 'The ganconer betrayed us. There was naething we could do—'

'I know,' Tahquil acknowledged grimly, 'you have not the power to match them. Where is he now, the ganconer?'

'He has gane. The swan draws him awa' frae here.'

'It is as I feared—they have mistaken Via for me.'

She sat down on the grass, bowed her head in her hands, and remained silent for a long while. Eventually, looking up, she said, 'Under my auspices my companions have suffered, despite that they accompanied me by choice. Out of friendship to me they have been brought to this pass. No mortal comrades have I now, and no ring of gramarye, no red vial of strength, no provisions, no means of making fire, no weapons or shields—but I have you, Tully, and you, Tighnacomaire, and I believe the swan remains my ally. In this terrible hour, I must abandon my journey to Arcdur and turn to the southeast, following the Hunt. If my friends live, I will rescue them. If not, I must know their fate, or else be unworthy of honour and deserve no fellowship.'

'A mad quest, Mistress Mellyn!' rejoined the urisk. 'Do ye not ken what lies east and south of this place? The orchards of Cinnarine give way to miles, nay, leagues of country untrod by the races of Men. Beyond that, the mazes of Firzenholt, or Haythorn—call it what you will—and beyond that, barren Wastelands stretch to the Nenian Landbridge. Few mortals be such mollymawks as tae try and cross that sea-causeway—it was ever a kittle road. And the Landbridge leads into Namarre.'

'If they have been taken to Namarre, Namarre is where I must go.'

'We dinnae ken for sure—'

The swan fluttered in over the treetops, fell awkwardly through them and emerged as a pristine damsel, demurely smoothing her feather cloak.

'What news of the Hunt?' Tahquil rasped peremptorily.

'Horse and hounds have hastened far with fair friends. Swan saw Huon fly where hedges wander. Swallows say he flies further to fallow, furrowed fields of war and salt-wind seashores.'

'To Namarre?'

'With certainty.'

It was a turning point. Once again, her path had changed direction.

She must abandon the search for the Gate to Faêrie.

Four hundred and forty miles lay, in a straight line, between Tahquil's turning point and the outskirts of the hedge-mazes of Firzenholt.

Eastwards and southwards galloped the waterhorse by night, tireless, jumping barriers of wood and stone, evading barriers of moving water, swimming across pools so still and clear they might have been forgotten shards of the sky. Swift and strong he was, beyond the powers of mortal horses. His rider must have fallen from his back many times, were she not fastened there by his sly magicks. Swift and unwearying also was the nimble-footed, leaping wight that ran like a goat at his side every time night's doors swung around, while away up in the airy heights a long-necked bird kept pace using slow, sure sweeps of her wings. It was a pace no *lorraly* beast could match.

Strange hawk and hound and horse.

Strange huntress, who is the quarry.

5
FIRZENHOLT and BEYOND
The Laurel Labyrinth

With skillful elegance she skims the sky
And rides the wind like foam upon the sea,
Yet mortal men for love of her would try
To steal her, in their bold effrontery.
Their fleeting hands of clay should not endeavour
To smirch the likes of she who treads the ground
In eldritch loveliness, unchanged forever,
While flowers spring like fallen stars around,
Or glides, spearheading chevrons on the lake,
Reflected there in lucid symmetry.
No lover nor true artist could mistake
This paragon of femininity—
Where else is such ethereal beauty twined
Than avian and damsel-shape combined?

Sonnet for a Swanmaiden

Riding upon the back of a waterhorse—what mortal had ever stayed in such a seat for so long? On a horse made of cold currents and liquid convergences, jests and trickery, pressed against a hide like the burnished seas of midnight, things looked different to the rider. It seemed to Tahquil-Ashalind that they ran through a different world, a world of shadow and incendiary lambency blown always by the forge bellows of shang winds.

If she was capable of musing at all, if the concepts and passions surging through her head were able to string themselves together in any rational sequence, she wondered if it were possible that Thorn, despite all the terrible risks he faced, still lived. If he did, Namarre would surely be the place to find him. As this fatuous hope took flame, she was drawn with redoubled urgency to pursue this mad, new quest.

They went by secret ways, for the Wild Hunt was active every night, screaming around every horizon. Five hundred miles long was their winding course over the wild, wide land. Five times the rising sun had opened its eye to behold that they had covered another one hundred miles or more, despite the brevity of the Summer nights. On the twelfth day of Grianmis they reached Firzenholt. But there on the edge of that place, among the outlying topiaries, they were forced to stop.

Before them lay miles of interlocking evergreen hedges, dense and high, formed of box, privet, juniper, cypress, fragrant laurel. Odd as it appeared to the newcomer, these bushy palisades were trimmed into formal shapes not usually associated with nature. The creatures that predominated in Firzenholt-Haythorn were peripatetic hedge-eaters. These small beasts with their scissor-like mandibles preferred the new shoots, and because it was their habit to travel on straight paths, ingenious cambers and geometric curves, eating as they went, they unwittingly moulded the hedges into smooth, rounded forms: wedges, overhangs, blocks, cubes, stairs, archways, cones, ramparts, pyramids and spirals, yet mostly into long, unbroken walls of pruned greenery.

Peculiar to this northeastern region of Eldaraigne, the hedge species of Firzenholt propagated themselves largely by suckers arising from their rootstock below ground level. These shoots always arose in straight lines, only turning corners when meeting an adamant embedded obstacle such as a knotted brain of granite globules or a smooth plane of shale. This gave Firzenholt's layout the appearance of having been planted in regimental rows by an overzealous and eccentric gardener. Long avenues and short walks forked or turned corners to become cul-de-sacs, concentric paths or a sudden series of elbows and doglegs.

Directly beneath these verdant walls a system of narrow channels and dry dirt paths ran between the thin trunks, with scarcely enough headroom for a fox to creep along without brushing its ears against the lower boughs. Things were wont to travel along these hidden canals and pathways, and other things lived above: small birds, squirrels and creatures that pranced upon the hedge tops.

Thus was Firzenholt.

At dusk, Tahquil lingered beside a glossy pool bordered with trees. Her long, slim fingers encompassed an orb of Fairbread that glowed softly like a pink pastel smudge beneath the long leaf-curtains of a willow. It was dusk. Soon the melting sun found the brink of the world and sank beneath it. As this occurred, the willow withies that trailed like slender rain into the waters of the pool suddenly trembled. It was the agitation of the water that had made them do so. Equally suddenly, the cause of that agitation came up, breaking the water's surface: a horse's head, its eyes rolling like white marbles in their sockets, ears laid back flat against its skull, water-weed like verdigris interwoven in its streaming mane, its dark lips drawn back in a rictus of tombstone teeth.

Tahquil jumped backwards and fell over.

'Fancy a ride?' queried the nygel innocently, heaving himself horsily out of the pool. He *nichered* in a self-satisfied manner and frisked about, shaking droplets from his hide.

'I would,' said Tahquil, picking herself up, 'but 'tis impossible.'

The nygel looked up at the high ramparts of Firzenholt, now ebony against the last magnolia smokes of sunset.

'Ah yes, I forgetted.'

He flicked his jaunty tail at an imaginary fly. Tahquil waited for helpful suggestions as to how they should proceed, but none were forthcoming.

'Can we go around?'

'Wild farrests creep tae the southern marches. Stony peaks cluster at the narrth. Baith are barriers equal tae this.'

'Och,' said the urisk, a wild thing crouched among willow roots.

'Och what?' said Tahquil.

'Merely "och".'

'I gather that you have no advice as to how we should cross this . . . this formal garden that wanders in its dotage?'

'I can gae its paths, for I am small enough that when I reach a dead end I can crawl underneath the bushes and out t'ither side. Nygel can swim the channels. Swan can fly over. But ye?' The urisk shook his crimp-haired head.

The swanmaiden reported, from green-shadowed torrents of withies, that according to her aerial inspection no route existed along the grassy walks between the hedges—all were blind alleys, at least in the western half of the maze. Beyond the midpoint, a route did exist, albeit a most circuitous course.

Tahquil pondered.

'I require,' she said at length, 'merely the materials at hand.'

With that she took the small knife that remained at her rope-belt and began slicing withies from the willow, stripping the leaves from the flexible stems. By the time the moon had risen, Tahquil, by dint of weaving and tying, had fashioned a pair of items which resembled the racquets with which the courtiers of Caermelor had been wont to play at shuttlecock—but without the handles.

'Hedge-shoes,' explained their maker. 'I intend to walk across Firzenholt. Without such apparati, the hedge-roofs will not support me if I should stand on them—my feet and legs would sink straight in amongst their twigs. Yet those twigs are strong and dense enough to hold up my weight when it is spread over a greater area. In any event, this is my hope.'

She tied the hedge-shoes to her own worn boots and practised walking, to the amusement of the nygel and the disdain of the swanmaiden.

'Ye've the gait of an egg-bound duck, dearie,' opined the urisk.

'Aptly described,' mused Tahquil. 'And oh, to be able to fly like one, but where might I obtain such flight-feathers?'

Tying the woven platters to her belt she tried to climb the nearest portion of the hedge. At the surface of the green wall, no shoot or sprout was stout enough—they all broke off in her hands.

Plunging her arms deep inside the yielding plush nap, she found twigs and sprigs. Further in, her fingertips met small branches. To these she endeavoured to beat her way, but the springy shoots pushed out at her face and body, and would not let her near their supports. Her struggles were in vain.

Inevitably, frustrated, she flung herself aside.

'The palace gardeners used to trim the tops of the hedges but they would use ladders to get up,' she said, panting with exertion. 'I have no ladder and my knife will not cut through any saplings thick enough to construct one. Is there truly no way around this maze?'

'It straggles far to the north and south,' said the urisk, 'until it meets forests and bleak hills. Beyond lies the coast. The swan says all the coastline is weel guarded at this time.'

'Ye need nae ladder,' said the nygel, just as Tahquil had lost all hope. 'There be a batter way. Jump an me back.'

'Oh no,' said Tahquil, as his proposed method dawned on her. 'That hedge is higher than a cottage roof-gable. If you overshoot, every bone in my frame shall be broken. If you undershoot, every morsel of flesh shall be stripped from me as I fall through the hedges.'

The waterhorse neighed and capered.

'D'ye think I am a *larraly* horse with nae marr sense than a fly? My aim never errs. It has never erred sae far,' he added lamely.

Knowing that this was of course the truth, since wights were unable to lie, Tahquil mounted the horse. Nevertheless, as he walked away from the hedge to allow himself space for a run-up, feelings of trepidation strangled her with blue and skinny hands.

The night drew in, caliginous, gelatinous.

Tahquil could only assume that the nygel was able to see the hedge better than she through the gloom. He began to trot, then to canter and finally to gallop. Sitting back on his rump she was glued to the wightish hide so closely that she felt she was fused to the powerful frame. The outer hedge of Firzenholt loomed, solid sable. With an abrupt lurch her body separated from the horse's as his hindquarters violently heaved up, and she was flung through the air. For a timeless moment she hung suspended in the night, between firmament and ground—next she was sprawled face-deep in a resinous, scratchy cushion high on the hedge top.

Shouts spurled from below. Crawling to the edge she peered over, waving to nygel and urisk. A winged thing dived at her head, hissing as it passed her ear—Whithiue. The swan veered away in a steep turn and faded to a glimmer on the darkness. Tahquil tied on her hedge-shoes, stood hesitantly, and looked around.

Up here, it is another world.

Acreages of black velvet roads spread around. A conglomeration of shapes like the structure of a city thrust up like cut-outs on the sky. It was a city whose arboreal buildings were bizarre and nonfunctional, whose roadside gutters were carved lethally deep.

And not a herbaceous rooster, not a foliate wishing-well, not a verdurate urn in sight. 'Tis most unlike the topiary gardens of the palace.

To call Tahquil's stilted progress across the hedge-roofs 'travelling', would be a description less than complete. She shuffled like a child wearing its father's boots, or like an old man crippled beneath the burden of decades. Her thoughts at this time were few—purposefully she shut them out. Around the wedges, overhangs, blocks, cubes, stairs, archways, cones, ramparts, pyramids and spirals of the hedge-city fluttered creatures of the night. There were owls and bats and the sweetsinging nightnoon northmoths sung of in ballads, making tiny melodies with the resonance of their arabesqued and azure wings. Also there fluttered, at odd intervals, a black swan. In her swan-form she—unlike the nygel— could not speak the Common Tongue. Throughout the night Tahquil received no tidings from her, but the presence of the wight, despite her overtones of hostility, was reassuring as the mortal damsel trod the black roads.

Magenta-flowering vines pleached themselves among the evergreens, their perfume a harmony. Red berries ripened festively on the junipers, and these were not bitter at all but sweet fare. At midnight and again at *uhta* Tahquil gave the swan the waterskin tied on a string. The bird brought it back clenched in her strong beak, filled with water from the canals below. At daybreak, Tahquil chose a comfortable helix and lay down on the lee side of it to rest. The hedge-eaters, which had retired into the hedges overnight, now surfaced. She watched them as they mowed across the dewy aerial lawns with their jaws like shears. They troubled her not, only trimming the shoots around her reclining form before obsessively proceeding on their way.

For seven nights Tahquil trudged, or waddled. She seemed alone, but she had company aplenty. There were the stars and the moon, and the whims of the swanmaiden, and the menace of the Hunt which, unseen, left the imprint of its clamour on the wind. And there was the pain of the Langothe, and dreams of Thorn so vivid she thought she had already succumbed to madness. Now that the ring no longer encompassed her finger, the agony of loss pierced more deeply. Gradually her strength was failing.

One evening she woke to see her wightish guide, manifested in humanlike form, perched on a leafy trapezium.

'Slow-walker has succeeded, fairly scoring the centre of Firzenholt,' said the swanmaiden. 'From here a floor-way follows hedges as far as the verges—a winding floor-way. Swan shall steer helpless human.'

'Helpless human hears helpful swan and is grateful,' replied Tahquil. Grasping a handful of hedge, she began to slide to the ground. Descent was simpler than ascent. Gravity pulled her, sprigs broke her fall. Between the two forces, she landed, not *un*scathed, but only slightly so, to be met by the urisk and the nygel.

'How now, loyal friends,' smiled Tahquil. Her hair was full of twigs—that very hair whose prodigal filaments held open the last Erith Gate leading to Faêrie. 'Are you hale?'

The calls of hunting night-birds were muffled now by the fur of the great cypress collars standing erect all around, towering into the sky, but the noise of water hurrying along the channels bubbled up from the hedge's foundations.

'Hale and hearty,' replied the urisk cheerfully.

They walked on, now guided by the swan who made low passes overhead to indicate which direction they must take. Once, curious as to the source of sounds of merriment in the hedges, Tahquil drew aside a curtain of fragrant leaves and peered inside.

A party of siofra was picnicking inanely on the banks of a channel, and rowing in leaf-boats on the water. They did not notice she who momentarily spied on them. The spy was intrigued at their unglamoured feast: the horns of butterflies, the pith of rushes, emits' eggs and the beards of mice, bloated earwigs and red-capped worms, mandrakes' ears and stewed thigh of newt, washed down with pearls of dew cupped in magenta flowers.

Later, the whirr of spinning wheels permeated the night, intensifying as the travellers passed beneath an overhang of thick foliage, and dying away at their backs. Once or twice, grinning faces like wizened old men poked out at the passers-by.

After a time the sameness of high avenues roofed by stars began to foster the illusion that they were journeying pointlessly, in circles.

'We're doubling back,' said Tahquil. 'I know it!'

'Sooth lass,' said Tully. 'But hae ye never walked the tricks and tracks o' a maze? Ye mun gae backwards tae gae forwards.'

'This is no proper maze—'tis a random affair. There's no logic to it. Yet I can do no less than to credit the swan with finding a path out of here. Tighnacomaire . . . Tiggy—will you bear me again, for the sake of swiftness?'

The waterhorse granted her wish. Five more nights she rode between the hedges then. Only down long boulevards could the nygel speed up to a canter—he must trot along the short lanes and walk around the sharp turns.

Sixteen nights have passed since Viviana and Caitri were taken . . .

It did not bear thinking about.

One eve they came to a place where the flowering vines were thicker than ever. Here, between the grassy path and the lower stems of the hedges, lay five long canoes of bark.

'The canals,' said Tahquil. 'Do they flow straight to the eastern edge of this place?'

'Almost straight,' said the faithful urisk. 'So says the queen o' birds.'

'And do you think the owners of these canoes will become severely enraged if I take one?'

'That I cannae say. I've not set eyes on craft like these. There's no knowing who made them.'

'Have you not lived since the world began?'

'Aye, but I've not travelled much. It's a hame-body I am.'

The nygel was absent-mindedly ripping vines off the hedges and eating them. Their scent dizzied the air.

'Well,' said Tahquil, 'I've a mind to ride on the water. It will be a route more direct. But how to get to the canal flowing beneath the hedges is a dilemma—there is little space between the lower boughs and the ground. Tiggy, how did you do it?'

In answer, the nygel turned around and with his hind-hooves vigorously kicked at the lower portions of the hedge. Broken branches flew in every direction. In a short while he had opened a gap high and wide enough for Tahquil to pass through, stooping. She dragged a canoe with her and slid it into the waterway. Four feet wide, the channel coursed along its low tunnel directly below the hedge wall.

'Prithee, hold this vessel still for me, Tully.'

She lay down on her back in the vessel of bark. With a splash the nygel sprang into the water downstream and swam away. The urisk pushed the boat. It began to move.

Tahquil glided under the arched trunks supporting the hedge, looking up into the hollow ribcage of the wall, the hedge worlds. The eyes of the dwellers therein blinked, the voices chattered, and they flung down flowers from the vines. Covered with magenta petals she drifted along the waterway, a horse's head going on before.

Another night, mauve and languid, floated by like a spent blossom.

At *uhta*, when many things happen, the nygel blocked the channel with his wide shoulders. The boat bumped against him.

'We have reached the edge.'

Tahquil opened her eyes—she had been dozing. Instead of the cavernous, ribbed grey vaults of hedge-hulls overhead, there opened a sky as delicately pink as a camellia petal, bedewed with a single star. She climbed from the canoe.

Instantly, a horizontal wind threaded strong fingers through her hair. Atop a soaring cliff she stood beside the waterhorse, beyond the last bastions of the hedges. The canal had indeed brought them to the edge. Now, in company with other waterways flowing out of the maze, it plunged over the jutting brink to tumble seven hundred feet down a sheer precipice. At the foot of the precipice some of the falls splashed into rocky basins which drained into underground systems, while others joined a river thinly meandering across a bleak plain towards the dimly shimmering line of a distant shore.

Pre-dawn light laved the landscape. Up there in the open, it was impossible not to immediately become intensely aware of the sky, which throughout Cinnarine and Firzenholt had merely been a frame for a picture. Now it unrolled to every horizon, becoming the picture itself, a moving portrayal of the moods of the climate roiling across the countryside in a paling, indigo vastness so clear and pure that you could drink it, so wide and dizzying that it seemed strange that the whole world was not spinning up into it.

Eastwards, the horizon was stained with a long crawl of brown smoke, underlit with a dull glare. At their backs the tall barricade of foliage marched north and south—the last ramparts of Firzenholt the Amazing. Before them the east wind, lifting the girl's hair, tossing the horse's mane and tail, came rushing up off the plain.

Armies were encamped on those wastelands: the Legions of Erith.

Oh, how I should like to go down and enter that camp, to discover who bides there! If my love is among them, I might fall into his arms and die content. . . Yet I may not visit, for speed is of the essence. . .

Questions tormented Tahquil: *Is the Prince with them, dear Edward of the sad gaze, who was like a brother to me? Did he survive the destruction of Tamhania, or is Erith bereft of royal leadership? Who is the leader of those armies? If a King-Emperor reigns, who might it be—James XVI or Edward IV?*

Yet it makes no difference. Should Prince Morragan's unseelie myrmidons have failed to destroy their most strategically significant target, should Thorn in fact live, I dare not approach him for fear of bringing danger upon him. Should he not, I have no reason for life other than to see my friends safe. And should they also have perished, then Morragan and his unseelie followers may do their worst to me. I shall care no longer. Ah, may cruel Morragan and all his race leave this my home, my Erith, and never return.

She lingered long over the scene spread out at her feet.

Down on the plain, a cock crowed. Dawn blazed over the horizon, the sun rising from behind Namarre and striking its rays across the Nenian Landbridge, across the wastelands, casting long shadows from the thousands of tents and pavilions, the makeshift Mooring Masts, the Windships riding at anchor—finally touching their golden tips to the face of the girl with blowing hair who now stood alone on the brow of the escarpment.

But is he there? Is he down there?

It was a hot Summer's day, fortunately for wanderers who would never have endured a life out of doors at another season. In the shelter of the easternmost hedge, couched in a niche at its roots, Tahquil slept, lulled by the burble and murmur of the canal as it coursed down its channel to fling itself out over the cliff into miles of air. Hawks hovered in the thermals. She did not see them. A bruised flower petal sashayed down from its vine to alight on her arm. She did not feel it. Wrens chirped from their inner bowers of cypress and privet. She heeded them not. The sun blazed on Firzenholt and Cinnarine, then submerged itself, sizzling, in the western ocean, engendering coloured steams which streamed out sideways like scarves of shot silk. Tahquil woke and filled her pockets with perfumed flowers, as a camouflage against the sensitive noses of wights.

A waxing moon saw her picking her way down the face of the escarpment, led by a goatlike creature who discovered paths and footholds where at first glance there appeared to be none. By midnight they had reached the ground below. There, thistles grew rank and weeds crawled over rubble. Patches lay bare of growth; shale or dust or hard-packed dirt. Stubby torsos of burned trees poked up like grim monuments. The wind came galloping, unchecked, from the direction of the sea. A waterhorse came galloping from the direction of the thin river. It shook itself as a dog will, drenching the urisk and girl, before rolling enthusiastically in a dust patch.

'Ye'll be bringing the Legions of Erith clamouring around our ears,' grumbled the urisk. 'Their patrols are sair vigilant.'

A damsel formed of shadows and reflections came walking from a clump of mortified trees whose fingers had woven darkness between them like a cat's cradle.

'Whither?' she questioned, laconically.

'Onward as before,' replied Tahquil. 'If your friends the swallows have the truth of it, Viviana and Caitri have probably been taken to Namarre.'

'Such happenstance is certainty. Swallows say Wild Hunt steers from fell habitation without variation—from formidable fortress on starry heights.'

'Huon and his chase use a castle in Namarre as their base?'

'Faithfully.'

'I'll warrant another bides in that same stronghold,' muttered Tahquil, 'and he greater by far than they—as a thunderstorm outranks a spark. How does the land lie between here and there? How shall I cross the Nenian Landbridge?'

'Hundreds of soldiers stay here in wastelands,' said the swanmaiden, 'vigilant fellows fending sallies of harassment. Savage wights violently hold slender strip separating seas.'

'If the wastelands are held by the Legions of Erith and the Landbridge by forces of Unseelie, my only option is to skirt the bivouacs of the Legions and cross the Gulf Perilous to Namarre by boat.'

'Seas of strait shelter fell wights,' insisted Whithiue. 'Vessels founder. Ships sink. Humans submerge and finish as fodder for ferocious sea-monsters.'

'If land and sea are dismissed, what remains? Is there a tunnel under the gulf, similar to the under-mine?'

'Tunnels,' said the urisk, whose speech forms were nightly adapting to Tahquil's, 'are iverywhere. They run aboot like lost worms, 'neath ivery land. Ye'll likely be standing above one as ye speak. The underground is riddled with roads—the Fridean make them, maistly, and keep them clear. But the passageway beneath the gulf is not for ye. It delves deep, sair deep, and there's no air in't—naught fa' mortal bellows tae suck in.'

'Air. By air, then—I'll go by air. I shall stow away on a Windship—'

'No craft of Eldaraigne will be crossing the Nenian Landbridge while Namarre holds that span.'

Tahquil clapped her hand to her forehead. 'Of course—you have the right of it. Methinks this diet of juniper is pickling my brain. Oh, to have wings to fly—' She paused and turned a hard stare on Whithiue, who was preening her long hair.

'Prithee, Whithiue, lend me your feather-cloak.'

The swanmaiden's eyes narrowed to two darts. She hissed threateningly, thrusting her long neck forward. Taking a step backwards she raised her arms from her sides, appearing to swell in size.

'Am I to take it that you refuse?' inquired Tahquil.

'Vehemently!'

'A swan's cloak to her is as dear as life,' hooted the urisk. 'Without it she would be forever trapped in humanlike form, never to take to the skies again.'

'Ah yes, that I know. I would guard it, I would return it—but no, I understand such a ban.'

And yet, how delicious it would be, to soar unaided, untrammelled, as a bird soars—to feel the lift of invisible currents under my own vanes.

'But if you will not do me that favour, perhaps you will do me another.' Tahquil tried to conceal the catch in her voice. 'When next you fly out across the land, will you try to discover whether he still lives, the King-Emperor of Erith? Nay—I shall be more precise to avoid confusion—'tis James XVI of whom I crave tidings, not his successor. Will the swallows know, or perhaps the other swans?'

'Swan will furnish favour. Swan will find word of sovereign.'

Emotion surged through Tahquil like a tempest.

'Swan is valiant,' she said sincerely.

All four of the nygel's hooves left the ground simultaneously, their owner's nose having been pricked by a thistle that thrust its spiny leaves and erect stem between two stones, its green head bristling with purple hair.

'Have ye heard a word o' our counsel?' asked the urisk. The nygel sneezed.

'I'll bear the mistress past the fighters and acrass the bridge,' he said, blinking as ingenuously as a newborn foal.

'How so?' demanded Tahquil.

'The night I cannat outrun a *larraly* habby-harrse av land arr sky is the night I pat an a harrness and start palling a plough. And an the landbridge what's wan mair waterharrse with a dinner av flesh glued tae its back?'

Stroking his goatee contemplatively, the urisk was a portrait of sagacity. The swanmaiden subsided. Borne on the balmy wind, men's voices drifted, inarticulate, from the distant encampments.

'Well said, Sir Nygel,' complimented Tahquil, 'I commend you. I believe your plan will work.'

Crickets drilled small holes into the dark metal of night. A thousand fires glittered, a scatter of fireflies across the plain. White moonlight and orange flamelight arced off steel: razor spearheads, thorny spurs, graven helms, shiny aiguillettes adorning uniforms. The wind brought the smack of smoke and snatches of sound—the clink and clash of weapons, the whinnying of horses, the jarring keen of a blade being sharpened on a whetstone, the bark of orders being rapped out, the crystal chime of a different wind on its way.

Two mailed sentries of the Third Luindorn Drasilliers, patrolling the outskirts of their bivouac, crossed paths and hailed one another. Both identified themselves as regulations demanded, to cancel wightish trickery:

'I am mortal, and loyal to the Empire.'

Thus greeted, they exchanged a few words to keep the vast, echoing voice of night from sending whispers of apprehension down their spines.

'What news, Fordward?'

'All is quiet in Slegorn Sector. And you?'

'The same.'

They leaned on their lances, the wind plucking at the corners of their chequered tabards. A darker darkness began to overcome the night, but the stars bristled more brightly, like fistfuls of pins; bronze, electrum, copper, silver-gilt.

'The Wild Hunt has been busy scouring the skies this half-month,' said Fordward.

'Methinks it ever heads northwest in its excursions,' said his comrade.

'Aye, yet 'tis glad I am of the wizard's weavings about our borders,' said Fordward. 'Feulath, and that new wizard who has arrived to replace the outlawed Sargoth.'

'The newcomer has performed with more gumption than I had hoped, considering he is but a backwoods conjurer from a Stormrider Tower.'

'The young Prince personally chose him, so I heard.'

'Is that so? Edward shows discernment, amongst many good qualities. The men love him well, and are keen to prove their loyalty. Thank the Powers he survived the tragedy of the Royal Isle.'

'Aye, thank the Powers,' Fordward agreed sombrely, nodding for emphasis.

A tinkling as of tiny bells lapped at the extreme limits of audibility. Neither man commented on the approach of the unstorm—it was an occurrence too common to be remarkable.

'I would fain see an end to this lull,' said Fordward softly. 'The sooner we ride against Namarre, the better.'

''Twill be soon, they say,' replied his companion. 'We are all eager to see action. Waiting overlong drives men to restlessness.'

They conversed a little more, in the same vein. Rarely was their exchange slanderous or vulgar. All the soldiery held the Dainnan in the greatest esteem and the majority therefore perceived the code of the Brotherhood as the measure of their own conduct. The Dainnan Vow—to right wrong, to punish the guilty, to feed the hungry, help the feeble and obey the King-Emperor's law—those vows of courage, truth, charity, fidelity and uprightness had made their mark on many of the warriors of Erith, as a shining cup casts reflected light on the beholder.

Hand-picked, these camp sentries were alert and watchful. Even when they met like this, for but a moment, their tongues might wag and their eyes rove but never did their attention lapse. There was no dozing off at the post, especially during the wighting hours. Unseelie incarnations of untold varieties had been straggling through these wastelands for more than a year, coming from the forests in the south or the peaks in the north, making for the Landbridge. Yet the leaguers were forced to position themselves here, camped in an unbroken semicircle around the old fort by the entrance to the bridge, because strategically, it was the best location from which to defend Eldaraigne from Namarran raids. On the naked plain they found themselves liable to be assailed from any quarter. Along the western line they had fenced themselves in with magicians' sorceries. To the north and south they had thrown up earthworks and spiked palisades.

To the eastern front the armies bent their gaze. To the east they soon would be ready to advance, challenging the wights holding the Landbridge in an effort to clear the way and march through into Namarre to put an end to the uprising. Meanwhile, scouts searched for signs of a possible early Namarran attack on the Legions. Due to the inability of Windships and Skyhorses to cross water, little was known of what doings fermented in Namarre. Only sketchy information had been gleaned from spies who had managed to sail around and land on its opposite shores—those few who had returned to tell of it.

The Wastelands altered illusorily as the unstorm swept down. Emerald faces of thistles bristled with amethyst spines. Ruby-eyed sand-mice with opalescent hides skittered amongst broken jewels pulsing with an ethereal diaphanousness. Numinous forces breathed a mockery of life into tableaux—untaltried men had done battle here long ago. Their graves had grown green these hundred years but still their simulacra fought on, long after their original moulds had mouldered. A Stormrider in haste crossed the airs of the plain. An aeronaut fell, windmilling, from a flying ship. A company of travellers was pursued by wights and bolted, screaming, their mouths round O's of silence under the white knobs of their popping eyes.

'Look there!' A sentry snapped to attention. Auburn light slithered along the murderous spike of the cavalryman's lance he hefted in his right hand. A distant fire winked out, winked into incandescence again. Further on, another winked off, winked on. Something was passing silently between the watchers and the fires.

'I don't recall seeing that 'un before.'

'It blocks the light. Therefore 'tis real.'

Shouldering their weapons they ran forward to investigate.

The untamed winds of gramarye raked through Tahquil's hair, sizzling in her blood like red-hot pokers plunged into mulling ale. She couched along the horse's spine, her brown-dyed locks escaping from her taltry to mingle into his grey. With eldritch life springing vital beneath her thighs and gramarye streaming hectically all around, she no longer knew who she was; whether a mote scudding through a void, a half-spelled urge winging its way to calumny, an illusion, a drollery, a flung burst of dust.

Like daggers honed on stony resolve, male voices penetrated this detachment.

'Halt. Who goes there?'

She was unable to identify them through the mirages shifting in the unstorm, nor had she the power to reply in any case; her tongue mimicked wood. For their part, in the fickle illuminations of the shang, the men-at-arms could not clearly make out the intruder.

'A horse—but ruled by a rider?' muttered Fordward.

'In the name of the King-Emperor, halt or be run through!' shouted his companion.

A spear-cast away, the horse propped, skittishly kicking up its fetlocks.

'No rider,' uncertainly said one man.

'It has broken loose from the pickets and strayed.'

'Or else 'tis some un*lorraly* killing-thing, bound for Namarre.'

'Nay—see? 'Tis only a pony—not a war-horse at all, and too small to be an aughiskie.'

'Unless it is glamoured.'

'I carry a strong charm against glamour and I see a pony.'

The object of their attention abruptly galloped away. In a flash it was beyond the range of their lances and had disappeared into the confusing backdrop of shanged fires and stars and plush velvet shadows.

'Raise the alarm?'

'Naw. 'Twas a nygel for sure, and riderless.'

They jogged back to their stations to resume their beats.

Coated with the thickly fragrant juices of vine-flowers and plastered like a four-limbed starfish to the nygel's side, Tahquil was carried through the unstorm and the encampments of the Royal Legions. The lightness of the nygel's hooves, the swiftness of his passing and the bewildering nature of the Wastelands under shang combined to conceal their passage from all but the keenest eyes—which, by the time they blinked, had lost their evidence.

The girl's cheek was fastened to the living hide. Unable to lift her head, she missed seeing the tall pennons and banners snapping in the breeze. Unnoticed, the King's Standard and the Royal Banner, the personal flags of the Royal Family, flew from the largest of the pavilions—that which bravely displayed a canopy of purple and the Royal Crest emblazoned in gold on every silken wall.

The shang wind released its hold on the memories of the elements and fled over the shores, out across the sea. The nygel passed beyond the last watchfires of the front line and thence into the ruthless darkness of no-man's land, where two days since, a skirmish had been fought. He darted past two sprawling, silent shapes with mortified claws where hands once had been, jumped over another that moaned softly, and eluded a strange hulk looming against the sky. He ran past the ruined fort standing deserted on the doorstep of the Landbridge. Foliots had found and claimed it, as they claimed most abandoned halls of men. The empty windows flared with their sudden lights and eclipses.

And then the nygel with its lopsided burden cantered onto the Nenian Landbridge.

In the wake of the unstorm, thick clouds had begun massing up from the southern horizon, until they blanketed half the dome of the sky. Out of the gloaming, eldritch faces leered, wightish forelimbs snatched, eyes darted like spiders on fire, voices sniggered, sobbed and gibbered.

The nygel did not stop. He did not turn his head to inquire after his passenger's comfort—such an idea never broke into the weird forests of his mind. He cantered on, joyously—for the smell of the sea came from all sides now, telling of swells like black glass mountains, and the heaving muscle of tidal forces, telling of whipped-cream wind-tickled wave crests, of spray and spume smashed against the sky, and cruel currents that mocked humanity, flowing as cold and sensuous as eldritch desire. Like all of their kindred, nygels loved best the sea, that mother of all waters.

Officially, the border between Eldaraigne and Namarre divided the Landbridge exactly in half. Tahquil, semi-insensate, and her steed had almost reached this midpoint when the twilight gave out an unpleasant surprise. Chrysanthemums of fire came blazing at them—brands brandished in the meaty fists of a band of Namarran warriors headed by one of their wizards. With yells of triumph they whirled lassoes above their heads in practised fashion. One man cast his rope. It struck the nygel's neck and fell short. At the touch of the hated halter, the wight uttered a scream of fear. Feinting and dodging so rapidly that few mortal riders would have remained mounted without the aid of supernatural adhesion, he eluded them, only to run into a second band, the ambushing compatriots of the first. Now desperate, the waterhorse flared his waterlily nostrils and caught the scent of his ultimate resource, that which was his native shelter, his natural—if such a term can be employed for the supernatural—element.

The two bands of wight-tamers converged, rushing together like breakers in a choppy soup. In a burst of desperate speed their quarry slipped out from between them and dived into a pool.

A brackish pool it was, lying so close to the sea: a damson-coloured water of rock and sedge and salty mosses and secrets. A drowning pool.

Deep under the water sank the nygel. All care for his burden had been chased from the kelp forests of his animus by the urge to escape, the instinct for water, the imperative to elude the rope.

Silently he sank and perforce silently Tahquil, attached to his flank, sank with him. A few bubbles rose up like hollow planets, sat like silver thimbles on the surface, and then popped.

The Namarrans, cheated, raged at the brink, cursing and flinging stones. A moment only remained they thus. One, more nervous than the rest and sharper-eyed, called out.

'Blood's death! A scavenger! A scavenger moves this way!'

A flurried chaos at the poolside, a clattering of stones, a swishing of bushes and the Namarrans were no longer there. Only the reflection of a single consumptive star floated wanly on the surface. In the dimness, something crooked shuffled towards the patch of water. Its shambling gait belied a remarkable swiftness of progress.

Down below, Tahquil's heart pumped frantically. The veins of her temples stood out, cords binding a skull turning inside out in agony.

Down below, the nygel felt a stirring at his side and remembered.

He sloughed her, braced himself underneath her expiring form and pushed. As she broke through the roof of his liquid haven he boosted her up, out and sideways, depositing her on the shore before subsiding anxiously and immediately. Had his recollection of her presence and mortality arrived an instant later, it must have been too late.

Tahquil lay helpless, coughing water in spasms of violence, retching, vulnerable, her eyes unfocused. A huge, stooped figure in grey rags bent over her. It swung a voluminous net off its back, dropped it on the ground and opened it. The net contained a large, irregular object. To this object, Tahquil was added, still racked and convulsed. The scavenger closed the net, lifted it on its humped back and shuffled away.

The dirty clouds moved north to muffle the entire sky. Only a greenish corpse-candle faltered along the marshy places of the Landbridge.

In this obscurity an urisk was standing beside a murky well. He knocked three times on the brackish water. A familiar long head came up and looked around.

'Vanished,' it said, in gloomy astonishment.

6
TAPTHARTHARATH
Smoke on the Water,
Fire in the Sky

Red Taptharthar: magma's pumping
Through below-ground veins, where jumping
Pressure points like hearts are thumping,
Setting mighty boulders bumping.
Up past thinner crusts they're humping,
Pushing past to swell the tumps. Stings
Of lapilli rain in lumps; rings
Opening in lava sumps bring
Boiling vomit for the dump, fling
Rock bombs high, to fall down crumping
And the slow morasses slumping;
Creeping ooze congealing, plumping.
Flames for trees, rock-melt for lakes—
Red Taptharthar burns and quakes.

NAMARRAN BARDIC CHANT

Metal beaks had embedded into Tahquil's ribcage, her left arm, her thigh. During the jouncing journey over the miles they had pecked their way in—the nodes, projections and sawing ridges on which she lay constricted by the tensile web. Throughout a long, strange journey she had lain stupefied, fading in and out of consciousness, shuttled between real nightmares and the nightmare of reality. The effects of her ordeal had been compounded by the Langothe, whose intensity apparently ebbed and flowed at random, or perhaps was driven by the whims of the various exigencies of existence. During her moments of awareness the longing for the Fair Realm seized her. Images of its star-jewelled mountains, its forests of mystery and its clear, singing rivers formed before her inner gaze; images of such power they seemed to haul the blood from her thundering veins, the tears from their bitter wells behind her eyes.

Hunger had not troubled her, nor thirst—she having lately swallowed enough to quench a hundred thirsts—nor, despite her damp condition, had cold. What she was rammed down on, that amalgam of iron rims and studs, was warm. In places it gave way to the yielding suppleness of skin—slightly hair-roughened but sensuous, as the metal was agonising, as though she reclined upon a cruel lover.

Nor could she, during periods of awareness, understand where she was or how she had come there. When the jouncing and jabbing ceased, there came a descent, a bump, a groan, the tension of the net slackening, a disoriented rolling, the beaks withdrawing and new ones digging in new locations. She stifled a cry.

The groan had not been hers.

A large presence hovered nearby. Its carrion stench hovered also. Perhaps it noted the paucity of life signs exhibited by its most recent catch. Yet unwounded, merely stunned and temporarily helpless, Tahquil retained a measure of hidden vitality. Presently her captor withdrew to the left. A juicy tearing and a crunching emanated from its proximity. After an aeon, the author of these munchings shambled away with footsteps like anvils being dragged through a quarry.

A moan welled again, close by Tahquil's ear. She tried to open her eyes but discovered that she had already done so. Bleary red smudges crowded in at the edges of sight, illuminating nothing. Her hands explored.

Across a landscape both unfamiliar and well known her fingertips travelled. Metallic ridges of armour, yes—and the sleek adamant undulations of living thews. A thicket of hair, a contoured field of stubble. A Midsummer breathing, irregular and strained. A slick syrup that might have been blood.

'Who are you?' she whispered, but the armoured man made no reply.

Once, in Gilvaris Tarv, Tahquil-then-Imrhien had seen Namarrans passing by. Now, by the shape of the armbands and the earring of this warrior, she knew him to be one of their kindred. His breathing deepened, bubbling and stewing in his chest. The unnerving rattle of it seemed to echo hugely, as though reverberating off the interior of some spacious hollow, a chamber of rock and stone. Perhaps they found themselves in a cavern. This did not matter to Tahquil. Of more immediate concern was the tangling snare which bound her to this doomed lover and his accoutrements, this warrior with his overlapping metal scales who, by the sound of his breathing, soon would be cold and breathless as a netted fish.

Her hand slid down his chest to his hip, to the scabbard belted there. A haft protruded. Hampered by ubiquitous cordage, she slid free the blade, groped for a strand and sliced it through. The dagger was keen. It severed the fibres with short, easy strokes. Feverishly she worked in the dark, once stinging her own hand with the paper-thin metal edge. Her fingers slippery with blood, she dropped the dagger, almost. Another cord sprang apart and another—now the gap was big enough. She wriggled through.

Cramp disabled her and she did drop the dagger. Falling, it rang on stone. She doubled over, gritting her teeth, trying to loosen the rigid spasms in her sinews and chafe sensation into seized-up limbs. Reviving ganglions prickled like pincushions, shooting outraged spokes from centres that had been crushed by armour's brazen knuckles.

Somewhere nearby, the Namarran stirred and sucked in an almighty gasp.

'Six heads have I broken this day,' he wheezed with foreign pronunciation, 'and yours shall be the seventh.'

After that he made some choking sounds and fell silent. She touched his chest: there was no rise, no fall.

Heat thrummed from the stones upon which Tahquil crouched. A vibration arose like the thump-thump of a powerful engine. The carrion stink curdled in her nostrils. How long would it be until the monstrous presence returned, dragging its anvil feet? She swung her head around. A dull red patch hove into view—a sulky smear of crimson chalk, not flickering like flames, but steady. For want of a better course, Tahquil began to crawl towards it. The floor of this chamber or cavern was littered with objects. She brushed them with her seeking hands, climbed over or around them, or swept them from her path; things of rock, things of metal, things of bone, scuttling things with articulated carapaces.

The red glow expanded. Jagged shapes became discernible, looming on all sides. Indeed, this was a cave within rock. Stalactites of solid limestone hung from its ceiling, stretching down towards their dwarfish counterparts growing up from below. Boulders of all sizes strewed the uneven floor. Between the boulders lay bones. Long and smooth were the bones, or small and knobbed, domed or socketed, hinged, splayed, jointed, crenellated, chewed. Weapons and pieces of armour rusted among these relics. Hot to the touch was the metal, and it had been eaten away by airborne acids. None of it was useable. Scorpions threatened from chinks. Aiodes with leathery hides of stone lay cracked open like eggs, revealing glorious agate linings. Over all, the blood-hued light's lurid ambience was thrown like frayed gauze.

Perhaps this red opening led to another chamber—to a maze of chambers like the mines of Doundelding. For surely this grave-cave must be underground. Who would hew an above-ground structure like this, with dismal furnishings such as these?

A hot, scarlet wind rushed towards Tahquil, bearing on its back a reek both alarming and sickening, a stench she knew well but could not immediately identify. It was not the rotted-meat smell roiling in the guts of the cave. Pulling herself upright, she lurched forward with as much haste as she could rally. The wind's furnace breath blasted stronger. The light strengthened and at length, trembling with synesthesia, Tahquil stepped from the cave mouth into the open air of a surreal landscape.

What the world would have seen, had it possessed an eye and that eye turned upon the girl standing framed by the stone orifice, was this: a figure as tall and slender as a lotus stem, clad in wind-

plucked rags. Matted hair, the colour of mud and as filthy, surrounding a smeared face so flawlessly beautiful that the eye, this
invented eye of the world, must travel over it again and again in
disbelief, searching for the tiny fault which must surely exist but
did not. So fair was this countenance, so exquisite the proportions,
that it seemed not flesh and bone but a painting come to life, or
a sculpture fashioned from the finest-grained and purest marble,
by the hands of the most expert artisan.

What the green eyes in that face beheld was this: a wasteland
of a new kind. No vegetation grew anywhere. Dark was the sky
and low pressed the clouds, underlit with the sullen glare. These
were not the fleecy clouds of Spring showers, nor yet the
moisture-heavy thunderheads of storms—this was a layer of
smoke and steam slathered thickly across the firmament. Sunlight
filtered through weakly, the day's eye showing as a noxious
yellow stain in one corner.

Near at hand, pools of water nestled in pockets of barren rock,
each one attended by its rising mass of steam. Around these pools,
the rocks were coated with a glittering substance like crystallised
ice or snow.

Small craters pockmarked the ground. Some gulped emptiness, like fossilised mouths, while others jetted gouts of heated gas
to mingle with the smokes and other vapours. Around these vents
clustered spiky growths of sulphur crystals, golden-yellow. Strung
between them were webs of fine, glassy strands like hair.

Grotesque formations towered up like giant versions of the
burned toffee scrapings thrown out by the Royal Confectioner in
Caermelor. Gaps between these preposterous twists of rock
afforded glimpses of a glutinous river, bright orange in hue. Slow-
moving, it glistened gold at the edges. Dark flakes tessellated its
surface. Further off reared terraced cliffs of ash, marching away
into a louring obscurity. In one place, torrents of amber honey
cascaded slowly down their walls like a ponderous waterfall.

Tahquil knew, then, that she had reached Namarre. She had
been brought here by a scavenger, a huge, slow-witted entity
whose sole intention at any time was to collect provisions for its
larder, its preferred fare being the flesh of humankind. Some

instinct or habit prompted these creatures to choose victims with enough life left in them that they might keep fresh for a short while, yet with not enough spark that they might offer serious resistance to the scavenger's culinary arrangements. These sick or wounded creatures they would take to their lairs, there to devour them sooner or later. This one kept his larder in Namarre, in that region abhorred by men which they called Tapthartharath.

From histories taught her in childhood, Tahquil-Ashalind had some knowledge of Tapthartharath. Even after a thousand years, the ground was still restless. Unimaginable fires surged and swelled beneath it. The reek of brimstone was the same odour that had heralded the last days of the Isle of Tamhania. Yet, restless though Tapthartharath was, it was not as dangerous as Tamhania. Its subterranean forces seeped, releasing gradually, never building up to a major explosion.

A road, or what seemed a road, passed near the cave mouth and led away among the fused-Sugar formations. Its surface was billowy and undulating, with a texture like sharkskin, finely detailed with miniature spines. In places this skin was wrinkled, as though formed from skeins and coils of rope, or like the tightly massed roots of a great tree which had turned to stone.

Goaded by an urgent need to get away from the cave of death, Tahquil-Ashalind set out along this way. Heat rose through her boots. She kicked against a scatter of brilliant zeolite crystals. Sweat trickled in runnels down her skin and her throat was scorched with every indrawn breath. At her neck, the iron belt-buckle seared her flesh. Further along, out of sight of the cave, she came to a portion of the road which had collapsed inwards. Tiptoeing warily to the edge of this window, Tahquil looked down upon a red glaze flowing only three or four feet below, moving along a tunnel beneath the surface. The road itself had been formed from the cooling skin of this lava tube as it congealed. In places it might still be only inches thick. Tahquil resumed her journey, keeping to the road's more solid edges.

Lava lakes lay like mirrors of polished ruby at the feet of slopes where fumes billowed upward in tall plumes, angled against the land like a forest of smoke-trees. Pillow lavas were piled everywhere like flattened balls. A myriad white bubbles of pumice stones spilled from smoky pits. Here and there, treacherous rubbles of scoria underfoot made each step uncertain. Tongues of flame spurted unexpectedly from fumaroles whenever the underground heat built up enough to boil the rocks to froth, releasing their flammable gases. As tall as Mooring Masts these flames leaped, white at the cores, deepening to dazzling colours. Abruptly they would flare out, leaving images burned on Tahquil's watering eyes.

An angry thirst plagued her. All about, water lay in sunken jars of stone, but none cool enough or fit to drink. Toxic steams rose from them. All day she walked along the rough flank of the lava flow, because of a need to distance herself from the scavenger's cave, because no other course of action had offered itself, and because to give up and cease moving would be to admit defeat and lose all hope. She journeyed at right angles to the sun, heading north.

As the smudged sun was blotted up by the western smokes, she found an ashy couch beneath an overhang which, seen from one angle, resembled a shipwreck and, from another, three broken lutes. There, she slept.

At morning, a gas jet ignited, flaring from a fumarole. Its light struck daffodil rays from the facets of sulphur crystals burgeoning like strange, spiky flowers along the rim of a basin. It struck silver glints from shards of black obsidian, and carbuncle glitter from red chunks of hematite. Through eyelets in pylons and tines of rock, thin gases streamed. Waking with a thirst that trammelled her with visions of the cool, clear lakes of Mirrinor and the saturated valleys of Lallillir, Tahquil steadied herself against the broken lutes and journeyed on.

The lava flow directed her through an area of bubbling pots in which domes of gas formed up through brilliantly coloured muds, to burst flabbily with *flumping, flupping* sounds, like simmering porridge. Splats of mud were thrown up and down like paint—vibrant blue-grey, scalding yellow or vivid red.

Amongst this garishness, one aqueous pond of tranquillity

attracted her. Parched cravings led her to its brink. As she stood undecided, watching steam scoot across the water's unblemished surface, a low rumbling noise started up beneath her feet. The pond gurgled. The girl dashed for cover. A violent explosion spewed a gush of water and steam high into the air. Taller grew the geyser, its head vanishing into the clouded air. A plump, hot rain splashed down.

When it was over, she took to the road again. By now, the tiny spines on the epidermis of the pahoehoe flow had wreaked a spiteful damage on the soles of her boots. The flow was veering to the right—ahead, the rounded grey-blue shoulders of ash dunes reared up. To save what remained of her footwear, Tahquil left the lava path and began to climb.

A dust of powdery ash-snow puffed from each footstep. Ankle-deep, she waded uphill. Below, a lake of lava gleamed like a shield of burnished bronze through swathes of dull vapour. Mirages shimmered on the dunes; alluring lagoons. When the sun dangled above her head like a withered dandelion, Tahquil seated herself on the lee side of a formation shaped like a dancing, six-headed bear. Ash and mud streaked her face, mixed with perspiration. Her hair hung rank with airborne particles, plastered down by condensing steam.

Darkness, when it snuffed out the guttering and jaundiced candle of the sun, discovered her there still, curled on her side in the listlessly shifting powders. A breeze blew cinders and dust from seemingly man-made walls protruding from the dunes—high, thin, long dykes formed of black stone blocks, manufactured by volcanic forces.

Dreams or hallucinations acted out plays on the final stage of Tahquil's thirst-induced trance. Thorn rode at a gallop through a rain-drenched forest, pearls of water being flung from his wet hair. Dripping gruagachs offered overflowing bowls of water in their outstretched hands. A transparent pool opened at her feet, its sheer surface marked only by a sprinkling of sparkles and petals of apple blossom in fragile flotillas. A fountain tinkled into a cool, marble cistern. A vision with hair of moonrays shored her up and brought to her cracked lips a cup containing rain, green with new-minted reflections. She gulped. Coughing, choking, she grabbed the cup, swallowing all its contents.

'Easy, mistress!' said the moonray visitation.

'More. I must have more.' *Mine eyes, let this be no deception.*

Brimming, the cup was returned to her. Again she emptied it and demanded further dividends. Repeatedly the cup returned, filled from a gourd by a second manifestation.

'The swan has been quartering the skies without rest, these two nights and days,' remarked Tully as he poured.

'May the fruits of joy be heaped upon you, all three,' answered Tahquil weakly. She gripped the green cup. It was the half-husk of a seed the size of her fist. She lay a while against the curve of Tighnacomaire's man-shoulder, her dust-clogged hair falling in tangled locks across her face. Beyond their shelter, the coloured smokes and obfuscating vapours of Taptharatharath glided by in the night. No speech passed between her two eldritch companions. Silence was as natural to their kind as poetry. With the patience of eternity they bided, while her body rehydrated.

Later, between love and madness, Tahquil said, 'The swan— has she discovered tidings of the King-Emperor?'

'Aye, that she has,' said Tighnacomaire. 'And mair. But whatever it may be, she has nat telled us.'

'I must speak with her. Is she near?'

'Who can say?' said the urisk with a shrug. 'She comes, she goes.'

'And I go, too. It is high time I left this fried bower. Yet, the night is dark—the fogs hide moon and stars. I cannot see two paces in front of me.'

'Ye shall nat need yarr eyes,' said Tighnacomaire. 'I shall bear ye.'

'Oh? And shall you drown me again? I believe the mud in the pools here is good for the skin, if one does not object to being cooked.'

Shamefaced, Tighnacomaire ballooned his cheeks and snorted.

'I'll nat be diving in these sizzle-pots, nay, nor any mair springs av water neither, with ye an my back, mistress. 'Tis sarry I am.'

''Tis feckless ye be,' added Tully.

'And if I ride,' said Tahquil, 'where shall you take me? Do you know the way?'

'The way to where?' vaguely said the pale-skinned, raw-boned horse-man.

'To the fortress, the headquarters of the Hunt, where my friends were taken.'

He slid away. With one fluid movement he left the shelter and trotted around the back of the six-headed bear. Tahquil had scarcely time to draw breath before he dashed back, in horse-form, kicking up swirls of ash.

'He kens the way,' said Tully. The nygel stamped a foreleg, switched his tail. Awkwardly, he lowered himself to the ground. Tahquil stepped astride his back. He stood again and away they cantered.

The incendiary landscape of Tapthartharath unfurled beneath the flying hooves of the waterhorse, and on all sides. Over the ash dunes they sped, and hills of coal-coloured pumice, and by the serpentine dykes, tall as cliffs, thin as coffins and black as hearses. The ragged edges of Tahquil's garments streamed out along the wind of their passing, like sombre flames.

Far away, a river of lava as thick and stiff as honey, moved like an incandescent crocodile. A side flow was diverging in a gout of tangerine syrup, carrying chunks of dark rock. At the head of the branching flow, a wall of burning rocks rolled forward by degrees, panting from thousands of dragon-nostrils. Little fires and spurts of steam and smoke were coming off it. Parts of its sides tore away, revealing glimpses into the golden flesh beneath the dark crimson and orange scales. The scabby crust pulsated sluggishly, like boil-ing tallow.

The land was rising. With each stride, the bright drums of the nygel's hooves hit the ground a little higher up. They climbed through pillars of smoke, columns of steam, and slanting gas tow-ers. They splashed through gaudy muds, leaped over glowing melts from which heat burst forth with incinerating vehemence. Long steams came racing and roaring along the ground in thick curtains, sucked out of smouldering fissures by the wind. Gaping red-lined throats belched white smoke rings. The pall of putrid emissions thickened, darkened, drew in and around like angry lynch mobs. In this obscurity, Tahquil lost sight of Tully, who had been running nimbly alongside. Spasms of coughing wrenched her frame. Seven million pins prickled her skin. Her eyes swam, wept like the sea, combusted in caustic juices.

'Tiggy, where do you take me?' she moaned.

He neighed a response. She thrust her face into his mane and simmered there in misery.

All night the waterhorse galloped between smoky walls alleviated infrequently by pockets of less toxic air. He seemed tireless. Many times Tahquil reckoned it must be morning, longed for morning. But when her eldritch steed eventually swung to a halt, no light welled through the blood-panes of her swollen-shut lids, yet the air was pure, clean and sweet on her raw lungs.

Tighnacomaire cancelled his stickiness and his rider slid off. Cold water sluiced her burning face. She drank and lay motionless, utterly exhausted. The combined torments of her recent travails and the Langothe's savagery had smothered her life-spirit until only a spark remained. Somnolence came like a midnight thief and stole her away.

7
DARKE
Evernight

Dark is the night that blinds the sight and, moonless, hides our paths.
Dark are the shadows of the madness gathered on our hearths.
Dark the storm-cloud, tall, wrathful, proud, whence tears of sorrow rain
And dark my heart that we must part. When shall we meet again?

LAMENT OF FAREWELL

'Lie still.' Tully's reedy tones brooked no dissension.

Tahquil opened her eyes.

Suspended in the profound heights of a sky as deeply blue as pure essence of amaranth and as intoxicating, brilliant stars, layer upon layer, dwindled to a crystallised haze at inconceivable distances. Indigo, raven and iridium were the colours of the night. In every direction, long, tree-clad slopes marched rank on rank, fading into the darkness. A tingling entered Tahquil's shoulder blades, seemingly welling up from the ground pressing into her back—black ground, stretching in the north and east to black mountains that raised their blocks along glittering horizons.

Away beyond the southern ridges, above the dimly written fish-bone points of the furthest fir trees, the stars fell short of the world's rim, obliterated by a wide belt of impenetrable gloom. The width of two fingers, held sidelong at arm's length, measured the height of it. Higher up, the pall dissipated, drawing back to reveal the silent stars.

Danger—the air vibrated with it, and other intuitions also: excitement, expectation. Tahquil, obeying the wight's orders, remained motionless.

After a time Tully announced, 'They are gone.'

'Who is gone?'

'*Unket* things,' he replied shortly. 'But there's no tellin' when they'll come by again. Cover yoursel' with muck, lass. Smear it thick, that they may not catch the tang o' ye. Blacken your face.'

Raising herself on her elbow, Tahquil tore up handfuls of moist soil and living leaves the colour of basalt. She did as he bade, then drank again from the seed husk's hull—long, refreshing draughts. Some way off, Tighnacomaire, in horse-form, was grazing.

'The night is long,' the mortal girl said softly, wonderingly, tilting her chin towards the silver magnificence of the vault rising, fathomless, overhead.

'No,' said Tully. 'Elsewhere the sun shines. This is Darke, the land of Evernight.'

'Is it so? Sain me! I have heard tell of this place. They say day never dawns here. But it makes no sense . . .'

'From the bottom of a very deep well,' said Tully with aplomb, as though accustomed to such venues, 'when ye luik upwards ye'll see naught but stars in a night sky, no matter gin the sun be shining up there or no. Darke is walled by a half-ring of mountains to the north, and a crescent of high smokes frae Tapthar to the south, which give the same result as a well's wall. By some trick o' the winds, the smokes ne'er blow intae this eye.'

'Evernight,' repeated Tahquil. 'A haven for nocturnal wights.'

'Indeed,' said the urisk. 'A pleasant land. If Men dwelled here in their snug cottages, fain would I stay and tend their hearths. But Darke is as much shunned by your kind as is Tapthartharath. Many things haunt here but few are mortal.'

'Few?'

'Ainly captured mortals. They dinnae suffer it for lang,' added

Tully uncomfortably. 'Ye shouldnae have come here, Mistress Mellyn. There's still time tae turn back noo, gin ye come tae your senses. The horse can carry ye back tae the lands o' Men, fleet as flight.'

'I cannot. I must seek my friends.'

'Och, but there's hobgoblins hereabouts, lurking in the stones, and other things even more *unket*. Darke is sair kittle for ye, 'tis perilous.'

'I doubt it not. But I must face the risks. Where is the fortress?'

'Atop Black Crag it stands, on the round, high plain, some seven leagues to the northeast. Long ago Prince Morragan had it built, as a retreat where he might take his leisure from time to time. Annath Gothallamor that stronghold is called—the Great Castle of Night, the Dark Fortress.'

Annath Gothallamor. It was a thundering name, like the chord from the bass tubes of some eldritch bellows instrument. A name charged with portent.

'Has it occurred to ye,' said Tully, 'that ye might be walking intae a baited trap?'

'It has. But now, let us go.'

Tahquil stood, swayed and collapsed. She rubbed her wrist across her forehead.

'I have not much strength. Do you carry food?'

'Nay,' Tully hooted. 'Water I carried, but here we'll not need it—springs rise everywhere. Fire I brought from Tapthar—see?' He uncovered a cone-shaped hollow stone. Within, a lump of rock glowed with inner fires. 'Heat-bearing rock—*cridhe-teth*. Hot-Heart, men call it. Warmth and light we have, but no food.'

'It matters little,' said Tahquil, levering herself to her feet again. She could not recall when she had last desired food. A greater hunger had her firmly in its grip. Her limbs weighed like congealed metal, her joints had rusted. Tighnacomaire raised his head and peered at her questioningly. His eyes were two gold coins in the night. Silently, she nodded and he trotted over. Soon they were on their way again.

She sat slightly hunched, a tangle-haired, unkempt rider on a pretty pony. Quietly now went her steed, with the cunning of his kind, his horny feet making no sound, scarcely dislodging a leaf of the grey sedges or strange grisaille grasses. A bubbling spring made a chitinous chinking as of glass goblets. The air stirred, wafting in soft fans against Tahquil's face. Balmy, it was fragrant with a glistening of secretive leaves—shy, shady leaves nodding in dusky forests, washed clean by starlight.

Beneath the canopy of eternal night they passed over marshy ground where pale lights bobbed, wandering—soft, acid green, soft lightning blue, their flickerings mirrored dimly in sheets of water. Through the waving sedges Tighnacomaire's sure steps found the ways between hidden bogs and sudden pools.

'I have seen a light like those,' the girl murmured, 'long ago. It almost led a good man to his doom.'

'Hobby-Lanthorns,' said Tighnacomaire. 'Will o' the Wisps. They love the wetlands, the boggy places.'

'As do your own kind.'

'Aye!' he nichered. 'I'd have a mind tae dance with them were ye nat riding.'

'I am flattered you care.'

'There's Joan-the-Wad and Jacky Lantern—I ken them all.'

Enticingly, a green luminance tinted a sheaf of ferns, a blue lambency highlighted a rocky prominence.

'Are they not death omens?' asked Tahquil.

'Ainly the spunkies and the corpse-candles are warners. As farr the rest av them, some are cruel as bogles. They'll lure marrtals intae sticky mires and drown them, orr lead them over the brinks av cliffs. But others are ainly seeking a laugh, same as tricksy boggarts—just seeking tae make a goose out av some drunken farmer weaving his way hame over the fens at night.'

'Few such farmers weave hereabouts. As for foolish mortals, this is a desert, for I am the only one. Why do they linger here, these marsh-lights?'

''Tis the Call. The Call is strong here. It broadcasts from Annath Gothallamor.'

'It is long since that summons first went forth,' replied Tahquil, remembering she had originally learned of the phenomenon in Gilvaris Tarv, while staying at the house of Ethlinn Bruadair.

With a faint rustle and a splash the three travellers left the marshes and cantered on under the stars, through a black and silver land, onward and upward, ever higher.

No rain fell in Darke, but every so often, mists rose from the streams and marshes, or rolled in from the sea, muffling the landscape in their thick wool. When they dissipated, they left glassy beads quivering on every leaf and twig, on every blade and web, and the damp loam seeping with moisture, the tree-roots digging deeper, the dark-green frogs gleaming as though oiled, the springs and soaks brimming, the flower cups filled with quicksilver, to spill again.

By degrees, Tahquil-Ashalind's vision adapted to the ambient illumination of Darke, subtle and changeless. Her perception was perhaps also enhanced by her contact with an eldritch creation. Bent figures she saw, limping amongst hummocks; grey trow-folk, lovers of silver. Swart grotesqueries she glimpsed, sneaking and cavorting in the black forests; hobgoblins, those wights more unseelie than bruneys, more seelie than bogles—pranksters whose tricks might be kind or cruel, or both together. In a forest clearing danced a circle of the vampiric baobhansith, like maidens clad in the colours of sunfall, with poisonous flowers plaited through the smoke of their hair.

From the nygel's back Tahquil watched the prowlings of these entities. Darke was alive with them. She felt secure, protected by Tighnacomaire's speed and skill, guarded by Tully's watchfulness, yet security was tinctured with a certainty that they approached something awful and momentous, and that there was no escape. Somehow, through her link with these eldritch companions, she was beginning to sense the Call.

There was, of course, one who stood at the centre of the Call—its source, its Supreme Commander.

Morragan.

Consideration of that grey-eyed Faêran prince induced panic and shock. It also invoked visions of the Realm. The Langothe sprouted claws and tore at her equilibrium. Weakened by starvation and care, crippled by the devastation of love beyond reach, Tahquil teetered on the brink of insanity. She fell forward on the nygel's neck and slept without awareness of the transition to oblivion.

A change in the lullaby rhythms of travel woke her. Tighnacomaire was slowing to a halt. Through the tendrils of his weed-twined mane, constellations dazzled. Feeling his hide release her, Tahquil dismounted. The waterhorse cantered off to a silken mere where the images of stars floated like blossoms. He entered. One circular ripple glided out.

'He was gettin' dry,' tooted the ever-present urisk. He raised a wiry arm, pointing. 'See there.'

To the north, a rocky butte thrust up suddenly from the land—a plateau wide and high. Thongs of water threaded the draperies of its precipitous sides. From its centre jutted a hill, crowned with an architecture of many towers.

'We're gettin' close now,' said Tully. 'Up there on the tabletop they call the High Plain, Black Crag looms. And atop the Crag, the Castle.'

Tahquil's heart fluttered.

'The story repeated,' she said, speaking her thoughts aloud. 'Another dark fortress. Another Tower Terrible, and he in it, and the Hunt as well. If anyone were to be standing at the edge of that tabletop, he might look out over the whole of southern Darke. Were such a watcher in possession of keen nocturnal vision he might see us, as specks moving through these stands of slim trees.'

'I'll warrant that all o' Darke is subject tae scrutiny, not ainly from the High Plain, but from the skies and *aiblens* from ither vantage points or scopes ainly available tae those who hold great power in their hands. Yet, they watch for warriors and for mortal spies unaccompanied by wights. For 'tis not usual—nay, 'tis unheard of, for eldritch and *lorraly* to form such a league as we four. Many times I have thought it strange mysel', that I should be hurryin' from my ancient haunts and traipsin' across the countryside wi' a wee lass. And for the horse tae bear ye as he does, and for the swan tae even speak tae ye—'tis a marvel.'

'Why do you come with me?'

He scratched his sparse triangle of a beard. 'I dinnae ken, rightly.'

'Good taste, no doubt,' she managed.

His pixie mouth stretched into a grin. 'Nae doubt!'

Palely glimmering, tree boles stretched up to a star-perforated lattice of leaves. Long tree-roots wound along the edges of a brook. Here, Tahquil lay, drinking. The water cupped in her hands was clear and invigorating, laced with a welter of scintillants dancing like disturbed glitter-dust, a swimming echo of the sky.

Tahquil looked up again, across the rising slopes to the high, black loom of the butte, overhung with its silver canopy.

'Let's away,' she said. 'I'll ride on.'

Even as she spoke, a black cross intervened between water and sky. It swooped down into a grove.

'*An eoincaileag!*' exclaimed Tully. After a moment, the swan-maiden emerged. Nothing about her disclosed the nature of her tidings—whether they were good or evil. Tahquil stood up, clutching a tree-stem for support.

'Say on,' she said quickly, and without preliminaries.

'*Heihoo!* Valiant human friend is wise, wending to Fell Fortress from southern side, from slopes of fire and fume. On far side, further from the Fortress, hosts forgather, summoned. Hordes seethe and swarm on the High Flat.'

'Dwell not on the manoeuvres of Morragan's armies! What tidings of James, King-Emperor?'

Tahquil looked into the lovely face of Whithiue. A curious anger was printed there. The swanmaiden would not say more, at first. When she began to speak again she informed her listeners that while she was seeking news of the King-Emperor, other tidings had come to her knowledge. The reason for it was not clear, but it was widely broadcast among wights all across Erith, that Prince Morragan was not the only Faêran lord to seek the yellow-haired maiden. Now the High King of the Faêran himself commanded that whosoever should find her must bring her to him.

'So, King Angavar too has woken at last,' Tahquil said, awed, 'and has heard of my story.'

Again she wondered why she should be hunted—whether her pursuers had guessed, or somehow discovered who she was, and that she had come from the Fair Realm by some secret way.

Whithiue said, 'Fain would swan serve Angavar and heartily

follow his will. He is sovereign. The world's fairly sworn to submit. Swan's fealty, homage and sentiment are his.'

'Pray do not betray me, Whithiue! I would not be a pawn in the games of the Faêran. You do not know why Angavar and Morragan seek me.' *And I shall not tell you! For, if they knew that I could open the Gates to the Realm, my eldritch friends would have me brought to these Faêran lords in a moment. I judge this High King would straightway force me to the Gate, if he got me in his power. Then, to take revenge on his brother, he would return to Faêrie with his retinue, leaving Morragan to give vent to his wrath by allowing unseelie wights to punish Erith until time's end. I want none of that. I want the Faêran all gone, every last bewitching, ruthless one of them.* Aloud, she said, 'These Faêran monarchs and princes would have no care for the fates of my stolen friends. In the conflict of lord against lord, insignificant mortals perish. Keep my secret, I pray you! Do not betray me!'

'I'll no' play ye false, lass,' said Tully, 'and neither will the horse. But dinnae luik sae unkindly on the Faêran. Ye would be well advised not tae speak ill o' them. And certain, they can be merciful and just.'

'Just arrogant!' cried Tahquil.

'Had swan secured summons from Faêran sovereign's very hand, swan would hasten to fetch human to his feet,' said the eldritch girl, tossing back her dark hair.

'Doubtless,' rejoined Tully. 'But ye've heard the King's edict from some witless sparrows or sullen trows. Can ye break faith wi' the lass for the sake o' their rumour?'

'Hearth-wight wheedles well. Swan's in sore straits,' said Whithiue undecidedly.

'Do nat be wildered,' said Tighnacomaire. 'Yarr bound tae the mistress by the feather.'

The swanmaiden bowed her long neck; a gesture of concurrence.

'When friend has viewed fate of sisters, swan shall fulfill vow of fealty to High Sovereign and specify her whereabouts.'

Tahquil, now temporarily safe, repeated impatiently, 'What tidings of James, King-Emperor?'

Whithiue replied, 'Sixteenth sovereign so-styled has fallen.'

A white-hot stone knocked in the throat of Tahquil. 'Say on,' she said, very, very softly.

'He failed to survive,' said the swanmaiden. 'Some heinous wight slew him. Swan speaks with fidelity. Seagulls voiced story, which wave-wights verified, who viewed his final hour.'

Thorn was dead.

With eyes like empty shells, the mortal girl stared at the immortal—she who was of the kind that could never lie. A heavy door slammed shut with utmost finality, leaving her desolate.

Night birds twittered and grieved.

A descant flute began to play somewhere in Darke's silver-grey coppices—breathy, burring notes. Others started up. The threads of their separate melodies entwined like tinsel streamers, creating harmonies to break the heart. The breeze was purple with the scent of violets.

'No,' said Tahquil-Ashalind. 'No.'

Reason left her then.

She could not hold back. Over and over the sounds burst from her, like water from a dam whose walls had been breached; a wordless, mindless keening, a long-drawn lament of anguish and desolation more bitter than she had ever known.

The high lamps of Darke shone steadily down on the dim meres and marshes, the groves and glades, the hills and hummocks. Their rays caught the satin sheen on the flanks of an eldritch horse racing up a steep shoulder of the plateau, with a rider on its back. They glanced from the horns of a short figure leaping in the horse's wake. They caressed the glossy feathers of a long-necked bird sailing the rising airs that flowed to the uplands.

High up, near the edge of the plateau, a shelf jutted. Barren and rocky, it was cut in under a cliff. On this shelf the horse stopped. The rider fell off. Seven hundred feet below the shelf, the twilight hills and lowlands of Darke spread out, the sumptuous velvet and brocade of the shadowy forests decorated with sequins and threads of water.

Tully sat cross-legged beside Tahquil, who lay as she had fallen.

'Wauken, miss,' he said, and he murmured a spell of home and hearth, one such minor working as urisks are capable of. She roused, bewildered, blank-faced, and peered around. The wind elevating from below lifted her brown-dyed hair up and back, spreading it out along the currents like ribbons of kelp.

Down a stairway incised into the cliff face drifted Whithiue in maiden-shape, comely as the evening star. She opened her feather cloak. Out tumbled fruity spheres as soft as teased wool, in hues of peach, apricot and melon. One rolled to the feet of Tighnacomaire. He sniffed at it, then, absently, ate it.

'Ye great lunk,' said Tully, smacking the nygel on the nose. 'Go and eat some eel-grass, or grass-eels. These are for the mistress.'

Tighnacomaire rolled his eyes guiltily and laid his ears flat.

Sorrow had gathered to Tahquil-Rohain from all its hiding places in the woods of Darke: from empty nests and buds untimely shrivelled; from a twig upon which a tiny owl sang a lament for his lost mate; from a mighty oak that had fallen on its side, whose last dry leaves, bunches of hands cut out of brown paper, clapped like a death rattle; from wind that grieved among the tree boles, whispering *farewell.*

The grey raiment of despair was drawn to her, and when she was clothed, the dullness of the garments flowed outwards like the rays of an un-sun, spreading smoky un-light and wrapping even the wild things of Darke in its ragged webs.

But stone and ashes do not weep.

I am sere. I am stone. Desperate, desolate stone, deeply etched with the acid of agony. Let stone turn to ashes, as the stones of Tamhania were burned away. I am nothing, a husk. I will walk on, but the flame has consumed me, then died.

For herself, Tahquil had little care now. She touched some Fairbread to her mouth, moving like one of the clockwork toys from Tana's gorgeous salons—but she might have been carved from milk-quartz.

If he lives longer, I must still go on. I will honour my inner promise to rid the world of the Faêran, if I can, and see my friends safe home, if it is possible. After that I will care naught about what happens to me.

'Far have we come,' said Tully, after the damsel had broken her fast with three small bites. 'Gin ye clamber up that stair in the rock, ye shall rise above the rim of the High Plain. Then ye shall see Annath Gothallamor.'

She climbed the stair. The steps were cracked. Mosses and tiny plants grew from the fissures, veiled with nodding white flowers. Near the top she paused, standing on tiptoe. She craned her head, raising her eyes two inches above the level of the plateau's brink.

The Plain rolled away like a floor flagged with jet and obsidian. Yet it was not devoid of vegetation. Short grasses sprouted, and in places, bushes squatted in round-shouldered clumps. On their immense black backdrop, the spiky stars glittered more sharply now, huge and close. Against them, climbing up the sky and obliterating the celestial radiance with its bulk, a sudden, massive bulwark rose like the topmost peak of a mountain. And from the culmination of this crag thrust a fortress topped with clusters of spired towers, belfries, conical turret roofs, toothed battlements and flying buttresses, its grim walls pierced by narrow slots with pointed arches. These slots, which seemed miniature by comparison with the great mass of stonework, shone with an inner glow tinted with the dilute blue of *uhta*, like the lingering colour of the sky on a Summer's eve, just after the sun has set, like the cold blue of glacial shadows, like wood smoke seen by moonlight. Menace was implicit in these hundreds of gimlet eyes.

A movement caught Tahquil's attention. Slowly, she began to subside behind the edge. Gabbling broke out above her head— there had been spriggans in the shadows of the High Plain. She hastened down the stair. When she reached the shelf, Tully pushed her into a crevice. Creaking voices called from above and stones rattled down. Tighnacomaire whinnied. Precariously close to the shelf's border, he curvetted, his small hooves balancing deliberately. The spriggans on top of the cliff watched him, gibbering argumentatively, then withdrew.

'Whisht!' exclaimed Tully. 'A close shave, that.'

For Tahquil, words would not form. She choked on them, as speechless as the duergar's lash had once made her. She strove for sanity, half wishing the Langothe would take her instantly, so that she would not have to wait for its slow-wearing effect to grind her down.

When at last she was capable of utterance, she asked, in a bleak monotone, 'How shall I cross the Plain? There is scant cover.' It was the first time she had spoken since hearing the swanmaiden's tidings.

'Strong-sinewed swans will hoist feeble friend's slight weight,' said Whithiue. 'Sea-folk will surrender a wide fish-net. Four swans seizing hems have strength for ferrying human freight from here to Fell Fortress, flying fast.'

Scarcely comprehending the enormity of this tardily offered privilege, Tahquil nodded. She felt removed from the scene, as though she gazed down a long tunnel at the three wights on this precipitous aerial perch among the night glitter. Reason stood there alongside them, but she was disconnected from it. Tully's reply to Whithiue seemed to come from a room behind a wall.

'It cannae be done. The Hunt would find ye, or else watchers on the ground would look up and see the shape o' ye outlined by the constellations. The lass wants tae creep intae Gothallamor, not be dragged there in chains. Twa prisoners in there is enow— what's the use o' three?'

'How is she to secure her sisters?' Whithiue now looked exasperated. 'What's a scatter-witted half-sensible human fit for? Her fancy's wandering, frantic. Who wists whether stolen wenches survive? Such a scheme is futile, certainly set for failure. Cease following such folly.'

Doggedly, Tahquil said, 'You *must* help me. Take me in secrecy to this Fortress. I will not be thwarted. I must find my friends before I perish.' She was dully aware that Whithiue looked insulted, Tully puzzled and Tighnacomaire vague. Deep in thought, the urisk stroked his straggly goatee.

'Tharr's the Icepipes,' suggested Tighnacomaire abruptly, 'the burrows undarr the Plain.'

'Never heard o' them,' declared Tully. 'Might they be tunnels o' Fridean delving?'

'Nat Fridean. Icepipes warr made by atherrs.'

'Such subways are sealed from swan's scholarship, veiled from her wisdom,' murmured Whithiue.

'Those who fly high see ainly surfaces,' sagely quoted the nygel. 'Waterr seeks the underr places and the secret.'

'Ye're no' clashin' on aboot underground streams are ye?' hooted Tully. 'The lass can hardly pass through tunnels filled with water.'

'Streams arr lower. Icepipes arr high and dry. Men made them, cleverr men, long ago. Wizarrds of Namarre.'

'How shall I find a way to these Icepipes?' asked Tahquil.

'Wait,' said Tighnacomaire. 'I seek.'

He jumped away. As though the steep cliffs were level parklands, he crossed them swiftly and without faltering, his hooves finding secure footholds where none were apparent. Evernight glistened on. The southerly breeze brought a distant croaking of frogs.

Tighnacomaire returned not a fly's wing-beat too soon. A commotion was developing at the cliff top above. Spriggans had congregated there again. Their spindle-shanked shapes ranged along the skyline like gesticulating hieroglyphs. Some were shouting, while others had already started down the stair.

'Ride now,' said Tighnacomaire. Scrambling onto his back Tahquil was borne away from the rumpus, along a narrow ledge, until they veered around an outflung spur of rock and the spriggans disappeared from view. Tighnacomaire's sinews bunched and released rhythmically. Beneath his legs, chasms plunged and great holes gasped, filled only by eerie winds. The stars were sparks struck from his hooves. Somehow, he clung to the cliff side and at length arrived at a vertical fissure, deeply cloven, dark and silent. Warily, he poked his nose around a tall boulder and sniffed. Then he stepped through an opening.

Darkness sealed Tahquil's eyes like tar. She felt the waterhorse under her, moving forward. At the sound of a voice she started and would have fallen had she not been fastened on.

'Och, where's a light fa' the lass?'

Reflected sound waves mocked Tully's words.

Unexpectedly, light blasted out. It stripped Tahquil's eyes of

tar, peeled them like onions, divested them, it seemed, of eye
hatches, of lenses, of cornea, of retina, until they were seared
sightless with a white blindness.

As swiftly as it had appeared, this glare vanished. The urisk,
who had posed the light question, uttered a short, explosive word.

'A wee bit stark, that,' he added.

This time he uncovered the glowing rock of Tapthartharath
more slowly. A slim ray shot out under the lip of the stone cover.
It bounced off a plane, zigzagged back and forth between multitudinous facets and splintered into a billion and three fragments.

'Oh,' sighed Tahquil, raising her awed head from
Tighnacomaire's neck.

'Oh, oh, oh . . .' the echoes murmured.

From every angle, rainbows dazzled. Wide and high was the
Pipe itself, perhaps eighty feet from floor to vault and fifty feet
from wall to wall. Here was a duct massive enough to accommo-
date rows of a dozen horsemen bearing tall standards.

The inclinations of the wall, ceiling and floor of this tube took
the warm tangerine-amber radiations of the Hot-Heart of
Tapthartharath and multiplied them to uncountable repeated
images, splitting them prismatically into subtle component hues. It
was like being inside a wizardly kaleidoscope, but in fact the Pipe
was the eaten-out heart of a crystal of unimaginable dimensions.
A majestic splendour, yet hard, cold and merciless.

Tighnacomaire stepped now from a wide band of greyish
rock—granite or basalt—which had lined the inside of the aperture; an outer casing in which the enormous hollow crystal of the
underplain was housed. As his hooves touched the cut-mineral
floor it chimed—not the dull *thunk* of a spoon tapping the bubble of a fine glass goblet and resting there, inhibiting the
resonances—quite the contrary. Sympathetic vibrations rushed
away from the point of contact, across the floor and up the walls,
to flow across the upper choirs, crossing and recrossing, acting
upon each other to produce new frequencies of nuance and pen-
etration, and all these ringing notes, clear as water, pulsated
against each other in a long, swelling chord.

Tighnacomaire halted, uncertain.

The last note faded, like a reminiscence of the stirring of the jewellery air. The crystal waited.

'Cannat walk in silence,' stated Tighnacomaire.

'Silence, silence, ence, ence,' sang the vaults, sending off sparkles like pieces struck from the sky, the sea, the sun, fire, ice.

'Risk it,' said Tahquil. (Iskit, iskit.)

Tully held high the Hot-Heart and they went forward into a song, a net of rainbows, a web of glory.

It was not unpleasant. Never did the insistent decibels rise to a painful level, nor did the soft illumination of Hot-Heart produce intense beams. Even when they sprang off the facets at their most concentrated, the beams were rods of amber, or scarlet resin, or bolts of gold silk—not swords. Darkness fell away and fled before the interlopers, then closed in behind. They moved in their own orb of radiance, crisscrossed by spokes of astonishing colours. Deep beneath the High Plain they pushed on.

Presently, the nygel stopped again. The last patters of his and Tully's hooves rang off into the crouching darkness in front and to the rear.

'Light draws attention,' remarked Tighnacomaire. (Tenshun, shun.)

'Indeed!' Tully snapped shut the stone lid, breaking off the rose-marigold effulgence at its stem. Blackness slammed down like an iron curtain.

They went forward, through a pitchiness so solid it seemed tangible.

Of course, the wights had needed no luminescence to see by; they had provided it solely for Tahquil's benefit. Yet, none of them had earlier considered the danger they invited upon themselves. Perhaps in the nygel's case this was understandable—his mind was a bell-jar full of dragonflies darting at their own reflections. And Tahquil, for her part, was verging on delirium. Tully, with the commonsense of a common domestic wight, should have known better. Conceivably, some enchantment in the chant of crystal, some oblique spell zinging off the obliques, something occult in the dark occlusions had laid hands upon his eldritch senses and dulled them, lulled them, culled them, gulled them.

Annulled them.

Tahquil nodded, drooping on the waterhorse's back. Indeed, when they first entered this place she had, in a confused way, feared instant detection, trusting only that Tighnacomaire, with his sharper instincts, would be able to turn and flee at the first sign of peril, and so outrun it. As they penetrated further into the Icepipes and nothing untoward occurred, she began to relax, turning her muddled thoughts to what obstacles might lie at the journey's end and how the Fortress might be entered and what might be found therein. Ideas rambled incoherently through her mind, in tablature. She could not pin them down, could not make sense of them. In this state, she was unprepared for the encounter.

The cavern filled with the susurrations of Tighnacomaire sniffing through the velvet pockets of his nostrils.

'Waterr,' he whispered. 'I smell it. And what else—'

The dark exploded.

A clamour went up on all sides. The brief flare of an ignition revealed that, straight ahead, the floor ended. A thin bridge, suspended from above on slender diamond fingers, arched over the chasm. From the centre of this span poured a scrawl of spriggans, brandishing weapons. In their haste they jostled one another. One fell over the side, his fast-receding shrieks overlaying the wild shouts of his fellows.

The nygel whirled to face the direction from which he had come. A second time, he stamped. His hooves ignited sparks. The flash illuminated haemorrhages of yelling wights exuding from cracks in the walls, cutting off the escape route. Their noise fed itself back into the crystal, amplifying with each circuit, drilling through Tahquil's ears. Under her, the nygel spun like a compass needle. Dizzy, she braced herself for the onslaught. Would these enemies attempt to wrench her from Tighnacomaire's sticky hide, flaying her in the process? Or would they merely spear her as she sat on his back? Death never seemed inviting, yet at this instant, neither did it appear entirely unwelcome. Her head jerked back as the nygel surged. He bolted. His haunches gathered. He jumped. The ground dropped away, her stomach flew to her gullet. Her arms and hair flew up over her head as she and the horse plummeted like iron weights. In front of her nose, her ragged shirt fluttered invisibly. Her blood thundered with fear and exhilaration. They were falling together into the chasm.

There was no time to scream, no breath for it. The terrible, whistling wind of their falling ripped it from her lungs. She was a rag doll on horseback, diving into a well.

Violently they smashed into a slab of adamant. Water filled Tahquil's skull like hemlock wine.

Pressure clamped down, roaring. Red bubbles popped and fizzed in Tahquil's eyes. The nygel was drowning her again. Her arms flailed vainly. Tides sloshed in her head. Her brain swam like a frightened frog, and a band of steel tightened across her chest. Her consciousness dwindled to a golden pinprick, yet that tiny point burned bravely and was not yet extinguished.

And then the pressure reversed, crumpling her against the nygel's shoulders and neck. Fluid streamed from Tahquil like a garment. Sweet air swirled in freely. Tahquil lay along the spine of the waterhorse, sobbing, deprived of sight and hearing, shuddering with the hoarse rasps of her panting and the racking coughs.

When these subsided, she lay quietly in darkness. There seemed to be no movement. The only sound was a gurgling, a whisper of liquid brushing against stone. She was up to her neck in water.

A long time afterwards, the darkness paled. Dimly, the head and ears of Tighnacomaire took shape. Beyond them, an ashen glimmer dawned. As it strengthened, Tahquil made out walls racing along at a staggering rate, and close above, a ceiling going by in a blur. They were not motionless after all, but travelling at enormous speed, propelled by the current of an underground stream. A low archway framed the source of light. Towards this they hurtled.

'Fear natt!' lisped Tighnacomaire, regenerating a vestige of her faith in him. Suddenly, the archway had them in its pincers. The current shoved them through. Suspended in midair, Tahquil closed her eyes.

They were falling once more, but it was only a short drop. It took them plunging down a hurrying sluice into a stream, deep and clear, flowing under the open skies of Darke. Tighnacomaire began to swim with the flow, angling towards land. Three hundred yards downstream, he climbed out on the shore, depositing his rider gently beneath the eaves of a coppice of unusual night-poplars. Leaves like coins of swarthy silver fluttered down.

Tahquil, sodden, weakened further by the aftermath of terror, lay dazed and ill, shivering, wretched. The stream, gurgled and babbled, flowing quickly beneath leaning willows and black alders. Glossy ribbons of starlight laced it. The poplars of Darke let their shining leaves drift down, winking bright and dark; leaves that thrived on nebulae of opalescent starfire instead of sunshine's golden downpour.

As in a dream, Tahquil saw Whithiue glide from the trees. The swanmaiden spread her white arms and between them stretched a space from which the stars had been erased. A warm snow fell on the prone form of Tahquil. It enveloped her in cosiness. Her limbs quieted. She slept.

Down the violet wind slid syrinx melodies, wild as foxes, mad as love, strange as awakening.

Whithiue sat nearby with her knees drawn up, hands clasped around them. She stared at Tahquil, her head cocked to one side.

'Friend is speckless, spick and span,' she said. 'Washed by fresh water.'

Indeed, the muck with which Tahquil had been disguising her scent was gone, and the waters under the High Plain had rinsed the dirt out of the roots of her brown-dyed tresses. Her locks now lay long and damp all around, in spirals and thick swathes, frosted by the starlight.

'Fair friend is valiant, faithful,' said the swanmaiden, observing the true colour growing from Tahquil's scalp. 'Vahquil of fulvous hair,' she mispronounced.

Boobooks called across the night. A stumpy bough became a tawny frogmouth, which spread owl's wings like painted fans and flapped away. Every detail of Darke was startlingly clear to Tahquil's eyes. The night was no longer murky, but luminous. The shadows' unlikely mysteries lay revealed.

Tully was perched between the spurs of a poplar. Like swan-maidens, urisks were associated with water. In domestic situations, they usually haunted their own pool. Tully had come through the underground stream unscathed. Now, he did not even look wet. Only one droplet, caught in the curls of his hair, shone pellucid; a fragile tear. A spider knitted a web between his stubby horns.

'They ken that we're here, noo,' he said grimly. 'They'll have spied ye on the horse's back. They'll have issued an alert, lass—their eyes'll be all aboot, on stalks, and they'll come for ye any time noo.' He squinted up at the veil of stars, as though hearing already the howl and thunder of the Hunt.

'I might run like the wind with ye, acrrass the High Plain,' said a man, or the semblance of one. Tahquil did not recognise him at first. 'But they wad catch us befarr we gat halfway,' Tighnacomaire continued.

It had been several days since he had taken his man-shape. In this form he lay on his side, idly scraping up a dirt wall across an ants' trail, to flummox them.

'So,' said Tully gently, 'your quest is at an end, mistress. Ye cannae get tae the grand fortress.'

White hares gambolled on the mouse-fur lawns of Darke, beneath the spray of silver lights from distant worlds and suns. Far off, voiced over and over, a kind of signal or summons echoed repetitively—*Ai-ee! Ai-ee!* Laughter, sometimes shrill and maniacal, sometimes low and coarse, wound through the night-forests. Heartbroken wailing and lamenting followed.

Tahquil said in a flat tone, 'If only to see Viviana and Caitri once more, or to know what has become of them, I will remain here and await the Hunt. Unprotesting, I will let them take me. There is no other way.' Careful, even now, not to thank the wights, she added, 'You have all been most kind.'

She lowered her lashes, shutters against the world.

The swanmaiden viewed the girl through half-lidded bird's eyes. She said, 'Vahquil has fed on Fairbread, seed-fruits of Faêrie. She has voyaged with waterhorse, seen with eldritch viewpoint. Has worn on her finger special circle of strong, shining sorcery.

Has sustained healing spell from horned hearth-faun. Vahquil-sister shares wight-ways. See, she's washed stainless.'

Whithiue stood up. She wrung her azalea hands, then lightly trod a few paces back and forth. For only the second time, the swanmaiden was not wearing the precious cloak of ebony feathers. Her gown seemed fashioned of mist and cobwebs. It was cinched at the waist with a girdle of flashing garnets. Her fabulous hair streamed along the light southerly breeze. She spoke again, hesitantly, her words aimed directly at Tahquil.

'Scorn surrender! *Fly* hence, to Fell Fortress. Wights won't hinder, won't waylay swan. Friend will venture forth in security. Settle within high walls. Have certainty, swan will visit subsequently, to withdraw feather-cloak. Have certainty, should feathers be spoiled or scattered, vengeful hostility of swan's family will follow forever.'

The swanmaiden's words jolted Tahquil's memory. What was it that covered her and kept her warm, even now, as she lay on the cool lawns of Darke? She looked down at herself. The feather-cloak spread glistening like polished coals over her body. It had warmed her as she slept—maybe it had guarded her from the probing senses of the eldritch night-things that roamed throughout Darke. Swan-cloaks could not be swapped easily from one wearer to another for, like the law by which wights might not step over a threshold unless invited, the use of such a numinous garment required the permission, freely given, of the original owner. What an honour the swan had bestowed upon Tahquil, that she, a mortal, should not only be given shelter by the wight's most treasured possession, but should be offered the full use of it, with all the powers it could bestow! Emotion welled in Tahquil like spring water after a storm. Her eyes burned. She searched for words. Thickly, she said, 'Whithiue is gracious . . .'

'Swan fragrance shall smother human stink,' interrupted Whithiue, and indeed a certain aviary odour arose from the feather-cloak, reminiscent of the Skyhorse stable-mews. 'When swan has found feather-cloak afresh, secure and flawless,' the swanmaiden subjoined sharply, 'fetters shall shatter.'

'Yes. After this deed is done, no longer shall you be obliged to me in any way. Never shall I ask anything from you again. This I swear. Rather, I shall be in your debt.'

But not for long, Tahquil thought bleakly, *for I sense my life-thread unravels. Thorn, soon I shall be with thee.*

Whithiue fixed her alien eyes on Tahquil. Far off, a wordless ululation of Darke from some unhuman throat rose like mist from a river, like a waterbird from the marshes. The swanmaiden nodded—an odd, abrupt gesture, like the darting head of a bird scanning for danger, or hunting the waters for bright, swift fish.

Indeed, for all their appearance, swanmaidens are not human. This must not be overlooked.

Reverently, Whithiue lifted the cloak from Tahquil's body. The damsel stood up. A thrill of fear shot through her at what she was about to assay.

'How must this feat be accomplished?' Her voice cracked.

Whithiue hugged the cascade of feathers in her arms as though it were a cherished child.

'Celebrate! Have faith!' she hissed, her eyes alight with anger, or grief, or fear, or maybe some eldritch emotion foreign to mortals. 'Fly forthwith!'

She tossed the cloak around Tahquil's shoulders. It settled there.

It settled snugly, warmly—*conforming.*

Screaming with outrage and shock, Tahquil felt every nerve of her body stretch into the bud of every quill, felt the breeze lifting the outer pinions, already suggesting lightness and flight. The scream became distorted, terminating in a whistling hoot. Unbalanced, Tahquil staggered, waddled. The wind enticed, plucked at her feathers. Except for sensing her connection to living feathers, she felt unchanged.

But the world had changed.

It had changed utterly.

From each eye she perceived one half of this novel universe. Her awareness altered drastically.

On the ground, Darke's eternal night had turned into a dim green day, as seen through viridian glass. The horizon was an iron band. Everywhere, water lay seductively. Before, she had not noticed so much water. Its glimmer jumped through the grasses and trees. Frogs gave off delicious sounds, like the noises of a kitchen.

Three figures stood nearby. All were very tall. Two seemed indistinct and the third was Whithiue, gorgeous, clad in a gown of stars. Like the beings of Cinnarine's orchards, these three were auraed by soft, spurling colours.

Tahquil turned her long neck up to the sky, and it was an unknown sky. With another sense, which her humanity translated as sight, she viewed a flow of energies netting the heavens and the ground; force-fields made up of infinitesimal particles threaded screwlike along common lines, like beads on wires. These currents curved from horizon to horizon, forming patterns over and under and through everything. They were of no colour she had ever seen—a new colour, indescribable—and they shimmered, seemingly sentient. In addition to their intrinsic motion they drifted slowly, circling the world anticlockwise. Sometimes they altered slightly, as though adjusting. In places, silent storms and substorms disturbed the patterns with violent discharges.

For miles up the fields extended, further than the reach of the atmosphere, until they met a kind of fast wind coming from the sun, which could not enter the magnetosphere. In this layer of rarefied airs, trapped particles whizzed. Although the south pole could not be seen over the horizon, the brain of the swan-mortal was imprinted with the certain knowledge that at the polar cusps the solar wind plunged these energised particles into the atmosphere to create the southern aurora. Immeasurably higher, the stars gave off similar radiations to penetrate the energy streams.

The trajectories of the currents pulsed in the sky reliably, as obvious as roads. Indeed, they were roads, or rather, signposts. They would serve as a navigational guide to fliers on their journeys anywhere in the world—over land, or over thousands of miles of ocean devoid of landmarks. Belonging to Aia itself as it revolved and rotated, these standing magnetic forces ensured that those capable of perceiving them would always find their way home.

Then Tahquil spread her arms wide. Unconsciously, she let the wind swoop in beneath them. The cloak had changed her, or changed the world. She did not need to be taught how to fly.

Wings beat hard.

A black swan flew up.

The world turned. Girding the world, the shang Ringstorm seethed; a wall separating Erith from the unknown northern half of Aia. Striping the world, shimmering flows of electromagnetic energy shifted delicately. The optics of the swan-mortal could perceive not merely the magnetic fields, but every form of radiation both visible and invisible to unchanged mortal eyes—from the long, low energy waves below red on the spectrum, through thermal infrared and dazzling ultraviolet, to the penetrating X-rays and gamma rays coming in from outer space. Yet all this extra information gave rise to order, not chaos.

The swan's eyes, unhumanly aligned, scanned along the frame of each of her wings. The strong feathers were working like muscles. Beneath these wings, seen from a height of two hundred feet, the High Plain jutting on its tableland was illusorily flattened against the ground. The fortress on its crag took on a curious perspective, its towers broadening towards their pinnacled crowns, tapering to slim bases among a jumble of roofs.

To the metamorphosed bird flying above with slow, powerful down-strokes, much activity was visible. North of the fortress, armies were massing in readiness to march—battalions of mortal warriors perceived as blotches of infrared. Their numbers were small compared to the Legions of Erith encamped on the other side of the Landbridge, but on either flank of their bivouac, somehow blending with rock and bush, large numbers of other incarnations swelled the forces of Namarre and these glowed infragreen, like sombre marsh-lights. They were not drawn up in lines, nor did they inhabit booths and pavilions. Wights they were, of many descriptions, with one trait in common—their ill will towards humankind. And although their methods of destruction did not resemble those of Men, they could be more terrible.

Some—in particular the hobyahs and spriggans—clustered in groups. For the rest of the unseelie host, there was apparently no discipline, no leader. However, this apparently lawless, motley force *was* governed, ultimately, by a Commander.

The swan-mortal's vision raked the landscape. Fleeting across the tableland towards the fortress galloped a horse. The jet-stream hair of the rider stroked the wind. Having caught hold of the horse's tail, a runner sped along behind, keeping pace. Southward, fast bands of spriggans patrolled the vertiginous edges of the Plain. Beyond them, on the far horizon, the smokes of volcanic Tapthartharath muddied the sky in a low band, intermittently lit by a dim red glare. And far out towards the west, towards the Nenian Landbridge, a shimmer, a line, as if the sea's edge trembled there, yet it was not the sea.

It was the war-harness of armies that glistered there.

The wind was kind, a cradle. The sky, with its guide chart, was half-known territory and liberation. Yet the swan-mortal's wings, unaccustomed to enduring such prolonged efforts, grew tired. She turned against the wind then, preparing to descend. With cool impetus the wind restrained her—but only for a moment. Her senses slipped again into flight mode and she located the buoyant spouts of air upon which a flier could glide without labour, spiralling down towards, and then amongst, the topmost battlements of Annath Gothallamor.

The eyes of the swan-mortal saw, without comprehending, a fantastical and licentious architecture soaring perpendicularly into the starry night. Forests of towers and crocketted pinnacles punctured the drifts of stars, stabbing up from amid decorated gables. Tall ogee arches sprouted leaf finials. Circular oriel windows projected, cantilevered from the facades. Quatrefoil windows bloomed lavishly with flowerlike traceries of stone. Square towers, round turrets and octagonal wings rose from low flocks of flying buttresses, their exteriors banded with fret and grotesque imagery. Dripstone moulding surmounted every portal and fenestration, fashioned in curious designs both rich and elegant. Gargoyles and waterspouts leered from every roof gutter.

Through these ramparts and keeps the swan fluttered, past arcadings of pointed lancet windows, high and narrow, ornamented with friezes of quatrefoils and other organic illustrations in stone. As she passed, she looked through the coloured glass of these windows, the lavender and indigo and violet panes. Chambers therein she spied—vast halls and small oriel rooms, long galleries and staircases. Slender colonnettes and tall furniture occupied these chambers, and sometimes there were forms moving between. Around she flew, again and again, her wings sagging with weariness. Small, wightish archers stationed on the roofs took some note, then probably dismissed her presence as unremarkable. Against a high window with a cusped ogee arch she flapped her wings, straining to see inside.

Abruptly, terror took hold of her, and she imagined a black sun rising out of the south. Wheeling through the barbs of the crocketted pinnacles she noticed three winged shapes in the sky, speeding towards the fortress, and knew them to be the Crows of War. Frantically, the swan darted around a corner, spied a rose window from whose centre the stone tracery radiated like the petals of a flower, and glanced within. Panic-stricken, she beat at the stained glass with her wings. In the chamber behind the panes the occupant looked up, but drew back. The swan sank, fell away down the tower's flank, touched down on a canting roof-surface and folded her pinions. She came to rest, and as she did so, the feathers uprooted themselves from her nervous system, parted from her flesh and transformed once more into a cloak, which draped from her shivering shoulders. Its edges lifted slightly in the broken airs, as if it wanted to fly again.

Two columns nearby were carved in the shape of robed men who seemed to be upholding the capitals on their shoulders. Pressed against a wall between them the mortal girl stood like the third statue while the funereal wings of the Crows swept by, their shadows as cold as forgotten sarcophagi. At their passing, even the archers on the battlements cringed. With a long and hideous cry, the birds vanished from sight.

A sharp, black feather floated down.

In the subfusc of the shadows Tahquil paused, frozen with indecision.

Like scraps of black silk, serrated bats flitted in and out of remote niches. On one side of the ridge the roof tiles slanted shallowly down to a lead-lined gutter fenced by crenellated battlements. Spaced at equal intervals, every three merlons apart, stone spires, sharp-tipped, stood like erect spindles wound about with thorns. Gargoyles like winged toads lunged motionlessly overhead.

It occurred to Tahquil that something was now approaching swiftly through the roofs, along the gutters. She scrambled back over the ridge. Here, the canting roof extended behind the tower until it met a high, steeply pitched gable running across at right angles. Stooping low, she eased her way along the tiles, hugging the cold stone of the tower wall. What she might do when she reached the pitched gable was uncertain—its gradient prohibited climbing. A precarious wall-stair had been cut into it, underneath the machicolations. But this led only to a small balcony parapeted with a row of pointed arches, which were draped with petrified ivy.

A narrow ledge jutted from beneath the lancet windows set into the thickness of the tower's wall. Tahquil glanced up, baulking in surprise. The stifling sense of a presence coming behind along the roof-walks seized her, almost immobilising her with horror, but she reached up and took hold of a projection, stepped on the ledge and pulled herself up, with the feather-cloak swaying at her back. Clambering into the embrasure, she placed her foot on a sill and swung in through the window, whose lower segment had been standing ajar. Clumsily, she sprang down to a flagged floor and stood immobile. Above, a malignancy passed outside the window, which shuddered slightly on its hinges. A raven cawed.

Then, stillness.

Annath Gothallamor enclosed her.

8
ANNATH
GOTHALLAMOR
Part I: A Fortress Fair and Fell

And whither have the heroes flown? Unto the bitter shore
And onward to the tableland they call the Plain of War,
O'ershadowed by the starry heights whereon the ravens soar,
To stand before the fortress grim: Annath Gothallamor.

VERSE FROM A NEW SONG CIRCULATING ON THE STREETS OF CAERMELOR

The stars shone like fields of violets behind the intricate patterning of the leaded panes. Suspended from a golden chain, a filigree lamp gave off a frosty moonlight luminance which smacked of gramarye—surely no *lorraly* flame burned within such a device. The intruder stood upon a landing between a flight of stairs leading up and another leading down. The balustrade was ornamented with repetitive cusped lancets and a trefoil frieze. Along the inner walls of the stairwell, the stems of slender colonnettes rose up, curving gracefully, like lilies, into complex vaults supporting the stairways. Softly, Tahquil began to ascend.

Her feet made miniature sounds upon the steps. The feathercloak brushed them, whispering. The air exhaled the scent of gramarye. Up she toiled, and now the exhilaration and artificial strength imparted by the swan's cloak began to fade. Tahquil was weary, as she had never been weary before. She plodded upward, and her mind could not be read, even by its very self.

Three flights she conquered. At the top of the third, a door stood open. She paused on the threshold, peeping in through the portal.

The interior was not large—it was the chamber of the rose window, a circular room. Large areas of the oak-panelled walls were pierced and glazed with coloured glass through which starlight fell in tides of powdered amethyst, shot through with the silver motes strewn by nine golden lamps. These lamps topped pedestals of solid gold, ten feet tall, arched, pinnacled and mouchetted. Their illuminations displayed, thirty feet above, a ceiling gorgeous with lacelike stone tracery and pendant bosses. The spaces between the stonework were stencilled with heraldic motifs.

On the floor beneath this lofty fantasy all the furniture was of oak, ornamented with traceries and carvings of marvellous expressiveness, upon which the greatest industry had been expended. Gilt-spined books rested in stacks on an octagonal table, its base decorated with recessed lancets, its top supported by traceried brackets. Nearby stood a writing desk with linenfold panelling, a lectern fashioned like a two-tiered tower on a baluster support, and an X-framed chair. Tall, canopied niches in each corner embraced stone urns on pedestals. Inscribed in gold lettering on a high archway, runes shone mellowly, spelling the words:

⊶ Is Truth So Hard To Find? ⊷

Along this wall, partly concealed by heavy velvet curtains held back by gold cords as thick as a man's wrist, recessed rows of bookshelves reached almost to the ceiling. Books crammed each level, their spines forming palisades of delicate aurum embellishment on blue vellum. One of these tomes lay open on the lectern. Seated on the X-framed chair, the chamber's occupant now ceased to study the pages.

A pair of eyes lifted and met Tahquil's. The intruder advanced three paces into the room, stretched her arms forward in a sad entreaty and dropped to her trembling knees on the tiles.

'Caitri,' she said, still reaching out.

'Are you mortal, and loyal to the Empire?' querulously inquired the seated girl, clutching the stiff folds of her pearl-encrusted kirtle in a white-knuckled fist.

'That I am—and you?'

'Yes!'

Caitri sprang from her chair. Kneeling beside Tahquil she cradled her in her arms, murmuring reassurance over and over in soft tones, like a cooing dove.

'My lady! Rohain!' the little girl said at last, in a voice charged with emotion. 'I can scarcely credit it, that I should find you again. What joy, to behold you. What pain, that it should be in *this* place.' Hurriedly wiping away tears with the back of her hand, she led Tahquil to the chair and bade her be seated while she poured wine from a crystal decanter into a chalice oppressed by sapphires. The wine was as black as liquefied night. Silver flecks floated in it, like drowned stars.

'You have the feather-cloak! Was it you,' said Caitri, 'the bird knocking at the window, the wild swan? I should have let you in, but I was afraid. You are ill! Do they know you are here? I shall hide you, take care of you until you become hale. Then you shall fly away.'

Spluttering on the wine, Tahquil shook her head. 'No, no!'

'Hush! They will hear you. In this place, there is listening done by things which you would not have believed could possess ears. Hush! Now, you must rest.'

The starry wine, no doubt, was not unaffected by the forces redolent in the air, thrilling forces being flung from the lamps, emanating from the walls, imbuing the furnishings of Annath Gothallamor down to the very tassels of the gold silk cords and the bullion fringes on the footstools. The potency of the draught diverged through Tahquil's veins to the very roots of her hair, to the tips of her toes, as refreshing as a fluid draught of the sidereal sky. Clear-headed, fortified, she laid aside the chalice and spoke.

'Where is Viviana?'

'She lies below.'

'Is she hale?'

'No—yes. That is to say, she lives and all eldritch longings have left her, but she sleeps in a kind of trance from which I cannot waken her.'

'Thanks be to mercy that I should find you both unharmed! Are we safe here? Can we whisper undetected?'

'Let us withdraw to the curtained alcove of the books lest something should look in on us.'

When they were concealed behind velvet draperies, questions began to tumble from Tahquil's lips. By degrees, Caitri's story unfurled.

'When the Hunt took us, I believed we should be slain,' she said, 'but the creatures, the terrible *things*, brought us here and we were taken before *him*.'

'Whom?'

'Why, none other than Morragan, Crown Prince of the Fair Realm,' said Caitri, and a certain nervous reverence breathed through her pronunciation of that name. 'The Raven Prince, he of whom you spoke after we came near Huntingtowers and your memory returned.'

A millstone thumped against the back of Tahquil's chest.

'And how did he deal with you?'

'We were questioned—not by the Prince, but in his presence. I think he did not speak to us directly but I, for one, could scarcely bear to look in his direction or to look away either, so I know not where my eyes rested or what I was saying. Never in my life have I felt thus. I was drawn by him, yet terrified all the while, for there is that about him which is truly perilous.'

'But you were not harmed?'

'Oh, no. In fact, Viviana was in such a state, "mewling and fretting" as one of the attending Faêran lords described it, that something was done to her. Whether it was by a slight gesture of the Prince's hand or some other means, I know not, but suddenly she quieted and straightened, then curtsied and stood as poised as the trained courtier I first knew her to be. All trouble left her. Glad was I, on beholding this change. She gave answer to each of their questions, and I suppose I did likewise. When he was satisfied, the Prince dismissed us. We were escorted out of that saloon and simply abandoned.'

'Explain further!'

'Our escort deserted us, and we were left to wander the lofty galleries and passageways and stairs alone.'

'With no direction? No limitation?'

'No—yes,' Caitri repeated. 'No wights harassed us, although frequently we glimpsed them passing along the ends of corridors, bent on their own business—disappearing around corners or up and down stairs. Yet, jailers of a sort imprisoned us—barriers we could not see, which prevented us from entering certain quarters, or from gaining access to Outside. Aimlessly we wandered, probing, seeking exit. When we spoke of hunger or thirst, we would enter the next chamber to discover wine laid on a table. When we spoke of weariness, we would come upon divans piled with cushions. We talked of laving ourselves and sunken baths would be filled with pleasant waters. Noble raiment was provided.'

'And when you spoke of leaving?'

'When we spoke of leaving—nothing. After some days, or weeks—I have no idea of time's passing—we began to confine ourselves to this tower—the Crossing Tower. It seems the most stable. Elsewhere in the fortress, there is a constant queer shifting of wall, doors, rooms. One can never be certain of finding one's way around—'tis too easy to become confused. In this way, Viviana became lost. When at last I found her, she lay asleep on the floor. I could not waken her. Some wightish servants came and carried her away. I followed. They laid her on a plinth in the Great Hall at the foot of the Crossing Tower. She sleeps there yet, with hands folded on her breast, but she breathes, and pink roses bloom on her cheeks, and her lips curve, perhaps, as though she smiles at her dreams. I feared lest the same fate should overtake me, but now you have arrived!'

'Alas! Poor Via! And you—how do you spend your days, if days they can be called?'

'Aimlessly. In changeless solitude. I walk the Tower Stairs, I stand beside Viviana and perhaps adjust a sleeve of her dress, or comb her hair. It grows so quickly, spilling over the plinth's edges to the floor. Sometimes I trim it with a little pearly knife. All the straw-yellow was rinsed from it in the cleansing waters of the baths—her locks have returned to the colour of chestnuts. At whiles, I retreat to this room, to look at the magnificent pictures in the books. Or I stare out of the windows at Evernight and remain in thought for hours. But I have so longed for companionship. Will you take some more wine?'

'Thank you, no.'

'We get no food here, only this strange and delicious wine. It is a beverage that sustains like food and drink combined, and whilst living on it, one has no need to perform certain,' she coughed delicately, 'functions of the body. These functions being a trait of mortal creatures, and unnecessary to the Faêran, there are none of the usual facilities in this fortress. Whether wights need to—er—execute the same processes as *lorraly* beings—'

'I understand, pray continue,' prompted Tahquil.

'Yes, whether they need to do that, I am uncertain, but if so, they take themselves far from the walls of Annath Gothallamor, lest they offend the Faêran. It is never cold here, nor hot. One may dress lightly or warmly, as one chooses. Often enough I have seen the fireplaces filled with flames which leap hugely, but are heatless. The fuel is curious, and never consumed or altered by the fire's rage. I have seen banks of flowers heaped in the grates, or jewels, or burning skulls. Vast and strange is this castle, like a foreign country.'

'And he—Prince Morragan—do you see him in your wanderings?'

'Never since the first meeting have I set eyes upon him, or upon any Faêran lord or lady. But now and then I hear the strains of music echoing through the high halls, and snatches of laughter or conversation. Such music—it moves me deeply. When I hearken, I feel that something surpassing fair, something rare and fine that I almost held in my hands, has slipped from my grasp and its like will never more be seen. Every note plucks at my heartstrings with hurt and longing.'

Caitri laid her head against the feather-cloak and closed her eyes.

'Caitri, my joy, my sister,' said Tahquil, 'be not sorrowful. I am come to rescue you.' The little girl's brow creased momentarily, then smoothed. Tahquil continued, 'How close to an exit may you approach before these barriers of gramarye forbid further passage?'

The child answered eagerly. 'Downstairs, in the Great Hall where Viviana lies, the walls are clothed in richly broidered hangings. Along one wall hangs a series of four tapestries, each one depicting a season of the year. Behind that of Winter, a cleft opens between the stones of the wall. Once I noticed the hem of the Winter arras was twitching by itself, as though a sly draught toyed with it. Lifting one edge, I saw behind it an opening some ten or twelve feet high, perhaps four feet wide. I felt no unseen wall of prohibition pressing against me; nothing forbade me to enter therein. But cold was the breath that issued from that cleft, and I had no mind to venture into its darkness. Perhaps it led Outside, perhaps not—but the icy draught had a tang on it of forest leaves. Lingering near Winter, I have fancied, on occasion, that I heard deep within the wall dim shouts, or a ringing of bells.'

'This I must see for myself.'

'But how, my lady, shall you rescue us?'

'As we speak, our three eldritch companions make haste towards Annath Gothallamor. It is a fact, they might well be already here. They will enter easily, unchallenged, and will search for me, for us, throughout the windings of this castle.'

'But how shall they find us?'

'You have already recognised the cloak of feathers I wear upon my shoulders. Whithiue has been gracious, but she will never rest until she regains it. No doubt, even among these currents of gramarye, she will be attracted by the cloak. Then Tighnacomaire shall carry us away on his long back, if we can but find a way past the invisible screens you describe, which imprison mortals. The gap behind the Winter tapestry sounds promising.'

Caitri nodded, pondering. 'This is good rede. I only hope it can be done.' She cocked her head to one side. 'Your hair is gold at the roots, m'lady. By this, and by your face and your scent, they who catch sight of you must surely know you.'

'The feather-cloak muffles the latter, and I can use it to mask my face in the hope that I might be mistaken for a swanmaiden. But will you darken my hair for me before we depart this chamber? I see an ink pot on the writing desk. Its contents will do the trick. None must recognise me, here. The cloak's bird stench baffles wightish noses but yellow hair stems would betray me, for sure.'

And so it was done—the hair was dyed again, this time with black ink. As she shook it dry by an open window, Tahquil looked out and saw, far below, a horse and rider pass beneath the outer walls of the fortress, with a runner close behind.

'I pray that there go Tighnacomaire and Whithiue,' said Tahquil fervently, 'and I may be mistaken, but I fancied a figure of slighter stature ran behind them, on two legs, which might be loyal Tully. Come, little sister, lead me to the Great Hall prithee, lest discovery prohibits completion of this enterprise.'

Like the upturned skeleton of a mighty ship, the enormous hammerbeam ceiling of the Great Hall rose one hundred and twenty feet above the floor. At the meetings of their angles, the mighty oaken brackets beneath each rib sported carvings of winged lords and ladies who seemed about to fly across the gulfs of the interior. Slender columns, grouped in clusters, rose from the piers to the springing of the vaulted ceiling, whose load-bearing ribs delineated the support lines of the roof. In the upper vaults, great pendants of stone dangled, suspended from the transverse arches. Beneath long friezes of leaves and grapes, hangings graced the walls. A carved, tri-part screen stood at one end of the Hall. Underfoot, tiles of coloured clay inlaid with terracotta stretched across the plain of the floor, depicting deer, wolves, birds, flowery patterns, and musicians.

Viviana lay like an icon, as Caitri had described, upon a marble plinth most gorgeous with sculptural decoration. Her hair swept back from the pristine flower of her face, swirling to the floor in weighty skeins of dark, honeyed silk. Her dark blue houppelande, bordered with brocade and cloth-of-silver and stitched with stars, was clasped by a girdle of ivory and bone. She was shod with slippers the colour of polished quartz.

'Fair Viviana,' breathed Tahquil, kissing her brow, which was warm and living. Tahquil watched for a sign, a flutter of the eye-lashes upon that apple-blossom cheek, but there came none. For a time she clasped the courtier's hand, until Caitri recalled her with a whisper.

'It is perilous to remain in the open!'

They ran together to the Winter tapestry. As they reached it, a corner of the sturdy fabric was pushed off the wall by a sudden draught. Bitter cold jumped out and smacked them. Tahquil forced back the heavy fold, revealing a rectangular portal delved into the wall behind. A tongue of whistling air whipped out and sucked the tapestry back hard against the portal's maw with a violence that almost pinned Tahquil to the stones.

'Ware!' Caitri hissed, and they shrank against the wall as a group of stooped grey shapes limped past a doorway at the other end of the Hall.

'There is no cover here,' said Tahquil as soon as the trows had passed. 'Let us return upstairs to the chamber of the rose window.'

They were not halfway across the floor when a clatter from beyond a nearby archway startled them again into flight. Pressing themselves inadequately into the angles of a cluster of colonnettes they ceased, momentarily, to breathe. The noises, as of horn striking ceramic, paused then resumed. An unhuman shape loomed monstrously through the archway. High in its skull, two lamps burned. *Clack, clock*, the horse's hooves rattled on the tiles. Tighnacomaire emerged from the shadows of the arch with Whithiue walking at his side. Uttering a low cry, the swanmaiden ran towards Tahquil.

'Safe! Safe!' she whistled.

'Take it!' Under no delusion that the swanmaiden was concerned for much more than the cloak's security, Tahquil thrust it at its owner, grateful to be released from the obligation of its care, yet panic-stricken at the relinquishment of her protective disguise. An instant she hesitated, before releasing her grip on the cloak. What glamours might be at work in Annath Gothallamor?

'Are you called Whithiue?' she demanded.

'Sooth, swan is so styled.'

'Then the cloak is yours,' said Tahquil, her apprehension invalidated. 'Tighnacomaire, you must take us on your back, this very instant. Discovery is surely imminent. Yet Viviana cannot be wakened—what shall we do?'

But the urisk had also arrived. With no preliminaries he stood already at the head of the plinth, murmuring his simple remedies of home and hearth—the same incantations and deft hand movements which had revived Tahquil after her dousing.

Viviana lifted her elbow. She rolled sideways, but Tully was there to catch her in wiry arms and save her from falling. The courtier smiled dreamily.

'Have I slept?'

'There is no time for explanations,' said Tahquil, joyfully, suppressing a desire to laugh and dance. 'Make haste, Viviana—climb on the horse's back. Caitri shall ride up behind you, and I last of all, as his back lengthens. Tighnacomaire—if you can find no other exit for mortals, a secret way opens behind that tapestry.'

Echoes chimed softly off the walls. Somewhere in the vicinity, voices had started up. Approaching footsteps rang on tiles and stone.

'Why, 'tis Tiggy,' said Viviana, wide-eyed and as yet oblivious of danger. 'Greetings, friend.'

The waterhorse extended one foreleg and bowed low before her. 'How charming!' began the courtier, stroking his mane. 'Such courtesy—oh!'

Tully's strong arms tossed her across the back of Tighnacomaire. The sounds of approach grew louder and the nygel began prancing in fright at the evidence of impending discovery. 'An they catch us, spriggans shall make us pay hard farr helping ye!' he warned, rolling the whites of his eyes. 'Get an! Get app!'

Viviana, now comprehending their peril, reached down towards Caitri. Their hands locked together.

'Jump as I lift you,' cried Viviana. But as the little girl sprang, a scream raged through the corridors of the fortress, a scream so terrible it could only have been spawned by nightmare. The cacophony came barrelling into the hall of the tapestries like a tornado, buffeting the walls, shaking the furnishings, stabbing through eardrums, boiling with the quintessence of fury, vengefulness and triumph. Tighnacomaire shied. It was a small movement—his haunches jerked away an inch or so—but it was enough that Caitri slipped and Viviana lost her grasp. In that instant, a flood of mischief, wickedness and madness came pouring into the hall on hooves and talons, on batty wings and large, flat feet.

'Begone, Tiggy, begone!' Tahquil shouted desperately.

Hooves clattered, wings whirred. The swan flew up among the high and draughty places of the hammerbeam ceiling. A great rectangle of stiff and heavy fabric lifted off the wall. Into the cold blast that drove forth dashed the terrified waterhorse. Down the hidden way he vanished, bearing Viviana on his back. Caitri picked herself up off the floor and looked about.

She and Tahquil stood beside Tully in the centre of a circle. Surrounding them was a crawling net of shadow, a seething assemblage of unseelie manifestations, their eyes burning wells of malevolence. One stood a little apart from the rest, and when she noted him, worms of visceral disquiet began to wriggle in Caitri's belly. Small in stature was he, and stringy as a dried-out stalk of a weed. He wore garments of mustard-brown and dandelion—indeed, the dagged hems imitated the deep scalloping of dandelion leaves. Small, furred rodents wriggled in his sleeves. Coins of yellow flowers were sprouting from the strings of his lank locks and in the goatee which dribbled from his chin like some fungous growth. His thin and raddled face, the colour of old parchment, was stamped with malice and as remorseless as disease. A look of triumph flickered over it and Caitri felt the blood drain from her head. Here was the source of the blood-curdling scream.

The fellow's pale lips twisted. From between them emanated a corrosive voice.

'Ill met by Evernight, *erithbunden*,' he grated.

A rat scuttled up his arm.

'Yallery Brown,' acknowledged Tahquil, dully.

'The very same, *erithbunden*, the very same. Long the chase, and sweet the ending. Spy, listener at the doors, stealer of secrets—you who know the Way Back—now you shall tell all and tell it willingly. Yet, willing or no, the penance for your false deeds shall be exacted.'

There was no escape. That fact had to be accepted.

'If so be your will,' replied Tahquil evenly. 'But release my companions. They have done you no wrong.'

'The bait, Young Vallentyne's erstwhile doxy, has been allowed to ride away—but that is not to be *her* fate,' the wight said, levelling a skinny finger at Caitri, 'or yours, either. As for the urisk, he's nothing more than a horsefly to be swatted, and matters not.'

Then, clear and commanding, a voice spoke out across the echoing interior. Immediately the crowd of wights dispersed—except for Yallery Brown—fleeing away into side passages and hidden galleries.

Three Faêran lords stood in the hall.

Light regaled them, emanating from their breathtaking comeliness. Their hair, crowned with chaplets of silver, seemed immune to gravity. It drifted up and out along invisible spates of air, or of gramarye, as though an unseen lake rose above the heads of these exiled denizens of the Realm. The same force billowed under their dark cloaks, spreading the fabric like fragments torn from stormy skies.

'Ashalind na Pendran,' gravely said the tallest of the three, he who had first spoken. In the simple saying of her true name, in the look of fierce yearning in their eyes, Tahquil-Ashalind felt the strength of their desire. They knew her. She represented their unlooked-for hope, their priceless key, their lamp in the night of despair. Here was the one who *might* show the exiles the way home.

'Lord Iltarien greets you,' said the tall Faêran lord, executing a bow in a manner that hinted at mockery.

'I pray you, release my friends,' she repeated. 'They know naught of this business.'

'Who is here, remains.'

'I know what you want of me. Yes, I returned to Erith after the Closing. I came through a Gate, but the memory of its location is lost to me. If the Faêran have sought it with no success, what chance have I?'

The face of Lord Iltarien darkened.

'Follow,' he said, turning on his heel, and Tahquil-Ashalind, with Caitri at her side and the malignant motivation of Yallery Brown at her back, must follow. But they left Tully behind, for the Faêran hindered him with their arts.

Through the soaring halls and exalted corridors of Annath Gothallamor they went, the two mortals unsure as to whether they walked or glided or somehow flew. Shadows flowed, the colours of the ocean. Light glimmered, radiations of the stars. Gramarye was rife, imbuing the air, crackling in webs between their fingers like handfuls of levin bolts. Yet it was not to be grasped, not by them.

Climbing a stair of amethyst, they came to a high place. The walls shimmered translucent, as though hewn from crystal. Through them, like fire through aubergine lace, sparkled the prismatic stars of Darke. Possibly, there were no walls at all—the Faêran did not love enclosure. Indeed as the mortals entered with their escort, a scent of woodland pine, or rainclouds, wafted through this spectral eyrie, this turret room, this prison, if such it was.

'Go forward,' said the Faêran lords. They themselves withdrew.

He was seated, alone, his back towards the entrance.

At the sounds of their presence he rose to his feet and swung around. Caitri uttered a short, sharp cry.

A shudder rippled through Ashalind at the sight of him—an odd, icy shock, and yet it was not terror or apprehension that she felt; instead it was like a gust of cold wind, or the sting of a chill rain that rouses a restless dreamer. Marvelling, she balanced between joy and terror and was again bereft of speech. His eyes were the colour of rain-filled clouds. The look he bestowed pierced like shafts of the sun.

'Thorn . . .' Ashalind's voice cracked. She went to him and paused, drowning in the ecstasy of his nearness, beholding him beholding her. A kind of paralysis gripped her—she dared not reach out and touch him lest he prove to be naught but a phantasm. But his smile was tender, wondering.

'Speak to me,' he murmured, in the low, melodious voice she knew well.

'Alas,' she said, 'they have made thee a prisoner here too!'

'A prisoner? Aye.' He placed his hand lightly on her arm—a gentle contact, yet it leaped through her like a lance.

He laughed then, giving her a curious and unfathomable glance. 'Indeed, thou'rt a treasure among maidens.'

'Oh, my Thorn, I have longed for thee as life longs for breath! Deep joy it is to find thee again, but bitter sorrow that our meeting should happen in this perilous place.'

His studied her, from head to toe. 'Love's desire, thou canst set us both free. Only say where lies the last Gate to Faêrie, and how it may be opened, if at all.'

'I perceive they have told thee my tale, beloved, though I know not how they found out the truth. Would that I might describe the Gate! I only remember that it lies somewhere in Arcdur, and may be unclosed by my hand alone. Would that I might send Morragan and all his kindred through, and rid Erith of that bane forever.'

'Most sorely dost thou rail against the Faêran.'

'Which mortal would not? They steal us and toy with us, they trick us and tempt us—to the Strangers, we are no more than playthings to be cast aside or broken. Their cruelty and callousness knows no bounds. In earnestness, my love, if I could recall that Gate I would, but in passing through it a geas was laid on me. To that geas I later lost all recollection, until the finding of this bracelet I wear on my wrist. On my seeing it, the vault of my brain was unlocked. Yet even then, memory was not wholly restored. The one fact I most need to remember is beyond my knowledge. Even if I regain that knowledge there is no guarantee that the gate will still be there, for 'tis a Wandering Gate.'

Into his arms he drew her, she half swooning with pleasure. Beneath the storm-blue velvet of his doublet the strength of him was lithe steel.

'Wandering or not, it will remain where thou last saw it. Recall thou *must*,' he insisted. 'As thou lov'st me, thou must.'

The hyacinthine torrent of his hair fell loose around them both, an enfolding curtain. Raising her hand, she wound her fingers into its luxuriance. Her own heartbeat filled her like the subterranean drumming of Tapthartharath. She was shaken to the core with every beat. Something took hold of her—something like a stirring of the Langothe, like a hunger so terrible it could never be sated, and she longed for his kiss, that it might soothe the agony.

'A beautiful tyrant is thy passion, at this meeting,' he said. 'Why should we deny it?'

She looked up to where the rich embroidery of his collar folded back, revealing the base of his throat, the gentle hollow at the meeting of the two straight collarbones. Above this rose the masculine curve of his throat and the hard swelling there, like a plum slipped beneath the skin, sliding back and forth with every modulated syllable he uttered. Her eyes traced every detail, following the sculpted lines of the jaw, clean-shaven but powdered with a darkness the colour of his hair, along the taut planes, the chiselled bones of a face so handsome that surely no woman could look at him but her heart must split asunder.

'Sigh no more, pretty bird. Thou shalt have enough of me, and more,' he said in tones of amusement and delight. 'I intend to take time to enjoy thee most thoroughly.'

Catching her up in his arms as if she were a child, he laid Tahquil-Ashalind upon a divan of damson silk, its edges embroidered with silver and seed-pearls. His beauty saturated her vision. Her thought focused on him, to the exclusion of all else. Starlight rippled down the length of his hair, striking a sheen from it like the glowing blue sky of evening. His long fingers unbuckled the knife belt at his waist. This, he thrust aside. The dagger's gem-encrusted hilt struck the floor with a bell sound, a light *chink*, which for all its softness, seemed incongruous, a peculiarly jarring note, and she was assaulted with a swift recollection of his hand upon her sleeve, moments ago.

Ashalind sprang to her feet, tearing the tilhal and iron buckle from her throat. The chain broke and the jade-leaved tilhal rolled upon the floor. She gripped the belt buckle in her fist. Caitri, until now forgotten, crouched in sudden terror at the furthest end of the room. Embarrassed by the intimacy of the exchange to which she was an involuntarily witness, she had been covering her eyes.

Having been blind to events so far, she was now frightened by the noise and sense of sudden movement.

'My lord,' Ashalind hesitated, swallowed and breathed deeply. 'I see that thou dost wear a dagger. How is it that our captors allow their prisoner to remain armed?'

A keen wind gusted through the eyrie.

Or so it seemed.

'The Faêran have no fear of mortal-wrought blades,' he coolly replied, regarding her steadily.

'My lord wears his dagger at his left side. How then may he draw it, unless with his right hand?'

He grinned, a white wolf-smile.

Ashalind's scalp prickled. 'Who are you?'

'Mistress, mistress, what are you saying?' Caitri appeared at her sleeve, plucking at it. 'Your Majesty, prithee, pay no heed. My mistress is overwrought—'

Ashalind pushed her away.

'*Who are you?*'

'Dost thou not know me, Elindor?'

His features shifted subtly, or else rods and cones realigned within her retinas, or perhaps certain synapses within her brain altered their impulses. Whatever it was that changed, it was not much. But it was enough.

'No.' Aghast, Ashalind vehemently denied, 'No!'

But yes. It was not Thorn who stood before her, nor—as she had feared for an instant—the wanton ganconer, Young Vallentyne of Cinnarine. She paled like an arum lily.

'Say my name,' he commanded.

Tears buzzed like wasps behind Ashalind's eyes.

'Say it,' he said.

'Morragan.'

'Even so,' he answered, without hurry. 'How tenderly the name of her first love is framed upon a wench's lips.'

'You are mistaken, sir. I never loved you.'

He watched her face with a knowing, half-mocking expression.

'Time after time thou hast taken great pains to seek me in my own domains—twice at Carnconnor, once at Huntingtowers, now at Gothallamor. On each occasion thou cam'st before me in rags. I see that this visit offers no improvement. Canst thou do no better? I might note you with greater interest, wert thou to present thyself in more advantageous fashion. Thou must needs try harder, sweeting, if thou art to win my regard.'

'I never sought you out of love.'

'Didst thou not choose to leave the Realm in order to join me in exile? Thou dost protest of course, as is seemly in a chaste damsel, but thine actions proclaim louder than thy words. It would seem thou canst not keep thyself from me.'

Doubt began to nibble at Ashalind, and in its train, horror. Some grain of truth seemed embedded in his assertions, but how could that be? Again, she averred—though less confidently, 'You are mistaken.'

Coldly, calculating, he returned, 'Thou wilt learn thine own mind. Be sure it is soon, lest I grow weary of the novelty of thy countenance, and spurn thee when thou com'st pleading. Thou'rt only mortal, prone to decay. Many, less perishable, vie for my favours.'

'Oblige them,' she dared to reply.

The walls, if walls they were, cracked. Veins of silver flame climbed them. Morragan caressed Ashalind's cheek, ran his hand into her hair and seized a handful. Her scalp caught fire. She resisted the pain, refusing to cry out.

'I wield iron!' she cried, thrusting forth the belt buckle in her open palm. 'Avaunt, or it will burn you!'

He laughed softly. Reaching over, he plucked the buckle from her nerveless hand. It lay in his own, coolly shining. He closed his fingers over the loops and tongue of metal, and when he opened them a pile of reddish dust trickled away.

Ashalind blanched again.

'Is it come to this?' she gasped. 'That a Faêran Prince would force a mortal? Where is your pride?'

'Easily could I make thee serve me.' His laugh was low, a lion's growl. 'And I mean to do so, yet not in the way thou dost infer. If 'twere pride that prevented me, foolish maid, be sorry, for this reason—that you postpone as sweet a deflowering as mortal maid has ever known. If 'twere scorn that hinders me, that I should disdain to squander my time on an incognisant, inconstant wench, then be awakened to thy status and hope to rise above it by pleasing me better.'

He released her.

'Go hence,' the Crown Prince of the Faêran said harshly, his elegant form outlined in stars and cold flames. 'Rinse and clothe thyself as befits a guest of mine, for guest thou shalt remain, until thou findest for me the Gate. As the water pours and the jewels set their brilliance to illumine thy ephemeral attractions, dwell on my words.'

Confusion tangled Ashalind in a web of indecision. The flames which had ripped seams from floor to ceiling burned silently, tongues of licking moonlight. She cared not whether they might sunder the weird fabric of the walls, causing them to shatter and cave in. For another revelation had flared like lightning across her consciousness, throwing the foundations of every principle into relief—a revelation as profound as it was shocking, and all the more sickening in its belatedness.

Her own longing had deluded her, much as a thirst that plagues body and mind may conjure mirages before the eyes. She who parches beneath the desert sun desires above all to behold an oasis. Soon, her frying brain will provide that sight, complete with shady trees. Clues to reality may be deliberately overlooked—until the stoup of cool water turns to a mouthful of sand. Then, illusion's veil is cruelly flung back.

On acknowledging the Raven Prince, Ashalind had lost Thorn and found him simultaneously. Exultance bore her spirits up, but froze in midflight. It was a betrayal. She lowered her lids, hoping that Morragan might not have divined her emotions from her reaction—a hope she knew to be fruitless. He had read her agony as plainly as he might scan a book laid out upon a lectern. His smile was derisive.

Before this meeting, the memory of the Prince's countenance had been unclear to Ashalind, lost with the image of the gate and other elusive memories. In the light of recollection, one thought tormented. One more question demanded an answer.

The chamber possessed an interior of coloured marble and stone. Fan-vaulting arced to the ceiling, the spreading ribs of the fans blossoming into carved tracery, while the ceiling surface between the vaults was closely decorated with scalloped rosettes. Narrow lancet windows shed starlight onto a floor of blue and gold tiles. Foliate ornament adorned the oaken wall-panelling.

All the furniture was of oak: a sideboard inlaid with ebony, walnut, box and holly; a painted cabinet on a stand; a great oak table, lesser tables, carved chairs, stools, screens, chests and stands. A jug of wine stood on a mahogany side-cabinet with mother-of-pearl and mirrored panels. Like towering scallop shells, wings of sheer electrum rose behind the head of a silk-draped couch. Massive copper candlesticks upheld waxen columns headed with silver flames.

Water gushed from a fountainhead set into a wall, each jet a chain of diamonds flung through the air until it reached the lower basin. There, it transformed to a turbulence of thrashed crystal, constantly flowing away down some hidden drain, constantly being renewed from the rain-showers above. So pure was the liquid that the marble remained stainless, whiter than sunlight on hawthorn blossom. Each drop, alighting from flight, gave out a pleasant note, imbuing the chamber with melody.

This remarkable chamber was forested with clusters of pillars that proved to be, in fact, living oak trees. They spread wide their boughs, clothed in leaves of bronze and verdigris.

Under these trees, Ashalind and Caitri wandered.

'The idea never occurred to me,' said Ashalind slowly, effortfully. 'How strange. Perhaps it was a side-effect of the geas of the Geata Poeg na Déanainn—incomplete recall. When first I met Thorn, I did not see the resemblance. I had forgotten everything, including the appearance of Morragan, Fithiach of Carnconnor. Later, I recalled much that had befallen me before the hound's kiss stole my memory in the under-delvings of Huntingtowers. Yet, three aspects of my former life always remained as mist to me. The third, the location of the gate. The second, why I should have chosen, at the last instant, to leave the Fair Realm, to renounce everyone I loved and endure the Langothe in Erith. The first, the face of Morragan, Prince of Ravens. When I saw him again, truly saw him, with vision not overlaid by my desire, *that* mist cleared. Before it did, I confused him with another, and even now I can scarce tell the two of them apart. How can two lords be so different in disposition and appear almost identical? For one reason only, I surmise, somewhat tardily—and that is—' she choked on the words, 'they are *brethren*.'

'Impossible,' said Caitri. 'The Raven Prince had arranged some glamour on himself, to make us believe him to be His Majesty.'

'No glamour. You overlook, the Faêran cannot lie. I spoke his name and he responded, *"Even so."* And it is so, I assure you, Caitri. I recognised him as Morragan. His countenance returned to me as I had seen it first in the halls of Carnconnor, under Hob's Hill.'

'But are you saying that the King-Emperor is an impostor? That he is not James D'Armancourt of the dynasty?'

'Many secrets I concealed from Thorn,' said Ashalind, speaking more to herself than to her friend, 'and many he held from me. Yes, he is an impostor. And for that, I thank fortune, while cursing fate. *For my lover is immortal.* He lives, and I can never cease to love him, meanwhile hating the Faêran race whose blood is his. I am reviled, for becoming the game-piece of such a one, and worse than that, for being so foolish as to love him yet, even when apprised of the truth. The King-Emperor of Erith, he who I know as Thorn, is in fact none other than the elder brother of Morragan—Angavar, High King of the Faêran.' Tears striped her beautiful face like glass ribbons.

'Impossible,' argued Caitri again. 'His Majesty's birth would have been witnessed, as are all Royal births. He was raised in the public eye, as are all Royal children.'

'I cannot guess how or when the substitution was accomplished. I do know that there is very little which is beyond the grasp of the Faêran, should they so desire it.'

It surged over Ashalind with redoubled force, the comprehension that Thorn was alive; more than that—he could never die. Ecstasy and aching sorrow collided like two worlds crashing together in a void.

With that, both girls lay down on the winged couch and sobbed inconsolably, until there were no more tears left to weep.

As the hypnotic fume of sleep finally seeped through her brain, Ashalind whispered, 'I hope with all vehemence that Via has escaped unharmed.' But Caitri's eyes were already closed, her lashes two crescents of dark cinnibar, and she was breathing gently.

Time was measureless in Darke, there being no days to mark the passing of it, no seasons to weigh the pendulum of the year. Ashalind and Caitri woke to find the chamber of the oaks unaltered, save that gleaming raiment now hung on the trees.

For Caitri there was an armazine kirtle the colour of a robin's egg, a houppelande of blue velvet stitched with white nightingales, a girdle of pearls, a cloak lined with rich taffeta and a headdress of silver lace sporting ibis feathers stuck all over with pearls. For Ashalind, a kirtle of patterned baudekyn with narrow sleeves long enough to cover, in part, the backs of her hands, and a tight-bodiced overgown of velvet the colour of the Summer seas, richly fretted with gold. The sleeves of the gown, cut in the bag pattern, were buttoned closely around the elbows. There was also a black velvet cloak powdered with golden lilies, lined with blue satin and fastened with a gem-crusted band upon two sapphire-studded morses. Her costume was completed with a jewelled torque, an elaborate girdle wrought like a chain of lilies, a crespine headdress of gold wire, and a long veil of silver gauze to flutter over her ink-dyed hair, down her back.

The two damsels examined the garments and accoutrements but did not don them.

'I do not care for bathing or dressing in this place,' said Caitri. 'I feel as if eyes are watching.'

Discreetly, they laved their hands and feet in the wall-fountain. The white enamelled bird on Ashalind's gold bracelet seemed to flutter helplessly.

'How I kept my father's gift with me over all the long leagues, I do not know,' she sighed. 'It is the one token left to me that I wear blithely. I'll not wear Faêran gifts,' she added, but as soon as she had spoken, a flock of crows flew from the oaks and set upon her, pecking and scratching at her clothes. The travel-stained garb of Appleton Thorn began to fray and unravel. Squawking, the birds flew off.

'Not only are eyes watching, but ears are listening,' fumed Caitri, struggling to help Ashalind into the gold-threaded kirtle before the rags fell from her back. 'Alas you have no tilhal, and mine was torn from my throat by the wicked abductors of the Hunt. Did those birds harm you sorely?'

'Oddly, I remain unscathed,' answered Ashalind. 'But alas, that we are subject to such indignities.'

'Shall you soon recall the location of this Gate, that we may go free?'

'Even should I recall it,' said Ashalind, pushing her arms through the bag-sleeves of the gown, 'the Faêran have issued no guarantee that they would free us. No promise has been given— only an impression. Equivocation is a specialty of that race. If anyone has been tutored on that subject, it is I.'

'It is of no use to look for escape, I suppose.'

'None at all. There is potent gramarye at work here and Morragan is the master of it.'

'Poor Via. I wonder where she is,' mused Caitri. 'Will Tiggy take good care of her?'

'If he has learned to cease hiding in pools.'

'Where will he take her?'

'Maybe across the Landbridge, to where the Royal Legions are encamped . . .'

'I still cannot credit that the King-Emperor is in truth the Faêran High King disguised,' muttered Caitri, fastening the sapphire buttons at Ashalind's elbows.

'Aye, 'tis a bitter cup to quaff, Cait. I find it hard to swallow. I pictured Morragan's elder brother as a greybeard of middle years. I was forgetting that the Faêran show no sign of age unless they wish it. Both brethren have lived for centuries.'

It struck home to Ashalind now, for the first time fully, and the recognition of it was like a dousing with ice water. Thorn was indeed the King, *the High King of the Fair Realm,* the mightiest of the most mighty race was he, and powerful beyond the reach of Men. The winds, the seas, the rain, the thunder and lightning, all were subject to the governance of Thorn-Angavar. The birds and beasts, the insects, the trees and flowers, the very rocks must heed his command. All wights must give him obeisance, even the most feared and unseelie. In the entirety of Aia, he was matchless. Only his brother came close. The High King of the Faêran himself had once, long ago it seemed, stood looking down at the face of a deformed damsel, on the road to White Down Rory, and he had said—

'. . . what would you truly ask of me?'

The thought flashed, unbidden: A kiss. She hoped he had not read it on her countenance. In her confusion, her hands faltered, bungling the signs.

<<I would like to tell you with my voice that I wish for your blessing on my enterprise. I go now to the carlin who dwells here in the hope that she might heal my face—restore something of what I was—I ask your good wishes for this undertaking.>>

He nodded and stood a moment as if pondering. Then swiftly, before she understood what was happening, he stepped forward, placed one hand gently under her chin and the other behind her head, and kissed her full on the mouth.

Only twice before had there been direct contact between them. Now, bolts like the Beithir's, only sweet as ecstasy, went through and through from head to toe, over and over, until she thought she must die; then he released her quickly and strode away up the hill, and she fled, stumbling, weeping, through the trees.

It had been Angavar himself who had placed his hand upon her throat, upon her mute and mutilated throat, once rendered voiceless by the lash of the duergar's eldritch whip. He had put his mouth fiercely and gently upon hers, with a kiss of piercing sweetness so agonising that it seared every nerve—a kiss scarcely to be borne, almost death to mortals. By this kiss he had bestowed the gift for which she had expressed desire—the healing of her face. It had been he, not the carlin, who had restored her former beauty—and more. The restoration had also enhanced her natural excellence, infusing it with a symmetry distilled from gramarye.

She knew at last that hers was a beauty only a Faêran King could bestow.

And the kiss of the Faêran sovereign was potent as all the forces of nature. Its healing virtues left an unlooked-for legacy, and from that day forth, dreams had returned to Rohain-Ashalind—memory beginning its long awakening. Thorn had intended to make her face and voice whole once more, yet being no less than a sovereign remedy, his power had flowed on, finally overcoming the greater part of the geas of the Geata Poeg na Déanainn.

How the winds had unseasonably raged, after Thorn's men had failed to discover Ashalind at White Down Rory! Disguised by altered countenance and persona, she had fled on foot and by carriage, to dwell at the Palace. The cutlery had rattled, the corridors had howled, the doors had crashed off their hinges in the turbulence of his fury—the Faêran King's intent was foiled, he having lost her. In their beauty, their power and arrogance, the Faêran were unaccustomed to being denied. With storms, he had given vent to his ire.

For he could govern the storms.

It was the essential nature of the Faêran to wield elemental powers. Their sovereign was intrinsically the Lord of all Weather-Lords. In hindsight it was easy to recall how he had worked the weather when it suited him, bringing days of idyllic sunshine when they went hawking in the Forest of Glincuith. When out riding, she would laugh up at him, flushed from the exertion, and a wine-gold breeze would fan her face, catching up his Faêran hair of black fire. Once, she had praised the loveliness of rain-showers, only to hear droplets beginning to tap like the hooves of tiny goats dancing on the roofs. In those days the weather had pleased her, had responded blithely to her whims.

During their first journey together, the signs had been plain to read, if only she had noted them. It had been Angavar-Thorn who summoned the Vector-dispersing winds in Mirrinor, who had healed Diarmid's hurts in Rosedale, who had inspired open admiration in the habitually shy trows dancing under the moon near Emmyn Vale.

If only she had revealed her entire story to him he might have returned to her all that she had lost, then and there—face, voice, complete memory, release from the latent Langothe. But then—

what? She would have recalled the Gate's location and shown Angavar-Thorn the way to return to his Realm. He might have left his mortal playthings in Erith, and never would those days of sharp joyousness at Caermelor have come to pass; those rare, incomparable days she clung to in memory.

It was clear to Ashalind that he had known nothing of who she was, during that period. Even to the hour of their final parting and beyond, he had suspected naught. Had he learned her history, he would certainly have seized the earliest opportunity to quiz her.

How much had he now discovered? Did he believe Morragan pursued her merely to punish her for the crime of eavesdropping, or was he aware she had passed through a Gate from the Realm and might possibly find a way back?

Yet for all his might, Thorn-Angavar had been sundered from Ashalind a second time. Morragan had sent the Crows of War to breach the barriers of Tamhania and stir its submarine forces to explosive rage. After the destruction of the Isle of Mists, what then for the King of the Fair Realm? Why had he not sought high and low for his betrothed, employing his dominion over land, sea and sky to reach her? Was her subterfuge so effective, or was it that he cared no longer?

Caitri sat at a marquetry dressing-table laden with pots of jewelled hairpins. She gazed into the looking-glass while Ashalind combed out her malt-brown hair. Raking and untangling the little girl's knotted locks, Ashalind began to uncoil her memories of Thorn—the words which had been spoken and the words left unsaid.

My Dainnan name is Thorn, he had stated at their first meeting, in the forest of Tiriendor. Never had he claimed the name of James D'Armancourt. His amazing looks and magnetism, his hunting prowess, his skill in every field, the way the goshawk and indeed all birds and beasts bent to his will—these attributes had once, long ago in the wetlands of Mirrinor, led Ashalind to suspect Thorn of possessing Faêran blood. Using the handspeak she had communicated this conjecture to Diarmid, who had rejected it.

<<The elder race, the . . . >> She had no sign for 'Faêran'. <<Fair Folk, the immortals. Is it possible he is of their blood?>>

'The Fair Folk? Ha! Such immortals passed into legend long ago. Besides, like wights, they could not stand the touch of cold iron. Sir Thorn wields a steel blade, steel-barbed arrows—his belt buckle too, I'll warrant, is of the same metal. Nay, I've no doubt he is a mortal man, but such a man—one of no ordinary ilk. A man for men to follow. Perhaps a wizard, I know not. But 'tis not couth to speak of him this way, behind his back, as it were—I will not discuss this further.'

Therein lay the conundrum—if cold iron was anathema to the Faêran, how might Faêran royalty be immune to it? Was their power mighty enough to thwart their own nature?

'A penny for your thoughts,' petitioned Caitri.

'Oh. I was thinking about the Faêran. About Thorn—that is, the King-Emperor.'

'Never berate yourself for your love of him,' said Caitri. 'Methinks you had little choice in the matter. All the Strangers are beautiful beyond description. My mother used to tell me stories of them. Their effect upon humankind is that we are bound to love them. The more they choose to reveal of themselves, the more we must love them. Ever have our kind been drawn to theirs. And sometimes it is the other way around.'

Each mental vision of Thorn was a spark, touching off a conflagration of joy and pain. *He lives! But he is Faêran—my love, my sorrow, my enemy.*

'All unions between mortal and immortal are doomed to end in tragedy,' Ashalind murmured aloud. A tear dropped, glistening, from her eye.

Before it touched Caitri's hair it had been captured, and lay on an open palm.

On Morragan's hand, the tear hardened to diamond. He closed his fist then tossed the jewel into the air, whereupon a white seabird opened its wings and flew away.

'A tear for Angavar,' softly said the Raven Prince, revealed in the mirror like a flame of darkness. 'Prey for the Eagle.'

Caitri jumped to her feet, upsetting the stool.

The dressing-table now stood in a glade of an oak wood by moonlight. Gone were the chests, the stands, the cabinets. Gone were the walls. The ceiling had soared skyward to become the fantastic vault of Evernight. Vanished, too, was the gushing wall-spout, yet its music remained in the songs of nightingales hidden among the leaves.

The stars overhead shone so brilliantly that their radiance fell from the sky like the dilute rays of a silver sun. In long spindle-shafts it struck through the pavilions of the oak wood. The mists which braided themselves like twine among the tree-stems filled each shaft with slowly uncurling smokes.

Carpets of nodding bluebells hazed the ground between the knotted roots, and from them seemed to emanate a dim, supernal ringing, as of miniature bells. Under the scalloped layers of foliage a sweet wind breathed upon the wild thyme cushioning the banks. Ox-lips and violets nodded there, lushly overhung with woodbine and perfumed musk roses. A company of lords and ladies reclined on these flowery banks or strolled beneath the boughs. Some wore gorgeous raiment, others were clad only in nakedness, adorned by the beauty of their bodies, ornamented by flowing hair pleached with flowers. Many were Faêran—to these, a soft glimmer clung, like candlelight on crystal. The rest were otherwise.

Ashalind and Caitri stared.

Yallery Brown was present, and Gull, the Spriggan Chieftain, once glimpsed long ago by Ashalind in the marketplace at Gilvaris Tarv. Bigger than the rest of his kind was he, a full three and a half feet in height. His child's size belied his strength, for he wielded a longbow almost twice as tall as himself, drawing it without effort to shoot at small songbirds amongst the branches. Present also was the malignant Each Uisge in mail like the delicate silver scales of fish, and a mantle the colour of seaweed. A fillet of pearls adorned the sleek horse-hair mane which framed the frigid and charming face, as pale as death, as cold as the under-belly of a lamprey. Flanking the Prince of Waterhorses, two dour and doughty men in ragged plaid and thick calf-hide each held a pike twined with dripping red filaments of spirogyra. Water streamed from their garments. Their eyes were blank as stones.

Ashalind recognised them as two of the Each Uisge's mortal slaves, sons of tragedy, Iainh and Caelinh Maghrain. Another waterhorse she also recognised at once, a dark-haired young fellow with fine, pointed ears half hidden by his dark curls. Noting her eyes upon him, the Glastyn bowed, unsmiling. This unseelie wight had failed to identify Morragan's quarry when he intruded with malevolent intent upon the cottage of Silken Janet at Rosedale, for her golden hair had been hidden from his sight. On that night, he had knocked at the door . . .

Instinctively she drew her taltry over her head, pulling it forward so that her appalling visage was blotted out under a cowl of shadow.

Louder this time—three blows landed on the door. Imrhien drew the bolts and opened it.

Only the thickness of a taltry had intervened between freedom and capture, for certainly the Glastyn would have reported at once to the Crown Prince, had he spied the Talith glint of her locks.

Additional ill-met acquaintances loitered with this eldritch company in the oak wood, including a slender young knight clad in white linen buckled over with silver plate and chain mail. Milky streamers of mist issued languorously from the short clay pipe he was smoking. As dark as depravity streamed his hair, and his eyes were the shade of blackthorn fruits. The comely face of this knight was stamped with the look of a brilliant poet doomed to an early grave. The bane of mortal women—Young Vallentyne, who had condemned Viviana to a lingering death.

Succulent damsels lolled among the bluebells. None appeared to be above the age of seventeen. Some played a game, tossing a golden ball. Here were some of the feminine counterparts of ganconers—the lhiannan-shee, customarily invisible to all except the mortal men they ensorcelled, and the seductive baobhansith, less subtle and more voracious in their lethal arts. They all passed for human women, if one did not scrutinise them too closely. At first sight they appeared lovely, clad in gorgeous raiment—gowns made from a fabric of living leaves, or from the skeletons of leaves laced together; bodices fashioned of cobwebs laid like silver lace over dark grey mole fur, feathered hats inhabited by owls, leather cloaks clasped at the shoulder by silver cockroaches and beetles with clicking mandibles, chinking ankle-chains and bracelets made from the tiny, gilded skulls of mice or frogs with peridots for eyes, plated earwigs swinging from ear lobes. Neat were the waists of these lovesome girls, graceful their necks and dainty their hands, but now and then, the swish of a hem would reveal a talon or paw where one would have expected a slim white ankle; or the toss of a pretty head would show, beneath the richly coiffed hair, the tufted points of fox's ears. A raising of lids might uncover the slit-pupilled eyes of a basilisk or a cat. A tasselled girdle trailing from beneath a petticoat might suddenly twitch, betraying itself as a tail.

As part of this assembly, pointy-eared spriggans and hobyahs crouched like toadstools. And, deep in the grey shadows of the wood, a horseman of massive stature, with an antlered head, rode down an aisle between the trees.

Half the members, at least, of the Unseelie Attriod are gathered here with Morragan. Has he become the leader of this Elite Septet of Unseelie, in the same fashion as his brother leads the Royal Attriod, the Chosen Heptad of mighty mortals? Only three of the Nightmare Princes are absent—the Cearb, who is named the Killing One, Cuachag of the Fuathan and the monstrous Athach. Mayhap these wicked lords, too, bide not far away.

Behind Prince Morragan's shoulder stood his cup-bearer and his bard. At the bard's neck a slender, diamond-patterned python stared with garnet eyes, and at his belt hung a set of wooden pipes. As soon as she set eyes on the quaint instruments, Ashalind knew them to be those which had once belonged to Cierndanel, Royal Bard to the Faêran. They were the Pipes Leantainn, the very pipes which had first brought grief to Hythe Mellyn and later bestowed power upon the sire of the wizard Korguth in Gilvaris Tarv. Memories of childhood twisted her belly, and a cry escaped her.

A swan-girl lay at the feet of the Prince. Three other swanmaidens mingled with the gathering—one of them, Ashalind noted with astonishment, was Whithiue, crowned with a circlet woven of eglantine. As Morragan's glance flicked over her, Whithiue curtsied deeply and gave a secretive smile.

Yallery Brown spoke up.

'My liege,' he offered, 'only give me leave and I will wring the recollection of the Gate from the skull of the *cochal*-eater. When her creamy flesh encounters fire and blade and rope, perhaps her memory may be jolted.' He threw a rat into Caitri's lap. It bit her, and she flung it into the banks of thyme. Startled deer jumped from the shadows but did not flee. A silver fox pounced on the hapless rat and ran away with the rodent dangling from its jaws.

'What wouldst thou do with my fair and forgetful captive, Brown?' idly inquired the Prince.

The wight outlined his proposition, sparing no detail.

'Inventive,' commented the Prince when the wight had finished. 'Invention deserves a reward. Gull, shoot down yonder pigeon, and Yallery Brown's it shall be.'

Scowling gleefully, the squint-eyed Spriggan Chieftain raised his longbow, notched an arrow and fired. The dart hit the bird, which dropped, still fluttering, into a bank of flowering brambles.

'Go and fetch it,' said Morragan to Yallery Brown. The wight stepped into the brambles and picked up the dead bird.

'Play for me a merry jig, Ergaiorn,' Morragan said to his bard. 'I would fain see some dancing.'

The Faêran musician put the pipes of Cierndanel to his lips and began to blow.

Long ago, the music issuing from those pipes had spoken irresistibly. To the rats of Hythe Mellyn, it had described enticing scenes of gluttony. Then, to the citizens the pipes had tendered a different air, promising ponies, swings and sandcastles, hoops and whistles. No man or woman had hearkened to it but they had wept, for they were swept back to the lost days of childhood. However, their feet were glued to the ground. No child heard it but they must cease their games and follow in quest of enchantment and delight. A generation ago these same instruments had forced the citizens of Gilvaris Tarv to leap about until they begged for mercy.

Now in the halls of Annath Gothallamor the pipes of Cierndanel played a fast and mirthful tune which set to dancing every wight who heard it. Only the Faêran and Ashalind seemed immune to this enchantment, although Ashalind's leg ached where it had been broken when she was thrown from her pony as a child. Involuntarily, Caitri jumped up. She began to skip and hop with the rest, a look of astonishment stamped upon her face. Amongst the brambles, Yallery Brown let the pigeon fall, and began to jig and caper. The louder the pipes played, the higher he leaped, and the more the thorns tore his garments and pierced his flesh, ripping to shreds his jacket and breeches. Black blood gushed from his legs and arms. Ergaiorn played all the faster, and seeing the distress of Brown, the spriggans shouted with laughter as they pranced.

'Gentle Highness,' gasped the unfortunate wight, 'prithee, bid Lord Ergaiorn cease ere your servant perishes! Let me go and I swear I shall never again offend you.'

'How have you offended me?' casually asked Morragan.

'I perceive now that Your Highness would not have me torment the captive.' The wight ended his frantic statement on a scream of agony.

'Jump out on the other side,' said Morragan with a silencing gesture to his bard, 'and get thee gone.' Yallery Brown made all haste, fleeing into the wood, pursued by the jeering of the spriggans, for the thorns had stripped him almost naked and he was covered in his own blood.

As soon as the music ceased, the spell shattered.

While the wightish dancers fanned themselves with pigeons' wings after their exertions, a diminutive figure offered Ashalind a cup of midnight wine.

'Tak' a wee drap, lass. 'Twill gie ye courage.'

'Oh, Tully!' Caitri exclaimed breathlessly, in joy and surprise. Without a word, Ashalind took the cup, drank, and passed it to her young friend. Witnessing the wight's torture had sickened her—still her stomach churned.

'I'm free tae come and go,' explained the urisk, 'at His Royal Highness's pleasure. He bears me no ill will, if he notes me at all.'

'What news of Viviana?' asked Ashalind, quickly.

'The young lass at this moment bides safely among the tents of the King-Emperor's Legions.'

'Good tidings indeed!'

'I wish we might join her. Can you help us escape?' asked Caitri.

'Nay, lass,' the urisk said with compassion. 'There's naught a little fellow like me can do. 'Tis laid on me that I may not e'en bear a message for ye. I can do naught aboot it.'

The Raven Prince set his boot against the marquetry dressing-table and overturned it with a crash. The high-backed mirror, instead of shattering, liquefied. Pots of jewelled hairpins spilled to become a confetti of flowers growing around a pool of water, lustrous as burnished platinum. Taking Ashalind by the elbow, Morragan drew her to the pool's edge, the pressure of his fingers sending arrhythmic shocks of delight through her heart's chambers.

'Kneel,' he said, and she must obey. She looked down through the gleaming meniscus.

Caught through the network of internal forces and currents and intersliding surfaces of the water were shifting impressions of the mighty, ponderous cycle in which each droplet churned forever—the great levees of blowing clouds like stately galleons, the slant of rain falling through a thousand feet of charged air, the dazzle of raindrops splitting asunder as they struck the world's upturned face, the effervescent tumble down stony gullies, the slow surge and pull of tides, the mist rising like ghostly herons from the sea. The water held its memories in the same way human histories were preserved by the shang.

Morragan spoke to the water.

'Reveal.'

Reflections of leaves and stars drifted. Their images warped, blurring as the surface shivered. When it cleared, the pool displayed an entirely different landscape.

Arcdur.

Before Ashalind's eyes unfolded the land of stone and pine, of water and cloud, of jumbled stones and scree slopes, where constant rain and wind swept the rocks clean. Only in the deepest cracks the mosses grew, and the tenacious roots of the blue-green arkenfir. The dove-grey stacks and chimneys rising hundreds of feet high were blemished only by patches of aquamarine lichen and interrupted only by the dark green of fir trees. Wind through the chinks in the formations chanted a threnody in counterpoint to the song of the chuckling, chiming rivulets.

The scene moved and changed, as if the mirror-pool were a roving eye seeking this way and that through the monoliths and piles. Impelled, Ashalind could not look away. It seemed the pool widened like the eye's pupil, engulfing the edges of vision until Ashalind thought herself propelled, a disembodied watcher, through the fissures and gorges of Arcdur, by the high ways and the profound.

'Seek,' said a voice like flawless steel, inside her head. 'Seek the Gate!'

There seemed to be a barrier to her searching. Time and again, there would come an impulse, a surge, almost, of recognition of a certain pebble or the set of a rocky outcrop. It would seem as though she glided with confidence towards this, only to be met with a wall of glass, slowly clouding from transparency to opacity, and the familiarity of the location would alter to confusion.

After a long time, dizziness overcame Ashalind. She tried to close her eyes, with no success. She tried to disengage herself from these rocky sites but was unable to do so.

'Let me go,' she said. 'I cannot find it.'

A scudding wind blew thistledown across her face. Like a receding tunnel, the frame of her vision shrank. Pink stone, pine trees and blue-green lichen faded. Against a sable sky, canopied oak leaves and distant stars shimmered in the mirror-pool. Puffs of thistledown hovered and a black feather boated on its own reflection.

Released from the spell, Ashalind shook back her hair.

A little way off, the Crown Prince leaned upon a gnarled oak bole, surrounded by the Faêran, his handsome face as grim and brooding as a wintry mountain. For a while he stood in thought, silent in the moonlight, while those around him waited. And then with a sudden impulsive burst of violence he smote the tree with a mighty blow that broke it in twain, sending the trunk and boughs crashing to the ground. Yet already, touched by a Faêran hand, the embedded roots were sending up new green shoots.

'Anon,' said the Prince, 'thou shalt seek again, Elindor.'

Ashalind remained kneeling among the pin-flowers at the poolside.

'*He* has set his seal on thee,' the Prince continued, 'and thus I am unable to bring thee by my power to full recollection. Only thou, or he, can do that. Approach me.'

She walked to where he leaned. He bent his handsome head to her, and his long hair fell forward, sliding softly against her face with a caress as light as a moth's wing, as exhilarating as passion.

'Finding the Gate shall be to thy benefit, Elindor, and mine. 'Tis my desire to take thee with me into the Realm.'

'And should I find the Gate and open it,' boldly said she, 'who *else* shall pass through it, and who shall remain in Erith?'

Caitri caught her breath nervously. Fear rippled amongst the courtiers, causing some to shudder, but Morragan replied, with a hint of derision, 'What dost thou augur?'

Like the others, Ashalind was afraid of him, but recklessness born of futile anger at her enforced subjugation made her speak out.

'I presume 'twill be those of your company who find favour with you. I'll warrant you shall have no qualms at leaving your brother to languish in exile.'

'As he endeavoured to exile me, and, so doing, ironically received the same punishment?' He smiled wonderfully. 'My brother has chosen to lord it among mortalkind. Let him persevere.'

'No . . .'

'Dost hope for his exile, Elindor, that I may leave him here in Erith for thee? It appears thou didst delude thyself into some attachment, believing him mortal, but how does so-called love permit such secrecy? Why should he not undeceive thee, if he truly loved thee? Make no mistake, he who masquerades as mortal, calling himself Thorn, is indeed my brother. Angavar, High King is he, my twin, the elder by a heartbeat or two. Heir to the Realm by virtue of an accident of time—the Fortunate Son.'

He gave her a long, slow look as if awaiting some response.

'Yes. This must be so,' she said. 'I know it to be no falsehood. And yet I am at a loss as to how such a strange thing might have come to pass.'

A flock of huge ravens swept low through the glade. One, cawing, alighted on a bough near the Prince. Morragan observed it for a moment. Something seemed to pass between the Faêran and the bird. Then the Prince nodded.

'Thine orders are clear,' he said. 'Prepare for battle.' The raven spread out its glossy wings and departed like hope. Morragan returned his attention to Ashalind.

'The mirror now displays time past. Gaze upon it.' He made as if to throw something into the water, but if anything left his hand, it was not to be seen.

A second time the pool's surface trembled, its frame expanded. For the space of a wingbeat, it seemed that a solemn face looked up out of the depths—the green-haired loveliness of an asrai water-witch. Then a fog blew away like torn cobwebs, or curtains parting on a theatre stage. The scene: a forest of elm, yew and birch. Dew upon the leaves. The primrose light of early morning dappling the grass like fallen petals of the sun. A sea-sound of rustling leaves, the pipes and bells of birdsong. Then, lashing across this tranquillity like the edge of a crimson whip, the stridor of a hunting-horn . . .

In the year 45 William, King-Emperor of Erith, went hunting one morning from his lodge in Glincuith Forest. The young King, though inclined to brashness and somewhat foolhardy, was brave and strong and he rode the best hunter in Erith. By midday he, following his dogs, had—unintentionally or otherwise—outdistanced his lords and huntsmen. Reining in his steed he found himself alone in a forest glade which gave onto a spacious clearing.

Without warning a magnificent stag flashed across the glade. Close behind it ran a pack of hounds so bizarre they were like no beasts that William had ever seen. Their coats glistened with a silver-whiteness purer than winter frost, and when the sunlight flickered on them through the elms their ears glowed as crimson as forge coals.

In an instant William and his own pack had reached the clearing. The outlandish hounds had already brought down the stag but William drove them off and set his own dogs onto the wounded beast. He ought to have known these were no *lorraly* creatures and that it would have been prudent not to meddle with them, but in his haste he was careless.

He jumped down, pulled back the head of the dying stag and slit its throat. At the same time there came riding into the glade a tall stranger clothed in dark green, mounted on a splendid grey stallion. The stranger reined in his steed.

'William D'Armancourt of Erith,' he said, 'I know you well enough, but I give you no greeting. Never before have I beheld a man of Royalty and good renown stoop to a deed so unworthy, so discourteous it can scarce be credited. Be assured—although I will not condescend to avenge this wrong by harming your person, yet I intend, nonetheless, to bring disgrace upon you.'

William looked up at the speaker. In his life, he had never known fear, yet meeting that wrathful gaze he was severely shaken. His discomfiture was compounded by humiliation and embarrassment.

'Lord,' said he, uneasily, 'I am most eager to make reparation for my churlishness, and would fain win your goodwill.'

'By what means?' asked the stranger.

'If you will give me your name, I will try to find an appropriate method,' William replied.

The tall rider answered, 'Angavar, High King of the Fair Realm, am I called.'

Then William was in no doubt about the peril he faced.

'Greatest of sovereigns, I wish you well,' he said. 'I understand now that I have offended no mortal huntsman, but the most powerful of all Lords of Gramarye. I beg you to bid me do anything within my power and I shall do it, in order to regain your high regard and be of accord with you.'

'In that case, hearken,' said the Faêran King. 'In the Realm of Faêrie I am plagued by the Waelghast, who is Lord of the Unseelie Host. My power is greater than his, for as you know well, I am mightier than any wight, man or Faêran in Aia. Despite this he is forever trying to contend against me, and his followers challenge my knights without cease. In his folly he boasts to his entourage that I shall never overthrow him.

'It has been decided that once in every Erithan year he and I shall encounter one another in a duel, and the winner shall be proclaimed the stronger. Already we have met once. We are to clash again, twelve of your months from this very morn. I commission you to do duty for me in that contest. If you will do this, I shall put upon you the semblance of myself, and send you forthwith to the Fair Realm, in my place. There, neither Faêran nor wight nor mortal visitor will guess it is not myself who comes home from the hunt. The glamour I will put on you cannot be penetrated by their arts.'

'Yet, if you have not prevailed in this duel,' said William, 'how shall I?'

'There is one way only. With your first blow you will sorely wound the Waelghast. He will fall to his knees and cry mercy, begging you to deal him a second stroke to release him from the torment of his agony. He will be in the form of a fair and chivalrous knight, and by his words he will try to elicit your compassion. Once I submitted to his appeal, and there is a good chance I will do the same next time. Under no circumstances must you be persuaded, however. Smite him a second time and he will arise whole once more. Deliver a single stroke only, and peace shall reign again.'

'Must Erith be ungoverned while I reside in Faêrie?'

'As I will give you my aspect, so I will take yours. In your stead I will go this day to Caermelor, and none will suspect I am not William D'Armancourt.'

William looked down at the noble stag whose throat he had cut. No longer did it sprawl on the greensward with the blood pumping from its neck like a welter of rubies. Its hide was whole once more, white as innocence. Clambering upright, it walked to Angavar and nuzzled his hand.

'A stag of Faêrie,' said Angavar. 'They are bred to the chase. Countless times have I hunted this beast and much sport has he given me.' To the beast he said, 'Go thou, Royal Cervidus. The Gate is open.' Then to William he said, 'Make haste—we ride this hour. We must reach the outskirts of the Fair Realm before sunfall.'

Together they cantered across the countryside. William was

not aware of passing through any Gate, but as the sun slid near the horizon, he perceived that the landscape had altered, and he knew he rode within the Fair Realm.

As soon as they approached within view of a mighty, ancient forest they drew rein. William looked across at the Faêran King and saw himself, astride his own horse. He glanced down, and saw the form of Angavar mounted on the grey stallion. In his amazement, his breath caught in his chest for an instant, and his heart jumped.

'Your new abode lies before you,' said Angavar. 'Return to the Forest of Glincuith in a year and a day. There I will meet you, and we shall revert to our true shapes.'

'Tarry a moment!' said William suddenly. 'One troublous matter has occurred to me. When I fight, my left hand is the dominant. You people will note this . . .'

'Fear not,' said Angavar, 'your handedness could not be more appropriate. I, too, am sinistral. Now, ride forth.'

They took their leave of one another and Angavar seemed somehow to melt into the woodlands. William, however, with the white hounds following in his wake, rode into the ancient forest.

Here was the abode of Angavar. It was a palace, but not after the fashion of the palaces of mortal Kings. Aisles of growing trees formed the corridors and halls. The chambers were greenwood bowers, hung with leaves and flowering vines instead of tapestries; floored with living mosses instead of carpets, and in places, with smooth, natural slate. This royal dwelling place was open to the sky, yet it was apparent that rain never spoiled the interior. It was lit by stars of extraordinary brilliance and by lamps hung in the trees, and by luminous flying insects. No form of comfort was lacking.

The Faêran lords and ladies welcomed him as the High King. They themselves waited on him, fetching rose-scented water for bathing, and wine for his refreshment. The dusty hunting garments they removed from him, replacing them with raiment of green and gold. Then he sat down to feast in a magnificent hall, wherein was provided every luxury a man's dreams could invent.

A company of noble lords and ladies occupied the table with

William. Their voices were clear and melodious as mountain waters; their faces were fairer far than those of mortalkind, and they were dressed in the richest costumes of gold and green and silver, glittering with gems. Glamoured as they were by the power of Angavar that clung about the interloper, even the greatest among them did not know William for a mortal man, and perhaps this was also a jest on the part of the Faêran High King.

Thus William ruled as High King in the Fair Realm, and so greatly did he relish that year that it fleeted past like a stag before the hunt.

The day for his encounter with the Unseelie Lord drew nigh, and the entire Fair Realm began to seethe in a state of excitement.

The duel was to take place at a river crossing. There, the Faêran companies met the Unseelie Host, and in front of this mighty gathering, one of Angavar's knights cried loudly, 'This is no quarrel between kindreds, but between our leaders. Hence, let an oath be sworn amongst us that we shall not offer battle to one another. Instead we shall accept the result of their combat and acknowledge the one who conquers as the stronger.'

A thundering shout of accord arose from both camps, and the Waelghast and William made ready to fight. As Angavar had foretold, the unseelie adversary appeared as a young knight of noble face and graceful bearing. His sword was buckled on his right side and his lance rest was on his left—in the nature of wights, he could choose to lead with either hand, and preferred to mirror his opponent.

Clad in elegantly sculpted armour, the opponents faced one another from opposite banks of the river and closed their visors. A horn sang loudly. At this signal, they lowered and levelled their lances, braced them firmly in the metal niches under their arms, and urged their horses forward. Glittering jets of water sprayed up from the hooves of their chargers as they pounded towards the middle of the ford. They met with a shock that drove down to the roots of William's heels, but his aim was true and he held steady. His weapon shattered the boss of the Waelghast's shield and perforated his body-armour. The tip of the lance entered just below the heart of the unseelie warrior, if such a creature could be said to possess a heart. No doubt the lance of Angavar, wielded by William, was saturated with certain qualities of gramarye, since it could inflict a wound on an eldritch entity of such essential power.

The youthful knight fell from his steed into the shallow river, and his black blood mingled with the waters. William leaped from his own charger and stood over him, drawing his sword.

The comely youth gazed up at him in evident agony and cried, 'Angavar King, I conjure you by all that you hold most dear in the Realm of Faêrie to put me out of my pain. Finish your task. Smite me a second time, and more mightily than before.'

As he gazed upon the young knight, the mortal king was reminded of the vigour, impetuousness and enthusiasm of his own recent years. He recalled many an occasion when he had stumbled at the feet of his fencing-master, or been thrown down by his comrades during a wrestling bout. For an instant he seemed to see himself lying there, reaching out his open palm to ask for help, and pity threatened to stir within his mortal breast.

The instant passed, as William recollected that his defeated opponent was not human but an eldritch wight, who had pleaded with him in the name of everything he loved in the Fair Realm.

He did not allow his stern countenance to betray his wry amusement, mingled with his natural compassion, triumph and horror. Bidding his heart petrify to frozen stone, he thought, *Had I been, in truth, the sovereign of this realm, he would have snared me easily with this sad petition. There is nothing here I hold dear. All things that I truly love are in my own mortal world of Erith.*

He lowered his blade.

'Your request,' he replied levelly, 'is refused. I will not strike you again.'

Perceiving the steel lacing the King's eyes, the Unseelie Lord called to his followers and bade them carry him from the ford, for he knew that before sunset all his power would fade and he would thereafter be but a shadow of his former self, a ragged, flapping, almost mindless thing, no greater than the least of eldritch wights.

Thus, with one blow, did William of Erith defeat the Waelghast, fulfilling his promise to Angavar and bringing peace back to the Kingdom of the Faêran. The Unseelie Host knelt before him to pay homage, and celebration blossomed throughout the realm. William, however, did not tarry longer than was necessary. He had kept his word and now his sojourn was at an end; he was eager to return to home and hearth. Excellent beyond description was the Fair Realm; yet it was not home to him.

Alone, he rode away to the Forest of Glincuith, seeking the glade wherein he had first set eyes on the High King of the Faêran. There, beneath the nodding boughs heavy with foliage, a horseman silently waited for him; Angavar, in his true form. Glancing down, William discovered that his own shape was already on him once more.

Their second meeting was in striking contrast to the first. This time the two Kings hailed one another in a spirit of joyous camaraderie. There was no need for Angavar to ask how William had fared in the duel; he was aware of all that had passed in the Fair Realm during his absence. Nevertheless, he listened with delight as William recounted his story, and he laughed, congratulating Erith's King-Emperor on his success.

'For my part, I have ensured your kingdom's prosperity and freedom from strife these past four seasons,' said Angavar. 'You may be assured that your subjects have not suffered during your absence.'

'Sir, I doubt you not!' said William earnestly. 'On my life,' he added, with a grin, 'I never had such remarkable adventures as I have enjoyed this past year in your domain. I am forever grateful, and I swear friendship to you for as long as I live.'

'And I to you!' replied Angavar. 'Rarely have I encountered a man so worthy of honour. Now we must part, but there is something I must do first, if you are to live contentedly from this hour.'

Placing his hand upon the head of William, he said softly, 'Forget. Forget desire and delight in the land beyond the stars.'

With that they bade farewell to one another, and William rode with haste to Caermelor. When he arrived his guards saluted him, and his household welcomed him back as though he had only departed that very morning. He exulted at the sight of his people and his home, but he was heedful also, and concealed his happiness.

On the following day he called his advisers together and asked them to tell him how they had liked his rule during the past year. They were silent for a moment, pondering why he should ask such a question, then the most venerable among them said, 'My liege, since you succeeded to the throne you have ruled justly and effectively, but in the year just past you have displayed greater statesmanship and discretion in all affairs of government than ever before. Not until this year have you hearkened so intently to the wishes of the people, and never to my knowledge have the known lands flourished as well as they do now. Appropriately have your subjects named you William the Wise.' Bending into a deep bow, he subjoined, 'May it please Your Majesty to continue to govern as you have governed this past twelvemonth.'

'I shall honour your request,' said William. 'Glad indeed am I to hear your report.' He looked at the honest faces of the councillors before him and noted the faint signs of perplexity written there. Merriment welled up in him until he could contain and hide it no longer. William was not a man who loved deception, and he had had his fill of it that year. 'No more secrets,' said he, laughing aloud, and to the amazement of his advisors he proceeded to recount the tale of his prolonged visit to the Fair Realm, concluding with the wonderful tidings of his alliance with Angavar, High King.

His audience rejoiced, yet they kept it a secret amongst themselves, and it was not revealed until after the King-Emperor's death many years later. For the rest of his long life, William retained his fast friendship with Angavar. It became their custom to meet from time to time and together hunt the Faêran stag in the Forest of Glincuith. Occasionally they would give presents to one another.

William the Wise did not die until after the great Closing of the Gates between the Fair Realm and Erith. Before the Closing, Angavar gave his mortal friend the Faêran-wrought gift of sildron, and advised him how to manage the shang winds which would be released by the rupturing of the borders between the worlds. After the Closing, Angavar in exile knew that some day he would enter the Pendur Sleep, the more easily to let the centuries roll past. Therefore he gave to William the Coirnéad, a hunting-horn of Faêran craftsmanship, promising his help to him and the sons of the House of D'Armancourt, should they ever sound the horn in sore need.

A silver-clasped hunting-horn, white as milk . . .

Ashalind's fingertips disturbed the water's surface. Where two Kings had stood, one old and frail, receiving a gift from the other, young and straight and strong, now there flickered only a dazzle and a haze. The vision dissipated.

'Thorn,' she murmured. Time had not scathed him. He was, then, as she knew him now.

A silver and ivory fish leaped from the pool and flopped among the flowers. Caitri touched it, but it was merely a leaf.

'The founding of this friendship between royal houses occurred before my birth,' said Ashalind. 'I have never heard it told at Court or anywhere else. A thousand years on, the story has been lost to mortalkind.'

'Save for a pocketful of learned bards,' amended Tully.

'Is the tale true?' wondered Ashalind.

'Even so,' Morragan affirmed sharply.

'Mistress,' said Caitri, who had been watching in silence, 'it seems that the Faêran King was too merciful to refuse the last stroke to his enemy.'

'Do not make me impatient, little one,' Morragan said gently to her, and there was that in his tone which struck Caitri dumb. Far off, a cry went up from the heart of the wood and, rising penetrating and high-pitched to the stars, faded and died on the wind. The nightingales abruptly ceased their melodies. The courtiers of the Prince murmured amongst themselves like a breeze through fields of barley, and in this solemn quietude, the Each Uisge broke into a horse-laugh, coarse and savage.

'There is more,' continued the Raven Prince, unmoved. 'Less than a dozen years ago, a time of sore of need arrived for the House of D'Armancourt, provoking the winding of the Coirnéad. Fortunately, my brother must have considered awakening a pleasant diversion. Even the Pendur Sleep grows wearisome at last. View the glass anew, gulled bird, and be apprised.'

The depths of the looking-pool swirled and cleared.

They revealed a seascape on a clear night. Waves rolled shore-wards, long lines of luminous lace. Two human figures, richly dressed and silhouetted in starlight, were strolling along a slender tongue of land that ran between a freshwater loch and the sea. At the nobleman's side the Coirnéad swung, yet it was not Thorn who walked along the strand. Here was a strapping young Feohrkind monarch, well favoured, walnut-haired—the prototype, in fact, of young Edward, the son of his body. This then, was the true D'Armancourt heir, King-Emperor James XVI, of mortal blood, and beside him his bonny queen. The scene unfolded . . .

When sojourning at Castle Taviscot by the sea, it was the wont of the King-Emperor James XVI and his Queen-Empress to bid their guards and courtiers to leave them, that together they might savour each other's company in privacy. On this night, as they walked beneath the stars, in love and with no presentiment of danger, they became aware of something coming towards them. Its monstrous shape struck fear into them, but with water on both sides they could deviate neither to the right nor the left, and they knew it was unwise to run from supernatural creatures. A glint of hope lay in putting on a bold face and not showing fear in any way, so the royal couple took courage from one another and went unfalteringly, if not swiftly, forward. As the thing approached, they recognised it with horror. It was Nuckelavee.

The lower part of this unseelie incarnation was like a huge horse with flappers like fish's fins about his legs. His single eye was red as a dying star. Where the horse's neck should have arisen, there grew instead the torso of a huge man, with arms that almost reached to the ground. Grossly three feet in diameter was his head, and it kept rolling from one shoulder to the other as if it meant to topple from the neck. The mouth was as wide as a shark's, and from it issued breath like steam from a boiling kettle. But what to mortals appeared most revolting of all was that not a shred of hide or skin covered the monster's naked body. Hideously, he was flayed all over. The whole surface of him was red, raw flesh, in which blood, black as tar, ran through yellow veins, and great white sinews, thick as hawsers, twisted, stretched and contracted as the monster moved.

The King-Emperor placed himself before his Queen, shielding her from Nuckelavee. The couple walked slowly, in utter terror, their hair on end, a cold sensation like a film of ice between their scalps and their skulls, and a cold sweat bursting from every pore. But they knew it was useless to flee, and they murmured to one another that if they had to die, then they would rather die together, facing what slew them, than die with their backs to the foe.

As they pressed on, fear threw their thoughts into confusion, tearing from them the ability to reason soundly. Precisely when it was most needed, they gave no thought to the familiar Coirnéad swinging at the King-Emperor's side, and its power of summoning help. The King-Emperor recalled only what he had heard of Nuckelavee's aversion to fresh water, and therefore, led his wife to that side of the road nearest the loch. The appalling moment arrived when the lower part of the head of the monster came abreast of them. Its mouth stretched open like an abyss. Its breath was a forge blast on their faces, the long arms stretched out to seize the mortals. To avoid, if possible, the monster's clutch, they swerved as near as they could to the freshwater loch.

James stepped into the shallows, kicking up a splash onto the foreleg of the flayed centaur, whereat it gave a snort like the rumble of a landslide, and shied over to the other side of the road. Seizing their opportunity they ran with all their might. The wind of Nuckelavee's swipe whipped the garments and hair of the mortals as they narrowly evaded the monster's clutches. Urgent need had they to flee, for Nuckelavee had whirled about and was galloping after them, roaring like a tempest-riven ocean.

A shallow channel meandered across the path ahead. Through it, the excess water of the loch drained into the sea. The couple were aware that if they could only cross the running water they would be secure, so they exerted every fibre to the utmost. Bravely strove the Queen, despite the heavy petticoats that hampered her progress. Her husband bore her up, half carrying her. She struggled, but royal, daintily shod feet were no match for

Nuckelavee's pounding hooves and the monster was gaining ground swiftly.

'The Coirnéad!' desperately cried Queen Katharine, knowing in her heart that already it might be too late. James reached for the horn but even now several moments were lost before he was able to grasp it, for all his effort was focused on helping his flagging wife reach the rivulet. As they reached the near bank, the long arms made another attempt to seize them. The couple made a desperate effort to spring to the safety of the other side, but they never reached it. Katharine fell.

Seizing her, Nuckelavee bellowed his triumph, but James jammed the horn to his lips and blew upon it with all his strength, before turning to fight the monster.

Pure and clear, piercing as water crystal the Summons of the Coirnéad rang out.

A wondrous and terrible sound was the call of the Faêran Horn. Even Nuckelavee raised his ghastly flayed head as the full and mellow note lifted to the sky like an awakening of the first dawn. The horn's music roused the blood of all listeners to leap like the waves of the sea. So stirring was it, it might have summoned the very trees to pull up their roots and walk, or bidden the very stones to burst up from the clay and turn over. Strong and compelling, it carried over hill and vale, water and wood, across the leagues of Erith to a certain green hill.

A tall hill was Eagle's Howe, and fair, the turf growing over it, dense and green, and a crown of oak, ash and thorn at the summit. A hill guarded by gramarye. In days of yore, men had titled it King's Howe. This was the resting place elected by Angavar and his exiled knights and ladies at the end of the Era of Glory when, growing weary of Erith, they chose to cease dwelling among men and enter the Pendur Sleep.

Here they slept yet.

Another Faêran hill, far off, had sheltered the followers of Morragan for some centuries—but the Crown Prince had already woken and departed forty years since. Some said that a shepherd named Cobie Will woke him, by accident and by foolishness, believing the knights of Faêrie to be warriors of legend who would lend their strength in times of need. Others would have it that those sleepers were not wakened by any mortal, that they woke of their own purpose, weary of sleeping, and that the horn Will blew was merely one of many accoutrements belonging to them and not an instrument placed there for the summoning of Faêran help by mortals in need.

Whatever the reason, the cavities of Raven's Howe lay empty. But it was to the vaults of Eagle's Howe, or King's Howe, that the urgent summons of the Coirnéad came winging like an eagle-owl on the night wind.

Beneath the verdant swell of the Howe there existed a vast and exalted hall, vaulted with ancient tree roots as thick as saplings. Between the arches of these roots the walls shimmered along living veins of precious metals. Gems winking scarlet and leaf-green tossed back light from the fire in the centre of the chamber. In the dim radiance behind the flames a hundred of the finest horses slept, and sixty couple of hounds. Fuelless, the fire flared like a giant flower fashioned of ripped silk, coloured tangerine and opal. Its soft, red-gold luminance lapped a hundred rich couches draped with padded velvets and cloth-of-gold. Hereon lay, like peerlessly carven tomb-effigies, the sleeping forms of the Faêran nobles who had been exiled with their King on the Day of Closing.

Some were garbed in fantastic armour, which had been wrought in the time since the fateful day of the Closing—harness whose lamellae gleamed with the sheen of nacre or emerald, with the polish of lamplight flaring on snow, of starlight dancing on water, of moonlight imaged in ice or sunset reflected in steel. Some wore half-armours and yet others were clad in finery that seemed stitched from leaves and shadows and stars. As for their faces, helmed or unhelmed, the beauty of all the Faêran lords blazed brighter than all the lights of the universe. Yet, one amongst them blazed more brightly than all the rest combined.

Into the long silence of the Howe's enchanted dome lunged a bronze spear of disruptive sound. Warm and strong, the Summons of the Coirnéad—'Awake! Awake!' as if in echo of the thrilling Call to Faêrie long ago, a millennium past. An instant after the sound reached the hall's bell-shaped interior, clanging within its shining walls, the Sleepers on their couches stirred. A few raised themselves up on their elbows.

But tardily they roused. Already the most sumptuous couch, occupied when silence ruled, had been vacated. Even before the resonances of the horn's beseechment had faded from the changeless air, Angavar High King, was no longer present.

Not yet fully awake, the knights of the Fair Realm lapsed into the Pendur Sleep once more.

On a starlit beach many leagues distant from King's Howe the silver mouthpiece of the Coirnéad was shaken from the lips of James of Erith as Nuckelavee, in the manner of a man cracking a whip, snapped the young King's spine. The monster's maw hung open, slavering, ready to clamp down over James and crush the last life from his mortal frame.

Yet at the last instant, the wight was stayed.

A voice thundered across the shore, a voice both dangerous and beautiful. A Word was uttered. A command wrote itself in letters of fire across the firmament.

James felt himself lowered gently to the sea-rinsed sand, his wife Katharine lying beside him. He could not move, could not even turn his head, but there was no pain. The lovely face of Katharine bore no mark of savagery and her eyes were open. They were grey-brown as driftwood, yet it was as though they had clouded over and she waited somewhere else, hidden behind those clouds. Away in the ocean Nuckelavee splashed and bellowed amid a flood of crimson, his almost-immortality on the brink of annihilation. The vengeance of the left hand of Angavar had been laid upon him.

The Faêran King knelt beside the royal couple.

'It is too late for thy lady,' he said to James. 'Death has taken her beyond the reach of my healing. Thee, I can still cure.'

But James sensed the vitality ebbing from him and glimpsed the same clouds drawing in as he had seen in the eyes of his love, and he considered that he might find her if he looked behind them.

'Nay, friend,' he said to Angavar, for there existed a bond

between them, although they had never before met, 'nay friend, I would not be sundered from my Kate. Allow me now to claim the greatest gift given to mortals. And if thou wouldst aid me for the sake of sworn friendship, promise me only this—take my place, as once you took the place of my longfather William. Remain waking, to protect my son Edward until he comes of age and is crowned King-Emperor. Let Erith believe her sovereign lives, lest she tremble on her foundations, lest war tears her apart again. Keep the Empire whole and well governed until it passes into the hands of my son.' He gasped for breath and a thin red ribbon unrolled at the corner of his mouth. 'Have I thy word on't, Angavar King of Faêran?'

'On this I give thee my oath, James of Erith,' said Angavar gently, as the light bled from James's eyes. 'I swear it shall be so.'

The bodies of James XVI and Queen Katharine were borne back to King's Howe upon Faêran steeds. There they remained within the atmosphere of enchantment, untouched by decay, to this day.

Three ripples shimmered across the face of the looking-pool and the exposition melted, subtly, into another . . .

When James's retainers came hastening at the call of the Coirnéad, which had reached their ears also, they found—as they supposed—the King-Emperor in disastrous straits. He was lying on the beach, half submerged in bloody sea-foam, the waves surging around him.

'The monster has slain Kate,' he said as they carried him from that place. But they never found her remains, only the severed arm of a man, part of a horse's hoof and some pieces of flesh, skinless, disgusting, washed to shore on the tide.

The best wizards were summoned. Under their auspices—presumably—the King-Emperor recovered his health and vigour. In those first days, with the glamour on him, Angavar perfectly resembled James, but while keeping his vow, Angavar desired to be seen as himself after all, and not to go about masked as another. Over the next years his appearance altered, so gradually that the changes went unnoticed by the populace. Simultaneously, the King's Heads on the coins of the realm metamorphosed, the statues changed, and in the paintings in all the halls and galleries of Erith, the face of James became, subtly, the countenance of Angavar. It was perceived that the King-Emperor had taken to dying his hair black. Therefore the courtiers, ever followers of Royalty's fashionable whims, emulated this inspiration.

Only four mortals knew the true identity of the King-Emperor of Erith: the young Prince, the two Dukes, and Alys of Roxburgh.

Edward was only five Summers old at the time of his father's death. As he matured he was told of the fate of his parents. For a time he grieved sorely, but Angavar laid his hand upon the boy's shoulder and the grieving was not so hard after that. As he grew, Edward grew also to love this extraordinary lord of gramarye who kept his father's honour and kingdom intact, according to his pledge.

In the King's Howe, seven mortals had slept the Pendur Sleep beside Angavar. Now he wakened them, to keep company with him during his seasons at Court.

Long ago, before the ways to Faêrie were Closed, before the moment Ashalind had first opened her eyes on the world, Thomas Learmont of Ercildoune and Tamlain Conmor of Roxburgh had dwelled in the Fair Realm.

The Faêran had hearkened to the harping of Thomas and they were enraptured by his bardic skill. Asrhydmai of the Harps entered Erith, to lead him along the Green Road to the Fair Realm and he went not unwillingly. He stayed with the Faêran for a long time, playing and singing for their pleasure at the Faêran Court. It was Asrhydmai who had gifted him with the geas of an ever-truthful tongue, as a reward for his music. Angavar was greatly pleased by Thomas, who became a friend to the Faêran High King.

Tamlain Conmor, Duke of Roxburgh, had also been taken to the Fair Realm before the Closing. Like Thomas, he became a favourite among the Faêran, who loved him for his valour. Dear in comradeship were both these men to Angavar and dearly did they both love the Realm. At the end of their time in Faêrie, Angavar released them from the Langothe, which would have destroyed them, and gave them protection from the ravages of Time. 'Go ye, Thomas,' he said. 'Truth and good fortune go with thee.' And to Tamlain he said, 'Take thee thy worthy bride, Alys. My benison shall be upon thee and upon thy firstborn daughter, who was conceived in the marches of Faêrie.'

Yet both men remained loath to sunder themselves forever from that place. When Angavar saw this he said, 'It need not be so.' And then Thomas and Tamlain dwelled half in the Realm, half in Erith, for they were under the protection of Angavar and he often invited them to join him in a Rade or hawking party, or at feasting beneath the trees.

Mesmerised by these scenes of long ago, Ashalind, kneeling at the poolside, blinked. A single tear dropped into the water; a single, lucent orb swimming with reflections. Glimmers expanded.

The revelations resumed . . .

The Lady Rosamonde was born to the House of Roxburgh, and after that three more bairns. Those years before the Closing were years of great happiness. But after Prince Morragan caused the ways to be sealed, the Bard and the Knight felt it in their hearts bitterly. They could not endure the thought of never more beholding the Realm. For, having walked upon the greensward of that land, having been caressed by its winds and breathed the storm's-breath, wild and Springtime-blossom scent of it, they could not bear to dwell on in an Erith bereft of all access to the Land Beyond the Stars. Even though the Langothe was not on them, they asked Angavar that they might go beneath Eagle's Howe and enter the Pendur Sleep until such time as the brushing of the winds of gramarye might cause the Gates to crumble, or else the world to end. So into the long and changeless Sleep they went, and Tamlain's family accompanied him.

A thousand years these seven mortals had slept without waking—alone at first, later joined by Angavar and his Faêran knights. Then, when Angavar was called by the Coirnéad and forced to become King-Emperor, he woke them.

'Will you keep me company?' he asked, and now they readily assented, for they wished to take up their lives again and live them out at last. The desires and whims of mortalkind may change, even in sleep.

Thomas went with Roxburgh and his family to dwell at Court.

The King-Emperor returned to them the estates that had been in their possession so long ago, forfeited to the Crown upon their disappearance. It may be that these chosen mortals, companions of Angavar, carried with them some Faêran glamour from beneath the Howe—in any event, upon their return and the restoration of their lands, all other mortal folk forgot that it had ever been otherwise. Prince Edward, Thomas the Rhymer, Tamlain and Alys were the four mortals privileged to keep the Royal secret. Even fair Rosamonde and her siblings were not privy to it, the recollection of their early days and the Sleep having faded from their brains in the manner of dreams, leaving only a legacy of vague wistfulness.

Thus, eight Sleepers from the King's Howe came to the Court of Caermelor, while the High King's Faêran knights slept on. But the city could not hold him for long, and often Angavar walked abroad. To confine themselves within castle walls, or any walls, was against the nature of the Faêran. And when he went alone or in company into the wilderness, he went as a Dainnan, as Ashalind had first seen him.

He wore a shirt of fine wool with wide sleeves gathered at the shoulders and rolled up to the elbows; over this, a tunic of soft leather reaching almost to his knees and slit on both sides along the length of his thighs, to allow freedom of movement. Beneath the tunic, leather leggings. At each shoulder, the Royal Insignia was embroidered—a crown over the numeral 16 with the runes J and R on either side. Around his right forearm was wrapped a supple calf-skin bracer laced with leather thongs. From a baldric swung a silver-clasped horn, white as milk, and a smaller, sun-yellow horn mounted in brass. At his belt, a water-bottle, a couple of pouches, and a coil of rope. From a weapon-belt depended a sheathed dagger and a smaller knife, as well as a short-handled axe.

He picked up a second baldric, heavily embossed, slinging it across his chest from his right shoulder. A longbow and quiver protruded from behind that shoulder now, and arrows crested with bands of green and gold, fletched with dyed goose-feathers.

At Annath Gothallamor, deep in the looking-pool, an architecture formed and locked together structurally. The liquid condensed, hardened. A fine gold-dust—the pollen of bluebells—scudded across the solid glass plane. The images of the past had evaporated. Ashalind sighed.

'For whom dost thou sigh, Elindor?'

The way in which Prince Morragan said this caused the human-like sirens sporting on the flowery banks to spill the golden ball from their lissom hands. It hit the ground with a thud. At the same time, some spriggans who had been leering out of oaken gloom leaped nimbly backwards, falling on top of one another in their efforts to retreat from the peril conveyed by those silken tones.

As of old, Ashalind found herself quite unable to reply.

'Come hither,' said the Raven Prince, and she must do so. His gaze was mesmerising. 'It is high time,' said he, 'those illusions of thine were shattered. Sighing for reflections does not become thee. Canst thou doubt that seeing in Angavar an echo of thy first love, thou didst deceive thyself?'

'Not so,' said Ashalind, yet her confidence wavered. Long ago, before she had first set eyes on Thorn-Angavar, Morragan had claimed her attention in a rare and extraordinary fashion. At the halls of Carnconnor he had offered a tantalising option.

She recalled it well.

'Thou hast another choice, Ashalind Elindor,' said Prince Morragan softly. 'To go out by neither Door. I have no love for mortals and would not be grieved if thy race all should perish, but thou'rt passing fair among mortals, and faithful, and acute. Bide here now, and I swear no harm shall come to thee under my protection.'

Beneath straight eyebrows, the smoke-grey eyes were keen and searching. Strands of black-blue hair wafted across his arresting features. This Faêran was indeed comely beyond the dreams of mortals, and he possessed terrible power. The Longing for the Realm pained Ashalind like a wound. For moments the damsel struggled, pinned by the piercing blade of his gaze, and then her pony blew on her neck and nuzzled her shoulder. She sighed and lowered her eyes.

'Sir, I must take the children home.'

Never before in her life had she been prey to such enticement. There was no doubt, she had been close to surrender. Could there be truth in the words of this marvellous Prince?

'Thorn plighted his troth to me,' she insisted. 'He loved me.' But she began to mistrust her own words.

At Morragan's laugh the swanmaidens shrank into their feather-cloaks. Young Vallentyne dropped his smoking dudeen in a scatter of sparks, and even the savage Each Uisge flinched. Caitri, gripped by dread of Morragan's wrath, thought she saw the sunless countenance of the Prince of Waterhorses turn a whiter shade of pale.

'It appears he toyed with thee a little,' said Morragan to Tahquil-Ashalind. 'In exile, time hangs heavily on immortal hands. Long-drawn pleasure is sought after. As much sport is to be had in the chase as in the kill. Reflect, now, Elindor mine. What words of promise did he say to thee?'

And she did reflect, and it was not too difficult, for certain moments were emblazoned on her psyche so thoroughly that she believed no spell or geas could ever remove them.

Isse Tower, at evening: a star-wreathed balcony and someone breathtaking leaning upon the balustrade.

'I have searched long for you,' Thorn said. 'Will you come with me to Court?'

'I will.'

'I want you to belong to me, and to no other.'

'That I do already. I will be yours for my life.'

'Do you swear it?'

'Upon the Star, upon my life, upon anything you wish to name, I swear it.'

He held out his hand. She grasped a levin-bolt whose convulsion sizzled from fingers to feet.

'Now we are troth-plighted.'

The trees in the oak wood shivered. The leaves withered on them like shavings in a fire. Caitri whimpered.

'He said . . .' Ashalind hesitated, distraught now. 'Ah, alas,' she was forced to admit, 'he never promised to be mine.'

'Art thou surprised, innocent?' Morragan mocked. He rounded on Whithiue, his blue-black hair swirling. 'Enlighten the mortal, pretty duck.'

The cup-bearer offered the Prince a golden chalice, which he dismissed. Beguiled by attention from the Prince—even were it insulting—the swanmaiden bowed to him and glided forward.

'Whithiue is no unfriend to gracious lord Morgann Fithiach,' she enunciated, using a wider range of initial phonemes than had been her wont. 'Neither is she thus to mortal damsels.'

Caitri started up.

'What?' she exclaimed. 'Before this, you used only words beginning with soft sounds. Do you speak the Common Tongue properly after all? Why have you kept that secret from us? And now you seem to take sides against us. We have been deceived in your integrity! What else have you hidden, traitoress?'

The swanmaiden uttered a sound like the rage of snakes and flung out her arms. The cloak fanned from them, a black semicircle.

'Why should Whithiue speak at all to mortals?' she upbraided. 'A race of thieves! Ungrateful! Ugly human words not worthy of swan's speaking. *Hooiss shoshalnai souhuena whai mahaan!* Yet, of courtesy to wonderful lord, she will speak thus to single-language maidens.'

Morragan shot a dangerous glance towards the wight-girl.

Recollecting her proximity to the Prince she subsided deferentially, subduing her natural antipathy, but the glint of eldritch haunted her avian eyes.

'Consider,' she said. 'How should the Noble Ones esteem your infected race? Humans, who gobble up the husks of food, who consume the flesh of swans and beasts and swallow down roots grown swollen in the mire. Humans, who dine on dead matter and then defile the world with their waste! How might aristocrats adore swine?'

'Thorn broke bread with me,' disputed Ashalind. 'Many times we dined together!'

'Easily the glamour of the Fair Ones dupes foolish mortals,' derided Whithiue. 'Did Vahquil indeed see with her eyes what she thought to behold? Only the *toradh* was taken and the *cochal* was whisked away. Or else, the *toradh* was wrapped in a mere semblance of the food, an illusion.'

That is true! Hindsight reveals I never did see Thorn actually put food to his mouth . . .

'Swans sup on worms in the mud,' remarked Caitri venomously. The blast from the beating feather-cloak bowled her over.

'Do not vent your vexation upon the child!' cried Ashalind. 'Whithiue, once you were our friend. Tell me, if the Faêran consider us so foul, why do they steal us?'

'As humankind keep companion animals in fond contempt, so might the Fair Ones be diverted by humankind,' lightly said the swanmaiden.

The wightish onlookers laughed uproariously at that, with howls and caterwauls and shrieks.

'No. You are wrong,' Ashalind declared, in the overloud tones of self-doubt.

'Who but a callow maid swimming in the depths of folly would believe the highest of the high would take a mortal to his very wife? To how many transactions most preposterous has Vahquil been drawn by her vanity?'

'No!'

'The swan prevaricates as deliberately as she mispronounces!' accused Caitri. 'She speaks in questions, with *may* and *might*. She has truly said *nothing*.'

'Betimes, union between mortal and immortal has occurred,' went on Whithiue, 'often under duress, begat by the stealing of cloaks or skins. All such unions have been doomed to tragedy—has Vahquil not heard?'

'I will hear no more.' Tahquil-Ashalind stoppered her ears with her fingertips. 'Go! Avaunt, swanmaiden! Once you were kind to me, as I thought, but now I see that you wanted only to facilitate my passage into the spider's lair. You are faithless.'

'*Whisthaey!* Vahquil mistakes Whithiue,' sighed the lovely wight, 'for swan speaks only to aid hapless human, to peel waterweeds from her obscured eyes. All that swan has done has been in goodwill. If Vahquil has no gratitude for Whithiue, it is a sadful thing.' And, gracefully folding her cloak about her, she withdrew.

'Dost thou now perceive Angavar's intent?' softly asked the Crown Prince, drawing near.

But Ashalind, sick to the heart and choked with emotion,

could not reply. Against grief, she closed her eyes. When she opened them the oak wood and its denizens had disappeared and the colonnaded chamber was reinstated. Withered leaves and golden dust strewed the marble floor. Only she and Caitri remained there with Tully. Riven, the marquetry dressing-table lay in ruins upon the floor, its looking-glass smashed to smithereens.

The echo of an injunction bled away in the shadows:

'Anon thou shalt seek again, Elindor.'

In hollow halls and shady dells
In oak woods blue with silent bells
On hilltops under cloudy skies
By well and water, stone and rise,
By brakes of thorn and hazelnut
The tall Gates stand forever shut.

FOLK SONG OF LUINDORN

9
ANNATH GOTHALLAMOR
Part II: The Eagle and the Raven

In your dark eyes translucent moonbeams glimmer
And, running swiftly, silver horses shimmer.
But dawn's whey-pallored light shows you are leaving.
Of pleasure and contentment you're bereaving
Me. Here I wait, shrouded by midnight's curtain.
I wait. This sunless place is so uncertain
I cannot know if 'tis a dream I'm seeing,
And even shadows from themselves are fleeing.

LOVE-SONG OF TAVISCOT

In the rose-window library of Annath Gothallamor Tully perched cross-legged on a carpet, a meadow of ripe hay-gold and cornflower-blue. He was playing his syrinx. In a chair by a leaded casement as tall as a spear, its panes standing open to the night, Caitri was seated. She sang:

'And where shall ye belong if not at home?
Devoid of native heath and doom'd to roam?
The rover's footsteps quicken as he turns
Towards the hearthstone, where the home fire burns.
Mere shelter may be varied frequently,
But home is where the heart knows it to be.
A wanderer may roam throughout his days
In pathless lands or winding roads and ways,

But in his secret thought, will always yearn
Towards the home to which he would return.'

'Ah, Caitri,' sighed Ashalind presently. 'Pray do not sing those verses. The Langothe is ever present and those words arouse it in me as a bellows awakens coals to flame. Only by delving into these antique books have I been able to divert my thoughts from sorrow and yearning. Poring over their pages is the single activity that can sometimes distract me from our present plight. Even sleep troubles me with heinous dreams.' She twisted the enamelled bracelet on her wrist. It was beginning to look worn and barbaric, especially compared to the sumptuous exquisiteness of the Faêran jewellery dripping from every garment.

On their solid gold pedestals the nine lamps threw their light up to the ceiling, causing the stone tracery and heavy bosses to flicker indecisively. Lamplight spun in stripes off the gilt spines of the books stacked on the octagonal table. On the lectern, another book lay spread-eagled. Ashalind, seated in the X-framed chair, perused it.

'Here,' she said, indicating, 'I see an illumination depicting a man with a smiling face and another with a weeping face. Between them lies a single red rose, which they are both regarding. How may two people look at the same object and react so variously? What can it mean?'

Her companions were as baffled as she. In silence, she read on.

'With what confidence,' asked Caitri of the air, 'might we trust the words of the swanmaiden, or of the Prince? No doubt both are truthspeakers—they have no option. But skilled are they in prevarication. They speak in questions and riddles. They palter and evade. Centuries of practice have made them experts.'

'True,' nodded the urisk, who by dint of keeping company with mortals had by now largely lost his habitual manner of speech.

'And what of the moving pictures shown in the pool?' Caitri continued. 'I do not give much credence to the ones purportedly showing the demise of the King-Emperor and his Queen. I know for a fact that they were riding horses along the strand when the dreadful Nuckelavee came upon them.'

'Give credence to the looking-pool, lass,' advised Tully. 'It displays the truth. 'Tis the passing on of words that twists veracity. Tales are apt tae alter with the telling. Spoken stories are likely tae be embroidered upon, if ye get my meaning. The fanciful addition of horses happened in much the same fashion as the spurious notion of the Faêran allergy tae iron.'

Caitri said, 'What do you mean? Are you saying that the Strangers do *not* fear iron, that it is not anathema to them?'

'Aye. 'Tis no lie. Cold iron is the bane o' wights but 'tis naught to the Faêran. They can wark wi' it as they wark wi' gold or sildron any ither metal. In the Dark Years the myth grew up amongst mortalkind, springin' from *our* hatred of the cold burning-metal. The Faêran were sleeping, never present tae refute the lie even had they bothered tae do so. The tale gained popularity, since it served the purpose of lending a tad o' superiority to iron-handling mortalfolk.'

'Knowledge is power, I have heard it said,' reflected Ashalind. 'Had I known the truth long ago, matters might have been different. It was only the sight of Thorn wielding iron that convinced me he was of mortal blood and not of the Faêran.'

'Then ye're a canny lass, for the Righ Ard made reet coofs o' the rest o' unsuspecting Erith!' chuckled Tully. 'Who'd hae guessed the King o' the Mortals was in truth the King o' the Realm!'

'What about the other wights? Did they not know his true identity?'

'Some did, I suppose, some didnae. I, for one, didnae. And those that were told, seelie or unseelie, were sworn not to reveal the knowledge tae mortal men, lest the Empire be torn asunder.'

'King Angavar is so powerful,' said Caitri. 'Why does he not make a new Gate?'

'Some things are impossible, even for the High King of the Fair Realm,' Ashalind said levelly. She returned to her book, and Tully to his reedy music.

A sad wind lamented around the gables of Gothallamor, speaking a hollow language. Presently Ashalind said, 'I have found the answer to the riddle of the two faces and the rose! The weeping man used to own a garden, the fairest and most extensive in Aia. Now, all that remains for him to gaze upon is this one flower. As for the laughing man admiring the rose, he once was blind.'

'Riddles, riddles,' mused Caitri. Her eyes strayed to the open window and the illustriousness of the stars, sewn like burning pearls on the ceiling of the sky. Below the window the tumbled roofs of Annath Gothallamor gave onto the High Plain, whereon movement could be faintly descried.

'There has come no unstorm,' she remarked, 'since we have been in this place.'

'The Fithiach has banned the shang from the vicinity of Annath Gothallamor,' explained Tully, 'because it waukens images of Men. While he is present at the fortress, the unstorm never comes.'

'Herein is an odd thing,' said Ashalind, reading from her book, 'a poem, written about this very fortress. Tully, what does this mean—*Riachadh na Catha?*'

'Why, 'tis the auld kenning for the High Plain,' said the urisk, 'and its meaning is the Plain of War, or the Battlefield of Kings.'

Ashalind raised her head to the gold lettering inscribed on the archway over the bookshelves:

⟁ Is Truth So Hard To Find? ⟁

'*Riachadh na Catha,*' she repeated, slowly. She closed the book.

Tully's reed-music wove a thin wire of melody through soft dunes of starlight sifting through lilac panes. It was a tune she had heard before, one whose words Ashalind could never forget. Once Thorn had sung her this song beneath the luxuriant eaves of the Forest of Glincuith, having crowned her with a garland of flowers . . .

The west wind is my caress,
Raindrops my kisses on thy mouth.
Clouds race at my bidding, sunshine is my blitheness.
My heartbeat is the tide, my wrath, the tempest.
Mist is my mantle, starlight my diadem,

Frost is my sword, fire, the passion of my heart.
Night and silver water am I,
Autumn bounty and the garlands of Spring.
The long leaves of the woodlands blow in my hair.
Temperate as Summer, I,
Grim as Winter, and as perilous.

The words were imbued with new meaning now. Where was
Thorn-Angavar, and did he think of her? Were the words of the
swanmaiden true? Had his desire to enjoy her been no more than
a passing whim? Such a notion was heartbreaking; yet far worse
than his indifference would be his anger. Doubtless it had by this
time come to his knowledge that she, Ashalind-Rohain, had lit the
flame in Tamhania's Beacon and ushered in the three Crows of
War. She, and no other, had been to blame for the destruction of
the Royal Isle. Who could blame Thorn-Angavar if this had
aroused his ire and cancelled his ardency?

Perhaps she ought to be grateful that he had merely chosen to
neglect searching for her, trusting that she had perished in the
conflagration of Tamhania. Worse might have occurred: he might
have sought her out for punishment.

Nevertheless he *had* sent out for her after all, as the wights
had made clear. Of course—like Morragan he must have learned,
eventually, that in some way she was the key to his Realm. How
terrible his wrath would be on receiving this knowledge, on real-
ising too late that the key had actually been within his grasp
before Ashalind, still guarding the secret, had slipped through his
fingers. Indifference or anger; these were to be expected. After all,
the proclamations of Pod and others were historically correct, by
all accounts: any union between mortal and immortal was
doomed to tragedy.

But how had Morragan first discovered that the intruder at
Huntingtowers was in fact a mortal who had entered Erith by way
of a Gate? A Gate which, as it turned out, had eluded the words
of his own geas and might yet provide passage to the Fair Realm?

The urisk finished his tune with a long and plaintive note that
declined into silence.

'Tully,' Ashalind said into the quietude, 'pray tell me all you have found out about the Prince's discovery of me, for that mystery remains and I would fain solve it.'

'That is mickle,' fluted the goat-man, laying aside the instrument. 'My ears have been waggling, I have been mingling aboot, catching up on a' that I hae missed during decades of solitude.'

He began to recount all he had learned.

After Ashalind's presence had been detected in Hunting-towers, after she had escaped and been hunted down and—as it was believed—had perished in a cave-in of the old mines, and after the fleeing duergar had been apprehended with a swatch of golden fibres half plaited into a whipcord—after all these events, some spriggans happened to set eyes on the skein of hair. When they approached it, they sniffed its scent and remembered it, saying, 'This hair is of a mortal who visited the traverse beneath Hob's Hill a thousand years since. How came she here? Long ago her bones ought to have mouldered to dust!'

For the spriggans were Scrimscratcherer and Spiderstalkenhen, the very spriggans who had escorted Ashalind through the halls of Carnconnor when she went to rescue the children of Hythe Mellyn.

Their news was carried at once to Morragan. One of his knights came before the Raven Prince, bearing the abundance of gilded threads, bowing low on his knee. When the Prince took up the tresses, a sudden hope awakened in his eyes—*hope* for the first time in the midst of immortal despair, that most appalling of all despairs.

He said, 'If the spriggans have the right of it, the maid who owned these locks is none other than Ashalind na Pendran, daughter of Niamh, who with her family and the city of Hythe Mellyn, journeyed to the Realm, there to dwell forever. How has she come to Erith? For certain, she was within the Realm at the time of Closing, that much I know. She has come through by a Gate from our world to this. To regain her is to regain a way back to the Realm. It may be there is now hope of an end to exile. She must be discovered!'

To the Unseelie Princes he said, 'Find the spy!'

'Your Royal Highness,' answered Huon, 'after the spy fled from my fortress the Cearb made the rocks to quake, crushing her covert. Doubt not, the wench lies dead in the old mines.'

'Then bring me her corpse,' commanded the Prince.

But by that time it was too late. There was no sign of a cadaver, at least not a recent one; a barrow-load of human bones was dug up, but they belonged to miners of yore. It was thought that the bold wench had been scratched up and eaten by wolves, but Morragan questioned the wolves and interrogated the wights and the birds and the beasts of the wild and none had seen a mortal maiden with yellow hair, either dead or alive, save for those folk of the Talith already known and accounted for across the lands. Wights were sent abroad to scour the countryside near and far, with no success. The spy had vanished from the knowledge of men and wights and Faêran.

'If the maid lives she will seek the High King,' said Morragan to the first among his knights. 'But ere she finds him, she shall come to me. And let it *not* be made known outside this circle why she is sought, for if there is a way back, that knowledge must be withheld from all who are not my steadfast allies!'

There, for a time, the situation remained. Morragan's knights of Faêrie and their servant wights and the Unseelie Attriod began a Vigil across Erith, watching for any sign of the Talith maiden. Meanwhile in Isse Tower a servant worked with his taltry tied over his ugly head, concealing the cropped stubble of his outlandish locks.

At the commencement of this Vigil, Morragan vowed to divert Angavar's attention to one place, in order to draw him from the knowledge of Ashalind's presence, as a cliff-swallow's aerial acrobatics draw the predator from its nest eggs. To this end, his wightish servants began allying themselves with the malcontents who were already arousing sedition in troubled Namarre. They stirred up unrest among the outlaws, furtively urging the chieftains of their bands to unite, to rise against the Empire. The wights made grandiose allusions to eldritch aid and the assistance of a powerful wizard, in return for the warm corpses and almost-corpses of their hewn enemies when battle was joined. The

Namarrans were led to believe that their hordes might crush the
Legions and pour down from the north to overrun all countries
and unseat the King-Emperor. Enticed by visions of glory and
wealth, the brigands joined together in a rough semblance of an
army. Morragan-as-Wizard put forth the Call and the Mustering
commenced.

It was a lengthy business, since its main purpose was not to
hasten war but to prolong pre-war manoeuvres. By means of forays and raids, Morragan's eldritch côterie intended to keep
Angavar-as-James occupied, to keep the Royal Attriod guessing, to
ensure that the Empire's focus was directed towards affairs at the
Namarran border. Besides, full-scale conflict was not the wightish
way. Like cats, they excelled at skulking, sudden strikes, and
ambush in the dark, rather than the direct assaults typical of
hounds and men.

This temporising served its purpose. No suspicion entered
Angavar's thought. The secret of the damsel from the Gate
remained with Morragan and the foremost among his knights. Not
even the Unseelie Attriod was given to know it. As for the two
spriggan sentries who had recognised the scent of the hair,
Morragan had them imprisoned in the lowest dungeon of
Huntingtowers where, deep in compost, they enjoyed the finest
worms and slothfulness, season after season.

The Vigil continued.

And this uneasy situation would not have altered, but for a day
in Uvailmis of the following year—the same day as the freeing of
the nygel. In the marketplace of Gilvaris Tarv, Gull, the Spriggan
Chieftain, had been lurking, bent on causing mischief among merchants and cheats. He had spied the yellow hair of Imrhien—as
she was then—spilling from under her hood. He summoned others and they gave chase, but the carlin Ethlinn Bruadair outwitted
the spriggans.

Fearing to inform Huon and the Prince of their failure, the
spriggans mounted their own search, keeping watch on the house
of the carlin. Again the wights lost track of the yellow-hair—it
seemed she somehow melted from under their long and sensitive
noses and they could not locate her again in Gilvaris Tarv. She had

eluded capture as before, but now Morragan knew for sure that she lived. By the colour of her hair he knew it, for the few Talith who remained in Erith could be accounted for, and would not be wandering the markets of Tarv. It only remained for the Raven Prince to claim her before she could be claimed by Angavar, should her existence come to the knowledge of the Faêran King.

Meanwhile, a mute girl and her Ertish friend languished in a *gilf*-house by the river, were rescued and began an ill-fated journey to Caermelor. Travelling in the wilderness under Thorn's protection, Ashalind remained, for a time, safe.

Ill-founded secrecy built a barrier that stood between the Faêran King and the girl with the clue to the Gate. His twofold identity was deliberately hidden while hers had been forgotten— yet they became linked, in those Autumn days as they travelled the Road together, and that linking was a passion forged deep and strong.

In the last week of the year the Royal Wizard Sargoth had stolen by night into the forest near Caermelor. There he stood and called out seven words. Soon, a darkness folded about his eyes and he was rushed through the trees to a place where he was brought before the Spriggan Chieftain, Gull. The wizard had long been involved in dealings with unseelie wights, as a few daring mortalfolk were wont in order to gain the favour of the eldritch and thereby be granted power over their fellow Men. Sometimes this worked, usually it did not. Most mortals lived to regret their commerce with unseelie. Only the arrogant, the ruthless or the foolish ever assayed it.

Sargoth had been acting the spy, reporting the deeds of Angavar to Morragan, for of course Morragan knew the role his brother was playing, and the ire of the Crown Prince had waxed the greater that Faêran Royalty should play at being mortal, concerning himself with human affairs. In return for his efforts Sargoth received from Gull various rewards—the setting of spriggans to ambush his enemies, the lending of trinkets fortified with gramarye to shore up the wizard's trick-shows, the promise of safe passage to wealthy travellers who bore tilhals 'spelled' by the Royal Wizard.

Primed by Gull, the venal wizard had also been on the watch for an unknown Talith damsel. When he heard from Dianella the news concerning the true hair colour of the Court's latest guest, he came straight to the Spriggan Chieftain.

'I have found the one your lords seek,' said Sargoth. 'But abduct her not from Caermelor, for I want no attention drawn to my part in this. I would be of no further use to you should my doings be discovered. Moreover, I require extra payment for this work.'

'It shall be so,' agreed Gull, eager to ensure that there were no mistakes this time. In any event, Caermelor Palace was ringed with subtle, strong wards that had been placed by Angavar to safeguard Edward. From the palace, the Talith girl might not be abducted at all. Dianella, and subsequently Sargoth, had suggested that the yellow-hair should be sent, unknowing, to Isse Tower; there to be seized by the Hunt.

'Who else knows of the wench?' asked the Spriggan Chieftain.

'Only Maeve One-Eye the Carlin, and her errand boy.'

The Royal Wizard returned to Caermelor, but Gull commanded that those of his folk who escorted the wizard on his way back should pinch and thump the man until he was black all over, in payment for his insolence in daring to demand additional remuneration.

The Spriggan Chieftain sent his wights after Maeve. She and Tom Coppins were forced to flee, seeking shelter down a dry well. Unable to reach them, the spriggans lidded the well and imprisoned them therein. Word was sent to Huon at Huntingtowers: '*Make ready.*'

At the pre-arranged hour the Wild Hunt descended on the stronghold of the Seventh House of the Stormriders. Had Huon arrived a day sooner, he would have been successful. Unfortunately for the Antlered One and for Gull, their plans again went awry. By then, the wizard's treachery had been revealed. Angavar-as-James had all along been aware of Sargoth's spying, and by supplying worthless information had hitherto used it to advantage. Now he came riding sky in fury, and routed the Hunt.

Thus the quarry eluded the Hunt at Isse Tower. The news travelled swiftly to Morragan: Ashalind had returned to reside at Court.

It was then, for a time, that the Raven Prince believed all was lost, for surely the identity of the Talith damsel would be revealed to Angavar. Surely she would relate her strange history and Angavar would be first to find the Gate. But the Raven Prince had not reckoned on the geas of the Gate of Oblivion's Kiss. Into this tale of disguise and false identity, so complex as to border on farce, there had entered another factor—forgetfulness. And so, while Ashalind believed Angavar to be James, Angavar, in turn, had no reason to suppose Rohain of the Sorrows was otherwise than she claimed. True to his Faêran nature he lived for the moment and scarcely bothered to explore the past. He knew no fear. The past held no terrors for him. Furthermore, his sovereignty over the very elements, his knowledge of the tongues of all creatures, these and other powers made arrogance inevitable in the High King of the Faêran. Omniscience needs not probe and question. Its only flaw lies in not recognising its own provisionality.

Gradually, Morragan came to ascertain the true situation. Understanding, he marvelled at his fortune.

When the King-Emperor voyaged north with his armies, Ashalind was taken to the protection of the Isle of Tamhania. Morragan gathered his strength to himself again, and put it forth, directing it at the island. He triumphed—the gates of the Seelie Isle were breached and Tavaal-Tamhania was drowned. But she who they hunted so desperately had vanished once more. In the turmoil of aftermath, the Attriod sought Ashalind. Morragan guessed that Angavar would have set some device on his betrothed to keep her from harm, and guessing this he tried the harder, yet she outfoxed her pursuers, slipping from their net a fourth and final time. Instead of choosing a path back to civilised lands as they expected, she turned north. In the wide leagues of the wilderness she became lost to them. They searched for her in vain.

Through the flowery meads, the gloomy forest, Appleton Thorn and the wet fells, Ashalind and her companions were glimpsed only by wights who rarely strayed from their haunts, who were so mild or lawless or solitary as to remain beneath the contempt of Morragan's Summons; wights who had heard no news from the greater world or cared little for it if they had. Until, in Cinnarine, a ganconer who was making his way eastwards happened upon three likely victims. Originating from populous haunts, Young Vallentyne had not failed to mark that the Unseelie Princes kept watch for a damsel journeying in secret. Having sated, with one of them, the inclination of his species, he sent a message to Annath Gothallamor.

'And the rest ye ken,' concluded Tully. Putting the syrinx to his mouth, he resumed piping.

The eldritch music soared like falcons in flight. Evocative, it freed Ashalind from thoughts of her capture, reviving earlier memories. From down on the High Plain, the flourish of a wightish horn came blaring through the library windows. Coarse and brazen though it was, it brought to mind the purer note of another such instrument, a Faêran horn, sounding the last Call to Faêrie on the Day of Closing. At that time, Ashalind had stood beside her father in the Watchtower while, beyond the Gate, Angavar and Morragan clashed in bitter feud . . .

. . . many fled the Watchtower; soon a flood of Faêran, wights, birds and animals poured through the Geata Poeg na Déanainn to aid the King's return. There was scant chance that they would reach him before the Closing—the combatants fought, in fact, more than a mile from the Gate.

Silently, Ashalind battled an agony of indecision. She lifted her gaze once more towards the knights beyond the Window, staring at the melee. And all at once she forgot to breathe. In that instant her spirit fled out of her eyes and into Erith.

In their reckless sparring the melee of knights parted for an instant, revealing a rider who faced the Gate, although his gaze was not directed at it. Noble of bearing, he moved with the power and grace of the sea. So dark was his hair that it seemed fashioned from the night, glimmering with the polish of water seen by starlight. The force and wonder, the sensual beauty of him knocked commonsense out of the watcher's head like coins from a flung purse.

'Father forgive me,' she cried suddenly, 'I must try to return . . .'

Aghast, Leodogran cried, 'But why?'

'Only that—' His daughter struggled to find words. *'My future lies in Erith, I think. If the High King does not return in time . . .'*

This newly recalled memory came as a revelation to Ashalind. Through the Gate, she had glimpsed a face—the face of Angavar, seen for the first time, and distantly. It dawned on her that the sight of him, and only this, had demanded her last-moment return, against ridiculous odds, to Erith.

'Of course. He is Faêran,' she murmured to herself, 'and all mortals fall at least half in love with that race as soon as they clap eyes on them. How much more potent must be the attraction of their sovereign? I have been allured, as a moth flies towards the lantern-flame. Yet it pleases me to recall this, that my reason for being here in Erith is Thorn. My love for him is confirmed—albeit not reciprocated. In any case, there would have been no future in such a union.' And her heart seemed to be suddenly squeezed in a vice.

Into her reverie there broke an interruption.

From the stencilled ceiling high above, a snowflake fluttered down, landing on the lectern. Tully snatched the reed-pipe from his lips. Unfolding the scrap of snow-white parchment Ashalind saw words glimmering there, scribed in ink of argentum which flowed like a living current. Puzzled, she read them aloud:

I have no arms but I reach across the horizon.
My feet for seven years do not walk.
Water is my table, the wind is my bed.
I have no ship but I sail the ocean.
I have no eotaur, though I ride the sky.
The chains of Erith do not bind me.
I, the navigator, overlook them.

A frisson of terror and delight chilled the reader.

'It is a riddle,' she concluded, nervously scanning the library, which gave the appearance of being empty save for Caitri and Tully.

'Gie me a wee moment,' said the urisk. 'I shall get the answer o' it.'

Strong wings beat at the casement. A huge raven alighted on the sill, its claws digging into the wood. Frightened, Caitri ran from her chair and crouched at Ashalind's feet. The raven's round eye fixed them with a frigid stare.

'I s'll be finding the solution forthwith,' said Tully briskly. He scratched his curly head.

'Never mind, Tully,' said Ashalind, her pulse beating like the threshing wings of a trapped bird. 'I know it. The riddle's answer is a seabird, the elindor.'

'Thou art overly acute,' said Prince Morragan regretfully. He stepped from somewhere, or nowhere, and extended his arm. The raven flew through the open window, to perch thereon.

The library brightened. Pellucid light poured down, for the chamber now lay naked to the sky, the ceiling having disappeared without a sound. The nine lamps flared, showing that the tall casements had melted like panes of ice. They left wide interstices through which stars dazzled and the wind careened. Between the empty window-frames the walls remained upright. Stripped of their panelling they revealed themselves as monoliths of solid basalt, capped by stone lintels. Within this primitive and monumental circle the carved furniture and carpeting remained unchanged—incongruous, decadent.

Figures drifted in through the gaps between the monoliths, the courtiers of the Crown Prince mingling with the various wights addicted to the proximity of the Faêran.

Amongst them sauntered the Each Uisge in field armour, a sculpture in metal: the curved ridge of the gardebraces jutted from his shoulders on either side, meeting the rippled shoulder-defences of the pauldrons at a smooth seam. The lamels on both the upper and lower cannons of the vambraces were layered and scalloped like the scales of a fish, adorned by rows of pearly rivet-heads, chased and moulded to match the breastplate with its foliate seaweed design.

The couter protecting the left elbow protruded in a great fan-shaped shell of steel, large by contrast with the winged-shell reinforcement on the right elbow. The lamels fitted him closely at the waist. From the body-armour depended shield-shaped tassets ridged and fluted with pointed arches, prolonging the defence of the skirt over cuisses embellished with jagged wave designs which differed on each thigh. Fan-shells glittered on the poleyns, at the outside of the knees. The wave-crests on the greaves arrowed down in reflection of the upreaching peaks on the cuisses. The gauntlets were silver lobsters.

He moved out of view.

Negligently, Morragan stroked Ashalind's hair, toying with a few tresses.

She burned.

'Gaze through the window, *lhiannan*,' he suggested.

Between two basalt pillars stretched the dew-silvered net of a cobweb. Its strands glittered and thinned, then dissolved. Behind this mesh, a scene was displayed—not the evernight of Darke, but the circadian day of clean-rinsed Arcdur.

Once more the Eye of Gramarye roved through the land of stone and pine. Once more Ashalind could recognise no clue to the whereabouts of the elusive Gate of Oblivion's Kiss, or if it seemed she was about to do so, some hindrance obfuscated it. Searching, she felt her strength drain away as though the pith was being sucked out of her bones. 'No more,' she pleaded, but there was no relenting. The search was long. Her shoulders sagged with weariness. By the time the beautiful voice of Morragan said, 'Draw back,' her sinews hurt as though she had been reaping in the fields for three days and three nights.

Just as the scene of Arcdur was fading, another landscape overlaid it for a while—a field of war at sunset. The sky ruptured into long red wounds. Behind a mountain, the merest sliver of a fingernail moon came up in a misty nimbus the colour of spring leaves.

Beneath the bloody light of the dying day Ertish troops confronted Namarran assailants. The troops were organised in battle formation. Each battalion formed themselves an oblong composed of three ranks consisting of heavy cavalry, spearmen, archers and crossbowmen, with light cavalry on the flanks. In the front lines, the spearmen knelt on one knee, holding their shields before them, the lower edges braced upon the ground. Their spears slanted towards the enemy, all at the same angle, like a forest of saplings bowing beneath the powerful vectors of a hurricane. The Finvarnans had rammed their spear-butts into the rocky soil. Behind them, the archers and crossbowmen were arrayed. The archers, also on one bent knee, protected themselves with shields held on the left arm, until the instant they sighted and released an arrow. In the third line waited cavalrymen, shielded by the infantry until the moment was right for a cavalry charge.

The rebels' horses refused to drive themselves at this bristling hedge of spears. As long as the Ertish infantry remained steadfastly in this formation, they were secure, although without mobility there was small chance of defeating the enemy.

For a long interval the rebel forces subjected the Ertish warriors to an incessant hail of arrows, bolts and javelins. The constant barrage under imposed conditions of impassivity enraged the Erts, to the point that their discipline eventually crumbled. Some of the spearmen sprang to their feet and began to advance. To ensure the integrity of the shield wall, the rest were forced to follow.

As the Finvarnan companies advanced over the rough terrain, their attention fixed on deflecting the onslaught of missiles, they were unable to keep marching in step. Breaches opened in their ranks and into these gaps charged two divisions of the barbarians' heavy cavalry, javelins levelled. Once in the heart of the fray they fought with sword and mace, hacking, hewing and smiting. Caught in disarray, the Ertish infantry had no chance of withstanding the cavalry charge. They broke ranks and scattered into the waxing darkness. As soon as the barbarian hordes saw their enemy giving ground, they attacked in full force. The Finvarnans were routed.

But this battle had by no means decided the contest. The greater conflict was yet to come.

Between the stone pillars, the image altered.

Early sunlight reached long wands across the Nenian Landbridge, stretching shadows from the long lines of horsemen who rode solemnly, nine abreast, into its oncoming radiance. Beneath their helms, the soldiers of the Legions of Erith narrowed their eyes against the glory of the dawn. Their spears and banners stood up in serried ranks like a glittering forest. Darts of golden

light glanced from their armour, visible from miles away. High
above, Windships rose and dipped among the clouds, and twelve
squadrons of Stormriders passed like flights of great birds of prey.
The jangle of stirrup and bridle came ringing faintly on the breeze.

There rode among the Stormriders Lords Voltasus, Ustorix,
Isterium, Valerix and Oscenis. Among the Legions was numbered
a soldier entitled Second Lieutenant Diarmid Bruadair of the
Emperor's Regiment, his tabard resplendent with the King's Lion
in regimental colours. Nearby rode a more lissom soldier with hair
alight and a long quiver at her back—Corporal Muirne Bruadair of
the Royal Company of Archers. Riding at her side was a taller
archer, young Eochaid of Gilvaris Tarv.

Further back marched companies of men in less disciplined
array. Their war-gear was flamboyant, one might say reckless,
being mainly of hard-boiled leather riveted with iron. Some drove
chariots, some rode mettlesome steeds, others strode afoot singing
lustily, not in the Common Tongue. Their hair caught and tossed
the fire of the new day. A roar of laughter could dimly be heard;
an ox of a man sat astride his war-horse, brandishing an axe and
shield. Sianadh Kavanagh it was, none other—a warrior singing
patriotic songs while following Mabhoneen, Chieftain of the Erts
of Finvarna and his rallied squadrons.

The Arysk rode with the Legions also—the Icemen, three
Rimanian battalions in war-harness glittering like sunlight on
snow. And the stalwart brown-haired men of Severnesse rode, as
well as those of Luindorn.

The Dainnan were there in silver-white mail overlaid by long
surcoats. Among them was Sir Heath with the knights Tide, Firth,
Dale, Flint, Gill, Tor and many more chivalry of their *thriesnuns.*
The Royal Attriod rode with the Dainnan—Tamlain, Duke of
Roxburgh, and Thomas, Duke of Ercildoune; Octarus Ogier, Lord
High Chieftain of Stormriders; John Drumdunach, Lord High
Commander of the Royal Guard; Richard of Esgair Garthen, Lord
High Sea Admiral; and Istoren Giltornyr, Lord High Sky Admiral.

And he who rode at the head of these *thriesnuns,* these battalions, these wizards and fleets and squadrons, *he* came forth like
a lion.

Called James XVI, King-Emperor, he stood out from the rest, mounted on his armoured war-horse Hrimscathr. The sword Arcturus was scabbarded at his side, its damasked quillons deflecting the sun's rays to blinding shards. He was exactly as Ashalind had once pictured him with thought's invention, shining in golden field-armour with its slender, elegant lines, cusped borders and shell-like rippling. Damascening glinted on the lames, studded metal roses were connected by riveted laminations to shoulder, elbow and knee, and adorned the breastplate. The Lion of D'Armancourt roared upon his breast. His helm was crested with a great golden lion, a star-tipped crown encircling the war-beast's shoulders. Beneath the metal nose-guard was a glimpse of the high cheekbones, the strong chin, the eyes as keen as knife blades. He smiled at one of his captains and the lean lines of laughter appeared at each corner of his mouth. The Royal Attriod in their plumed splendour surrounded him, armoured cap-a-pie, light splintering off richly ornamented chausses, vambraces, coudieres, genouilliers, tassets, gauntlets. Flanked by standard-bearers, a trumpeter, the Dainnan, the Legions of Eldaraigne and battalions from the armies of every country in Erith with their banners and gonfalons, the gay pennons unfolding their points along the breeze, this sovereign of a lost realm looked towards the wide lands opening out from the Landbridge and advanced steadily into Namarre.

All these scenes came and went in a flash. As Ashalind watched, dusk veiled the landscape and stars shone through it. Knights and men-at-arms dissolved into indigo shadow—the skies of Darke caught in the spider's net between the monoliths. Limply, Ashalind draped her arms over the sides of the X-framed chair and rested her head upon one of them.

'Thou must do better in thy search, if thou'rt to soothe me,' said Morragan, and this time there was a perilous edge to his tone. With a flick of his hand he signalled to his cup-bearer. 'Shouldst thou not soon find the Gate, Elindor, martial conflict shall recommence in earnest.'

'Would you make war against your brother and sworn sovereign?' Ashalind cried, starting up.

Morragan made no reply. He strode away, his cloak unfurling like violent smoke.

The Faêran cup-bearer leaned to the girl, saying: 'The stirrings of this strife were begat long ago, after thy sly visit to Huntingtowers. A duergar was in possession of a skein of zircon locks and by this love-token, the reality of an active Gate was revealed. Namarran insurrection was engendered in order to distract Angavar from the discovery of thee.'

'How could you all be so certain the High King was not aware of the Gate?'

'On learning of its existence, Angavar would certainly have ridden for Arcdur with nine and ninety Faêran knights and ladies. Had he done so, we should have known it instantly. Dost thou underestimate us even now?'

'The purpose of distraction was achieved. Let there now be an end to conflict.'

''Tis His Royal Highness's desire to crush those who have leagued themselves with Angavar—the Legions of Erith, the Dainnan and the mortal Seven. Mighty are the forces of the Unseelie Host now gathered. Mighty are the Princes of the eldritch Attriod. Namarran warriors have allied also themselves with the Host, although beside the rest, their puny strength is as a javelin of water. By now they understand more than their own ambitions are at stake, but they see the fulfilment of their goals as an adjunct to any war against the Empire.'

'For no good reason does your liege harass the men of Erith,' Ashalind said faintly, collapsing back into the chair and accepting the goblet from the cup-bearer's hand. 'They have done him no harm.'

'Spies and thieves are all men,' said the Faêran cup-bearer scornfully, 'liars and meddlers, glutted on greed, lack of generosity, rudeness and selfishness, gloominess, untidiness, disorderliness, undue curiosity, slovenliness, ill temper and bad manners. Yet for all these faults the Fithiach would not deign to wage war upon humankind if not for Angavar, who loves them.'

'I repeat, there is no reason for war games now that I am here!'

Lord Iltarien stepped close to her, saying, 'Now that preparations have proceeded this far, our Prince has decided to carry the business through to its apposite conclusion. Angavar is aware thou dost bide with us in Gothallamor, though too late has he arrived at this wisdom. He also knows our Prince is behind the uprising. He will attack. Already he pushes across the Landbridge into Namarre. We are ready.'

Quoth the stylish Each Uisge, gurgling like a drain:

'The Raven's wings will spread wide across Erith's skies when Angavar Iolaire yields and is made a haggard.'

'Then you are conspirers and treasoners to your King!' shouted Ashalind, flinging the goblet and its contents at the Faêran knights. 'Treasoners all!'

The globules of wine solidified in midair. Teardrops of jet and diamond rattled to the floor like a beaded fringe, bringing down in their wake a curtain of darkness so thick that nothing could be seen, and through this utter absence of all light tore a howl of pre-ternatural menace. A subsonic pressure pounded at Ashalind's ears and she heard Caitri's thin scream like a scratch on the edge of a vitreous chalice. Then something seized her and flung her to the ground.

10
THE BATTLE OF EVERNIGHT
Of Love and War

Green hills rise up against the skies; behemoths of bygone time,
Silent beneath soft rain, bright sun, and silver star and frosty rime.
Grass covers, like a velvet cloth, the sunken halls where sleepers lie.
Stone caverns hide the gleam of gold, of armour and of jewellery.

Magnificent in splendid state, adorn'd with gorgeous pageantry,
Scutcheons blazoned with a sign—knights of mystic errantry.
Whyfore sleep these men-at-arms as centuries roll slowly past—
Untouched by time, ageless and fair? And what will wake them at the
last?

VERSES FROM 'THE SLEEPERS', A BALLAD OF YORE

The Faêran singer ceased the song of the Sleepers, the harpist's fine fingers stilled. The Lady Sildoriel, a member of Prince Morragan's exiled Court, spoke to Ashalind. She wore a gown sewn of butterflies' wings and peacocks' feathers: azure, turquoise, iridescent green.

'Mortals have been slain,' she said, 'for slighter insult than thou hast offered, Innocent. Yet here thou dost recline, gazing upon our feast. Truly thou'rt favoured—for the nonce, at least.' She smiled, a smile partly of fire and partly of mystery. In truth, to behold the smile of one of the Faêran was to stand, exhilarated, on a height. It was to look out over a plain that stretched to distant hills and was canopied by open sky, and to feel the wind come rushing across vast spaces to lift you. It was to fly.

'Fortunate,' gasped Ashalind, somewhat short of breath, 'am I.'

She shifted closer to Caitri, on their flowery knoll. Her latest gown, of brocade and shot silk, brushed heavily across living buttercups, cowslips, forget-me-nots and clover. A garland of wild-flowers adorned Caitri's brow, placed there by one of the Faêran, but her young face was bloodless. Untouched, a golden dish of strawberries lay on the sward, swelling crimson hearts capped by fresh green coronets and tenderly quilled with tiny seeds. Tully picked one up and bit into it. The crescent-shaped bite revealed, deep beneath the rose-red layer, ice-pink flesh surrounding the delicate albino eye of the core.

After provoking a fit of Faêran outrage and being thrown upon the floor of the library, Ashalind had succumbed to an unexpected and overpowering sleepiness. How long she had slept she could not tell, but she had woken in another place, another interlude or ventricle of Gothallamor. Here flowed a lucent stream where willows leaned, and the elfin faces of green-haired asrai girls peered curiously up out of the depths. New gowns hung from the boughs. The old garments had begun to melt away, ephemeral as moths' wings, perishing like ancient fabric which had lain for decades in a cedar chest. As soon as the girls had clothed themselves, a wooden boat, wreathed and posied with flowers of the meadows, came floating along the water by itself. Gently it bumped into their shore. They embarked, for there was no choice but to do so. The vessel bore them through a long, green tunnel of overhanging leaves, which opened out onto an orchard.

Here, it was like a twilight of late Spring. Apple trees were lathered with pale blossom which seemed to glow with its own radiance, like stars wrapped in translucent tissue. In moonlit glades, and through the trees, lithe figures danced to the liveliest yet most poignant music to which mortal ears had ever hearkened. Ashalind and Caitri watched, entranced and joyous, and it was some while before they comprehended that Tully had joined them. As the dance came to an end, three ladies of the Prince's Court strolled to where the mortals reclined, spelled with wonder. They rested beside them until the song of the Howe-Sleepers also concluded.

'It is always dark here,' said Ashalind, silently quelling her inner anguish, 'but the music evokes mornings of sunshine. I long for the sun. Why does the Prince dwell in Evernight?'

'It suits his temper, currently,' said Sildoriel. 'But thou mightst alter that.'

Ashalind turned her face away.

'Soon thou shalt lose thy chance,' the Faêran damsel said. 'For this feast and revelry marks the leaving of Gothallamor.'

Ashalind whirled around. 'The leaving? Where are we to go?'

Sildoriel smiled. 'Thou'rt not to leave, daughter of Niamh. Battle will soon be joined in earnest. The Prince departs, soon, for the fight. Thou'rt to remain here, awaiting his return.'

A sudden wrench of desolation forced Ashalind to clench her eyes shut. Firelight played behind her lids. She bowed her head. Her hair, flowing free, poured into her lap like wine.

A small, long-eared wight with bulbous cheeks and knobbly knees approached meekly. He was quaintly dressed in a jerkin of lizard-skin and breeches of zebra-hide, and he offered a dish piled high with seashells mottled and whorled with shades of brown and cream. Caitri drew back.

'Oh no! These sweetmeats are formed of dried mud!' she protested, waving the wight away. It made as if to scurry off but one of the companions of the Lady Sildoriel stayed it with a gesture.

'Wait,' said the Lady Gildianrith. 'I see, sweet nightingale, that thou art not acquainted with the delights of *xocohuatl*.' Taking up a shell like a long, spiral horn, she snapped the point of it, which broke off to reveal not a calcined hollow, but a solid interior, composed of a smooth compound. '*Xocohuatl* is made from the seeds of a Faêran tree which was brought to Erith and grows now in hidden places. Inform the *erithbunden*, Snafu.'

The wight squeaked importantly, 'Roast beans. Squeeze butter out of some. Pound up the rest, squash 'em, bash 'em, mix with milk, *xocohuatl* butter and Sugar. Slop into moulds, make cool, make hard. Eat. Yum.'

The Faêran aristocrats eyed the wight with obvious distaste.

'Pray, perform the chemistry of dining,' Sildoriel urged the mortals.

'True Faêran fare,' said Tully. Blissfully, he crammed a cinnamon-coloured shell in his mouth and helped himself to a handful more, adding, 'Chocoluatl!'

'Brown stuff like that would never catch on at Court,' whispered Caitri in Tahquil's ear.

The mortals declined the sweetmeat. Snafu scuttled into the trees and was pounced on by a scrawl of hobyahs. Gobbling sounds shortly emanated from that direction, while Snafu escaped, squealing.

'Your strawberries, my lady,' observed Caitri boldly to Sildoriel. 'Or rather, these victuals we see before us—they have the texture, the fragrance of strawberries. No doubt they possess also the taste and the goodness. Are they real?'

'The nourishment is real,' said Sildoriel with a shrug, 'and the taste and fragrance, all that is to be enjoyed. The image only is illusion.'

'Where then did the goodness come from?'

'Somewhere in Erith, little maid, there are strawberries which are devoid of goodness. They are merely husks, tempered with a semblance of taste. Whosoever shall eat them shall derive no sustenance therefrom.'

'The *toradh* has been stolen then,' said Caitri, prudently keeping reproach from her tone.

'Indeed, 'tis so,' affirmed the lovely courtier, with no trace of remorse. 'Hast thou never noted that some folk may eat lavish amounts of victuals and yet they waste away to skin and bone? Those folk are eating only *cochals.*'

'Why,' said Caitri, hotly now, 'do the Faêran take nourishment always from certain mortals, while other folk are permitted to grow fat?'

'I perceive a note of disapproval in thy tweeting,' casually said Sildoriel, taking Caitri's chin in her hand. 'Take heart, for the Faêran choose randomly or in jest, from here and there, as is our *right*. But when wights steal, like as not they will steal always from the same victims. Their thieving is done out of spite or jealousy.' She released the little girl, laughing at the expression upon her face, knowing full well the effect of the touch of the Faêran upon mortals. After Gildianrith, Sildoriel and the third Faeran damsel had arisen with a rustle of peacocks' feathers and left the knoll, Tully spoke quietly to the damsels.

'I hae tidings for ye,' he said, 'frae the battle-sward.'

In dread and eagerness, they attended to his words.

'Not long past, mortal engaged against mortal in western Namarre, beyond the bounds of Darke. The battle began wi' the archers and crossbowmen firing at each other frae baith sides, in an attempt tae cripple the enemy's infantry line. The spearmen stood their ground, tae protect the archers. For aye and aye, naught happened but a rain o' arrows and bolts. I hae witnessed this sort o' infantry siege before in bygone battles o' men. Both sides try tae goad the enemy intae makin' the first charge.'

'Who attacked first?' asked Caitri, breathless and wide-eyed.

'Och, the Imperial troops are weel disciplined. They refused to be drawn by the Namarrans despite continual skirmishing between the archers and light cavalry. Angered by this, the Namarrans in their wrath acted impulsively and launched an opening attack.'

'Was it successful?'

'Nay, the first charge niver makes much impression,' articulated Tully with the air of a seasoned campaigner. 'Neither side gained the upper hand. The Namarran captains employed their infantry to mask the mustering of their cavalry, after which they ordered a succession of assaults. Meanwhile the Imperial battalions held their defensive formation, letting the Namarrans tire out their troops, like waves dashing fruitlessly agin a cliff. When they judged the rebels had exhausted their strength, they launched a brief, incisive counterattack, winning the day.'

'Praise Fortune!' said Ashalind in an undertone. 'So the King-Emperor is advancing further into Namarre?'

'Aye,' said the urisk, 'further towards us. By now his Legions are no more than one league from the fortress.'

'So close!' A pang of agonising delight, mingled with hope and fear, shivered through the damsel.

'Yet by night,' the wight added grimly, 'unseelie wights take toll.' He was about to say more when the music of hornpipe, shawm and sackbut started up. The dancing resumed. High-pitched giggles and melodious laughter mingled, streaming through the flowering trees. Someone came towards the gathering on the knoll, someone who seemed to shape himself out of the twilight. The Faêran princesses hastily rose from their latest flow-ery couches. They curtsied deeply, three graceful herons admiring their reflections in placid water. Ashalind and Caitri found them-selves on their feet also. Without a word, the Raven Prince extended his hand to Ashalind. She took it, although it was as if she grasped the blade of a sword, and she feared her own hand must surely be cut to the bone. Merely, he led her to the dance.

To that measure, in such a place, with such a partner, neither description nor poesy nor flight of fancy can do justice.

The topmost turrets of Annath Gothallamor climbed the sequined sky like black-visored sentinels. On the apex of the high-est perched an iron weathervane in the form of a crow holding an arrow in its beak. Chimneys jutted from roofs of mossy slate. Small bridges crossed from turret to turret, and the mouths of water-spouts gaped.

High on the battlements spread a wide courtyard onto which opened several archways leading from the interior, each voussoir chiselled with the raven emblem of the Crown Prince. Out from these mouths rode knights in silver armour, with their eldritch ser-vants following behind them. The machicolations resounded to the ringing of metal plate, the jingle of mail, the clink of harness, the hollow clopping of hooves on stone, the raised voices of rest-less warriors eager for combat. Yet to battle they were not bound—not yet. Instead they made ready to ride to Arcdur, to search again amongst the serried stones for some hint of a hidden entrance, some chink or flaw which might betray the last Gate to Faêrie. No sildron crescents shod the superlative horses of Faêrie, who could stride across nothingness borne by the power of gra-marye. But jewels adorned their caparisons, flashing with the glacial colours of Winter.

Indeed, the capabilities of the Faêran were such that they might have flown unassisted, yet the atmosphere of Aia was not their native milieu; compared with the rarefied airs of the Realm, those of Erith were as syrup to these Faêran knights. To fly horse-less was to proceed slowly. Their elfin steeds were better adapted to the world of mortalkind, and able to make swifter progress while levitating.

Here were the Faêran chivalry of Morragan's retinue, those who had been amongst the hawking party, too far from the Gate when the Last Call to Faêrie had sounded. As they moved, starlight glittered, pure as hoarfrost, from every plane and flute and scallop of their fantastic armours, from every point and edge of their weapons. Proud was their bearing, easily they rode their wingless Faêran steeds.

So astonishing was the sight of this gathering that they appeared to be carved from ice crystal and darkness, hammered from iridium and shadows, embossed with moon-fire. The soft radiance of gramarye clung about them like a mist. They laughed, calling to one another in jest, scenting the fighting in the west as the hound scents the stag. Not one among them was not a warrior of surpassing skill, battle-hardened over centuries. Not one rode among them but he was in the prime of his power and prowess. Like drifts of blossom, the ladies of the Faêran passed among the concourse. Every knight wore a lady's favour on his sleeve.

At the very edge of the courtyard, where no wall marked the boundary between solid stone and insubstantiality, Prince Morragan stood. He looked out upon the High Plain. At his back, his Faêran equerry waited beside the head of a war-horse some nineteen hands high, and black as the moon's eclipse. Harnessed with caparisons of silver was this destrier, this noble charger. He shone with the richness of myriad jewels, although the horses of Faêrie needed no trappings and were thus decorated only for the sake of the Faêran passion for loveliness.

The Prince's squire slid a short-sword into a scabbard at the pommel. Morragan turned towards Ashalind and a wind roused, gusting across the battlements. It pushed Ashalind off balance, for despite the invigorating nature of the black wine, she was greatly weakened by the Langothe. Steadying herself against a wall, she regained equilibrium.

'Know this,' said the Prince. 'As long as thou dost believe in thy love for my brother, thou shalt search in vain for the Gate. When the veil lifts from thy cognisance, when thou dost perceive that this purported love is no more than an image in a glass, when thou dost eschew the strutting eagle and take flight with the raven, then it may be that thy memory shall become translated.'

In her heart she said, *You prevaricate. If I did not love Thorn, I should still search in vain, for the last remains of the Gate's covenant still bind me, and will not yield the final memory.*

When she made no reply, he said, 'Now fare I to Arcdur. Meanwhile, the freedom of the fortress and of the High Plain is thine. Use thy time well. Reconsider. If I return unrewarded, thou *shalt* endeavour to compensate me.'

The Prince swung himself up onto the war-horse with a movement so fluid it seemed never to have occurred. Grasping the reins in one hand he lifted the other, signalling to his knights. With one last glance down at Ashalind he urged his horse forward, leaping over the brink with a swift ringing of silver metal, to race away into the sky at the head of his cavalry.

But not before his last words had echoed off stone—*'I will not be denied.'*

Ashalind stood at a window, dressed in a layered gown of lavender samite whose intricate lace hems trailed upon the flagstones. Her heart was eaten out like a worm-raddled apple. As ever, she directed her gaze away towards the west. In the chamber behind her, Caitri rested languidly on an opulent couch, one arm crooked behind her head. 'Why has the Prince left the fortress at this time, with the King-Emperor's troops not a league away?' she wondered aloud.

'Perhaps he has no real care for the battle's outcome,' said Ashalind. She mused awhile, then said quietly, 'Once, in Caermelor, in the days when I rode with glory and fame in the company of great ones, and all the land seemed to lie spread out at my feet, and my hands were heavy with riches and the sun shone daily, you said to me this: "Mistress, I would wish you fortune, but 'twould be in vain, since you lack for naught—neither wealth, nor beauty, nor happiness nor love." And I gave you this answer: "Caitri, no one may possess every thing unless they hold also a guarantee that all their fortune shall forever remain immutable. Wealth, beauty, happiness, love—all are constantly in jeopardy and may be snatched away in an instant." Knowing this, the wise woman lives for the moment. The foolish woman dwells in apprehension. Both wise and foolish are we.'

Caitri answered, 'Be like the smiling man in the riddle of the rose, or like the thirsty optimist who sees a cup filled to midway with wine and rejoices that it is half full, whereas the pessimist, perceiving the same vessel, laments that it is half empty.'

'Is it not the so-called optimist,' argued Ashalind by way of diversion, 'who is truly the pessimist? For had he not expected the cup to be completely empty, he would not rejoice at its being half full. The so-called pessimist, on the other hand, is disappointed, since his expectation was for a measure overbrimming—thus he is in truth the optimist.'

'Well then,' Caitri responded merrily, 'you have outfoxed me with words!'

'That's as may be,' countered Ashalind, glancing over her shoulder at her friend. 'Words of wit have ever been my allies and my downfall. I have no great strength or swordsmanship. Only may I avail myself of wit and wisdom and knowledge for help in this our time of need. And craft.'

She turned back to the casement.

'Behold, all the wights have gone. The Plain is empty. Only armies of stones marshal themselves there, and their shadows are ordered to march at the whim and the wheel of the stars. Yet methinks I spy some movement—indeed, I believe a horse wanders there. Could it be Tighnacomaire? But no—my eyes deceive me. 'Twas naught but a trick of the starlight.'

The slow, dark breeze of Evernight, sharp as rock and jagged silver, slid in at the embrasure and blew Ashalind's long hair across her face. Between thumb and forefinger, she took up a strand of the dark tresses. 'See here, Cait—where drops of the Faêran wine spattered in my hair, its original colour is restored. The ink is bleached out. Flecked am I with pale yellow, like the spotted cats of Avlantia.'

'Ah yes,' acknowledged Caitri absently.

'You are uninspired. But invention strays into my thought. A bowl stands on the table there, beside a ewer filled with wine—will you wash my hair for me now, prithee?'

Ashalind shook the last droplets from the brightness of her new-washed Talith locks. Long necklaces of jewellery spilled from a casket on the table, and some of these she lifted, letting them slither in glittering festoons between her fingers.

'Your hair is beautiful. Will you let me dress it?' Caitri asked.

An unstorm was on the way, pricking through Ashalind's bones, lacing her blood, unlacing her clean-rinsed hair, stirring it with the premonition of its coming. Fine strands of brilliance lifted and floated about her face, the golden fire of the sun an aureole framing a pale and flawless oval from which her wide eyes stared—jewels of eyes, windows looking upon a distant place.

'The Prince is not here to forbid uncombers,' stated Caitri. Having attended to Ashalind's coiffure, she picked up the bowl and tossed the washing-wine out of the window, then leaned out and looked down. 'And so, I see one comes this way now. I won-der, what spectres will the shang wind disturb, here on such a high and lonely plain? What human events might ever have taken place here, where wights and Faêran have ruled for so long?'

'I can guess what it may arouse,' replied Ashalind, walking towards the door to the stairway.

'Where are you going?' Dropping the bowl, which broke, Caitri sprang to accompany her friend, a note of urgency and dismay lift-ing her tone. Ashalind paused.

'*He* said we are permitted out upon the High Plain, but no fur-ther. His words and wards permit no escape past its borders. Out there I intend to venture, now that wights have deserted its stony wastes and moved closer to the front line.'

Caitri, horrified, protested: 'Are you to simply stroll about down there in that pitted desert of rocks and take the airs as though it were some garden park of Caermelor? Why?'

'Because I grieve for what is lost, and am half killed by the Langothe. Because I long to escape these un-walls. Because the shang storm approaches.'

Caitri laid her hand on her mistress's embroidered sleeve.

'Do not go out . . .' she faltered. 'I am afraid to follow you there.'

'Stay here,' said Ashalind with a wan smile. 'Neither be afraid nor follow. Wait for me.'

She kissed Caitri's brow, and in a moment was gone.

The unstorm came up over Black Crag to the Plain. It blew across the fortress, lighting the pinnacles with tiny brilliants which outlined every ridge, every crocket and gargoyle, in shimmering pulses of bluish-green, like strings of diamantes. Annath Gothallamor rang and sang, chimed in its interstices and recesses like a mighty carillon, vibrated to the resonances of power in eerie currents of the unnatural wind. Within the castle's chambers furniture wavered, seemingly transmuted to burning crystal. Walls melted to translucency; the great pendant lamps caught fire and flowers of flame rained from them, vanishing as they touched the ground. Bats with emerald eyes flew in and out. The flagstone floor turned as black as a sink, appearing to subside away altogether. Caitri climbed onto a winged statue upon a pedestal and clung there, hiding her face amongst its stone feathers. Things flew and darted about her ears, rustling like Autumn leaves in a mighty forest, glittering like untold treasure-troves, and a weird singing arose all around. When she dared to open her eyes all fear fled from her and she was filled with wild, unreasoning exhilaration, so that she jumped from her perch onto the midnight floor which after all remained there to catch her, and danced in the wind and was even borne up by it a little, her feet hovering a hand's breadth from the ground in their satin slippers.

Later, after the shang had passed, when the walls of Annath Gothallamor had resumed their usual grim appearance and shifting habits, Caitri searched for Ashalind. Through cavernous halls webbed with fine tapestries she could not find her, and she sobbed with terror that she might never see her again. Some dismal trows followed her for a time, then trailed off into subterranean ways.

An arched doorway, high as a man on horseback, opened onto a stair leading down to a courtyard. Its architraves were thickly carved with wreaths of oak leaves and acorns. Here Caitri loitered alone. She sat with her back resting against the wall. Presently she dozed. A small sound awoke her—a light footfall, merely. Ashalind was not there, and then she was.

'Are you mortal and loyal to the Empire?' Caitri demanded reflexively, ever distrustful of appearances.

'I am Ashalind. And you?' warily responded the other.

'Your own dear friend Caitri!' With relief, the two damsels flung their arms about each other's shoulders. 'And have you walked through the storm on the High Plain?'

'I have. First I rode, for I found Tighnacomaire lurking there, and he bore me on his back. To ride through the shang on the back of a waterhorse—oh, that is a wondrous ride indeed, a dream! But not for too long, lest it steal one's sanity. After that, I walked. Tiggy yet lingers beyond these un-walls, not daring to enter but not wishing to desert us entirely. He has found some darkling pool or puddle to content him for now, although he is forced to share it with one or two other manifestations less seelie than him. I believe he cares not a jot. Now let us to the rose library, if the way makes itself available to us. There on the lectern lies an ivory-handled quill-trimming knife with a sharp blade. I want you to take it, Caitri, and cut off my hair.'

Caitri, disbelieving, demanded, 'Are you mad? Has the unstorm addled your wits?'

'My wits were addled long before this,' said Ashalind dryly. 'Since the Day of Closing, I believe, when I looked through a Faêran window, past a Faêran Gate, upon a Faêran face . . . Come, if you will not help me, I must do this thing by myself.'

To the rose-window library they went, the two mortal damsels. There, Ashalind seated herself in the X-framed chair while Caitri gathered heavy handfuls of her bullion hair and sliced them off close to the scalp. When it was done, Caitri stepped back and surveyed her shorn mistress, whose tresses lay in swathes at her feet, like a golden tide.

'Now,' said Ashalind, '*he* will not like me any more. He has no use for ugly mortals and will put me from him. We shall be made free.'

She lifted her hand to her head and felt the short stubble there. For an impossible instant it seemed she was back in Isse Tower with Grethet. Shrugging off the memory, she smiled.

Caitri said, shaking her head, 'It is no use, of course. It makes no difference. You remain beautiful, still.'

'Well,' said Ashalind, 'I have another reason for wanting him to think of me as the Shorn One, a mere simulacrum of my former self. I hope he might come to consider that the real Ashalind has slipped from his grasp and been replaced by another, plainer, less adequate copy. He might then be shocked if he should ever glimpse me as I was.'

'A vain hope.'

Ashalind seemed not to hear.

'Let us burn this harvest,' she said, plucking a lighted candle from its filigree bracket.

Hours beat by like blind crows. A tapping started up in the walls; knockings and hammerings reminiscent of the tunnels of Doundelding. Sudden lights flared in high windows. A grinding noise emanated from below a hearthstone in the rose library, as though someone were churning underneath the floor, and an ill-favoured hobgoblin was seen in the corridors and byways, prowling on splayed feet. Once, darting through a doorway to hide from this creature, the mortal prisoners came upon an unfamiliar stair. On climbing it they discovered a candlelit turret room, small and round, wherein sat a bevy of—ostensibly—little old women, industriously working at whirring wooden wheels. The scene recalled the spinners in the mines of Rosedale. Entering the room, Ashalind slammed the door behind them. One of the wizened hags looked up from her work. Her long nose was hooked, and her chin turned up to almost meet it in front of her mouth.

'Come in, come in,' she croaked belatedly, without missing a beat of her hobnailed boot upon the treadle. 'Sit ye down.'

'There's a hobgoblin on the stairs . . .'

'And he'll not bodder ye here,' replied the goodwife comfortably.

'Aye, he'll not bodder ye,' chorused the rest of the spinners.

'But we are mortal,' Ashalind pointed out. 'Do you not mind if we stay and watch you?'

'Tisk task,' chuckled the goodwife. 'Dere's more to ye dan mortal by now, daughters. Do ye not ken it?'

Reassured by the clucking and nodding of the seelie wights, the damsels seated themselves on three-legged stools to watch the spinning and await the departure of the lurking hobgoblin. Beside each wheel lay bundles of straw, which the little women were spinning into gold thread. Beyond marvelling, the girls made no comment but merely sat listening, alert for hobgoblin sounds outside the door.

'And we're spinning dis tread to be weaved into cloth o' gold,' explained the goodwife. 'Maybe 'twill be used to line a cloak for *hisself.*'

'Aye, for *hisself*,' nodded the rest, as their wheels whirred and clacked and the spindles grew fatter, like golden cocoons, and the straw never ran out.

The rhythm of the machines was a lullaby, and the fragrance of the straw was warm and friendly, the rich, amber aroma of a haystack on a Summer afternoon. The visitors were in no hurry to leave, and as an added incentive, the spinners began to tell stories amongst themselves. Mostly, their tales concerned Prince Morragan—sagas of adventure or famous hunts, descriptions of his prowess at games and sport and love, of his generosity, of his vengeance upon mortals who breached Faêran rules or otherwise displeased him.

'It were *hisself* as bade Nuckelavee assail da mortal Queen-Empress and her man,' the spinners mentioned in passing. 'He *itched* to make mischief on mortals.'

'Itched and itches,' rejoined one, sagely.

'And some say he did it to make her man sound de Coirnéad and waken Angavar King,' rejoined the goodwife. '*Hisself* was bored in his exile and craved comp'ny of da Fair and Royal kind.'

Ashalind could contain herself no longer. 'Wicked is the Prince!' she exclaimed, outraged. 'Wicked and hateful, to order such a terrible execution!'

With a clap all the candle flames went out. As the eyes of the mortal damsels readjusted, starlight revealed to the visitors all that remained in the room—some aged candle stubs and a few heaps of mouldy straw strewn about the floor.

'Well,' commented Caitri thoughtfully, 'the Prince may not have *intended* for Nuckelavee to slay the Royal couple. He might have supposed that King James would blow the Coirnéad immediately, so that Angavar would have time to save their lives . . .'

'Are you too under his spell?' cried Ashalind scornfully. Heedless of hobgoblins she flung open the door of the turret room and strode downstairs. Fortunately, the prowler was nowhere to be seen.

An uncanny wind swept through the fortress. The building, if such it was, trembled on its foundations. Thunder boomed from one quarter, then another. From the distance, a fanfare threaded down the wind, liquid notes strung on the starry airs of Evernight like chains of water.

Minor wights went shrieking through the halls of Annath Gothallamor.

'What is happening?' Caitri wondered, clutching Ashalind's hand. The two friends stood within a remote and barren ventricle of the fortress, peering through a slot in the wall that faced west.

'I do not know.'

Soon, they learned.

With a patter of small hooves, Tully came running in.

'Where have you been?' they exclaimed.

'Luikin' out for ye, lasses,' he panted, 'gleaning tidings. Morragan returns from Arcdur. He approaches now.'

Ashalind's heartstrings twisted like snarled cordage. All at once she felt ill. A desire to hide came over her, absurd because there was nowhere to hide. Caitri's face greyed to the colour of wet chalk.

'What shall we do?' she moaned.

'What else *can* we do,' answered Ashalind, 'but wait? Our fate is not in our hands, not yet.'

'What do you mean?' Caitri plucked at her sleeve. But there was no time for explanations. The thunder roared again, closer, and mixed in it, the ringing of silver caparisons on Faêran horses whose hooves pounded against the great pressure patterns that were the roads of the sky. A magnificent host galloped out of the west: black-maned horses, dark-cloaked riders, flashing with metal and jewels like flocks of splendid birds. They barrelled in amongst the roofs of the fortress, which shook under the force of their landing as though it must surely topple. Shouts and cries of command pierced the thunder.

As the last outriders circled before landing, Tully said quietly, 'Well noo. It seems the Fithiach is back.'

A thread of steel tautened across Annath Gothallamor.

Ashalind drew a heavy velvet cowl up over her cropped head. Its shadow draped across her face.

'Mayhap he will not notice,' agonised Caitri, wringing her hands.

'It will scarcely escape *his* eyes. No doubt he is already aware of my new mode. Squirm not! Do you consider him our tutor, to rap our knuckles for misbehaviour? As though there has been some wrongdoing? And if my hair is cut off, what is it to such as he?'

'He will be angry. It is certain.'

'A fig for the wrath of Morragan,' said Ashalind carelessly, but she trembled.

An odour of brine and rotting vegetation penetrated the dreary chamber. Two men appeared under an archway festooned with stone ivy. Around them, spriggans emerged from the shadows, their tails switching with vindictive impatience. The wights bowed peremptorily to the damsels, then twitched and jumped as though they had been stung. Obviously it sorely irked them to be forced to make obeisance to mortalkind.

'You—come,' their driftwood voices creaked.

The two men stood rigid, still, impassive. Passing close to them as she and Caitri joined the spriggan sprawl, Ashalind noted they were the doomed mortal servants of the Each Uisge, bound in eternal, ageless servitude. Pallid as drowned flesh, blank of eye, they turned with precision to fall in behind the damsels and their unseelie entourage, completing the escort.

'May we all be *sained*,' muttered Caitri in tones of dread, snatching a glance at the identical Maghrain brothers who strode silently, their sea-blue Ertish eyes fixed on some point in eternity. Caitri's hand fluttered to her neck, where a tilhal would have hung, had the charm not been torn off during the wild flight with the Hunt. Ashalind pulled the velvet cowl a little closer around her face and the spriggans jabbered peevishly amongst themselves. She longed to ask them for some tidings of battle, but their malign and sidelong glares deterred conversation.

Through the spacious halls of the fortress they hastened—halls wide and high as clearings in an ancient forest, which diminished those who passed through their mighty interior spaces, making of them mere beetles crawling across the floor. Fifty feet above, in the intricate beamwork of the ceilings, grotesque or beauteous faces peered down, smiling serenely or scowling. Tongues protruded obscenely, cheeks bulged like iris corms. Most of these effigies were fashioned from wood or stone. Others were not.

'Do you mark something?' Ashalind asked Caitri from the corner of her mouth.

'No. What?'

'The sounds of mining in the walls. They have ceased.'

Caitri listened past the rusted-hinge phonetics of the spriggans.

'So they are!' She shuddered. 'Even dunters dare not arouse his ire.'

Ashalind glanced back over her shoulder.

'Iainh!' she called. 'Caelinh!'

The men of the Isles made no response. Not by so much as a flicker of an eyelid did they indicate whether they had heard their names uttered.

'Sons of the Maghrain!' Ashalind called. The spriggans now hopped as though they danced on a red-hot griddle. Their tails spun madly, their squinting eyes flashed.

'No talking!' they screeched. 'Be silent!'

Their slanting slits of eyes glinted with malice. The prisoners did not speak again to the human slaves of the Each Uisge.

On they wended, ascending many vast and tortuous stairs, across a pillared courtyard of green marble where sunken pools brimmed with languid reflections. Leafy vines twined about the pillars; from them, flowers budded, sprinkling pink petals on the water. Here was a window—which was not a window at all, but an interval between the crook of two branches, framed by a collage of leaves. A glimmer there caught Ashalind's eye, and breaking away from their escort, she climbed into an embrasure, a bower of foliage. Peering through the trelliswork of the tree boughs she saw across a great distance, as though the clear air of Darke magnified her perception, mysteriously allowing vision far beyond the borders of Evernight to the west of Namarre.

In the gloom of *uhta* two armies, ranged rank on rank, faced each other across a strip of heathland severed by a stream which gleamed like a metallised ribbon. On the Namarran side, a few clumps of pine trees pointed up into the pre-dawn sky, like spindles from thorny undergrowth. The sparsely wooded land swept up to a ridge, whereon stood the ruins of an old stone castle. Western Namarre lay breathless, silent, brittle as dark crystal; a lacuna of uncanny stillness.

At an appointed moment, a roar erupted from the throats of thousands of Imperial troops. A tremendous barrage opened from the Imperial side, with a deluge of arrows and the thunderous explosion of burning projectiles from Windship-borne catapults. Instantly, the Namarran lines across the intervening space of No Mortals' Land broke into one long seething flame of white-hot bursting naphtha. Hurled by Imperial catapults, blazing missiles as large as barrels of cider, with tails of fire as long as lances, thudded into the ground like volcanoes. The soil came down like a hailstorm for minutes afterwards.

Under cover of this fire, Imperial troops threaded their way in single files through the tangle of undergrowth to the centre of No Mortals' Land, with arrows tearing overhead on their way to the Namarran lines. There they paused, awaiting signals from platoons supporting on either flank. The barrage from the Royal Archers and armed Windships was already creeping forward, and, fearing to wait longer, the Imperial troops began to advance. Soon they came up to the curtain of fire which had reached the Namarran front line and their rate of advance from then on was simply regulated by the speed of the barrage. They crossed the enemy front line without stopping. Such rebels as survived had fled to the shelter of the pines, from which they emerged later to surrender in small groups. Some of the legionaries ran into their own barrage and fell, wounded.

'Come away!' hissed the spriggans at Ashalind's side. They tugged at her elbows. 'Hasten!'

She ignored them, intent on the unfolding scene.

Following the barrage closely, the Imperial troops crossed through a denser belt of pines. Some twenty yards behind this belt ran a ditch, occupied by a number of the enemy who fled at the sight of the Imperial forces. They were all shot down.

Up the slopes of the ridge yellow naphtha fires flared like unnatural flowers, stinking of brimstone, gushing oily black smoke. They burned fiercely, yet without spreading out of control in the rain-soaked vegetation. Throughout the area behind the Imperial line there was keen elation at the news that the whole attack was going successfully. The reserve battalions, taking up position on the slope of a hill, looked out upon the ridge opposite and on the whole scene: the Windships flying and fighting against a dawn sky striped with carnation and topaz, the naphtha missiles punching black smoke plumes from the ruins on the summit, the troops for the later attack lining up under the coloured flags of their battalions, chariots marshalling in the shadowy meadows, companies of cavalry moving up through the heath with a jingle of metal plate, and the reserve archers swiftly stringing their crossbows.

The first objective having been taken, an infantry brigade continued its attack up the southern shoulder of the ridge, west of the stream, with the King-Emperor's Battalion still advancing immediately east of the water. Meanwhile, a company of knights pushed forward along the top of a low rise west of the stream. By their watchfulness, it appeared they expected strong opposition at the ruins of the old castle in the Namarran second line. This ruin, a few low piles of stones overgrown with brambles, sheltered many barbarian warriors. It lay immediately behind a wide ditch, screened by a narrow hedge.

The spriggans began to pinch Ashalind's arms. Impatiently she pushed them off.

'Budge now!' they creaked. 'Too long at the window she has spent.'

'I shall come soon! Soon!' said Ashalind, unable to wrench her gaze from the battlescape.

By now, dust and smoke from burning projectiles were making it impossible to see for any distance. Unable to take their bearings from landmarks, the chivalry pressed on, following the rising ground, keeping as close to the barrage as possible so as to be able to make the best use of their striking force whenever opposition was encountered. These tactics proved effective. On several occasions, at the instant the barrage lifted, the Empire's troops rushed to attack, causing the enemy to scatter in panic. Some hand-to-hand combat took place, the combatants hewing at each other with sword and axe, but generally the opposition was feeble.

By now the spriggan escorts were dancing up and down in a fury of panic, trying to stamp on Ashalind's toes. With no compunction she kicked out at them.

'Hurry! Hurry!' they squawked. 'Must answer the Summons or master will be angry!'

'One moment—just one moment more,' she cried.

The Royal Company of Archers with infantry, assailing the defences immediately north of the ruins, had been met by the discharge of two rapid-fire mangonels emplaced on the top of a stone buttress. This forced the troops in that area to ground, and the check seemed likely to become dangerous. For a few moments they watched the barrage of projectiles play on the place, and as it lifted and the enemy arrows commenced to whine, they charged. One of the Royal Archers, an outstanding markswoman, slew three of the shotmen attending the mangonels with swift arrows from her longbow. The rest fled. Assured of the idleness of the war-engines, the captain rushed forward with a lieutenant and the men nearest them. The moment they surged past the crumbling walls, panic seized the Namarran defenders. In a solid line, they abandoned their weapons and fled, many of them shot through by arrows as they ran, others being killed as they ran into the continuing catapult barrage.

The fight was over in a very short time, and two catapults captured. The Royal Archers stood among the ruins along the horizon and shot the rebels down, doing great execution and taking vengeance for crimes by land and sea. The Severnesse Eighth and the King-Emperor's Battalion bivouacked at their final objective, one hundred yards beyond the alignment of the old castle. Reserve divisions were brought up and it could be clearly perceived that it would not be long before the entire ridge was securely held, all objectives taken.

The Legions of Erith were advancing towards the High Plain. Morragan's raiders and brigands fell back before them, retreating without putting up much resistance. Of unseelie wights, oddly there was no sign.

Ashalind drew away from the window.

'Master will be wrathful! Depart instantly!' creaked the spriggans angrily, hefting their pikes in their grimy paws. Leaves fell into place, obscuring the view.

She whispered to Caitri, 'The Imperial troops have the advantage!'

As they left the embrasure, Ashalind looked back at the leaf curtain. Had it been but fancy? It seemed there had been a certain flash of gold upon the small finger of a hand, the ungauntleted hand of the Imperial Army's Supreme Commander . . .

The green marble courtyard gave onto a luxurious salon, carpeted in sombre yellow. It was filled with massive wooden furniture upholstered in tawny shades of marigold and spice. Here and there, fires burned in small, pierced braziers of bronze. Lizardlike saurians darted on bats' wings from fiery nests to mantelshelves, their lithe forms armoured in copper scales. The chairs were adorned with hideous feet, clawed and taloned. Grotesque faces grinned from chair backs. One of these moved its mouth and spoke. It was in fact attached to a shrivelled body which sat like a toadstool in a squat chair, its hands clutching the armrests.

'You thought yourself rid of me, eh, *erithbunden?*'

Yallery Brown grinned like a row of old candles. A skinny rat peered from among the withered dandelions growing in his hair. Ashalind heard Caitri's sudden indrawn breath. She herself flinched, but hurried on after a brief glance at the unsavoury wight.

'Make haste, make haste,' he jeered at their retreating backs. 'Yallery Brown will not be far behind!'

The yellow salon opened onto a gallery the colour of apricots. Underfoot, fallen leaves made a carpet. Sombre amber paper lined the walls, stamped with leaf motifs. The furnishings and hangings were of coppery velvet. From the crevices of the bracketed ceiling high overhead fell a continuous shower of leaves in Autumn hues: ochre, scarlet, saffron, umber. The spriggans pranced and capered in the rustling drifts, sniffing for larvae.

Stolidly the foundered Maghrain brothers marched on behind their charges. Here, time seemed drawn out, spun like thread from a sack of lint. As they walked, one day might have passed, or several—doubtless one of the tricks played by the bewitched fortress, but surprisingly, the two damsels experienced no discomfort or undue fear.

'The Lady of the Circle arrives!' a clear and lilting voice declared.

Two Faêran lords stood on either side of a door. Lofty was this portal, Winter-white, hinged and studded with lustrous metal. Indeed, it soared thrice the height of the Faêran knights. Ashalind tightened her grip on the folds of the cowl beneath her chin. Leaves whispered, swirling in gouts and streamers, lightly brushing her cheek. *Had Morragan's lords found the Gateway in Arcdur?* Doubtless not—they would not appear so equanimical had they discovered their way home. The eyes of Lord Iltarien rested upon Caitri, not unkindly. Leaning down, he laid his hand lightly upon her head.

'Accompanied by her pet nightingale,' he added to his previous announcement. Stepping back, he said, 'Enter!'

The white door swung open.

A blast of icy air assaulted Ashalind and Caitri, and went hunting after the swirling leaves. The mortals walked forward into a parlour wherein miniscule motes drifted like swans' down.

A snowy ballroom.

It seemed Winter dwelled here. Icicles depended from chandeliers, where slender tapers burned with a glacial flame. Snow sifted like Sugar-dust across the floor and piled up in banks against the legs of couches and sideboards, the walls of shimmering ice. Star patterns frosted mirrors. Rime edged everything with silver stitchery. Through this freezing haze, the shapes of furnishings loomed indistinct. Slowly the mortal girls wandered into the mist.

The Prince's bard appeared.

'Someone left the window open,' commented Ashalind.

Ergaiorn laughed. With a movement so swift it might have been imagined, he cast something from his hand. Gratingly, like the rim of an iron wheel on gravel, a sphere of crystal came rolling along the floor. It ground to a halt in front of Ashalind. Her gaze was drawn and clinched into its limpid heart, where an image developed.

'Behold!' said Ergaiorn. 'The Legions of Erith are come to Evernight.'

Below gaunt turrets, the outer walls of Annath Gothallamor dropped, sheer and vertical, to join the folded and crevassed skirts of Black Crag. A narrow road wound down to the open flat of the High Plain which spread out to form a circle half a mile in radius. Gibbous rocks covered this tableland—curious, lumpy stones in odd shapes and sizes, some of which seemed to roll of their own accord, or to suddenly sprout skinny limbs, or to dissemble into shadows between equally queer-shaped bushes and stunted trees racked by the wind. The High Plain teemed with wights.

Visible beyond the rim of the plateau lay a vast sea of winking lights: the campfires of the five armies of the Empire.

'See the Legions of Erith,' said Ergaiorn as Ashalind contemplated the crystal's moving pictures, 'encamped some small distance from the foot of the escarpment. They have defeated the mortal brigands of Namarre—all are taken prisoner or slain or fled. Far have the Legions advanced, but they are mistaken if they believe victory is within their grasp, for although the wights of eldritch have harried and harassed them, they have not as yet mounted any genuine adversity. Having beguiled the Legions with a hollow simulation of battle, giving ground before them to lead them on, now the Unseelie Host is ready for encounters more devastating. Should eldritch powers in earnest be brought to bear, mortals shall find themselves sore oppressed. And though the men of Erith might zealously use the tight-sprung limbs of their battery against these saucy foes, they shall fling missiles in vain, for gramarye eludes brute force and passes it by, to smite with stealth from the flank most unguarded, using the very frailties of men to great advantage.'

Ashalind dragged her gaze from the jewel's heart. In the Winter room she stood at Caitri's side, and despite the snow her blood ran warm and rosy. Ergaiorn's hand enclosed the crystal sphere. The Leantainn Pipes hung at his side, ebony wood mounted in silver.

'What frailties?' she demanded of him. 'Hearts that rule our heads? Fear of the dark? These are not *frailties*. Merriment lacking in deep joy, passion that knows no true love—those are true frailties, and they belong not to *my* race!' She stepped closer to the Bard, driven to boldness by sorrow and anger. 'Have you a conscience, Ergaiorn? You are forsworn! You and all of Morragan's gallants are forsworn! By opposing Angavar, you have broken your oath of fealty to your sovereign.'

Coolly he replied, 'Only because thou art favoured of the Fithiach do I have reason enough to justify the deeds of Faêran knights to thee, *erithbunden* maid, and because of the beauty of thy face. Ephemeral beauty remains ever a cause for leniency among us. 'Tis true, all Faêran lords swore never to take arms against our High King. This vow we keep intact. We swore never to succour his enemies. This vow also remains virgin. No promise was made to hinder his enemies and we hinder them not. Wights may plague the human race as they have done for millennia—what is it to us?'

'Then you contrive at semantics,' cried Caitri, 'like the lawyers of Erith, to thwart and pervert the very purpose of the contract!'

'Thy tongue rattles overloose in thy head, sweetness,' warned the bard with a cold smile. 'Beware lest it grow so long as to trip thee and make thee fall. The Legions of the Empire outnumbered the defeated barbarians,' he continued, tossing the translucent orb from hand to hand and spinning it on his fingertip, 'naturally. They have advanced into Evernight. At Plain's Edge the vanguard is forced to halt. At that place they are vulnerable to attacks launched from the plateau above, from secret forests on either flank and from Fridean delvings underground. Be not mistaken, the battle plan has been drawn. The strategy of the Fithiach is certain. When the Imperial forces threaten Annath Gothallamor they shall find themselves at the mercy of the Raven. With but a simple gesture, how easily the Fithiach might strike them down.'

Carelessly, he threw the ball into the air and let it fall. With a harsh clangour that forced a squeal from Caitri, it smashed to brittle diamonds on the floor.

'But the men of the Empire have a protector,' Ashalind challenged tremulously.

'Dost thou believe that Royalty would use gramarye against Royalty? That Angavar would use it to oppose his brother? True, the High King and the Crown Prince have drawn lightswords against each other before the Gate at the Hour of Closing, but no more than that.' His voice roughened. 'Should the Royal brethren unleash upon one another the fullness of their powers, why, then the forces of nature would be waked to a struggle which must shake the very roots of the mountains, and cause the seas to boil and overbrim. They would darken the skies with wild storms to lash the cities of men with terrible winds and cast down living things with utmost violence. Nay—lords of the Realm have no desire to be the destroyers of Erith. Full well do we love the land of mortals despite its several shortcomings and uncouth inhabitants.'

'Uncouth!' cried Caitri, her vexation again breaking its bonds. 'How can you so miscall mortalkind? Is it couth to keep us here against our will?'

'The nightingale's throat has lost its sweetness,' said a masculine voice.

A darker figure shaped itself out of the pastel haze, moving with the gracefulness of vitality, emerging and sharpening into the form of a tall warrior, staggeringly handsome. He was clad in the close-fitting buckled leather harness usually worn beneath armour. At his back, nebulous others seethed and waited.

Here stood Prince Morragan, of that there could be no doubt. Snowflakes did not dare to touch him, or maybe they melted if they did.

The mortals curtsied low, fixing their gaze on the floor, for there was that about the Prince which hurt their eyes when they tried to look directly at him. Words rose like dust in Ashalind's throat, stuck there and disintegrated. Inside the icy shell of her flesh she burned like a cresset.

'Fly away,' said the Prince. At the caress of his hand, a bird flew up from where Caitri had been standing. It circled once, twice, thrice, then, with a piercing cry, winged its way towards a high, dim window and disappeared.

Aghast, Ashalind stared into the swirl and mist.

'No! 'Tis too cruel. What will become of her?'

Without replying, Morragan stripped the cowl from Ashalind's head. Snowflakes nipped and brushed her ears, the smooth white dome of her skull, her bare neck. She stood silent while he studied her intently. His features remained without expression, betraying no sign of any passion. Presently, at his signal, his cupbearer came forward. After pouring some wine, he presented the goblet to the Prince with a bow.

'Drink.' Uttering this command, Morragan held the rim to Ashalind's mouth with his own hand. She could not help but sip and swallow.

Instantly, the liquid raced through her blood, like molten gold from a crucible. This was not like any wine she had known. It drove through her veins, branching and rebranching as wildfire races along the limbs of a tree to its outermost extremities. She choked, spluttered, caught her breath, and now the wine's intolerable potency rushed into her fingertips, her toes; it fountained upward into her skull and filled it, pushed through the scalp into the roots of the hair and exploded there with a great lifting and a bursting forth. The blood roared in her temples. She squeezed shut her eyes, tottered and fell, was caught by lightning and let down, crumpled, to the floor.

Her lids lifted.

Ashalind kneeled within an arbour curtained with gold filaments, through which streamed primrose light. Gold rained down past her shoulders and waist to her knees, in a falaise of hair thicker and more luxuriant then ever before. With her hands she parted the curtains and shook back the heavy tresses, opening her view.

The snow had ceased to fall in the elegant, white room.

With a look which might have been anger and tenderness mingled, Morragan spoke her name.

'Recall the Geata Poeg na Déanainn,' said he, 'or consider thyself the destroyer of the Legions.'

Rising to her feet Ashalind recalled instead, something Tully had once told her.

'For the Fair Ones to take arms against mortals, there is no honour in that.'

'You would not use your power to smite mortal men, who are without gramarye with which to defend themselves,' she said, rallying her resources. 'You are more chivalrous than that, sir. Your threats are merely implications.'

'In sooth I would not treat them so, *lhiannan*, nor would my knights. Howbeit, there are many here who joy in bloody work amongst mortalkind and would fain be hard at it. With one recollection canst thou restrain them.'

'Should you set all the wights of unseelie upon the men of Erith, still Angavar would force them back!'

Thorn's true name tasted strange on her tongue.

'Shouldst thou desire to make a test of it?' mocked Thorn's brother.

Visions of large-scale slaughter unfurled across Ashalind's mind. At once she could no longer meet the challenging gaze of the Prince, whose piercing grey eyes seemed to penetrate her very thoughts, almost to unlock that final memory. Averting her face she let the new-sprung hair swing across for concealment. After a moment she said, 'No. Let me search for the Gate once more. I will try to find it.'

Another mineral bubble was placed into her hands, cool and hard. Distantly, Ashalind wondered at the fact that her blood ran warm, even in the wintry room. Then the oracular pearl seized her concentration.

Scarcely had the search begun when it was interrupted. The new-budded images of Arcdur clouded. She looked up. A messenger had been conducted into the room and was bowing on one knee at the Prince's feet.

He was a mortal warrior, a doughty Dainnan captain—none other than Sir Tor of the Fifth Thriesnun. Leather armour covered him and his buckles were of bronze. He bore no iron—as an emissary he was bound to come unarmed and unshielded to the stronghold of the enemy. Beneath his walnut-brown beard, his visage was the colour of ashes. No comely man was he, yet she looked long and lovingly upon him, as the first mortal—other than Caitri, Viviana and the supernaturally preserved Maghrain brothers—she had seen since leaving Appleton Thorn.

'Disgorge thy tidings,' languorously bade the Raven Prince.

'Your Highness, I bring word from the King-Emperor.'

Immediately, a dullness clung about Ashalind's head as if wadding had been applied to her ears. The Dainnan captain spoke, yet his words were muffled, unclear, as though spoken under water. When he ceased, Prince Morragan's voice cut through the wadding like a glaive.

'Bold mortal, to enter these walls. Brave servant of Angavar, thy false sovereign. Hasten not to return to him, for other harbingers shall expedite my answer forthwith.' A net of fire, the cold hue of lightning, rippled over the Prince and dispersed. 'Get thee hence, lout, get from my sight.'

With that, the frozen walls clarified to transparency. From high in the battlements a chilling cry came sliding like a steel rasp grating ice. Sir Tor, backing away, shuddered and grabbed a rooster tilhal at his breast.

A storm of flapping ashes swept down from above, with the clamour of mad dogs. The Wild Hunt, led by Huon the Antlered One, catapulted forth from Annath Gothallamor like a swift thundercloud. But the Hunt was not unaccompanied. Like distorted reflections in an ill-made mirror, the Nightmare Princes of the Unseelie Attriod rode with them—the Each Uisge mailed in his cold malignancy; Gull, Chieftain of Spriggans, the pitiless Cearb, the Killing One who had caused the cave-in at the mines of Huntingtowers, Cuachag, the most terrible of fuaths; and the Athach, apotheosis of shape-shifters.

Westwards the mounted Host sped, until they reached the winking fires of the encampment. Blacker than the night sky, smoke against the stars, the Unseelie Host swirled and spiralled, swooped down on the Legions of Erith. And although the attack was taking place at least a mile off, it seemed to Ashalind that she heard the blood-baying of hounds, the snap of jaws, the twang of bowstrings, the whirr and smack of arrows and the clash of blades, the sizzle of sparks as swords smote armour, the yelling of men, the shrilling of horses, the hideous clangour of riven metal, the long, desperate pumping of mortal blood. Her heart was bursting with terror.

'I pray thee, put an end to this slaughter,' she begged, but she might as well have pleaded with a stone. Morragan turned his shoulder and paid her no heed. He remained watching the scene of the attack, the elegant fingers of his right hand resting upon the jewelled pommel of his sword. The Raven Prince was not to be approached.

A dirty ice-carving in a corner now proved quick. Thin cracks zigzagged across its surface. Sloughing jagged fragments, Yallery Brown took to capering hideously, his elbows and knees akimbo, delighting at the devastation wreaked on the men of Erith, which was clearly visible from the tower.

The unseelie creatures that had been assembled on the Plain now flooded down towards the encampment. Yet the battle was not one-sided, for the Lords of the Royal Attriod were everywhere, protected by powerful tilhals bestowed on them by their sovereign. Even Thomas Rhymer, the gentle Bard, rode with the light of battle-lust shining from his eyes. It drove him on. Perhaps he was shielded by some gramarye lent by the High King of the Faêran. Indeed, an aura surrounded the seven chosen comrades of Angavar; a soft, quivering light which gave them the appearance of warriors from ancient sagas, cast in the mould of the Faêran, and it might have been by this power they were able to withstand the onslaught of the dire and unseelie manifestations which sought their heart's blood.

The page boy from Caermelor Palace who had once been a cabin boy was now a standard-bearer. He hoisted high the King-

Emperor's oriflamme, tied to a lance. Of bright red samite, with three tails and with gold silk tassels between, the flag was as conspicuous as befitted a rallying point in the confusion of combat. From the boy's open mouth issued the battle cry of the King-Emperor's Battalion. Tall black figures against the flames, men strove against the forces of the uncanny with blows that rang by stone and wood.

Overhead the Host soared and dived, eluding the ponderous Windships with their aerial manoeuvres, outracing the Stormriders as the falcon overtakes the blackbird. Where Cuachag and the Cearb stooped, men fell. Where Gull and the Athach plunged, tents collapsed and went up in flames. The Each Uisge galloped in horse-form through the encampment, cutting a trail of blood and slaughter.

Ever at the head of the airborne fray charged the rider with the terrible branches rooted in the bone of his skull: Huon the Hunter, his longbow bent in his brawny arms. He was an engine of slaughter, continually drawing and firing with uncanny accuracy, until a rider like a comet flew against him and Huon plummeted from the skies, the great racks of his antlers hacked from his severed head by the sword in the left hand of Angavar. For it was indeed Angavar who fought in the thick of the engagement. Power and assurance declared themselves in his every movement.

Then, from far away, arose the clarion call of a Faêran horn. In Annath Gothallamor, an infinitesimal ripple murmured among the audience of Faêran chivalry and courtiers. They appeared instantly charged with expectation, or perhaps amazement. They leaned towards the source of the call, strained towards it, poised, riveted.

Faint in the southwest a fragile membrane of light opened and began to grow, and it was like the pellucid light of dawn, where dawn could never be. Described by its radiance, a company of riders. Tiny brilliants glittered from their arms and armour. Their trumpets sang out a paean of challenge. Pale wings of radiance streamed from their hair.

'The Awakened!' cried a voice Ashalind knew as her own, and it seemed that a multitude of other voices cried out simultaneously.

The watchers stirred at the sight.

The approaching riders were tall and terrible, beautiful. Their swords flamed and spangled, their spears glistened. Their hair was a total eclipse woven with stars.

Against the Unseelie Host rode the Faêran knights of Angavar, newly roused from their slumber beneath Eagle's Howe. In the formation of a spearhead, the avengers rammed through the black helix, broke it apart, scattered the unseelie hunters, hewed them out of the skies with bright Faêran blades. The Unseelie Attriod and those eldritch horsemen who escaped the shock assault fled in disarray through the sky, while on the ground below, the unseelie flood retreated into the forest, or sank beneath pools or rocky crevices underneath the ground, vanishing from sight. Dimly, there arose across the Plain a mighty cheering from the throats of thousands of men.

Ashalind's joy at this turn of events was short-lived.

The stirring within the fortress had become tumult. At a word from their Prince, Morragan's knights armed themselves and sprang upon their fretting horses, eager for action. Some feral wind, spawned in gramarye, raged in gusts through the Winter chamber. It shattered the ice walls, darkening their translucency, transmuting them to ruined stone. Through crumbling rifts the Faêran chivalry launched their steeds, leaped out and away from the fortress.

Yet already the Knights of Eagle's Howe were careering towards the plateau. Having vanquished the Hunt, they drove its remnants before them. Over the rim of the High Plain they came flying, at the same moment as Morragan's retinue descended from the heights. Unseelie things scattered from beneath the hooves of the Faêran horses while they landed on the Plain in faultless formation. The two companies reined in, wheeled and surveyed one another without engaging. They held their long lances upright, starlight glinting off the points as it glittered off their harnesses of gold. The streamers decorating these shafts fluttered out horizontally over the nodding plumage of the knights' helmets, the gently blowing lambrequins of gold and silver tissue attached to the backs of their helms, mantling their shoulders.

In this manner they poised, motionless.

Each party regarded the other across a wide strip of gibbous rock from which scribbled shapes vanished like the sea at low tide. Below the Plain, the Legions ranged across the lowlands of Darke roared and clashed their weapons on their shields, eager to advance and seek vengeance, though their commanders held them now in check. Around Annath Gothallamor, rearward of Morragan's knights, unseelie wights moved within a pitchy darkness they had gathered about themselves like veils of black muslin, from which issued howls and laughter, screams and sobbing, sudden frenzied knockings and threatening silences; an orchestration realised from fevered dreams. Among Prince Morragan's company, his knights took precedence, while the five who remained of the Unseelie Attriod must fall back into the shadows, mingling with their own kind.

Macabre slouched the shadows, luminous gleamed the highlights on the rocky Plain beneath the vigilance of the stars. Faêran armour—etched with running vines, strapwork arabesques and double-knots—shimmered with an ethereal sheen. Its gold was tinged with cobalt amongst the knights of the Crown Prince, while those who surrounded the High King glinted with a tint of alizarin, as though sunset flowed in fluid lines of flame over their war-harness.

For he was there at their head, of course—Angavar, mounted upon winged Hrimscathr, with the sword Arcturus now scabbarded at his side, starlight glancing off its damasked quillons. He wore no helm. The dark blaze of his hair framed the sculpted cheekbones, the eyes as keen as swords, the unsmiling mouth. The Royal Attriod flanked him, armoured cap-a-pie, their horses in full bard.

Morragan, Fithiach of Carnconnor, looked down from the towers of the fortress upon those who stood forward in challenge and those who awaited his command. He looked upon the face of Angavar, his brother, sovereign, rival.

'Iltarien,' he said to one of the three Faêran lords who had remained at his side, 'go thou down to the Plain and speak on my behalf. When my brother issues his challenge, tell him this.' And he gave Lord Iltarien a message in the language of the Faêran.

That tongue was unknown to Ashalind and yet familiar in some deep and inexplicable way, as the song of birds falls upon mortal ears and is almost understood, as the peal of bells or the roar of the ocean calls to humankind. When Morragan ceased to speak she was left with no knowledge of his words, but a lilting melody which danced round and round in her head.

'Victory is almost within my grasp,' murmured the Prince as Iltarien's horse launched itself from the stonework. 'Yet a premonition assails my thought. To go down to the Plain is to go to meet my doom. There is one who shall betray me—shall it be thee?'

'Master,' said a weaselly voice, 'should the *erithbunden* prove perfidious—'

'Yallery Brown, this is a daughter of mortalkind. How canst thou expect other than treachery? A daughter of Men, no less . . . but one who might have been more.'

Morragan bent his head towards Ashalind.

Every particle of her lightened and drifted apart until she became part of the plenum, and the plenum invaded her existence, and her blood flowed with the currents of rivers, and the ocean surged in her skull, whose tides were the slow heartbeat of the moon. Long green leaves streamed from her scalp and sap rose in her veins with the Spring, and a soft wind like dark hair swept across an unexplored landscape. She was lifted up to a region where stars shone out from behind the panes of her eyes, and somewhere within, the deep fires of the sun ran molten.

The Raven Prince had brushed his mouth against hers.

'Wight,' he said presently to Yallery Brown, 'if thou shouldst harm so much as a hair of this maiden's head, I swear I shall unseam thee from nave to chaps.'

The Prince's Faêran breath was as sweet as cloves.

Far below, Iltarien's steed came to land among the chivalry of Raven's Howe, and Angavar held converse with him. Clearly, Angavar challenged Morragan's tenure of the High Plain and the fortress, and demanded something more besides. Grim-faced and proud, Lord Iltarien delivered the reply his Prince had conceived with foresight, for who should foretell another's motives better than his twin? There could be no doubt of the tone and intent of that reply. Challenge was met with challenge. Nothing was conceded; no ground was given, no hope of reconciliation.

Angavar's voice rang out strongly in the common tongue, for all to hear.

'Then, my brother, since there is to be no accord between us,' he cried, 'thou must needs face me in battle.'

With that, he ordered his own Royal Attriod to ride back through the lines of his loyal knights and down the ramps over the rim to fall in with the Legions below, leading and defending them against the forces of Unseelie.

But upon the Plain, trumpets sounded. The lances of the foremost ranks of both companies of Faêran chivalry, which had been pointing to the black and zodiacal sky, were now lowered to the horizontal. The knights couched the butts of the weapons in the lance rests beneath their armpits. In the middle ranks, swords slid from scabbards with a long ringing rasp of thirsty steel. War-horns sounded a second signal, and both sides charged at full gallop. With a terrible roar they met like thundering ocean breakers, and the shock of that collision caused the ground to tremble to its uttermost foundations.

As the Faêran knights engaged, down in the lowlands Attriod rose against Attriod, and a thick mist poured out of the forest and from every well and waterway, to twine about the struggling Legions. Through these smokes, fell shapes could be glimpsed issuing from among the trees, from pools and subterranean clefts, and there could be no doubt of their murderous intent. Yet eldritch manifestations of another kind moved also in their midst, defending the soldiers of Erith. Never visible to a direct stare, they could only be seen from the edge of one's eye—urisks, and fierce men with silky grey hair wielding tridents, black dogs as large as foals, stunted fellows hefting pickaxes, cowled figures upholding lanterns, and other beings too elusive to perceive at all.

Faêran blades rose and fell, a-glitter with stars. The conflict appeared to Ashalind a milling chaos, a jostling, seething dance of death and destruction. She, transfixed in disbelief, could only watch from the ruined tower, unable to deflect her gaze.

Angavar did not join his knights in their battle. Instead, he galloped through the ranks of the knights of Morragan, ignoring them, as though they had never taken part against him. In amazement, they fell back at either flank without offering resistance. Splendid he rode in vengeful majesty, and the chivalry of Raven's Howe were reminded afresh that he was indeed their King, that they themselves were treasoners.

On powerful pinions the eotaur Hrimscathr bore Angavar to the lowlands, where he fought beside the Royal Attriod, opposing their malevolent counterparts, defending the mortal Legions. The great Cuachag fell beneath the blade of Arcturus, and the Athach also was overthrown, but Octarus Ogier was toppled from his eotaur by Gull, mightiest of spriggans. He fell among the blazing tents, to be ripped limb from limb by the Each Uisge, while the Cearb impaled bold John Drumdunach through the heart before Angavar could hew his way through the melee to aid his comrades. When this happened, it was clear that Angavar's wrath reached greater heights and he began to smite the incarnations of unseelie right and left with a terrible vengeance. The clear light of Arcturus became dimmed with lurid blood.

High in the blasted keep of Annath Gothallamor where ivy sprawled over the corroded stones and lilies sprang within crevices, a Faêran stallion pranced agitatedly, scraping the floor with his silver forehooves, throwing up his long head. His master's eyes rested thoughtfully upon Ashalind. He was armoured now, she noted dully, and some steady purpose resided in his glance.

She was angry with herself for being unable to deny his Faeran power, even though she was aware that it would be useless for any mortal to try to resist. It hurt her pride to know that although she might rant and struggle, it would do her no good. What little dignity remained, she clutched to her like the remnant of a torn cloak. She did not and would not protest, knowing that to do so would not only be futile, it would bring humiliation. Thus she appeared compliant, while beneath the facade her passions seethed.

The Prince lifted her up. He placed her sideways on his horse's back and sprang up behind her. They travelled not through the air, but clattering down the tower stairs, out through the main gates of Annath Gothallamor, to descend the road which twisted itself about Black Crag. At their backs rode Morragan's cup-bearer, his bard and the ladies of his court. A multitude of wights followed in the wake of the Faêran.

The Crown Prince was going to parley with his brother.

Through her indignation, and the delirium induced by the nearness of Morragan's Faêran vigour, and the dizziness brought on by his every incidental touch, Ashalind alternated between dread and desire for the fast-approaching rendezvous with Angavar-Thorn. The imminence of the meeting thrilled her. She longed to see him again, but to what measure he might scorn her was difficult to reckon. His slightest revulsion would be too much to bear.

'And how dost thou like riding upon my Faêran steed?' murmured Morragan at Ashalind's ear.

The uncharacteristic posing of the question struck a warning note. Ashalind made to reply but a coin of lead weighed upon her tongue and she could not lift it. Morragan laughed. She felt the thrum of his laughter through her shoulder.

'Didst thou think I kissed thee for love?' he said. 'Vain and foolish damsel. Alas, that thine expectations are dashed.'

Outrage and despair laid hold of Ashalind. With his kiss, he had rendered her mute. Her one fragile thread of hope had depended on the use of that intrinsically mortal weapon—the lying tongue. Once more she had been deprived of speech, and for an instant there came on her an irrational dread that all the other injuries would befall her again, and she would become mis-shapen, abandoned, reviled and amnesiac. Somehow, the foresight of Morragan must have warned him of her intentions— *There is one who shall betray me—shall it be thee?* For in truth, she had intended to cry out and betray him, if she could, and now that gate was closed.

Yet, even while she rode with the Prince down Black Crag, an alternative aspiration born of desperation took form, feebly, and began to grow.

As Morragan and his entourage approached the battlefield a

great shout went up from the Faêran chivalry, and the two companies disengaged, drawing apart. Faêran chargers wheeled to a halt
and a stillness spread from them like ripples in a tarn. All across the
lowlands the fighting paused, as unhuman things suspended their
quest for mortal blood. Drawn by some elemental intuition, the soldiers of Erith turned their heads towards the High Plain.

The Eagle and the Raven converged.

A short distance apart, all riders dismounted; however,
Morragan kept hold of his captive, encircling her wrist lightly with
his fingers. Seeing Thorn again triggered in Ashalind a rush of
excitement. Warriors made of flame and shadow, tall heroes out
of legend, these Royal brothers who now faced one another in bitter feud were both handsome enough to stop the heart and take
the breath away. Dangerous they looked, and too beautiful to
comprehend.

This was the first time Ashalind had set eyes on Thorn without the screens of assumed personae, the first time he had beheld
her stripped of all pretence. No reproach stained his glance, no
bitterness that she had not confided her secret to him. He looked
upon her with such fervent intensity and sorrow, it came to her
that if it were possible for the Faêran to love deeply, then such a
passion she was perceiving in his eyes. At that she marvelled, and
was overcome with joy so intense it was torment. And she felt
humbled, to think that she had doubted him so undeservedly and
was chastened by understanding, at last, perhaps too late.

Angavar-Thorn did not smile at her, nor, after his first brief
flicker of appraisal in which so much had been conveyed, did he
look at her again. He seemed to turn his full attention to
Morragan, dismissing Ashalind from further consideration. She
knew him well enough to be aware that what appeared to interest him least actually intrigued him most—that his ostensible
carelessness cloaked his prime focus. He was, in fact, conscious of
her every movement.

'I have the key in my grasp,' said Morragan coolly, without
preamble.

Angavar replied, and the clear tone of his voice was gentle,
like a calm ocean concealing lethal undercurrents.

'No key, but a damsel. Hadst thou the key, thou wouldst now be standing upon other shores.'

'She *is* the key, as thou know'st,' returned Morragan, 'knowing too late. I might slay or petrify her with a thought, before thou couldst prevent it.'

'An thou dost so, where is thy key?'

'An thou dost act against me, what care I if the key is destroyed, as long as thou art denied access to the Realm? What care I for exile if it means thine exile too?' The Prince's smile was insulting.

Ashalind wanted to say to Angavar-Thorn, 'He would not do it, he would not hurt me,' but her tongue was a wooden stick in her mouth and her wrist burned where Morragan's fingers encircled it.

Angavar said, 'Thou wouldst not harm this *caileag*. Thou dost forget, I wist thy humours.'

'Not I,' said Morragan. 'Others might.' Furtively, Yallery Brown, who had sidled close, fidgeted.

'At thy bidding only,' parried Angavar evenly.

'Shalt thou put me to the test?' inquired his brother.

Silence descended—a hot, tense silence of barely leashed fury. The two Faêran lords held each other's gaze without flinching, as though an iron girder joined them, eye to eye. So terrible was that regard that no mortal could stand to look at them, and they must turn their heads away.

'An she dies at thy command, I shall never rest until thy heart is riven by my blade,' said Angavar in bizarre echo of his brother's earlier words. 'I swear it.'

'How tedious, to be without rest for eternity.'

Another silence, more imminently dangerous than the first.

'Thus we return to the beginning,' Morragan remarked. 'Stalemate.'

'There is no gain to be had in this parley,' said Angavar, harshly now, 'or in full-scale battle. Our knights are equally matched. I might vanquish thine unseelie hordes single-handed. Further slaughter is without purpose. Thou and I shall meet in single combat, *without use of gramarye,* to decide the outcome.'

'We shall cross swords if thou dost like it,' answered Morragan offhandedly, 'at another time. For the nonce, I have something thou dost want. If thou carest aught for it, swear to lay down thy weapons.'

Angavar spoke in a voice of steel. 'Thou hast tarried long in thy dark keep, *mi fithiach*. Thou hast been missing the action.'

'Better action was to be found in the fortress, brother,' said Morragan provokingly, 'since the company *there* was pleasant. Fain would my weapon remain oft in the sheath, it filled that receptacle so well.'

From some abyss beyond time blasted a frost-bitten wind. The gusts lifted the long hair of the High King in streamers that flowed from his brow like the rays of a black sun. Now softly spoke Angavar, and perilously.

'Is the sword at thy side so rare that you are loath to notch it, Crow-Lord? They say the coward's blade never needs reforging.'

Morragan's hand jumped to his sword belt.

'He who fights carrying no shield is called a swordsman of valour,' continued Angavar, throwing a swift glance towards Ashalind. 'He who shields himself behind a woman deserves a worse name.'

At that, Morragan thrust Ashalind aside and Lord Iltarien caught her. There came the sweeping rasp of a crystalline *zing!* as sweet and poignant as morning bells. The Raven Prince had drawn his sword, Durandel. Arcturus was already in the grip of Angavar.

Angavar's lords started forward to wrest Ashalind from the grasp of her guard.

'Stay!' Iltarien roared at them. 'It is to be *single* combat. Do not try to take her!'

The Faêran King weighed his sword deliberately.

'Now,' he said to his rival, 'feel the wrath of the left hand of Angavar.'

All of Erith was centred around the vortex of the storm's eye. From every corner of the known lands, beings both mortal and immortal grew still and looked towards Namarre.

In the forests, mortal woodcutters, well guarded by charms, stood beside trees part-hewn, with their axes hanging limply in their hands and dusty sweat trickling unheeded from their brows—they knew not why. From verdant waterways the asrai water-maidens lifted their lovely forms, ivory draped with green silk, with innocent, passionless gazes fixed upon the distance. By village ponds, goose-girls forgot to shepherd their wayward flocks. Their long whip-sticks of willow dragged on the ground, but the geese had given up their honking. They grew tranquilly vigilant, craning their long necks towards the horizon.

Under Rosedale, eldritch spinning wheels lost momentum and ran down. The spinners raised their large heads from their work; the thread ceased to run through their knobbed fingers. Beneath Doundelding, all sounds of industry were interrupted. Not a pick-axe, not a hammer smote another blow; not a wheel performed another revolution. Out in the oceans, the wild seal folk emerged to sit upon rocky isles, hearkening to the north wind.

In Stormrider stables, winged horses quit their whickering and stamping. Not a pinion bustled, not a stirrup jingled. Blacksmiths stood idle at their forges. Farmers ceased their toil in the fields. Wizards left off supervising esoteric experiments and hiring out their astute observations. On Windships and Seaships, captains found themselves giving orders to slacken the sheets and lose the wind. Sails flapped as slack as empty bellies, until the wind tapered off too and they dangled limply.

In the abodes of Men, the hearth-fires died down as if they crouched to listen. Where rain had been falling the clouds dried up, withholding their bounty. The leaves of yew and myrtle, pine and lime hung poised as though splintered from precious stones. On walls of dominite stone, tiny lizards stopped their scurrying and became statues of miniature dragons, or tiny, jewelled brooches. The ocean itself waxed calm and slow, with the watchful, awful serenity of controlled violence.

Amber lions woke watchfully in the tawny ruins of Avlantian cities where red leaves scraped cracked pavements. In Finvarna, the herds of giant elk browsing on the grasslands swung up their heavy heads, their gigantic racks of antlers upholding a racing sky.

In Rimany, the snow bears paused like carvings upon icicle-draped cliffs. Spiders hung transfixed upon the lace wheels of their webs in the spidersilk farms of Severnesse.

Flocks of swallows gathered in the skies of Erith, swooping to perch amongst the topmost boughs and sway there, beaks closed, heads cocked to one side. In the wide, rolling lands beneath a peppercorn tree, there existed a horse-shadow the colour of translucent quartz. The *cuinocco* jerked its finely made head, flourishing the glistering icicle jutting from its brow, and looked to the north.

Sheep and cattle stood immobile in the meadows, as though embroidered on green baize. Fish hovered in deep caverns of indigo gloom. Heartless mosquito-queens folded tenuous wings about their wasp-sting forms. Flies swarming above the marsh-lands settled like iridescent beads on slender stems of water-grasses. Silent, Erith held its breath.

And no birds sang.

Perhaps even in Faêrie they felt it, even behind closed Gates—this conflict between the mightiest of Faêran lords.

Ruby and sapphire the Faêran broadswords flashed upon the High Plain, and never was such swordsmanship seen in Erith, before or since. So swift was every parry, thrust and riposte, that mortal eyes could not follow—could only make out a brilliant, glittering star-burst, like crystals shattering repeatedly—the awesome, bright shafts of the light-swords clashing together in a wicked storm of sparks like sharp flames of ice, like jagged shards of cobalt and copper. And somewhere in the core of this icy blaze, glimpsed or imagined, two terrible warriors met in a deadly dance of unimaginable precision, speed, strength and timing. Thunder shook the roots of the mountains of Namarre. Lightning climbed, aghast, the skies of Darke.

The onlookers had pulled well back from the site of the duel, giving the combatants a wide berth, careful not to step within range. Such virulent sparks could burn a tiny hole right through flesh and bone, through bone and sinew, through the very essence of being, drilling through body and spirit a keyhole or porthole to look out upon the long, grey desert of annihilation.

In a wide circle the mounted knights of Eagle's Howe and

Raven's Howe viewed the struggle, intent, their Faêran vision missing nothing. The survivors of both Attriods watched also, despite their wounds, and so did many men-at-arms of the Legions who had ascended the cliffs of the Plain. Dainnan warriors and Stormriders were there, and wights both malign and benign, including scrawls of spriggans, sprawls of hobyahs and the mad goblin Red Cap with a dead, red rooster swinging from his belt.

Yallery Brown was close by, and Withiue and Tully, holding the mane of Tighnacomaire. The goblin Snafu was there, and the enchanted brothers Maghrain, and Young Vallentyne with brother ganconers, Romeus and Childe Launcelyn, and other wights too numerous to mention.

The eyes of all the Faêran were dark with pain.

'Has it come to this?' muttered Lord Iltarien. 'That the best among us, the jewels of the Realm should take up arms against each other? Cursed was the day I followed the Fithiach, yet I could not do otherwise, for I hold him dearer than a brother and my loyalty cannot swerve.'

'Thus we continue to support him,' murmured Lord Ergaiorn, 'out of fierce comradeship, and honour, and perversity, and beloved folly.'

As they watched, it became apparent that Angavar and Morragan were well matched, for neither was gaining the upper hand. But Tamlain Conmor cried out, 'Angavar King is already weary from battle. Morragan is fresh from the fortress. There is no justice in the Prince's advantage!'

At his words, roars of agreement and disagreement broke out on both sides, but no one could gainsay him, and Ashalind, standing untouched but helpless at Iltarien's side, felt the chill of fear. The blue sword flashed so swift, so keen, every stroke a masterstroke.

Abruptly, all argument ceased, for the two masters of land and sky and sea and fire had drawn apart. Throwing off their armour by means of gramarye, they stood challenge now in shirtsleeves and full-length breeches. For a time they stood, gasping, flinging back their long hair which was wet with the sweet sweat of their exertion yet fragrant as pine. It was a respite from their mighty striving, mutually admitted. Appraisingly they regarded one another, readiness to retaliate against sudden attack written in the tense lines of their stance. Morragan spoke fleeringly to Angavar in the language of the Strangers. Angavar replied in kind.

Apparently by chance, Angavar had positioned himself facing Ashalind, to whom Morragan must necessarily turn his back to keep up his guard. In full view of Angavar, Ashalind's hands gestured silently.

Catching her eye, he nodded, almost invisibly.

Many of those who looked on realised that some communication had passed between the two, but what it had conveyed they could not fathom.

'False bitch!' squalled Yallery Brown springing at Ashalind, but Lord Iltarien repulsed the wight. Before Morragan could glance back over his shoulder Angavar had lunged at him, uttering a wordless cry from deep in his throat, and with an answering roar from Morragan, the duel began anew.

'What hast thou done, *erithbunden?*' Iltarien cried, but Ashalind, her tongue paralysed by the gramarye of Morragan, could only shake her head.

Then, penetrating the profound rumblings of thunder by virtue of contrast, there came a tintinnabulation as of sequins falling gently upon bells of glass. It had been approaching for some while before the playful breeze started up, darting between the storm gusts generated by the Faêran combat to snatch at cloaks and hems, to snip at hair, to stir the manes and tails of horses.

The High Plain darkened further, and broke out in sudden, pricking lights.

Pincushion stars glowed incandescent, fanned by the bellows of the unexpected shang wind, and Riachadh na Catha, the ancient Battlefield of Kings, awoke.

Pale monarchs stood up once more to fight, their antique crowns and armour alive with a preternatural sheen. Once before, in recent time, the shang wind had swept its random tides across the High Plain. Then, Ashalind had walked out from Annath Gothallamor steeped in grief and taltryless, etching her image wherever she went—a ghost among ghostly warriors, to keep faith for her in unvarying repetition should the shang rise again.

And risen it had, just now, at Angavar's command.

Sure enough, at this moment Ashalind now looked upon that ghost, the image of herself-who-was, walking away across the plain, lifting her skirts to step lightly over the stones. The simulacrum halted and looked back. Ashalind saw herself as others saw her, and was amazed. Her hair, shining like moonlight on bronze, swept past her waist. Ropes of pearl and sapphire were loosely braided through those tresses. Edged with miniver, her layered gown of lavender samite was richly netted in gold braid and seed pearls, the full sarcenet sleeves foaming with delicate white lace. And the face—an oval of flawless symmetry, of darling enchantment. A mask to hide sorrow.

At that moment, Angavar glanced towards this evocation and cried out. Stunned by the passion of that cry, Ashalind felt three heartbeats pass before she comprehended he had called her name.

Morragan, however, had responded instantly. He turned his head, looked straight at the shang image and faltered. It was only a blink of distraction, before he realised the vision was a sham—a hesitation so brief it took less time than a moth's wing incinerating in a candle flame, yet it was enough. So evenly matched were these adversaries that one of them needed merely the slightest opportunity to slip past the other's guard and drive the advantage home.

A tongue for telling lies had not, after all, been necessary.

Sianadh's tale of Callanan, the hero who tricked the warrior woman Ceileinh with such a ruse, had remained with Ashalind; had inspired her.

<<Bring unstorm,>> she had signed to Angavar in the silent language she had once taught him in the forest of Tiriendor. <<My ghost walks therein.>>

A momentary suspension of commonsense had been sufficient to distract Morragan. Beginning to tire, concentrating solely on the tactics of swordplay, it had taken him the space of a fleeting thought to comprehend the truth of what passed before his eyes.

Prince Morragan regained his judgement too late—by then

Angavar's blade had pierced his side. Blood trickled from the wound—not black in the moonlight like the blood of Men, but crimson, tinged with Royal blue. He staggered, yet did not fall. Angavar drew back, lowering his weapon.

The Lord Iltarien uttered a shout. Seizing her chance, Ashalind fled from him, but scarcely had she darted forward when Yallery Brown had leaped up to drive his rat's teeth and venomous talons into the flesh of her shoulder, biting to the bone, clinging to her like a steel trap. In agony she screamed, once, then Morragan was at her side. He threw off the wight, who rolled over the stones of the Plain. With an assured, cruel movement and supreme effort, Morragan brought his sword down and fulfilled his oath to Yallery Brown. A blackness fizzed and dissipated on the stones. A leprous cockroach crawled under one of them and Morragan set his boot-heel on it.

With his right arm, Angavar gathered Ashalind to him. His touch went through her like a javelin, healing her instantly and obliterating all physical pain.

But Morragan's effort had cost him dearly. The violence of his exertion had torn apart the wound in his side. The blow of Angavar's sword alone had not been ruinous, but the effort expended in smiting Yallery Brown severely exacerbated the injury. The blood that had been a trickle now gushed, and a look of wonderment crossed the Prince's face: he, the immune, made vulnerable, the immortal glimpsing the void at last, as fate came to meet him. He fell to one knee. His fingers opened and the sword Durandel clattered to the ground.

'Farewell, *lhiannan*,' he said to Ashalind, with the slightest and most haunting of smiles, which did not reach his grey eyes.

The numbness lifted from her tongue.

'Nay sir, pray do not leave us . . .' she blurted. Words petered out in futility and hot tears.

'Weep,' he whispered, swaying, 'for me.'

The sword Arcturus stood up, shivering, where Angavar had cast it aside. Its point was stuck fast into the rock of the Plain. The Lords Iltarien and Ergaiorn, the Prince's cup-bearer and all the chivalry of Raven's Howe gathered around the Prince on their knees, their heads bent, silent. They had taken off their helms. The Eagle knights and the Royal Attriod dismounted also, and all the kindreds of beings upon that Plain bowed down. The upper sleeve of the Faêran King was slit open—a long red-purple scratch showed through the fine linen. Now he knelt by his brother. Morragan sank down further, until he lay stretched upon the ground with his head and shoulders cradled in the arms of Angavar.

Softly, compassionately, the Faêran King spoke to the Raven Prince.

'I cannot heal this wound,' he said, 'or any wound begat by my own hand. The blow was not lethal, yet by thy subsequent actions thou hast made it so. *O, ionmhuinn brathair, mi cairdean, mi fithiach de cumhachd, laidir a briagha*—dost thou recall the Fields of Lys? We fought and sported there, but never was the sport so hard as this. Alas, how pride has cheated us. Do not depart, I pray thee. Not before thou hast walked again with me upon the sward of home—' His beautiful voice cracked. He bowed his head and spoke no more.

The Plain glimmered like a galaxy. Slowly the warrior kings of the unstorm faded.

Murmuring, Morragan spoke in the Faêran language and Angavar replied. Then the Crown Prince made to say something more, but before he could do so, his head fell back. In stark contrast against the coal-black satin of his hair, his beautiful face seemed chiselled of fine-grained marble, pale as paper. Still and silent he lay, with all of Erith still and silent about him.

Once, long ago in the Realm of Faêrie, a chorused cry had ascended when the Gates were Closing, exiling Angavar and Morragan. The second time Ashalind had heard such a cry was when the Awakened Knights of Eagle's Howe had appeared to do battle on the High Plain.

Now a third cry issued from myriad throats, and it was hardest of all to bear, and this time not all of the voices were Faêran. It seemed to come from near and far, from high above and deep below, and in it was an anguish, a sense of loss past compare.

From Angavar's arms a huge raven flew up on wings of shadow.

Empty-handed, Angavar rose to his feet and watched it fly away. The tranced stars went out in the shape of a cross and blinked once more alight.

Metallic, frosty, gigantic shone the stars. It was as though the sky were a pane of black glass against which unnumbered comets had flung themselves, smashing pinholes from which glistening lines of fracture radiated like the spokes of wheels.

Morragan was gone.

A shouted order came up from the lowlands, followed by the twang and purr of arrows in the air: a salute from the warriors of Erith. Ten thousand arrows shot straight up against the sky, hung poised at the top of their arc and rained down harmlessly, rattling upon the encampment. Then Ergaiorn put a golden horn to his mouth and blew the '*Ceol na Slán*'—the 'Song of Farewell'. At that music, even hardened warriors wept.

Those serried ranks of fair and noble knights who knelt on the Plain remained on their knees. They paid homage now to the victor, the High King of the Fair Realm. All wights of eldritch also made obeisance to him, save for the remnants of the Unseelie Attriod, who were nowhere to be seen, for they had fled far away.

Around the standing sword, where the blood of the Raven Prince had spilled upon the stones, there sprang now a garden of strange poppies with translucent petals like flames of white samite.

'These flowers will multiply,' said Angavar in a voice that rang across the landscape, 'until they cover this stone table. All of Riachadh na Catha will become a garden. But I will banish the *siangha* from Erith. Never more shall they wander pathless, the winds of gramarye.'

He took Ashalind's hand, making a sea-storm of her senses.

'Let us go from here, Goldhair *eudail*,' he said. 'Now thou must needs teach me how mortals grieve.'

Farewell, black bird. Under the stars
On silent wings, begin your flight.
It seems a sudden shadow flees
Across the night.

Fly swift, black bird, on faithful winds,
With rhythm strong, soar straight and free.
Yet something wonderful and rare
Shall leave with thee.

Fly on, black bird, do not look back
At those from whom thou must needs part.
Thy wings thresh airy currents like
A beating heart.

Fly high, black bird—do not look down.
Thy destiny is in no doubt,
But somewhere in the world below
A light goes out.

And didst thou wist so many hearts
Would go with thee?

ERGAIORN'S LAMENT

(TRANSLATED FROM THE FAÊRAN)

11
THE BITTERBYNDE
Part I

Faêrie, have my bones. Forever may I live,
But of deathless years I vow that I would give
All, to walk once more beneath thy singing trees,
Else to glimpse again the jewels of thy seas,
Or to breathe once more the wind that scours thy sky.
Faêrie, have my bones, and peaceful shall I lie.

A Song of the Exiles

Upon the back of the Skyhorse Hrimscathr, borne on the tumult of his wings, Ashalind rode with Angavar down to the encampment on the lowlands. For her, the boundaries between wakefulness and sleeping had blurred. In a drowsy suspension of awareness she thought she viewed herself from a vast distance, as though her movements were no more than images printed on a shang parchment while her real self hovered or floated elsewhere. But Angavar's arms encircled her, and that was all that could be desired—sufficient to numb the senses and ward off all painful reflections, for the nonce.

She leaned against him. Beneath the warm folds of the linen shirt his heart beat, slow and strong. Three rings shone on his hands, which rested, empty of reins, along her forearm. Any steed he rode would obey him without the compulsion of harness. Once, the ring-finger of his right hand had carried the heavy gold signet ring of D'Armancourt, but no longer—the Seal of the Fair Realm took its place now, marvellously wrought, set with jade and emerald. On the smallest finger of his right hand, halfway along, he wore the gold leaf-ring which Ashalind had bestowed on Viviana as protection—afterwards restored to Angavar. Twisted into a thin band on the ring-finger of his left hand, three golden hairs glinted.

She looked up. Past the curve of his throat, the sculpted jawline, past the fall of hair the colour of ripest black cherries spilling luxuriantly down over his shoulders, shone the multitudinous stars of Darke. The sky was a sheet of polished silver metal, spattered with ink-drops.

'My friends,' Ashalind murmured against the susurration of the wind. 'Viviana and Caitri.'

The Faêran King inclined his head. His breath was warm against her neck, spice scented.

'Cured of all ills, thy lady's maid waits at the tents to attend thee. Hast thou mislaid the child?'

'Caitri was spelled into a bird's shape.'

'Then birds shall send to seek her.'

'The goshawk Errantry—he would likely kill a wayward fledgling.'

'Have no fear of that, *ionmhuinn*.'

As graceful as a swan, Hrimscathr alighted beside a booth of rippling gold sendal, pitched near the Royal Pavilion. With a sound like airstreams rustling through poplars, the war-horse folded the great arcs of his wings and allowed himself to be led away by an equerry. Angavar and Ashalind, accompanied by a retinue of officers, passed along an avenue lined by Royal Guards standing to attention, and entered the lamplit tent. Within walls glowing like the cupped petals of a great primrose, Ashalind was met by Viviana. Many were the tears of joy they shed as they embraced. They conversed at some length, and at last Ashalind asked, 'What did you see that made you fall into such a coma in Annath Gothallamor?'

Viviana could not account for it. Possibly the Faêran had tired of her and put the sleep on her, or else some of the wights did it, or some stray gramarye mesmerised her. It remained one of the many mysteries of the stronghold on the High Plain.

Soon, exhausted by travail, Ashalind lay down to sleep on a fur-strewn couch, with her friend seated alongside. Angavar departed with his officers and passed swiftly among the Legions to heal the wounded as only he could heal, with the touch of gramarye.

The interior of the tent was luxurious, furnished with a table and chairs of carven ash, a lectern of rosewood. Light tapestries lined the walls. At one corner, pieces of armour and mail hung on a stand, shining sombrely like dislocated seashells and spiderwebs ravelled. Awake now, Ashalind swallowed the last morsel of the meal she and Viviana had shared.

She ached.

Angavar entered. His courtiers waited outside. With a smile and a nod to Viviana, Angavar both acknowledged her and bade her leave. Wide-eyed, the courtier bobbed a curtsey and backed away, casting many glances towards Ashalind. Her flushed face and flustered movements betrayed her excitation as she darted out through the tent flap.

'Quietude at last,' said the Faêran King to Ashalind, throwing down his cloak. 'Now we may compensate for much lost time without converse.'

Lightly she touched his sleeve.

'I must ask a boon of thee,' she said, in pain.

'Anything.'

'The Langothe consumes me—'

'The Langothe is it?' He probed no further—merely, his eyebrow flickered. 'That is easily assuaged. Look to me.'

Her eyes locked with his. Long he looked at her with his Faêran eyes, grave and attentive. Deep and far off, a world spun behind that gaze.

'Forget,' softly he said at last. 'Forget desire and delight in the Land Beyond the Stars.'

And the Langothe, that bone-gnawing heart-freezing longing which had become so familiar it seemed part of existence, like breathing, was gone.

Ashalind felt a boundless sense of freedom, as if her spirit had become a swan.

Angavar said, 'Long ago, when we parted on the doorstop of White Down Rory, I was nigh to asking thee if ever thou hadst visited the Realm. There was that about thee which hinted of it. Yet I thought it impossible. I did not trust my own senses, did not believe it could be true. Would that I had asked.

'Soon thou shalt unlock thy memory,' he continued, 'and next the Gate, that we may return to my kingdom, there to be wed among my kindred. Fain would I hie thence without delay, but my pledge to James binds me yet. Until Edward is crowned, I cannot leave Erith.'

As though she had not heard him, Ashalind remained as motionless as a jewel cached in the heart of a mountain. Like a curtain, the Langothe had been withdrawn from her inner vision.

All was now clear.

Where the longing had ached, a picture opened. Here had lain the source of the pain—birth and death, the exacting portal, the wellspring of Langothe which had beckoned to Ashalind and drawn her relentlessly, calling to the very essence of her being, although she had not known it.

A tall grey rock like a giant hand, and a slender obelisk leaning towards it, coloured as the lip of a rose petal. Both monoliths capped by a lintel-stone shaped like a doorstep. Near at hand in a granite hollow, a dark pool of water fed by a spring.

'I see the Gate of Oblivion's Kiss,' she murmured, 'etched upon the air.'

At her side, Angavar abruptly stilled, as utterly as some wild creature sensing hunters on the wind.

At length he said, in a controlled tone, 'And the way to reach it?'

'Not that, not yet. But I know the Gate now, I recognise it. And I will find it.'

'How does it appear, the Way to Faêrie?' His voice was almost casual now.

All she could recall, she told him. There was a keen and desperate restlessness in him, a longing so urgent, so terrible she feared it.

'Methinks thou dost want to make haste,' she said. 'Shall we take ship straightway for Arcdur? Even if thou mayst not leave Erith yet, we can locate the Gate in readiness. It can be opened, and thy subjects will be able to pass to and fro.'

A shadow darkened his features. He brooded. 'Nay,' he said. 'Mayhap, during the days and nights of Arcdur, those three strands of thy hair have blown away or been washed forth or subtracted by beasts of the wilderness.'

'Is it possible the Gate has closed by itself?'

'Even so. Yet while naught is confirmed either way, the chance remains that the Realm may be regained at last. For the nonce, I prefer to dwell with that chance, rather than realise bitter disappointment. There is no need for haste. The last day of eternity draws no nearer.'

'But while we hold back the chance grows fainter—for the rain and wind and the beasts and insects of Arcdur are as busy at their work of displacement as they have ever been.'

'No, they are not.'

Of course—she had overlooked the extent of his governance. His influence was such that he could arrest the eroding effects of natural forces. A smile tugged at the corners of her lips. *The west wind is his caress, raindrops his kisses on my mouth* . . .

Against the dandelion shimmer of the tent walls, her mind's image of Arcdur hung dissolving like a grey stain. Unwarned of, a flapping darkness crossed her vision, fragmenting it. Ashalind shook her head as if to clear it of confusion. Her face sharpened into an expression of wistfulness.

'The Raven . . .' she murmured.

'What of him?' Angavar flung back with a frown.

'He is gone,' she stammered, bemused, 'yet remains with us, in a way. Will the Raven fly into Faêrie, when the gate is opened? At the least, he can now no longer demand that second boon of Easgathair White Owl. The Gatekeeper has fulfilled the first—he locked the Gates, as Morragan demanded. It was no fault of his that I was enclosed inside the actual structure of a Gate, hidden neither within the Realm nor without it. Now that Morragan has lost his Faêran shape, surely Easgathair is not beholden to the second pledge—or even if he is, Morragan has no voice to command it. With the Password to unseal the Casket of Keys known to all and sundry, all the Gates may be reopened, never to be locked again. Faêran and mortal may traffick again, as in days of yore!'

'In Raven form,' sombrely said Angavar, absently twisting a strand of her hair around his finger, 'most of his powers have indeed been bled away. Not all. Some rudimentary power of speech remains. He is of Royal blood—it is not easy to disable us. Should he meet again with Easgathair White Owl, the Raven yet has a chance to command obedience. I would fain discover him, render him mute, else bind him with gramarye, or by his own word. I would find him, but he is not yet to be caught. Thus, it remains perilous to open any Gates.'

'Why didst thou let him fly away?'

''Twas mercy that stayed my hand. How could I, who showed mercy to the Waelghast, do less for my brother?' The attention of the Faêran King seemed to turn inward, his beautiful countenance tempering to the bleakness of a Winter sky. 'My brother, in whose downfall I played a significant part.' After a brief pause, he continued, 'I was uncertain whether he might merely fly off to some remote forest, seldom to be glimpsed again, or whether in the strange reaches of a bird's mental flickerings there existed a desire to regain the Fair Realm. And my qualms tendered him the advantage.'

Wide, her eyes drank him in, noting every detail. He was a fire and she a candle too near. He drew her close. Catching the cinnamon scent of him, she pulled away. He did not smell of sweat and leather, his breath did not reek of onions nor his hair of wood smoke. She could overlook no longer—this was no mortal man.

Perplexed, half angry, he said, 'Do not withdraw from me!'

She hesitated, unable now to meet his gaze.

'Thou art of Faêran blood. I am not.'

'What's thy meaning?'

A cudgel pounded on the inner cage of her chest.

'How *canst* thou love me?' At the backs of her eyes, tears welled. 'To thy kind, we must seem as beasts.'

'Never say that!' he exclaimed in a voice rough with some elusive passion—and then, incredulously, 'Dost thou *doubt* me?'

'I am of the imperfect race. By my troth, if I view my kind through Faêran eyes—'

'So. It seems thou *dost* doubt my love.'

She raised her face to his at last, and what she read thereon threatened to stop her pulse.

'No.'

He said, 'Never doubt me, Goldhair. Never.'

Ashalind's throat ached, as though she had swallowed her own heart.

'Long have we been parted,' she said, 'yet never hast thou been from my thoughts. Day and night, I have seen thy face before me. In my mind thy voice spoke. Each brush of the wind was a touch from thee, every dream a reinvention of thy form. At this instant thou art before me, and sometimes I am afraid. For I might blink and thou shalt have vanished again. Ah, but every fibre of my being cries out for thee.'

'And mine for thee, be assured of it.'

From beyond the tent came the rumour of men's conversation, distant singing, a medley of muffled hoof-beats as horses moved about the camp.

Ashalind recalled Morragan and his provoking words to his brother—*Fain would my weapon remain oft in the sheath, it filled the receptacle so well*. Another Faêran way of twisting the truth; using ambiguity to deceive without perjury.

To Angavar she now said, 'Taunting thee he implied that it was so, but Morragan did not lie with me.'

'I know it.'

He gathered her into his arms, resting his face against the top of her head. His hair poured down over her and she became lost in the maze of it, each filament a fine chain to bind the heart, a line to lure thought astray.

Among his race, the act of love was commonly regarded as sport and pleasure rather than as a mutual celebration of lasting passion. Tales of the Faêran made this clear. To hold him, feeling the tension through his shoulders so vehement that he trembled, to be kindled by the heat of his heartbeat—to know the effort it cost him, resisting his own nature; this moved

Ashalind profoundly. By this, she understood how he esteemed her.

As instinctively, as irresistibly, mortals were attracted to the Faêran. The immortals of the Realm were designed for love and for laughter, as birds are fashioned for flight. In showing equal restraint, Ashalind acted with no less honour than her extraordinary lover.

In denial, affirmation.

'It is my wish to honour thee,' he whispered. 'Soon shalt thou be my bride. When we lie together, thou and I, there shall be delight such as mortalkind can only dream of, and rarely do—such joy as might prove unendurable.'

'Two worlds dost thou rule,' she said. 'Thou lack'st for naught, some might say. Gold thou mightst have in oceans, and rivers of jewels. I cannot give such treasures. Yet, when we have made our wedding vows, I can only surrender to thee a gift that no one else in either world can bestow, and which can only be given once, by any maiden.'

'A gift to be enjoyed lifelong.'

It suddenly struck Ashalind that her lifespan and his would be unevenly matched. Mortal years could be prolonged in the Fair Realm, but humankind could not become immortal. He might continue to walk the green hills of Erith for many lives of kings, long after she rested beneath them. She dismissed the thought, vexed that she had allowed it to mar happiness.

A soft breeze stirred the tent's fabric, causing shadows to waver as though underwater. The wind carried the sounds of the bivouacked armies more clearly through the thin sendal partitions—songs of victory, laughter, the jingle of harness. Flaring campfires threw the shadows of armed men on the rippling walls. Sentries marched along their circuits, messengers went to and fro.

'Long have I searched for thee,' Angavar said gently, 'sending birds and beasts and eldritch wights to the task. All that time, every road and byway was watched. Every city and village in the populous regions was under the surveillance of my servants. Thou didst confound them with both thy fragrant disguise and the unexpected path thou didst pursue. Of recent days, thy bodyservant has told

me much concerning thy travels. Would that I had known then
what I know now. Time after time my searchers returned, having
failed to gain even a hint of thy whereabouts, and tumult would
surge again within my heart. It seemed thou hadst vanished out of
all knowledge. Fain would I have sought thee myself, yet I could
not be spared from the effort of the Legions. What makes thee so
clever at concealing thyself from me? Few could achieve such art-
fulness! I have dominion over the sea, the sky and all the corners
of the land. The Royal Raven may hide from me, for the nonce, but
no mortal could do it—save thee. And twice thou hast done so!'

Ashalind shook her head. 'I know not why, unless due to luck,
or ill luck, or fate. Alas, would that thou hadst been able to save
Tamhania from destruction!'

'I knew naught of the isle's danger until too late. No one at
Tana heeded the warning signs, therefore they sent no early plea
for help. When at last the ill tidings came to my ears I sped there
forthwith, but by the time my Skyhorse reached the latitude of the
Royal Isle, all was in ruins.

'After the island was drowned, didst thou not presume I had
perished during its fall?'

'The denizens of the sea reported thou wert not numbered
among the dead. Yet then, for a time, I did think thy life had
ended, for my servants had scoured Erith and thy absence
appeared to indicate thy total destruction. Shouldst thou have
been slain, and thy body rendered unrecognisable, then they
would never have discovered thee.'

'Unrecognisable? In what manner?'

'Crushed, dissolved, incinerated, eaten. But let us speak no
more of hateful matters. I have found thee, Goldhair. That com-
pensates for all.'

'Now at last we may enjoy the company of one another,' she
whispered, somewhat shyly.

'Even so!' he replied. 'And share our full histories as previously
we could not and did not!'

In a corner of the Royal Pavilion, Errantry roosted on a tall
stand. At the centre stood a table carved of walnut and oak, inlaid

with hawthorn wood. Ashalind found Thomas of Ercildoune and Tamlain of Roxburgh seated at this table with Richard of Esgair Garthen and Istoren Giltornyr, battle-weary yet unwounded—or if they had been wounded there was now no sign of it.

'It is a joy to meet again with the Royal Attriod,' said she.

They bowed, murmuring their greetings. True Thomas kissed her hand.

'Valiantly you fought,' she said to them.

Roxburgh's face was grim. 'Aye lady, but our success was not timely enough.'

He fell silent.

'Drumdunach and Ogier are sorely missed,' said Ashalind, seating herself at the table.

'Those who slew them have paid the price,' answered Roxburgh heavily. 'Now at last peace has returned to Erith—' He glanced at Ashalind and she saw in his look that same hunger she knew so well. 'And there is a way back . . .'

She nodded. 'Yes. There is a way. I shall find it again.'

A page poured wine, but the goblets stood untouched.

'They say you have discovered our secret, my lady,' softly said Ercildoune, 'as we have discovered yours. For if you are a thousand years old, we are older. Our exploits of yore are the stuff of legend.'

'Indeed,' Ashalind replied. 'I recall, when I was a child in Avlantia my nurse used to tell me tales of the Bard who dwelled half in the Fair Realm and half in Erith. Even then it was thought to be moonshine, a fabrication of the Storytellers to while away long Winter nights. But what of you, sir?' she said to Tamlain Conmor. 'I surmise that you also were once in that place, but I cannot fathom how it came to pass.'

'A distraction from our present grief would be welcome,' said the Bard, before Roxburgh could reply. 'Allow me to regale you with that story.' She nodded, and he proceeded.

'There is on Roxburgh land a green vale called Carterhaugh,' he began. 'In that vale lies a secret bower, filled with wild roses in Springtime. Long ago, before the Closing, strange things began happening at Carterhaugh. It came to pass that roses bloomed there all year round, even through the snows of Winter, and they were double roses, gorgeous blooms with richly coloured petals like flounced silk underskirts, the like of which had never before been seen in Erith. The fragrance alone, it was said, was enough to intoxicate anyone who went near.

'Few dared go near, for this unseasonable burgeoning was a sure sign of supernatural activity in the area. Indeed, parents forbade their children to venture there, lest some harm overtake them. But the attraction proved too strong for some, especially for young maidens who wished to pluck these extraordinary roses for their sweetness, in order to strew the petals amongst their linen or wear the flowers twined in their hair.

'After a time a rumour began to fly about. It was whispered that any mortal maiden who strayed in Carterhaugh would be captured by a young knight who appeared as the guardian of the roses. He would not let her go free until she gave him a token, and that token was either her cloak or her maidenhead. Knowing that if they returned home without their mantles they would incur their parents' wrath and inquisition, and perceiving this strange knight so well made and bonny, many a maiden came home with her mantle still upon her shoulders and nobody the wiser.

'Yet truth has a way of revealing itself.

'Soon the infamy of the unknown knight of Carterhaugh became widely known. It was said that he was one of the Faêran, and now with even greater urgency and direr threats, fathers forbade their daughters to go anywhere near Carterhaugh. But one headstrong—and some would say foolish—maid, the daughter of a nobleman, decided to venture there despite the warnings, or because of them, for she wanted to see this comely knight for herself. This was somewhat of a contrary wench. She was wont to wear green and flaunt it, just to show her indomitable spirit. Without breathing a word to anyone, she went to Carterhaugh alone.

'When she arrived at the bower of roses, the scent of them filled her with a joyous languor. She looked about amongst the nodding stems, which bowed almost to the ground beneath the weight of those heady blooms, but no sign could she see of any living thing.

'Greatly daring, she began to gather the roses. She had not plucked more than two when the young knight stood before her.

'"Lady, gather no more," said he. "Why come you to Carterhaugh without permission from me?"

'Boldly this saucy maiden planted her hands on her hips and looked him in the eye. "I'll come and go," she replied, "and ask no leave of you!"

'She returned to her father's hall that night with her mantle still wrapped about her, but her gown was crumpled and there were some small rents in it as though it had caught on some briars. Nobody thought anything of it, for this maiden was not one to care overmuch for the daintiness of her garments. But she went often to Carterhaugh after that, and no one suspected.

'Then one day her father came to her. He was a kindly gentleman and he loved his daughter well—perhaps too well, for that was why she had been able to get her own way for so long.

'"Alas, daughter," said he, not angry but mild and meek, "I fear you are with child. Name the father and if he be one of my knights you shall have him to wed."

'"Well, if I am with child," she made reply, "myself shall bear the blame, for there's not a knight about your hall, father, who shall give his name to the baby. I'll not exchange my own true love for any knight you have."

'"Then who is your love?" her father appealed.

'"Alas!" cried the daughter in her turn. "He is not of Erith, but a knight of the Fair Realm. The steed he rides is lighter than the wind. Its forehooves are shod with silver and the hindhooves with gold."

'Then the father bowed his head in sorrow, for there was naught he could do.

'As soon as she could, this young gentlewoman combed her hair, put on her golden snood and hastened back to Carterhaugh. There she saw the young knight's steed standing alone, but there was no sign of its rider until she had plucked a rose or two, and then he stood before her, and he was full bonny, there was no denying.

'"Lady, gather no more!" said he. "Why do you come here

breaking roses? For to lie with me might kill the bonny babe we made between us."

'She was not afraid.

'"Tell me, my love," she begged, "were you ever a knight of Erith? Are you a mortal man?"

'"Aye," said he. "I was out hunting in the greenwood, and I rode swifter than the rest and outstripped them. I was alone, and eventide had fallen, when I spied a strange and splendid procession riding at leisure through the trees. At its centre was a green silk canopy borne on four spears by four mounted knights, gloriously accoutred. Under the canopy rode a Queen of the Fair Ones, on a white palfrey. At once all sense of peril deserted me and it seemed that I must catch up with her. Spurring my horse, I rode furiously, but no matter how fast I galloped, I could not catch the slow-trotting pageant. When at last I came near my heart's appetence, my horse stumbled and I fell from its back. I might have died from the fall, but that she caught me—a Queen among the Faêran, Leilieln of the Yellow-Flowered Broom. She took me to the Fair Realm to bide with her, for she saw I was comely of face and strong and lithe, and there I have stayed for nigh on seven years. Pleasant it is to dwell there, but now I have reason to wish to leave, and that reason stands before me now.

'"A right-of-way opens from the Fair Realm into Carterhaugh," he said. "I am permitted to pass through it and linger awhile, here in the world of mortals. But I must not stray too far, for my task is to guard the roses of Leilieln, exacting a pledge from thieves. But tonight is Jack o' Lantern Eve," the knight continued, "the night when the Faêran Court ride at the murk-and-midnight hour. Those who would win their true love must go to the well at the crossroads, and bide there."

'"The Faêran will know I am by," said she, "and will try to conceal you in their midst. How shall I know you amongst all those brave and gallant knights of Faêrie?"

'"Lady," says he, "first let pass the black horses and then let pass the brown. Quickly run to the milk-white steed and pull down the rider. I shall ride on the white steed, nearest to the town, for I was a knight of Erith—they give me that fame. My right hand will be gloved, lady, and the left hand will be bare. My hat shall have a feather in it and combed down shall be my hair. Those are the tokens I give you. I shall be there."

'"How will they try to foil my purpose?" said she.

'"They will turn me in your arms into a newt or a snake, but hold me fast and fear not, for I am your baby's father."

'"I will hold you fast!" said she bravely.

'"Then they will turn me in your arms into a bear and then a roaring lion, but hold me fast as you shall hold our child, and fear me not."

'"I'll not be afraid!" she said.

'"Then they will turn me in your arms into a red-hot cauldron of iron, but hold me fast and fear not for I'll do you no harm."

'"Their tricks shall not drive me away," declared she.

'"Then," said he, "they will turn me in your arms into a burning sword. Throw me into the well-water and I'll be a naked knight. Cover me with your mantle and keep me out of sight."

'"I heed all you have said," she answered him.

'That evening she went alone to the well at the crossroads and hid herself. All was deadly still and silent. The face of the silver moon was the only other face she saw. In the middle of the night, she heard the ringing of bells and bridles, and after the silence of Jack o' Lantern Eve, she was as glad of that sound as of any *lorraly* noise. The Faêran Rade came by, riding at a trot. Richly caparisoned they were, and many fair ladies and comely knights rode among them. First the black horses passed by the well, and then the brown. As soon as she saw the white horse, the girl ran and pulled the rider from its back.

'When the Faêran Queen turned and saw what had happened, the storm of gramarye arose. This mortal damsel, Alys, she was no laggard, no milksop. She had heeded well what the enchanted knight had told her and she held him fast throughout all the shapes of horror they put upon him, and she won him and covered him with her mantle.

'Then Queen Leilieln of the Yellow-Flowered Broom spoke in anger, saying: "She that has got this knight has got a stately groom.

Woe betide her ill-faur'd face! An ill death may she die! If I had known what now this night I see, I'd have looked him in the eye and turned him to a tree." So pronouncing this curse, she rode off with her Faêran company behind her.

'But Tamlain Conmor wed his victorious sweetheart, and the child that was conceived in the blossomy bower—a traverse between Faerie and the realm of mortals, where numinous roses bloomed, touched by gramarye—that child they named "Rosamonde".'

'With her mother and me,' said Roxburgh, taking up the tale, 'Rosamonde entered the Pendur Sleep beneath Eagle's Howe.' His grim features softened when he mentioned his daughter's name. 'After we awoke she accompanied us to Angavar's Court. Rose and Prince Edward spent their childhood together, and a bond of steadfast friendship has grown between them, as doubtless you already know.' Indeed, the affection between Edward and Rosamonde was common knowledge at Court, and it was expected that some day they would wed.

'What of Leilieln's curse?' asked Ashalind.

'Angavar brushed it aside.'

'A marvellous tale,' she said. 'I am now enlightened! But Thomas, how could your honest tongue evade revealing these stories?'

'Cannily,' said Ercildoune, giving the ghost of a smile. 'Much as the Faêran and wights are experts at verbally skirting the truth, so have I also become a master of prevarication.'

'And now we are drawn together,' said Ashalind. 'Three mortals who have walked there, who have breathed the air of the Realm and gazed upon it.'

'As perhaps we were drawn from the first moment you entered Caermelor,' said Ercildoune, 'recognising a fellow traveller in some ineffable way. There is no mortal who can enter the Realm and return unchanged.'

'Shall you discover the open Gate?' asked Roxburgh suddenly. There was a wildness to him as though his warrior's blood, roused to battle, had not yet cooled.

Earnestly Ashalind regarded the Dainnan Chieftain.

'I shall do all in my power,' she said. 'This I vow.'

Amid the tents, all talk centred around the wonders that had taken place, not least of which was the sight of the King-Emperor wielding a Faêran sword to fight a Faêran Prince. Angavar commanded the Royal Attriod to inform his captains of the true tale at last, so that it might be passed on to the men. Edward now was of an age to be crowned and take his rightful place on the throne—Angavar's pledge to James was nearing fulfilment. Word spread like the plague through the Legions: 'King James is dead, long live King Edward!'

But many of the men could not fully comprehend what had happened, and thought that the King-Emperor had been slain in the recent battle; thus, in later years, despite the celebrations soon to occur in Caermelor, the truth eventually—inevitably—became reshaped and altered by historical perspective. And the songs made by the bards about the sovereign they loved, about the wise and just reign of the Faêran King, in future years became songs about King James XVI, the sire of Edward.

Angavar passed sentence upon the defeated chivalry of Raven's Howe, banishing them indefinitely to the Pendur Sleep beneath the hill. In this he was lenient: high treason was a crime punishable by execution.

'Already you are exiles,' he said to them, 'and now you shall remain so, at my pleasure. When we return to the Realm, traitors will not be among us.'

But while the knights of Raven's Howe knew only blackest despair, the knights of Eagle's Howe were jubilant, knowing the time approached when they might regain the Fair Realm at last.

Not so Ashalind. On silken cushions in the gold tent, she wept with a desolation she could not define. Even Viviana could not comfort her.

The curtains parted with a faint *swish* and Angavar was there once more, returned from the Royal Pavilion where he had held council with his commanders and the Attriod.

'Leave us,' gently he bade the courtier. Viviana withdrew, curtsying awkwardly, overwhelmed.

Without haste, Ashalind raised her face to the Faêran King. She could not yet look at him quickly—her breath would catch in her throat and choke her wordless until the shock of seeing him had faded.

'What ails thee?' he asked.

'Grief, it is,' she admitted. 'I have found thee, beloved, and that is my greatest happiness, but I feel have lost something I cannot name . . .'

For a damsel not yet eighteen, she had witnessed much horror during the Battle of Evernight, and the aftermath of shock lingered. Coming on the heels of all her other travails, it was no wonder such strife had engendered a melancholy mood. As well, she could not help but recall, again and again, the downfall of Prince Morragan.

On her attainment of freedom, Viviana had relinquished the leaf-ring, returning it to the King. He had worn it since. Now he replaced it on Ashalind's finger, drying the tears from her face with kisses like the touch of the sun.

'Yea, the loss of such a one as *he*,' he affirmed, 'is a weapon to slay joy.'

Then he amended, 'But not forever.'

It was not in the nature of the Faêran to allow themselves to be touched deeply by sorrow, or for long.

Ashalind returned to Caermelor with Angavar and Viviana, borne in the Windship *Royal D'Armancourt*. There, Prince Edward waited. Against his own wishes the Prince had been sequestered at Caermelor, prevented from joining the fighting. As sole heir, his life was too precious to be risked.

As the Windship plunged out of the smokes surrounding Darke, and her flying keel once more broached the bright, sun-rinsed airs, the goshawk Errantry stooped from high altitudes with a half-dead bird clutched in his talons. He dropped it on the surging deck, where it became the pale and crumpled form of Caitri, lying streaked with blood. Angavar raised her up with his hands and she stood before him, healed but dazed. Ashalind kissed the little girl and held her in her arms.

'Cait, no longer must you serve me, or anyone,' she said. 'You and Viviana shall be given your own estates, your own house-holds. Until your affairs can be made ready, I invite you both to remain with me at Caermelor Palace.'

Even before the Windship approached Caermelor, a troupe of riders on eotaur-back came barrelling from the clouds, with Prince Edward in the lead. Having received the news from Stormriders, he was eager to greet Angavar and Ashalind upon their triumphant return. Skillfully he steered his steed to alight on the decks, where-upon he dismounted, doffed his helm, knelt and bowed his head.

'Majesty and matchless lady, I do heartily recommend myself to you.'

Bidding him welcome, Angavar raised the young man to his feet, but as Ashalind looked into Edward's face she perceived his skin was pale, his cheeks hollow, his eyes shadowed as though he had scarcely slept for weeks, or had suffered some illness.

'I have been sorely troubled, due to your absence,' he explained, his eyes flicking from Angavar to Ashalind. 'Mightily glad am I, at your return.'

His brow was flushed, as if fever burned there, and his chest rose and fell like that of a drowning swimmer.

'Are you hale, Edward?' Ashalind asked, concerned.

'I am hale,' he replied, flashing a warm, yet strained smile. 'This welcome homecoming has made me so.'

'Then let us rejoice!' said Angavar.

So it was that she who had been called Butterfly and Lady of the Sorrows and Warrior, now entered again the Royal City. Once, she had entered it alone, in a carriage; once riding on a horse's back with the King-Emperor, and this time—yan, tan, tethera—she came in a ship of the air, on the arm of a lover to whom only the words of poets might do justice, and all truths were at last revealed.

Yet their story was not ended.

On foot and horse, the Legions of Erith departed from Darke and returned to the lands of daylight. Through Namarre they passed, across the Nenian Landbridge and into Eldaraigne. Thence they travelled towards Caermelor to parade through the city in a triumphal procession, before dispersing to their native lands.

As they marched, they found themselves constantly overtaken by unseen presences which caused the hair to rise on their necks. They were disturbed by flickerings and flittings which disappeared when stared at directly, and by noises in the night and troubling dreams which woke them in a foment of horror. Yet these phenomena were naught but the ebbing of a tide, the return of unseelie wights to their traditional haunts of old—to well, stream and spring, to mine and cavern, to hilltop, mountain and wood, to roofless towers and the forsaken buildings of humankind. Fewer wights returned than had set out, just as fewer soldiers returned to home and hearth, for that is the equation with armies and battles.

Overhead, vast flocks of birds darkened the soft blue skies of late Teinemis like an unseasonable migration, despite that the lovely waning of Summer was on Erith, wreathing the known lands with flowers tied up in corn-yellow ribbons of sunshine. The legionaries sang as they tramped, and looked up at the flocks wheeling like torn nets of black knotwork, seeing this as a portent of some sort, or perhaps a celebration of their victory, or merely another manifestation of the restlessness in the world about them. For the entire land seemed to have awakened; the rivers and streams purled swifter and more joyously, the winds blew sharp and clear, excitement laced the leafy depths of the forests, the blossoms sprang more vigorously, and wild animals, shedding their timidity, were glimpsed with unprecedented frequency everywhere except near the columns of the travelling armies, whose troops were wont to shoot them for food.

Summer, the blithe girl with corn-silk hair, gave way to mature, red-haired Autumn and Arvarmis, the Cornmonth. In Caermelor a tumult of rejoicing greeted the Legions. The triumphal procession, showered with flower petals, wended down the main thoroughfare. Amid the celebrations, preparations were set in train for the state funeral of King James, whose remains were to be brought at last from Eagle's Howe for interment beside his Queen in the Royal Crypt. A ceremonial farewell was held for the two fallen lords of the Royal Attriod, Octarus Ogier of the Stormriders and John Drumdunach of the Royal Guard.

For nigh on a year, lavish arrangements had been underway for the forthcoming coronation of Edward. At the palace, the Seneschal—who was responsible for the supervision of feasts—worked frantically, by night and by day. The Lord High Chancellor, the Head Steward and others of the Senior Household collaborated. Gifts began to arrive for the Prince, who was to reach his sixteenth birthday on the day of the coronation. Added to this frenzy of activity, the common people were making ready for the imminent Samdain Festival of the Autumn Equinox with its harvest fairs, apple cider, vines, garlands, gourds and cornucopias.

To the astonishment of the citizens and nobles and courtiers of Caermelor, the gorgeous knights and ladies of Eagle's Howe went openly among them in high merriment, telling tales and singing songs of the Fair Realm. Borne on a wave of ubiquitous jollity, Ashalind put aside the melancholy induced by witnessing the violence of war, and cast off the ineffable impression of bereavement that had been plaguing her. After the funeral for King James, there were many, many reasons to rejoice. Only kindness, justice, hope, goodwill and love surrounded Ashalind. Laughter rang through the halls of Caermelor Palace and along the streets of the city.

Sianadh was back at Court, limping ostentatiously due to a leg wound he had received in some mysterious manner (and which had been healed seamlessly by Angavar). He roared and clapped people heartily on the shoulders, broadcasting his bold feats as a Windship captain—which increased in valour with each telling—to all and sundry. Diarmid and Muirne accompanied him, having themselves won glorious reputations in battle. The carlins Ethlinn and Maeve were invited to stay at Court for the celebrations, with Eochaid, Roisin Tuillimh and the carlin's lad, Tom Coppins, who was always willing to recount the story of how he and the carlin fled to the well in the woods, and were besieged by wights, before being rescued by the Dainnan.

Far and wide, Relayers rode sky bearing more invitations to the coronation. Silken Janet Trenowyn arrived at Caermelor with her father, her newfound mother Elasaid, her seven wild, rescued brothers whose hair was as glossy as rooks' plumage, and a small black rooster sitting upon her shoulder. On her left hand, the smallest of Janet's fingers was missing.

'Frostbite, me dove,' she explained unconcernedly to the King-Emperor's betrothed. 'T' fingerlock was freezed.'

Janet's garden had become a talking point for miles around Rosedale. It burgeoned luxuriantly and unaccountably. In its fertile soil strange plants sprang, producing the best of fruits and flowers. The insects that flew there were the biggest and most brilliant, attracting colourful songbirds. And the hens that roamed about eating the insects were huge and glossy, each laying at least two eggs per day.

'It was dust from Faêrie that made your garden bloom,' whispered Ashalind to Janet.

As for the sons of Trenowyn, for so long had they remained under enchantment that their nature was still influenced by it. Boisterous as rooks they were, rowdy and untame. They did not fit well with the ways of city folk; indeed, these sturdy lads seemed half to belong to the world of eldritch. Like the beauteous Rosamonde of Roxburgh, the childhood of these mortals had been touched by gramarye. They seemed no longer quite human, as if they had more in common with the Faêran, to whom they were greatly attracted. For their part the Fair Ones were as fond of the boys as they were of any wild creatures.

Some old friends were absent. The death toll from the destruction of Tamhania had been high. Roland Avenel had perished in the sea; his body was never found. Yet somehow, in the exigencies of the storm, he had saved the lives of Annie and Molly Chove, the two maids from Tana. The Wade family, naturally, had survived—theirs was a close tie with the ocean. Georgiana Griffin had sailed out of peril in the company of Master Sevran Shaw. Soon afterwards, they were married.

With joy and surprise, Ashalind greeted the Caiden family, the fisher-folk who had once lived in the cottage near Huntingtowers. Tavron and Madelinn beamed as she loaded them with gifts. Tansy and Darvon brought the white whippet on a leash. It jumped up and tried to lick Ashalind's face. Laughing, she gathered the dog into her arms and caressed its ears.

'Your tongue is as wet as it is loving!' she exclaimed. 'But the geas is lifted—you cannot wash away my past now, little rascal!'

A Windship was dispatched to Appleton Thorn. It returned bulging with passengers. Almost the entire village had accepted the once-in-a-lifetime invitation. Ironmonger and Wimblesworthy came dressed in their brigandines and mail, highly oiled and polished. Bowyer, Cooper, Spider, the new water bailiff, Farrier, the Village Hornblower, the reeve, the village bailiff, the steward, the Keeper of the Keys and the constable all arrived with their families. Betony and Sorrel Arrowsmith were among the passengers, but their brother did not accompany them. There was a new Village Master—he who had been the water bailiff, Falconer by name.

'Galan never came back,' said Betony sadly. 'Only his horse returned, with a bit of seaweed tied in its mane.'

'And yet,' ventured Sorrel, with the air of one who seeks hope in the wastelands of despair, 'my heart tells me we might well greet him anon.'

Lord Voltasus, Storm Chieftain of the Seventh House, had fallen in battle. Lord Noctorus—the new Chieftain of Stormriders—unexpectedly posted the heir of Voltasus, Lord Ustorix, to a lonely port at the Turnagain Islands. Controversially, he announced that Ustorix's sister Heligea would become the new head of the Seventh House. She was invited to Court and travelled to Caermelor by Windship, accompanied by her mother Lady Artemisia; the Lords Sartores; Isterium, Callidus and Ariades; their new wizard, Andrath; and several servants from Isse Tower, including Brand Brinkworth, Keat Featherstone, Dain Pennyrigg, Tren Spatchwort, Carlan Fable and Teron Hoad.

Above Caermelor the clouds billowed and surged like drifts of blown apple-blossom. Keels sliced through the vapours, which frayed to reveal towers of piled-up sails bellying taut, straining with the wind. Windships sailed in from each of the Twelve Houses of Stormriders, each escorted by squadrons of outriders. Heligea's sister Persefonae attended with her husband Valerix, Lord Oscenis of the Fifth House, and Lady Lilaceae.

The Lady Dianella had been betrothed to an elderly earl in the

Sorrow Isles. She was not invited to attend the festivities. Of her uncle the wizard Sargoth, a hunted man and an outcast, there were scant tidings. Some while ago a group of foresters in eastern Eldaraigne had glimpsed a vagabond, barefoot, wasted to the bone and clothed in rags. He had shrieked incantations at them, warning them to beware, and not to approach him, for he was a wizard and could easily cast them down. Yet, he was bereft of wizardly contraptions. The foresters laughed, and passed the madman by.

The towering, square bulk of the keep overlooked the Autumn Garden of Caermelor Palace. The five-lobed leaves of the ornamental grape, deep crimson, embroidered the stone walls of the park. Beneath the spreading tupelo trees with their long red leaves and tiny fruits of vivid blue, clipped hedges burgeoned richly with scarlet berries. The hedges were a glorious medley of autumnal vegetation—the purple barberry, whose oval leaves were turning from deep bronze to flame, the garnets of glossy evergreen cotoneaster, dense, dark holly hung with bunches of blood-red beads, and the orange-crimson baubles of pyracantha, the firethorn.

Around the roots of the winter cherry trees bright hard orbs lay scattered, as though necklaces of topaz and carnelian had broken, spilling their gems. Lilly-pillies scattered the shiny cherries of their own fruiting, deep magenta, like rose quartz struck with light through purple glass. Errantry sat brooding on the boughs of a ginkgo tree, whose fanlike leaves stood out crisply against the cloudless sky of morning, a striking display in clear, bright yellow. On the flowering cherries, standing erect and columnar, the foliage was changing from green-bronze to red-veined amber. Camellias bloomed, their rosy or creamy petals pleated like dancers' petticoats. Leathery-skinned coppery fruits the size of a woman's fist were ripening on the boughs of the pomegranates. Immobile among leaves piled up like surf, a watch-worm twined its rainbow coils about the pediment of a mounted statue of King William the Wise. A thick, sweet fragrance permeated the garden, exuded by the double flowers of gardenias, white as starched ruffles. Birds were singing.

In the days leading up to the coronation of Edward, two richly dressed people strolled along the paths of the Autumn Gardens, deep in conversation. As they went, they pushed aside the long branches of golden willows which drooped to the ground. The withies formed softly swaying curtains. Their faded yellow leaves fluttered through the air, as thick as snow.

Over a dark-green tunic, Angavar wore a long, dark-red sur-coat of velvet, worked with his own Faêran Royal Arms: the eagle gorged with a star-tipped crown, wreathed with hawthorn blossoms. A magnificent cloak covered his shoulders, fastened by a jewelled strap across the breast, lozenge-shaped clasps and golden cords. Its heavy folds were stitched with a pattern of hawthorn leaves. Holly-green breeches were tucked into cuffed boots reaching to midthigh, and a plain golden fillet encircled his brow.

His companion was clothed in a gown of rustling, lime-coloured silk, embroidered with gold cinquefoils. Its tight-buttoned sleeves extended well down below the wrist. About her neck she wore a collar of red-gold studded with emeralds and rubies. Her heavy hair, which shone like the flowers of broom, flowed loose. It was garlanded with Autumn leaves and berries on gold wire, fashioned from beryls and carnelians. Strings of miniature emeralds were wound loosely through her tresses. Her costume included a super cote-hardie lined with ermine, which was caught up on one side to reveal the silken gown beneath. Her girdle was composed of a series of square, jewelled brooches to match the collar.

'How did it all begin?' mused Ashalind aloud. 'Thou didst go hunting, and William of Erith tried to steal thy quarry. Yet thou wert lenient with him, and thus the bond of friendship sprang up between Erith and Faêrie. Now, methinks thou dost no longer savour the chase.'

'Faêran stags run no longer in Erith,' he replied. 'It is Faêran practice to hunt only beasts of gramarye, which do not perish but spring to life after they fall. Such beasts are well versed in evasive manoeuvres, and great skill is necessary to outwit them. They do not fear pain and death, for there is none. They take joy in the thrill of the chase, much as children delight in their games of hide-and-seek.'

He reached up to touch a sprig of fading willow leaves. 'From years of dwelling amongst humankind I have grown to honour the fragile lives of mortal creatures as never before. But this new compassion has become a great burden to me.'

Ashalind understood. Her lover possessed a kind of reverence for life which the Faêran did not normally own. It was against his nature. He had lost something of the carelessness innate to all immortals. Immortals could not care too deeply—it would destroy their hearts and minds. For who could know better than they that forever is a long time?

Sunlight through the willows dappled Ashalind's skin, its touch like syrup. He who walked like a tiger at her side was the fragrance of leaves, the essence of sunlight. His hair glinted as though droplets of dew were caught therein. Fragments of an old, clumsily translated Talith song strayed into Ashalind's thoughts.

> All the day was his, and the night,
> Wind and rain, sun, moon and stars,
> Snow and ice, frost, fire, stone.
> His was the power of the storm and ocean tides,
> And of the quake that sunders rock,
> Of the fire-mountain, the whirlwind, the o'ertowering wave.
> The drop of dew quivering on a web,
> Caught in a spangle of dawn glow,
> The painted butterfly's wing,
> The jolly bud, the leaf nodding on the twig,
> The blackbird's song—they were his also.
> The white owl in the hollow tree,
> The red fox and the golden eagle,
> The carp leaping the waters, mailed in silver,
> And all that was fair and wondrous,
> Every thing rare, joyous and awe-ful.
> Laughter, merriment and song,
> Wrath and vengeance, these were his too.
> And the rising of the sun was his,
> And the going down of the sun.

Her spirit was suddenly moved with a desire to see the Realm again.

'I can give the world to thee,' said Angavar, pausing among the amber-threaded willow curtains. 'Is there aught thou dost desire, which is not already in thy possession?'

Against the rim of her awareness, a black bird brushed its wings. Ashalind ignored it.

'Yes!' she cried. 'Together, let us right all wrongs. Let all slaves be sought out and freed, and slave-traders be pursued unmercifully. Let the beating of servants be outlawed, and domestic wights be installed in all domiciles, especially of the Stormriders, to enforce this precept. Let the treasure taken from Waterstair be distributed among the deserving poor of Gilvaris Tarv and wherever else they may dwell!' The words tumbled forth as she warmed to the subject. 'Let us gift Appleton Thorn with a new gorse mill, a sturdy plough, a dozen scythes of Eldaraigne steel and twenty stout draughthorses. Oh, I have so many aspirations—I shall think of them all presently. Not least, to revise the dining etiquette of the Court!'

Lean lines of amusement briefly bracketed Angavar's mouth. 'As thou wish'st,' he said, 'so shall it come to pass. But do not forget, it is Edward who must henceforth decree new laws for Erith, not I.'

'I am assured of his agreement, should the suggestions proceed from thee. He loves thee well, and honours thy wisdom.'

'As perhaps thou dost not—it appears thou wouldst upset my erstwhile governance willy-nilly!'

'Not at all! Fie—thou dost tease me! Hadst thou been aware of the mistreatment of servants, thou wouldst have remedied the situation straightway, I'll guarantee! When I was a child in Avlantia I never heard of such ill handling as later was laid upon me at Isse Tower. I feel certain that no such cruelty towards menials occurred in those days when thy people passed often to and fro between Erith and the Realm, seldom glimpsed by mortals. They deplored unjust abuse and would have punished hard masters.'

'How dost thou know aught of Faêran practice?'

'In Hythe Mellyn the lore-masters taught us what they knew of

Faêran ways. My teacher was Meganwy, a carlin well versed in the code followed by . . .' Ashalind faltered. All her life hitherto, whenever conversation had touched upon the sovereign of the Fair Ones, he had loomed as a fabulous figure in her imagination, a remote and glorious legend enduring since time's birth, only to be dreamed of, never to be glimpsed, no more to be reached than the stars. It was difficult to reconcile this entrenched vision with the fact that he was standing beside her, that she was speaking with him, that he was *Thorn*. '. . . the code followed by thy subjects,' she continued shyly, for a moment incapable of looking in his direction. 'I know how strictly thy laws are enforced.'

'We condemn slovenliness,' observed Angavar frankly. 'Slatterns deserve punishment.'

'Perhaps, but not with blows,' said Ashalind. 'That is where we differ, thou and I.' She hesitated again then spoke, though hardly knowing what she was saying: 'We differ in many ways. The more I know of thee, the stranger it feels.' Her breath escaped in a soft sigh. 'But how that strangeness stirs my blood . . .'

'Boundaries,' answered he, 'can be crossed.'

He leaned towards her, holding out a small jar of enamelled glass as green as flames from burning copper wire. Intricate decorations of foliage and birds twined about the sides, so beautiful and lively that they put Ashalind in mind of the leaf-ring.

'Wist thou the contents herein?' he asked.

A lock of his long hair swung from his shoulder, brushing against her cheek like thistledown, and for a moment she was unable to speak. From the highest boughs of a gingko tree a blackbird whistled three notes. Ashalind cleared her throat with a discreet, dry cough and regained her equanimity.

'I have not seen its like before, and yet methinks I know of something similar—I have heard a tale.' Angavar twisted off the lid, revealing an ointment the colour of new spring grasses. Dipping a fingertip in the stuff, he touched it to her eyelids. She blinked. 'Good faith!' she said in wonder. 'And is that not the self-same salve accidentally used by the midwife in the tale of Eilian? The old woman who attended Eilian in childbirth, after the damsel wedded a Faêran lord?'

'Even so.'

'Now I shall be able to see thy people, when they are hidden to other mortals!'

'Indeed. No mortal can see the Faêran unless they wish it. But, anointed, thou mayst see them whether they wish it or no. And thou mayst pierce all eldritch glamour besides.'

'A useful faculty! Yet all appears unchanged,' she added uncertainly.

'No illusion is yet nigh.'

Gleefully, Ashalind laughed. 'This is fun! Thou'rt indulgent with thy gifts!'

'Ask for more. Thy pleasure pleases me.'

'Yes I will ask for more. A boon comes to me now. Would that it had occurred to me beforetime—long have I yearned for the freedom of the servants of the Each Uisge, whose lives were ruined in a single moment of youthful folly.'

'Ere the sun has thrice set, they shall be discovered.'

She laughed again, in amazement and relief. How easy it all was!

'I can scarcely credit that this should be happening.'

Angavar's slow smile was beautiful, a stab of sunlight.

'Believe it,' he said.

Never had the Court of Caermelor seen such a gathering.

Like living jewels the Faêran danced and strode among them. Their poetry and songs enchanted mortal hearts with a keen delight, despite that sometimes the last echoes of the lyrics might leave the hearers imbued either with heart-bursting joy or an ineffable sense of tragedy and loss. The villagers of Appleton Thorn, servants from Isse Tower and Tana, an ebullient family from Rosedale, a crazy Ertishman with his swaggering niece and nephew, a chandler from Rope Street in Gilvaris Tarv, children with webbed fingers and hair the colour of pewter—all were welcomed as equals with the courtiers, whose initial dismay at this motley concourse turned first to fascination, then to pleasure. The cut-glass manners of Court, seen as baffling and pointless by the newcomers, quickly became redundant. The lords and ladies of

Caermelor Palace found themselves charmed and diverted as never before. Goblet the Jester formed a firm friendship with Sianadh, which proved dangerous to the dignity of almost everyone. There was no end to the larks of these two, but most folk learned to take their mischief in good part.

Others were glimpsed at Court, usually by night—in the gardens, or the Royal Quarters. It might be an urisk, or a small innocuous looking waterhorse, or a dark-haired youth dressed in leaves and moss, with a small pig trotting at his heels. At times when Angavar walked beside the leaf-strewn pools of the Autumn Garden with his betrothed, a gorgeous swanmaiden dallied there too, her slender frame reflected in the water like a burning hibiscus. Soon the Autumn Garden began to be shunned by the courtiers and most of the mortal visitors—it was considered to be haunted. Rumour had it that the ponds were connected to the sea by underground waterways, that merfolk and benvarreys and silkies came up through them, and sea-morgans also, and merrows, and the *maighdeanna na tuinne*, and something completely festooned with shells which laughed inordinately, and dripping gruagachs with the sheen of flowing water gleaming down their ankle-length hair. Of course, the citizens were not surprised that numerous eldritch manifestations should be attracted to Caermelor Palace, because the tidings of an amazing event had spread—the High King of the Faêran had come to Court with his retinue. For that same reason there was not a lady's heart that did not yearn, not a single human being who remained unmoved.

Vinegar Tom and various domestic imps lurked among the Autumn Garden's rufous hedges. High in the golden fire of the trees small figures moved, laughing and chattering in an arboreal language of Khazathdaur, stringing up ropes and ladders until the treetops of the garden were webbed with them. Like butterflies, the coillduine flitted rapidly in and out of the crystalline brilliance of the foliage, trailing auras of soft fire. Unseelie things also gathered to haunt the palace domains, for they loved the Faêran no less than their seelie counterparts—but some enchantment prevented them at this time from wreaking their mischief upon the mortal citizens of Caermelor.

Even Finoderee loped in one evening, dressed in his new clothes.

As for Edward, now King-Emperor uncrowned, he seemed at once merry and melancholy. The members of his Household whispered understandingly that the prospect of sovereignty surely filled the young man with both eagerness and dread.

'I urge this upon you,' Edward said to Ashalind, 'that you go now with Angavar to seek the Geata Poeg na Déanainn in Arcdur. Now, before the coronation. You must go by sea, for there are no Mooring Masts in that northern land. All my Seaships are at your disposal.'

'If we pass through into the Fair Realm it might be years before we come back to Erith,' Ashalind reminded him. 'Besides, Angavar's vow to your father is not yet fulfilled.'

'Then do not yet pass through the Gate but mark it only, and set guards upon it to await your return.'

'You are eager to find the Gate.'

'No. But I wist well how Angavar and the others of the Faêran yearn and cannot rest. Mayhap, finding it shall soothe them, for a time.'

'You are generous.'

But when she put the proposal to Angavar, he looked sombre, thoughtful.

'Edward suggested this?'

'Yes, and I am glad to discover what has been vexing him, for of late he has been as doleful as a—' She had been about to say 'crow', but thought better of it. '—as a weeper.'

'Methinks it is not the restlessness of the Faêran that eats him.'

'Then, what? The approaching coronation?'

But he would not say.

All over Erith, people wondered where the shang winds had gone. No longer did tableaux glow and shimmer in a numinous twilight, no more did ancient cities awake from slumber to relive their glory days. Angavar had banished the unstorms. As days and weeks went by, folk began to realise that the shang would visit them no more, but they were reluctant to abandon the old, ingrained habit of the taltry.

Since the return to Caermelor, Angavar laid aside the Lion of D'Armancourt and openly displayed his own eagle escutcheon, the sigil of Faêran Royalty. The couriers and everyone in the kingdom who knew him by sight were fully apprised of the truth—King James had asked the Faêran High King to rule in his place until Edward came of age. Surprisingly, or perhaps predictably, this truth did not affect history as it existed in the minds of the soldiery and the majority of the citizens of Erith, who recognised the face of their sovereign only from crudely stamped images on coins. The King-Emperor had come to be regarded as a sovereign without parallel, a paragon, the most popular ruler in history. The people would have followed him into any sort of danger. They found it difficult—nay, impossible to accept the idea that the entire Empire had been under glamour's illusion for so many years, that this monarch they loved was in fact not of their race. Popularly, the obvious explanation was that the King-Emperor had been slain at the Battle of Darke, and his ally the Faêran High King had subsequently arrived to stamp out those of his enemies who remained alive.

Now from every country came, at last, the Talith. The scattered remnants of that race gathered at Court to meet the Lady Ashalind, the betrothed of the Faêran King—she whose hair now glimmered with a daffodil sheen to match their own. Old and young, they came—the few who were well off and lived on the bounty of their estates; the few who were poor and who generally sold their tresses for wigs or who had gone into service, such servants being much sought after for their looks; and the majority, who dwelled in middle-income comfort. If the Talith wondered at this newcomer in their midst, in their delight they put aside their questions. It may be that their natural curiosity was dulled by the gramarye hanging in heavy veils about the palace, drifting like incense through the corridors and halls. Avlantia's dispossessed formed a coterie about Ashalind, reviving ancient songs and lore of their northern land, polishing their innate skills of eloquence, sharpening their scholarship, revelling in poetry, music and theatre, showing off their skills in the sports of field and track.

With her anointed eyes, Ashalind perceived the wakened

Faêran of Eagle's Howe here and there at Court, sometimes where others could see them, sometimes not. They preferred to spend their time in the gardens, or riding and hawking in the Royal Game Reserves of Glincuith, rather than enclosed within walls. She thought them selfish, sternly moral, callous, cruel and kind, with a love of courteousness and an infinite capacity for joy. They were as swift to punish as to reward. She glimpsed them helping people with a wave of their hand, or bidding small (also generally unseen) wights pinch lazy servants and frowzy courtiers until their flesh appeared smudged with cobalt and charcoal.

Yet it could be argued that they were neither better nor worse than mortalkind, and this sanctioning of vice and virtue was not a frequent occurrence. In general, the Faêran ignored mortals, taking more interest in their own affairs. Sometimes they mingled with the Talith, but only half a dozen mortals commanded their whole-hearted attention—Ashalind, Prince Edward, Ercildoune, Roxburgh, Alys and young Rosamonde.

One evening a flight of eotaurs came hurtling out of the sunset. Stormriders had brought tidings of the brothers Maghrain.

'Your Majesty,' panted the Wing-Leader of the Royal Squadron, bowing low, 'they were found as you described, standing beside the black loch. The waters were boiling, as though some violent storm raged beneath the surface.'

'A storm indeed,' said Angavar.

'As we speak, the Dainnan bring them here aboard a patrol frigate.'

'You have done well.' The King dismissed them.

That night the Dainnan Windship docked at the Mooring Mast of Caermelor Palace. The Maghrain brothers were brought before Angavar and Ashalind.

She looked with joy and horror upon the red-haired men. They stood to attention, their faces blank. Neither spoke. Water trickled from their clothes. Kelp was tangled in their wet hair.

Turning to her betrothed she said, 'Enchanted they remain! Wilt thou free them, prithee?'

'Goldhair,' said Angavar, 'these men have existed in Erith far beyond the span of their years. Unlike thee, they have lived and breathed every mortal moment of the last millennium. Dost thou understand what will happen, should the spell be broken?'

She paled.

'Oh,' she said. 'That I had not considered.' She paused pensively, for the space of six heartbeats. 'Does one still speak only untruth, while the other is honest?'

'Nay. That was laid on them only for the purpose of thy test. Yet two words only may be uttered by them. Down the centuries they have been permitted only "yea" or "nay", for the Each Uisge detests the sound of men's speech.'

She went to the Ertishmen, searching their dispassionate faces.

'Do you wish to remain enchanted?' she asked.

'No,' replied one of the brothers. A vein stood out at the side of his neck, pumping hard. Every sinew seemed knotted, as though he strove against some mighty force. Yet he and his brother faced no visible opposition.

'Do you know what will become of you, when you are freed?'

'Yes,' said the other brother, whose brow was beaded with seawater, or possibly sweat. His jaw was clenched, his knuckles white, as though he strove to speak but could not.

Ashalind bit her lip. She kissed each brother on the cheek. Cold was their flesh, which for centuries had known only the touch of water under stone.

'Then may goodness and mercy go with you, and the sun to shine upon you, and the wind ever at your backs.'

Angavar placed a hand briefly on each waxen brow.

'*Sain* thee,' he said.

The brothers turned towards one another. Expressions of joy slowly spread across their faces. With hoarse shouts they opened wide their arms to embrace each other, but even as they leaned into the embrace, time caught up with them. Before they could meet, two columns of dust rained down upon the floor. So fine was this pollen that a slight breeze was enough to lift the particles, and they blew away.

It could sometimes be a terrible thing, to be at the side of the Master of Gramarye.

But it could also be exalting.

Always, to be in the presence of the Faêran was an exhilaration. It was like experiencing the prelude to a storm when the wind rises, the skies darken and the air is charged with magic. On the doorstep of storms the world is an altered place where anything is possible, where you become so buoyant that at any moment that gusting wind will whip you off your feet and carry you up, over lashing treetops to its elemental domain of turbulent air and purple steams. That is what it was to be with the Faêran.

How much more intoxicating to be close to the Faêran King.

'When I am with thee, I believe I can fly!' Ashalind exclaimed.

At that, Angavar laughed aloud.

'It would please me to see thee take thy pleasure of the sky,' he said, and he took her flying.

To fly, without visible means of support, is an ancient dream. Mortals have forever desired to fly like a bird—this was *not* that way of flying. It was not the way of a swan, dependent on muscular effort and skillful balance in gliding the lofty currents. Nor was it the sildron-borne way, the courtly, mechanised glissanding, with a flying belt for hoisting and ropes for propulsion.

The Faêran manner of levitation was like that of a mote, of thistledown, of a butterfly, a leaf, a fly, a blackbird, an arrow, an eagle, a firework a storm cloud, an ideation and more, combined—for it permitted ascents far beyond the reach of the highest flying birds, to thousands of feet above the ground where temperatures dropped to extremes and the sparse air would have been hard to breathe, had not the forces of gramarye sustained life in effortless comfort.

It was to float, weightless, amongst lofty leaves on fragile twigs, passing through bowers of foliage which swung like green spearheads—as birds could never do without breaking their feathers. It was to hang suspended above a limpid pool or the wavelets of a wide, grey mere, and then to let down one foot and dip the toes into the water. It was to jump from a cliff top, arms widespread, and hurtle out into the abyss, descending in a gentle curve, only to bank and climb into the low cumulus, or catch an updraught back to the cliff top, or alight halfway down the rocky face on some precipitous ledge, impossible to gain by any other means. It was to be as light as gossamer, to walk across a bed of flowers without crushing a single petal, to ride on the back of a storm with the thunder exploding in your ears and the wind racing unchecked through your veins, the outraged thunderheads towering all around like a giant city. It was to feel every nuance of change in air pressure, wind speed and direction, yet to master every fluctuation; to be as conscious, as capable of altitude and flying speed and navigation as perambulatory land-bound creatures are sensible of the act of walking.

Yet for the Faêran, flying was purely a leisurely pastime. It was no use for long-distance travel, for it was too slow—especially in the heavy airs of Erith. As a swimmer labours in the wake of a sailing ship, as a walker falls behind a chariot, that is how Faêran levitation compared to riding on winged horses or voyaging in Windships.

Thus, Ashalind and her lover made a progress on eotaur-back, visiting many of the regions of Erith they loved best. When they arrived at each location they dismounted and flew, unsupported, except by gramarye.

In Lallillir, they swooped over the misty fells and down into the damp river-combes where gruagachs, like slender iris flowers, combed their buttercup hair beside reedy pools.

To Haythorn-Firzenholt they rode. There they alighted on hedge tops, disturbing their close-growing foliage no more than would a fallen leaf, for they could walk light-footed where any Erith-bound creature would sink into the green mass. At twilight in the rolling hills of *cuinocco* country, a slender white 'horse' shyly approached the couple and bowed its horned head, trembling with delight as Angavar's hand caressed the moonbeam arch of the neck.

'My people title him *unicorn*,' he said.

In Rosedale the briars bloomed out of season, powdering the entire valley with a profusion of pink and white rosettes, dainty as kittens' paws. How different Erith looked, seen from above, as the sun's eye saw it. Forest leaves reached to the source of light, spreading their arms so as to receive its fullest outpourings. Tender shoots of palest green and gold hid the old and faded bark below.

The swan-girls of Mirrinor gathered around Ashalind and Angavar like dark flowers, as in a boat of glass the couple skimmed the placid lakes or stood balanced on the water before slowly sinking together into the diaphanous world of the asrai. The laval meres of Tapthartharath scorched them not, and they flew among the black spires, immune to vapours and noxious gases arising from that desert landscape.

Flying itself was a source of hilarity. Far from the eyes of courtiers—indeed, out of range of human vision—the fliers tumbled on aerial currents as pups play on a lawn. Free from gravity's constraint and garbed in the woodland *dusken* of the Dainnan, Ashalind learned how to somersault in the air, how to make loops, dives, steep turns, rolls and other aerobatic manoeuvres. She was a child again. Not since the age of seven, a millennium ago, had she indulged in such foolishness. Never had she been abetted by such an accomplice in frolicsome absurdity, lawless in the streaming air, a dance partner whose beauty made her weak.

Errantry looked on with a frigid eye. To raptors, flight was a livelihood.

'I would like to remain in levity always,' said Ashalind, floating with Angavar among the outermost leaves of an oak. 'Gravity is too grave a condition.'

'Alas, thy race is not designed for constant lightness,' he said. 'Their bones lose density, their sinews shrink. In idleness, the mortal heart shrivels.'

'Then I call it a shame!' said Ashalind, swimming in deepgreen, scalloped foliage. 'Yet it matters not, if I may fly with thee sometimes.'

'Where next?' inquired Angavar.

'To Tiriendor, now. I would fain see that fair forest in Autumn, as I shall always love it best.'

In Tiriendor, the liquidambars were formed from jewels of light showered from the sunset, and the oaks were hung with balconies of bronze. The air had a dreamlike cast, as if a haze of gold dust floated through the trees. Bright leaves bubbled past, whirling, escaping in sudden outbreaks from the boughs, glimmering and whispering in the sunlight. They lay on the ground, palms upturned and empty, like begging hands. Wild quinces ripened on their boughs like gold-green lanterns, and scarlet-capped toadstools resembling goblins' caps thrust up from the mould.

This time, brambles failed to catch at Ashalind's apparel. Briars and thorns waved themselves aside. Nor did animals and birds flee—on the contrary, they came willingly to Angavar's hand, docile and unafraid. Some, he called to his side; others came seeking him. Timid fawns and wary wolves, gentle doves, falcons, bears, squirrels—all approached him with trust, seeking his caress. Even the white moths of eventide fluttered in circlets above his head, crowning his dark beauty with cold flames flickering palely.

'Why did the animals not gather thus when first we passed this way?'

'I bade them stand aloof. Wouldst thou not have suspected a Dainnan with a retinue of wild creatures?'

'I suspected thee nonetheless!' she answered with a smile.

More flocks of swanmaidens visited them, and the baobhan-sith in great numbers, and wights of every kind. Few had discovered the true identity of Erith's erstwhile King-Emperor. His Royal glamour had remained too strong, impenetrable. Those few that had learned of it had heard the truth from the Unseelie Attriod, who had been apprised of it by the Fithiach.

Seelie or unseelie meant nothing to the Faêran, who had naught to fear from wights. Whereas a mortal King might have punished them, Angavar had made no reprisal against those of the Unseelie Host who had answered Morragan's Call. According to Faêran Code they had done no wrong. It was neither treasonous for wights to gather at the summons of a Faêran Prince, nor criminal for them to harry mortals and assail them. Customarily, the Faêran did not concern themselves with dealings between wights and mortals.

While fulfilling his pledge to protect the Empire, and when fighting his way through wight-invaded Isse Tower to find

Ashalind, Angavar had ridden against the Unseelie Host. Yet the greater part of the wights who had been defeated at the hands of Angavar and his knights bore no malice against their conquerors. Even the Waelghast, once Chieftain of the Unseelie Hosts, had challenged Angavar out of pride only, and a perverse desire for sport, no matter how perilous. They might at times provoke an engagement with the Faêran, for it was in their nature to be battle-hungry, but it was nigh impossible for wights of eldritch to nourish hostility towards them. There were, perhaps, exceptions to this rule amongst the remaining lords of the Unseelie Attriod, but they were now scattered.

Underground they passed, Angavar and Ashalind, with their Faêran retinue. Below the graves and sarcophagi of men, they visited caverns of the Fridean, and the workings and delvings of knockers and eldritch miners. Everywhere, diminutive fellows crowded around, laying down their picks and shovels, bowing low in awe.

'Is it *hisself*? *Hisself* indeed!' they twittered amongst themselves, drawn irresistibly by the presence of the Faêran King.

To the land of the fells their Skyhorses flew. The true wolves of Ravenstonedale, beautiful and dignified, approached the Faêran King and his companion with timid grace. They offered no hurt, and even proudly brought their cubs to show to the visitors. It seemed they had complete trust in Faêrankind—faith enough to accept Ashalind's presence with merely a sniff of query.

'In the manner of their species,' said Angavar, fondling the ears of a playful cub, 'they are not wont to prey on thy race. Their howls are not the voicing of hunger and blood lust, but a communication between their kindred. The fireside legends humans spin amongst themselves do great injustice to the wolves. They hunt for food, play with their young and dwell in harmony with the forest.' He laughed. 'As merciless killers, they cannot begin to approach the achievements of humanity!'

Plundered of their Faêran-wrought treasures, the halls under Waterstair stood empty. They echoed to strands of mortal and Faêran laughter that intertwined like chains of field-daisies and stars.

'Verily,' confirmed Angavar, 'this treasure was wrought by my people during the Golden Era. Before we went under the hills to lie down in the Pendur Sleep, we hid it away. The writing on the portal—these are the words of the swan-music riddle. If the word "swan" is spoken aloud in the Faêran tongue, the doors will open.'

'True Thomas was able to translate the riddle for us,' said Ashalind. 'Do swans indeed sing as they fly? I have been a swan. I did not notice it.'

'Thou hast not been a true swan, Goldhair. The feathers of true swans possess unusual properties, and make a poignant music as they glide through the air,' said Angavar. 'But not all ears are able to hear it.'

Above mountains Ashalind floated with her lover, and across sunset seascapes. They drifted over the riven snowscapes of Rimany, the filatures of Severnesse, the crocus fields of Luindorn, the wild shores of Finvarna and Avlantia's ruined and forsaken cities. In the long, long rays of equinoctial radiance it seemed forever to be the beginning of a golden day. The sun glided low in the northern sky, mellow and amber, sweet as a honeyed peach, its attenuated beams casting spindly shadows across the land. Low-angled, the light was richly tinted. The season brought not the hard white-gold of Summer hammering straight down from the noon arc, but soft, malleable bars of yellow-gold which speared slantwise through the trees. They changed every leaf into a sliver of stained glass, panes of old gold, blood-garnet and russet, and they painted each tree with translucent gilt on one side, freckled shadow on the other. Eternal morning reigned in that long, low, corn-yellow light—Autumn Evermorn.

As the season's glory deepened, they returned to the bustle of Caermelor.

In the solar of the palace a pile of logs and pine cones burned in the grate of a fireplace luxuriantly carved with the arms and supporters of Eldaraigne. The walls of the solar gleamed with a faint gold tinge emitted by the chromium compound which had been mixed with the plaster. Against this lily sheen the tapestries stood out in startling, brilliant colours. Two brindled greyhounds lounged on the patterned hearthrug, wearing strong collars of rubies. Near them stood a small inlaid table of oak, with a chess set of jasper and onyx disposed on top of it. On another table squatted a jewel casket with etched and filigreed lock-plates, its matching keys lying carelessly alongside. Forests of candles blazed in chandeliers and atop tall candelabra.

A footman stood to attention, bearing a silken cushion. A musician leaned upon a high stool, dreamily plucking the strings of a great golden harp. Notes rained from it like frozen tears of the sun, for the young sovereign was here in the solar, and he was rarely without music.

Viviana and Caitri sat in the window niche, busy at embroidery and whispers. Edward had consented—with a distracted wave of his hand as though they were may-flies he brushed away—to their remaining seated in his presence. A roseate glow silhouetted the demure profiles of the two girls. Beyond the embrasure, the sky seemed slashed and split like a ripe persimmon. The red light of sunset streamed in, clear shafts; elongated crystals of ruby. The uncrowned King-Emperor, Edward, stood resting an elbow against the mantelpiece. Moodily, he ran the toe of his boot along one of the fire-irons. Beside him stood Ashalind.

'Prithee look at this, Edward,' she was saying. 'What is your judgement? Do you think it will be to my lord's taste?'

Edward turned his attention to the small, glittering circle in her upturned palm. He took it between thumb and forefinger. The outer wall of the band was worked cunningly with a pattern of eagles' feathers entwined with seabirds' plumes. On the inner side were engraved the words 'I love thee'.

'It is a noble thing,' the young King-Emperor commented, examining it closely. 'Excellent work. One would expect no less from the Royal Goldsmith.'

'I gave him my white bird bracelet to be melted down,' explained Ashalind, touching her wrist where the ornament used to encircle it. '"This gold is only twelve carats," said he to me. "When it is purified there will be less metal to work with." "Enough for a ring?" I asked. "In sooth," said he.'

'But your bracelet!' protested the scion of D'Armancourt, handing back the ring. 'Did you not tell me 'twas your father's gift?'

Ashalind slipped the ring into a small pouch of green velvet, tied with gold ribbon.

'Yes, but you see, Edward, it was the only article in my possession which my lord has not given me. My father would not think it amiss. To me, the value of the bracelet extends far beyond its material worth. I desired some rare thing to give my betrothed in token of our vow. And the ring possesses a secret. Pressed snugly within an internal conduit are three strands of my hair.'

'How inventive,' said Edward, scrutinising the flames.

The harp stilled. An unfamiliar silence stalked the solar.

'Play,' Edward said over his shoulder. Instantly the musician's hands found business.

'Your birthday approaches so quickly,' said Ashalind, finding cheery words to dispel the discomfort which seemed inexplicably to have arisen. 'To gain the age of sixteen and to be crowned King-Emperor on the self-same day—what a momentous day for you.'

Good sooth! she thought. *I myself am only seventeen Winters old. There is no great number of years between us. Or maybe a thousand . . .*

'Have you seen your latest gifts?' she continued hastily, hoping to smooth his furrowed brow with lively chatter. 'There are so many, they have been forced to store some of them in the Upper Wardrobe.'

'People are generous,' he murmured. 'As we speak, a gift that I have commissioned for you is being crafted. 'Twill be something else not given you by Angavar.'

'What is it? Tell me, prithee!'

'A gift to suit you perfectly. A looking-glass . . .'

She caught her breath, coughed discreetly behind her hand to cover it. There had been that in his tone, and in the way he lowered his head, darting a quick glance at her, which suggested some hidden meaning. But then he looked away.

'There he is,' squeaked Viviana, letting her embroidery fall and pointing out the window. Both maids craned forward to look into the grounds below. A captain of the Royal Guard strode past. Glancing up, he saluted briefly, giving a wry smile.

'Your heart's out the window, Vivi,' said Ashalind. 'You may follow it if you wish, but use the stair.'

'May I?'

'Of course! You too, Cait.'

The two damsels curtsied gracefully and exited the solar. As they did so, a page in Royal livery entered, dropping to one knee in front of Edward.

'Speak,' the young man said brusquely.

'Your Imperial Majesty, I bring greetings from Lady Rosamonde of Roxburgh, who awaits in the antechamber.'

'Gramercie, Griflet. I shall call for her anon.' Edward waved the page away. 'Anon.'

'Pray excuse me, Edward,' said Ashalind, clutching the green velvet bag. 'There are matters to which I must attend.' She curtsied.

'Queens do not curtsy,' he said. A roughness edged his voice.

The blood rose to her cheeks.

'I am not yet a queen. You, now, are my King-Emperor, my sovereign.'

He did not reply, but took her hand, kissed it and nodded. As she went out the door, he turned back to the fireplace.

Ashalind descended the spiral stairs and followed a darkening hallway. Her footsteps seemed to echo, which was odd, because rich carpets covered the wooden floors. The echoes slowed, although her pace did not slacken. She stopped in her tracks. Something familiar was nearby. She could smell it.

The silence was utter.

Neither the buzz of conversation from the Great Hall, nor the soft-footed shuffle of pages lighting the lamps and flambeaux came sifting down the corridor. From the courtyard, not the creak and scrape of the well-winch, nor the dusk cooing of doves in the dovecote, nor the barking of hounds in the kennels, nor the clatter of hooves on the cobbles—none of the normal sounds of the palace could be heard.

'Come out,' she pronounced into the quietness.

Nothing altered.

'Come out, you,' she insisted, more loudly. 'I know you are there.'

The hallway remained dark and still.

Impatiently she cried, 'If you do not show yourself, I shall have you squeezed out, like whey from a cheese!'

A small figure slid from a wall niche. It stood twiddling its thumbs nervously.

He always made her irritable. She pitied him, he with his pathetic sidling about in dark places, his abstruse fears, his club-footed limp: pitied him, fearing him the while.

'Well,' she said at last, 'good luck be with you, Pod of Isse. I see you stowed away after all.'

Pod twiddled his thumbs faster. His face was blank as an unwritten page.

'Why did you come here? Do you seek me? Or a cure, per-haps—do you seek the High King of the Faêran, to cure you of your deformity? He will do so if I ask him—'

'No!'

The lad had shouted. The shout crashed off the walls, cuffing Ashalind's ears. She took a step back.

'Well, what then?' she snapped, hiding her discomfort with peevishness.

'I wanted to see the palace. Wanted to get away from Heligea.'

'Heligea too came hither, simple gull. And I'll warrant she does not know you exist.'

'Does.'

'Does she not like you? Why? Did you tell her something she would rather not have heard?'

Pod's lip trembled.

'Don't be vexed,' he said. 'I'm hungry.'

Ashalind softened. 'That's easily dealt with,' she said. 'I'll show you the way to the kitchens. Come.' But he held back.

'Too many people.'

'Oh. I understand. You and I, we avoided company, we never cared for the staring, did we? Come down to the kennels. The hound-boy will give you bread and meat. Only he and the hounds shall see you. Howbeit, you can be healed, like I was. *He* can heal you, and maybe you will grow up to become a great wizard or the like. You have a gift—'

'No,' said Pod vehemently. 'You shan't take it!' He stared at her in horror, or hatred.

'Nobody can take away your gift. Who should wish to do so?'

'The henk, the henk I mean, you holiday fool!'

It came to her now that he believed his club foot was connected with his random capacity to prophecy, much as a carlin's sacrifice of faculties was a prerequisite for power.

'Should you be healed, your gift would remain with you,' she stated. He thrust out a sullen lip. 'If you do not believe me, hear it from my lord, who cannot lie!' Pod remained obstinate. 'You stupid boy,' she cried at length, exasperated. 'Why do you refuse help?'

'Don't want your help,' he blurted, looking wildly about as though she had trapped him and there was no escape.

'Then I will offer it no longer! In any case, you are not as clever as you thought. Your predictions are not worth a pinch of snuff. They are fickle and maggoty. You said that he and I should never find happiness together—you were wrong. Wrong—do you hear me? I am to wed my lord in the land of Faêrie, and no thing shall ever come between us!'

An inexplicable feeling of dread came over her as the words left her mouth. Fervently she wished that she had never spoken them. Once, she had heard Thomas of Ercildoune quoting, in a rare moment of pessimism, 'At man's moment of utmost happiness, that is when the axe is about to fall. Some contend that great joy is in fact the harbinger of great sorrow.'

Ashalind waited without breathing. Pod's eyes glazed over. He opened his mouth. 'Such as you and he—'

'Hold your tongue!' she cried, her hands jammed over her ears. 'I will not listen to you. I will not!' She turned and fled. So that the dire words would not penetrate, she began to sing a ditty Caitri had been warbling that morning before breakfast—a silly love song in an outmoded tongue.

'Sweven, sweven, sooth and winly,
Blithely sing I leoth, by rike.
Hightly hast thou my este,
Mere leofost.'

Down the passageway she hastened, *sweven, sweven,* and around a corner, *sooth and winly, blithely sing I leoth.* But even through thicknesses of stone, and filtering between her trembling fingers, the last intoned words of the warped boy came trickling—
'. . . shall never find happiness together . . .'

'Sorrow take you, lying wretch,' she sobbed. 'Sorrow take you!'

But already, it had.

The coronation of the new King-Emperor, Edward IV of the House of D'Armancourt and Trethe, High King and Emperor of Greater Eldaraigne, Finvarna, Severnesse, Luindorn, Rimany and Namarre, King of His other Realms and Territories—this investiture took place on a bright day in Gaothmis, the Windmonth. Contrary to its usual wont at this season, the wind was not strong or gusty, for it had been prevented from becoming anything but the lightest breeze, merely enough to send a sparse confetti of leaves wafting through the mild air to shower as lightly as kisses on the procession. Blue were the skies, as acres of cornflowers. Billowy clouds piled up around the horizon in opaque puffs edged with silver.

The quality of the daylight was notable. It poured from the skies like clear water, sparkling with the lustre of crystal. Nightly, the sky was an ebony shield lavishly pitted with silver, and the air wafted in mild currents, exceptionally balmy for the time of year.

Kings and nobles gathered from every corner of the Empire to swear their fealty to the new King-Emperor and do him homage. Six thousand guests attended the coronation festivities, which lasted for three days and nights. Each day as the sun westered, open-sided pavilions were set up on the tourney field. Upon the high embankment at the northern end, the Royal Pavilion stretched the width of the field, glorious in purple and gold. In the glow of afternoon, the entire site bloomed with colours like a flowered meadow, forested with tall poles from which streamed flags including the Banner of the Fair Realm with its eagle, crown and hawthorn, the Empire Standard, the Royal Banner of D'Armancourt, the Eldaraigne Jack, flags of the other countries of the Empire, the Standard of the Royal Attriod and numerous standards and banners of the Dainnan, Wizards, Stormriders and other nobility; Windship flags; tattered oriflammes from ancient battles; pennons; a hundred and twenty pennoncels three and a half yards long, charged with shields of the Royal Arms; four and eighty streamers thirty-two yards long, of red worsted, charged with gold lions and white lozenges; fifty streamers forty-five yards long, decorated with swords and lilies; fifteen hundred small swallow-tailed flags called gittons, with swans, stags, greyhounds, watch-worms and falcons; hundreds more gittons striped red and white; and three hundred streamers thirty yards long chequered gold and white, sprinkled with green and red roses.

The Coronation Festival of Edward IV became known as the Festival of Wonders, for with discretion, the Faêran had influenced every aspect of its organisation. At the nightly feasts, courses were served in number and deliciousness far surpassing any feast in history. Never had roasted meats tasted more succulent or worts more savoury, never were sweetmeats more fragrant and appetising. None could recall wobbling jellies which towered higher on their dishes without collapsing, whipped cream that melted more agreeably on the tongue, or richer truffles, or more plentiful.

A hundred tuns of purple grape wine from newly broached casks was pronounced the best vintage ever. In addition there flowed sarceal, paxaretta and topaz, three hundred tuns of ale, one pipe of hippocras and a cordial of wine and spices.

A partial inventory of the food included fifteen hundred quarters of bread, one hundred and four oxen, six wild bulls, twelve boars, nine hundred sheep, three hundred and four calves, three hundred and four herons, two thousand geese, a thousand capons of high grace, two thousand pigs, a hundred and four peacocks, assorted pigeons, pheasants, grouse, hens, rabbits and curlews, eleven thousand eggs, five hundred stags, bucks and roes, fifteen hundred hot pasties of venison, six hundred and eight breams and pikes, twelve porpoises and seals, a hundred and twenty gallons of milk, twelve gallons of cream, thirteen hundred dishes of jelly, two thousand cold baked tarts, ninety gallons of hot and cold custards and countless Sugared delicacies and wafers. The variety of dishes was improbable. Each pie was made with forty-eight different kinds of meat, except for the largest. When it was opened it proved to contain twenty-six live musicians, who, on being revealed, struck up on their instruments. The tourney field was filled with harmonies played on sackbut and serpent, on ophicleide, gittern and lute.

Such divertissements took place between the courses as were discussed by the guests for years to follow. Every entertainer performed his act flawlessly—even a novice juggler who, awed by the multitudinous and splendid company, allowed his concentration to lapse for an agonised instant, found the dropped bottle somehow back in his hand and immediately whirling through the air with its fellows as though naught had ever been amiss. Not one of the musicians plucked or blew a wrong note.

By virtue of the sight conferred on her by the green ointment, Ashalind perceived more than did the other mortals at the feasts. It took some time for her to be able to differentiate between the sights visible to all, and those visible only to herself and the Faêran. The first time she spied a Faêran lady passing among the guests and taking food from their plates, she was scandalised.

'Oh, why should Lady Lindorieth be thieving so brazenly?' she whispered to Ercildoune. 'The guests will object, and then she may become angry and put some spell on them. Is there nothing to her taste at the tables of the Faêran?'

The Duke frowned and looked blank.

'Your reference eludes me, Ashalind,' he said.

Angavar sat so close by Ashalind that his hair caressed her shoulder when he moved, and each time, a tingle ran right through her skin. He now raised one eyebrow. Only a whisper was necessary.

'Lindorieth takes what she wants, where and when she desires it,' he murmured. 'As is her right. Some among us choose to waive that right. Others do not.'

Ashalind saw then that none of the diners whose plates had been looted seemed to notice their lack. The Faêran lady, exquisitely lovely, was taking only the *toradh* of the food, leaving its semblance still on the dish.

'But she removes most fare from the platters of the lean guests!'

'Which is why they are lean.'

'There is no logic in this.'

Angavar bent his grey gaze on her. 'Thou hast much to learn of our ways, Goldhair,' he reminded her.

'I believed that the Faêran habit was to penalise overeaters.'

'Dost thou note the way that those singled out by Lindorieth wolf their fare? They eat and yet wane, never waxing.'

'They do not appear hale. Yet others look enviously at them, for being able to consume so much rich fare and remain as slender as reeds. Is taking their toradh a punishment or a reward? It is a mystery . . .'

'To thee.' He appeared amused by her perplexity. 'Look there!'

He indicated a table lined with bejewelled courtiers. The face of the Marquess of Early—whose waistline threatened to split the gorgeously embroidered silk of his doublet—bore a look of pain. He had pushed his gilt and velvet chair back from the table and was using a lace-edged satin handkerchief to mop his brow. A lithe young Faêran lord had just prodded his bulging abdomen with a crosier, in passing. Another, without breaking stride, casually trod on the toes of the gouty marquess. The elderly gentleman groaned, picked up his foot and massaged it.

'The Marquess suffers for being an overzealous trencherman,' remarked Ercildoune, following the line of Ashalind's stare.

'No, no,' she protested indignantly. ''Tis Faêran mischief.'

'Thomas speaks only the truth,' said Angavar. 'The man is a glutton. He requires lessoning.'

'These laws of thine are hard,' sighed Ashalind. 'If Early can be persuaded to change his habits, wilt thou cure him of the gout?'

'He will then cure himself,' laughed Angavar.

The sound of his laugh, and the look of him, promptly drove all speculation about the Marquess of Early from Ashalind's mind. Angavar's Faêranness dizzied her with an inebriation of the mind she was hard put to resist. With an effort she recalled her thoughts, blinked and focused again on the tourney field.

Every evening, as the trestles and pavilions were being disposed, Feulath—now Royal Wizard in place of Sargoth the Discredited—would put on a show of fireworks so spectacular as to disgrace all his former displays as a bonfire makes pallid a candle. After the fireworks were over, pastel-coloured orbs of light would spring up around the revellers, lining the edges of every tent and flag, lying strewn upon the grass. They could not be picked up, and vanished when anyone tried, only to reappear later.

Around the tourney field, elevated stages had been set up for bards, and for the pie musicians, and there were platforms for dancing. To the delight and astonishment of the dancers, their feet skimmed the wooden boards like soap bubbles blowing across water.

Throughout the feasting many a song was sung, many a speech orated, many a cup raised in honour of Erith's new sovereign, and the Faêran King from under the hill, and his bride-to-be. Following the orations and toasts for the two Kings, True Thomas jumped to his feet and made a speech in praise of Ashalind. Without divulging the complexities of her past, he expounded upon her travails in the wilderness in such eulogistic frames that, listening with amusement, she began to wonder whether it were she he was talking about, or some stranger. Sianadh was lauded as the champion who had helped on her first journey, while Viviana and Caitri were extolled for their loyalty and resourcefulness on later treks. The roles Diarmid and Muirne had also played were not forgotten. Ercildoune courteously concluded his speech with a mention of having once danced with Ashalind at Court, and how honoured he felt to have partnered the next Queen of Faêrie.

It was only then that Ashalind fully comprehended the enormity of the step she was about to take. The excitement of the past few months had kept her from seeing it. In being wed to Angavar-Thorn she would become the Queen of the Fair Realm itself. It seemed improbable, a wild dream—exhilarating yet terrifying. Her gaze rested upon her handsome lover. He was of the Faêran—the terrible, beautiful race that loved and hurt her own kind. And unions between these two kinships had always been doomed . . .

yet such tragedies all lay in the past. For certain, matters could be different now!

Beyond the barriers and gyves of difference, her love for Thorn was strong and steadfast—as it were, the steely shaft of a pin that could clasp together two halves of a brooch, the one made of diamond, the other of glass.

There were toasts to Sianadh, and to Viviana and Caitri. Then, from a table set a little apart from the rest, a man stood up. He bowed in the direction of the high table and the company fell silent.

'Speak,' commanded Edward in a clear voice. 'You must know, all sealfolk are welcome amongst us. Your fealty is sworn and the sea-gifts you have brought are deemed most worthy.'

By the grey sheen of his shaggy head, Ashalind now saw that the standing man was in fact Galan Arrowsmith. On his right sat a girl-woman. Her smile was enigmatic, her hair the colour of the ocean illumined by lunar reflection. To his left were seated Betony and Sorrel, now joyously reunited with their brother.

Arrowsmith said, 'Our Sovereign of Erith is generous. Long may he reign.' A murmur of approval ran through the gathering. He resumed: 'We have heard how the Bear of Finvarna has performed many services for Lady Ashalind. This may be so, but once, not so long ago, I too accompanied her along her perilous way. My lady, had I known to whom you were betrothed—'

She interrupted, 'Galan Arrowsmith—to you, my friends and I owe much.'

He bowed.

'You gave us the shelter of your village and more,' she continued. 'You lent us your steeds and your strength. Such kindness shall ever be remembered.'

'Yet methinks that for all I did 'twas not enough,' said Arrowsmith. He added wryly, with a momentary glance at Ercildoune, 'And I never danced with thee, my lady.'

There was a sudden, tense silence. Then a ripple of laughter spread around the speaker. Ashalind glanced at Angavar and saw that he was smiling. Perched on his chair-back, Errantry roused his feathers fiercely.

'Well then, get up on the floor,' Ashalind challenged the half-silkie, and she left her seat.

He strode up to the dancing-floor, where Ashalind met him. He kissed her hand, the musicians struck up, and the two danced a few steps to the accompaniment of cheers and applause. When the music stopped, Arrowsmith bent over her hand once more.

'Methinks it will take me a good while to soothe the hammering of my pulse,' he said loudly, but only half in jest. Flicking his gaze towards a table dominated by Ertishfolk, where Sianadh sat, he added, 'Kavanagh, devour your red heart!'

Sianadh, drunk as a lord, roared a jovial but unintelligible reply and saluted Arrowsmith with a brimming tankard raised aloft, spilling ale on all and sundry.

'I never danced with him either,' said Ashalind.

Arrowsmith turned his fey sea-eyes on her. All at once the company fell silent again, hearkening, watching both Angavar and the couple on the dance floor. Those assembled were fully and horribly cognisant of what the jealousy of the Faêran, if aroused, could mean.

'Ah, what he missed!' Ashalind's dance partner audaciously pronounced.

At the high table, one corner of Angavar's mouth twitched.

A sigh fled through the gathering.

Gallantly, Arrowsmith conducted Ashalind back to the high table and dropped to one knee before Angavar.

'Your pardon, Majesty, if I have offended you.'

'My betrothed dances with whomsoever she wishes,' said Angavar, clearly untroubled. 'That she has chosen you is a panegyric, for the lady knows how to choose well.'

He was merely amused at the seal-man's bold praise of his betrothed. Jealousy was far from him—he knew Ashalind too well to doubt her, and besides, he was Faêran and had every reason to be complacent.

A murmur of laughter came from all sides. All tension broke like an eggshell, and relief flooded over the guests. The festivities resumed.

By day, the field was cleared for sports and games, jousts and tournaments. The Faêran knights eagerly took the field for a hurling match, that being a favourite game of theirs. Following its conclusion, where the vanquished team had stood, suddenly they stood no more, and a horde of flying beetles went up over the tourney field, darkening the skies. The price they must pay for defeat was to fly across Eldaraigne in this form, but they took no harm from it and good-naturedly endured the penance, which they would have inflicted on their opponents had their fortunes been reversed.

But eventually the day was over, and all festivities came to an end. Soon a Seaship—the *Royal D'Armancourt*—would depart from Caermelor. Escorted by six Dainnan cruisers she would set sail for Arcdur's stony, lichened wastes, carrying Ashalind and Angavar, Ercildoune, Roxburgh and the other survivors of the Royal Attriod. They would be accompanied by the Faêran knights and ladies of Eagle's Howe, all of them desperately keen to find the gate. Such a mighty entourage must prove invincible against any lingering dangers that might be encountered along the way. Yet their foes had been conquered; what could possibly threaten?

Ashalind's parting from Edward had been painful.

'You must go,' he had insisted, at a private moment. 'You must simply leave, the sooner the better.' He could not hide the fact that he fought against tears.

'But we shall not be apart for long,' she reassured him. 'When my lord and I find the Gate, all Gates will be opened once more! Time will no longer run awry between the worlds, for my lord has promised that when we return to Faêrie he will match the time-stream of the Realm with Erith's continuum. Everything shall return to the way it was before the Closing, save that the inconsistent passing of years in one realm and hours in the other will be annulled. There will be open exchange between the worlds, and you and I shall be able to visit one another at any time.'

'That is not what I mean,' he said, and she finally understood how blind she had been.

'Besides,' he stammered, 'somehow, in my heart I fear the parting will be longer than you surmise. I fear . . .' He could not go on.

'Have no fear. How can there be harm, when I am beside him?'

Immediately she regretted this statement. He threw her a look of anguish.

'Yes. He can give you anything,' he said. 'Everything. I love you both. I wish you both every happiness. Of all mortals I have ever seen,' he added earnestly, 'I have never beheld such exquisite beauty. When you use the looking-glass, think of me.'

In sudden confusion, she could only nod, tight-throated. Thus they took their leave of each other.

From Caermelor's estuarine docklands the Arcdur expedition departed by Seaship in the morning. The masts of the clipper *Royal D'Armancourt* pierced a pale blue sky. A light, fresh breeze was blowing. The passengers looked back at the pier and the numerous docks and jetties where ships and boats of all sizes were moored, rocking gently, their masts and rigging seeming to knit and unravel like some crazy spider's web. Southward, past the stern, the crag of the Old Castle thrust up out of the water. The tide was high, wavelets covering the causeway. Facing this gaunt sentinel of rock stood the hill of Caermelor, its skirts laced with foam. The palace, at the summit, loomed dark against the sky. Its roofs, towers and turrets were alive with flags which snapped and flapped like hundreds of wings. A sudden spear of golden light glanced off the armour of a guard moving high on the battlements. Pennants flew also from the roofs of many of the buildings perched on the hillside, in celebration of the coronation.

To starboard the land rolled back into an Autumn haze, the shoreline curving around to a headland, the Cape of Winds. To port, the open sea sparkled like a polished goblet of crystal filled with blue-green wine, clear and cool. The water flashed as though strewn with diamond chips. Far off in the waves, sleek shapes dived. Sometimes they surfaced near the ship, calling greetings, waving to the Faêran and mortals on board.

The ship was steering northwest, hugging the coast. She kept on that heading until she rounded the Cape of Winds. From there, the captain turned her north to cross the mouth of the Gulf of

Mara. In the days that followed, her great keel passed over the place where once the fair isle of Tamhania had risen from the ocean. There was no sign that an island had ever existed. The sea rolled bland and innocent over Tamhania's sunken tomb, and the Autumn sun shone upon it softly, a yellow pearl. At one point, the ship hove to and the voyagers paused while songs of remembering were sung, and flowers were strewn over the water.

Angavar summoned a brisk southerly airstream which sent them on their way again. The clipper heeled over and now she began to plough the waves, slicing through them, keen as a honed blade. She plunged in up to the hawse pipes and bounded up, water pouring off her hull like ribbons of molten glass. A curling wave, foam-ridden, opened out in a long chevron from her bows. Tier upon tier, the great crescents of her heraldic sails snapped taut and hard, brimming with the power of the wind.

Those aboard could see, away to the east, the low grey line of the coast. It drew nearer as they approached the Cape of Tides. Soon the cliffs of the promontory loomed on the starboard side and the ship was passing through a narrow sea lane between the mainland and the islands of the Chain of Chimneys.

After that, the shoreline retreated once more. They turned northeast, the wind obligingly swinging with them. Remaining parallel with the coast they sailed on at a rapid pace, retracing the journey Ashalind had once made in a fishing boat. A sense of unease grew on her as they neared Arcdur. Too many memories came crowding in. As she stood at the rail watching the approaching shore, a line of dark birds rose flapping from the trees and flew away inland. High in the rigging, Errantry opened his hooked beak and screamed. It seemed some sort of omen.

A shock jolted through her. She looked up to see Angavar— he had joined her, unnoted, and placed his arm lightly around her waist. Together they stood, looking out across the intervening water towards the land.

'Why did the Raven's knights betray their King?'

'Thou hast set eyes on him, Goldhair. Thou hast been subject to his influence. Almost, thou didst allow thyself to be lured.'

Ashalind cast her mind back, to Hob's Hill in Avlantia, and a traverse which passed beneath it—a long green tunnel of overarching trees beyond which shone the hills of Erith in the saffron morning. Larks were singing, and a merlin hovered in the sky, and the hedges were bare and black along the fallow fields, and blue smoke stencilled the distant skies. Somewhere, bells were tolling.

There had been a clear and compelling voice, like dark metal, and that voice saying,

'Bide here now, and I swear no harm shall come to thee under my protection. I can take thee through fire as through castles of glass. I can take thee through water as through air, and into the sky as through water, untrammelled by saddle or steed or sildron. Flight thou shalt have, and more. Thou hast never known the true wonder of the favour of the Faêran.'

That voice had pronounced her name, and she had stumbled. But the warm, hay-scented breath of her pony had recalled her to Erith, and the sound of children's footsteps pattered through her brain, bringing visions of her lost brother.

'Ashalind.'

This time she fell to her knees and could not arise. The children hurried by. To look over her shoulder, to see one who governed gramarye standing there with the whole of the Fair Realm at his back and that world promised to her—it would be so easy. So sweet it would be, to watch him pivot on his heel and walk away, and to follow. Slowly she clambered to her feet. Despite her desire, she neither looked back nor turned around. She pressed on, her feet and legs heavy, as though she waded through honey.

How could this Prince have nursed such bitter hatred against humankind? How could she have allowed such a one to twist the strings of her heart? That he no longer lived, except as a kind of abstraction, suspended her between relief and sorrow. The tugging of the opposing forces was perplexing, tearing open a wound with no comprehensible source.

Recalling her attention, the deck of *Royal D'Armancourt* rocked under her feet. Angavar was watching her, quizzically. She said to him, 'Now I understand. The charisma of Morragan lured them to it. They loved thee first, but they loved him too. You were absent— and there was no pony, no child to remind them of their fealty.'

'Few could resist his influence should he decide to make them change their path.'

'I did.'

'That I know. He knows also, too well, and he never shall forget.'

'But the power of gramarye is lost to him now!'

'A bird lifts itself on the air. It stoops to kill. Is there no power in that?'

She could find no reply.

'I regret allowing him to fly forth, the Raven,' said Angavar, turning his eyes towards the horizon. 'I ought to have captured him, caged him. For all his lack of strength he is out in the World now, free to cleave the skies like arrows shot by a mad archer, choosing targets at random.'

The clipper's slim bows slid into a deep natural harbour, a rocky sound. There, between high cliffs of gaunt stone, she came about. The indigo-coloured sails lost the wind, hanging in great soft loops from the yards, their golden lion devices obscured by the folds. From the gently canting deck, crewmen clewed in the canvas, hauling hard on the lines, throwing back their heads to squint up at masts so tall they tapered like ladders into the sky. The anchor was lowered with a rattle of iron chain. Ropes were flung ashore and tied to trees and rocks. As the first mate barked orders, landhorses and baggage-laden packhorses were led down a ramp from the fo'c'sle where they had been stabled, and across the gangplank onto dry land.

The passengers mounted their steeds. The expedition set off, winding northwards through the landscape of tall stones and natural, granite-lined wells.

The news of the Geata Poeg na Déanainn had spread rapidly, and all creatures of eldritch were by now aware of the possibility that a way back to the Fair Realm might indeed exist. All the Faêran knew it, but only a few mortals had been made party to the knowledge. The tidings had not been broadcast among the mortal populace of Erith, for the Faêran considered it was their own business and not a matter to be bandied about by gossiping humankind.

Thus it was that few mortals rode amongst the company. The ninety Faêran lords and nine Faêran ladies of Eagle's Howe accompanied the expedition, and Thomas of Ercildoune and Roxburgh as well, and Alys beside her lusty husband, although Istoren Giltornyr had remained at Caermelor with Richard of Esgair Garthen. With such a fellowship no force of mortal wizardry or men-at-arms was required, and besides, who would stand against them now? Nonetheless the two powerful carlins Ethlinn and Maeve had come to Arcdur, and the best knights of the Dainnan. And there was Sianadh, who had lost his Windship in a card game and, undeterred, was looking for excitement; and four of Silken Janet Trenowyn's unruly brothers, who had gained some fey qualities while under the influence of enchantment, and who sought the same goal as the Ertishman.

Yet it seemed to Ashalind that she and Angavar were escorted only by the mortals of the retinue, for the Faêran passed noise-lessly and swiftly among the monoliths, as outriders. She caught only fleeting glimpses of them riding through the landscape on either hand, and they seemed to her like beautiful images in watercolour, painted on the most fragile of tissue, so ephemeral they were already fading into the rain-washed pines, the rills that tumbled, tinkling, through jumbled stones and the moss that clambered over the rocks.

Cradled in the interstices between the monoliths, mists nestled like teased handfuls of raw silk. Lichen, like pale blue-green forests in miniature, clung to rocks. Heat and cold had worked upon the rocks of Arcdur's bones. Flakes of granite which had split from the parent boulders lay like tiny islands of lichenous leafage. At their old sites, clean-cut shapes remained; perfectly matched facets of pink rock.

Arcdur's outward appearance had not altered much since Ashalind's last visit—save in one marked respect. Throughout all her journeys through the lands of Erith, she had been accustomed to seeing wild birds and beasts flee at the approach of humankind. Now, on the contrary, the creatures of the wilderness came eagerly to the sound of their horses' hooves. Birds flew close and alighted on rocky ledges within arm's reach. At whiles Angavar would bid Errantry fly far off. Then he would raise his hand and small birds would come down to perch on his wrist. Sleek foxes and untame, topaz-eyed goats emerged from crevices to watch the riders pass. Lethargic snakes uncoiled. Glittering beetles spangled the air and lost themselves in the arcane drifts of Angavar's hair. Even nocturnal animals roused themselves and came forth from their hiding places to greet the Faêran riders and their King.

If the outer character of the land had changed but little, all else was different. Once, the scars and crags and granite stacks of Arcdur had withstood the attacks of wind and water with equanimity, even indifference. They had stood dreaming for millennia, lost in some remote mineral reverie, wreathed, from time to time, by mists, while year by year the ancient lichens flourished and grew on their hides at a pace so slow as to be apparent to no mortal creature.

Now, it seemed to Ashalind, the stones had awakened, and the trees and the waters also. She sensed a watchfulness, an excitement, everywhere. The air and the ground seemed charged with a kind of eldritch awareness. It was not difficult to guess the cause. Now that Angavar had thrown off his mortal guise and allowed his identity to be known, there was no thing unliving or living, no entity either *lorraly* or eldritch, that could be near him and not be stirred by the presence of that elemental power. As birds and beasts were attracted by this fair company, so also were the incarnations of eldritch. They, who typically would have fled or vanished in the blink of an eye, now showed themselves openly.

Large numbers of wights were seen by the mortals of the retinue. Many more were visible to the anointed eyes of Ashalind, and she saw they were diverse: hideous and fair, malign, tricksy and beneficent. She shuddered, and was thankful that she rode in the company of one who might subdue them all, if he chose.

Lesser wights crowded in rocky crevices or lingered on gravelly shingles by the brinks of winking pools. The waters of those pools would flurry momentarily. Sly eyes squinted from beneath sills. Beside a pebbly beck, the ferns abruptly twitched and nodded, as if something had waited amongst them but was already gone. Seated high on giant boulders, in places impossible for mortals to reach save by mountaineering or the use of sildron, pale damsels serenely combed their hair. At times, faint snatches of music rose from beneath the horses' hooves. Every shadow, every gnarled trunk, every crag seemed inherently, subtly, to harbour some manifestation. Every well and water sheltered some weird distillation, and if one watched for long enough, the lines of the land might shift to reveal another form. Even when the wind soughed through the pine needles, it sang with voices other than its own.

Angavar was fully aware of the attention, and permitted it, and did not ask for salutations or other acknowledgments of his sovereignty. That was not the way of the Faêran. That he alone was the ultimate sovereign of gramarye was incontrovertible. It needed no further proof, no validation.

From horizon to horizon, this country afforded an almost unimpeded view of the sky. The cloudscape arrayed it with awesome spectacle. Purple-grey cumulonimbi were piling up to great heights, crowding in from the west, borne on the back of a keen salt wind. They overtook the sun, blotting it out, haloed in silver by its hidden light. A dim veil of shadow crept across the landscape. Three strands of hair escaped from Ashalind's headdress and fluttered about her cheeks. A heaviness weighed down the air, a presentiment of rain. Like the quick stab of a pin, a single, miniature water-drop fell on the back of her hand.

Angavar was riding ahead of her, leading the party, for the country was so rocky they must progress in single file. The goshawk rode on his shoulder. She saw Angavar glance skywards. That was all—he did not gesture with his hands, nor did he call out some incantation. If he murmured any words at all, she was unable to catch them.

The wind veered. It swung around to the south, and now, overhead, the towering castles of mist were moving with it, as though on wheels. They billowed and altered shape, seeming to slowly explode from within and reinvent themselves in fantastic forms. Ragged holes and rents appeared, letting sunlight fall through in patches. As the rain clouds drew away from the sun's cool face, a wash of pale gold spilled over the stony heights of Arcdur, rinsing bluish shadows through chinks of rock.

Her servants rode at her heels. She heard them murmur, 'Behold, *he* has averted the storm.' Her maids and all the Dainnan remained in awe of him, of what he had become. Angavar turned in his saddle and smiled at Ashalind, and at the brilliance of that smile her heart was lit, and sped like a hunted thing.

'Do we continue upon the right path?' he asked.

She nodded, endeavouring to calm her pulse. 'I believe so.'

And indeed, recollection and some inner voice told her that their heading was correct, that somewhere to the north lay the place from which she had stumbled in the rain, long ago, driven from the delights of the Fair Realm of her own volition, gripped by a need to live in the same world as one whose face she had glimpsed through a window, more than a millennium ago.

Soon she would pass through the Gate at Angavar's side. Then she would ride into his world, a fantastic world, wild and strange, where dwelled her family, and her friends, and all the Talith who had abandoned Avlantia. She would meet them again, embrace them. And this time, she would stay.

The path which was not a path widened, and Angavar dropped back beside her. A small rock-goblin jumped squeaking from beneath the hooves of his Faêran steed. Angavar's laugh was captivating, contagious, and she must laugh with him.

But the landscape of Arcdur continued to roll monotonously by, offering no familiar sign to Ashalind.

'Is it possible,' she said anxiously, 'that the outward appearance of the Gate has changed during the years since I last saw it?'

'Possible,' Angavar said, 'but not probable. Wind and weather would not alter the stones much in such a short span, although if the ground has shifted, the angles of the rocks may have subtly altered—some may have fallen.'

'But if a trembling of the ground has moved the foundations of the Gateposts, then the Gate itself may have snapped shut or been thrown wide open!'

'Not so. The gramarye of the traverses is not easily tampered with. No mere quaking of the ground may open or close a Gate between the worlds. Be assured of it.'

It had taken several days for Ashalind to cross this region of Arcdur on foot, wandering pathless and weak from hunger. This time, the sun set only once upon her journey. That night they rode on for many leagues under the stars until the mortal riders grew weary.

The sky over Arcdur was filled with a jewelled splendour so brilliant, so vast, it was as though the land was roofed by a dome thickly encrusted with crystals in a multitude of sizes and intensities, prisms which split their own light into every twinkling colour.

'There once was a time,' said Angavar as they rode on, 'when the peoples of a world now in ruins dwelt in mighty cities so wreathed about with smoke and fume, nightly so ablaze with light powered by the harnessing of the energies of levin-bolts, that they could but dimly view the stars, if at all. These people of an era long past could not understand why their ancient poets praised the glories of the night, for they saw the stars merely as faded pinpricks in the crown of the firmament. Only by journeying to the highest desert places, furthest from their cities and closest to the sky, were they able to behold their stars as we now behold these of Erith. As for the stars of the Realm—why, those they glimpsed only in dreams.'

As he spoke, Ashalind watched him. His face glimmered with the sheen of far-off suns; his hair eclipsed them. Wonder and passion exulted her spirits with a force that was almost palpable. And it may be that the Faêran were sensible to such forces.

After a while, Angavar said, 'I love thee. How I love thee.'

He chose to make their bivouac in the shelter of a great stand of arkenfirs, down among the roots where fragrant needles had fallen in layers season after season, building up deep, dry cushions. Bolts of satin were thrown over these cushions, and the softest of beds they made. Lights kindled themselves amongst the boughs, and fuelless fires sprang up, whose flames gave out gentle warmth yet did not blacken the resinous mulch. No silken pavilions blossomed, decked with proud banners to proclaim that this was the stopping place of a king. There was no need for shelter. The rain would not fall upon them, nor would any wind steal into their midst like a thief to pry at their garments with fluttering fingers, or slip keen edges between their ribs. It was not necessary to set a watch for danger.

Beneath the arkenfirs a feast was held. Afterwards the Dainnan found repose, and Ashalind's servants also, and Ercildoune and Roxburgh.

'Good night,' whispered Angavar as he left Ashalind's side.

But she lay waking among her maids, twisting the leaf-ring about her finger.

'Fear no harm from wights now, betrothed,' he had told her, 'nor from any mortal creature. For when I am with thee, thou'rt safe from all harm. When I am not, I shall leave thee in the care of others who can protect thee, or else thou shalt bide in some secure place.'

Overhead the bristling boughs nodded, black against the pale night sky. She watched the stars moving in slow arcs of monstrous magnitude, uncounted miles away. She was tired, wanting to sleep, but she ached for Angavar's presence and her lids and ears were held open by the songs of the Faêran, whose forms she glimpsed like pastel glows drifting among the rock formations. For the Fair Ones did not sleep, not on this eve—she wondered whether they ever slept. All through the night they roamed in distant groups, singing songs so deeply moving they made her want to laugh and weep, and when she did find slumber, it was filled with the most poignant of dreams.

Next morning, the expedition crossed a ridge clothed with conifers. To the west, a glimmer along the horizon betrayed land's end, the ocean-washed shores. In a shallow valley below the ridge a clear beck chiselled its way through rocks of chalcedony. Their horses splashed through the water, kicking up spray which glittered like crystals threaded on a thousand silver filaments.

They were climbing then towards the sky, the wind soughing in their ears and pushing against their backs as though to nudge them on their way. Reaching the next hilltop they reined in to survey the land that lay before and below them. Errantry soared up and was lost in the sky's pearl-blue expanse. Choughs gliding on updraughts darted after winged beetles. The grey pallor of the stacks and chimneys was broken only by patches of pink lichen and a few stands of blue-green arkenfir. Wind chanted through the chinks in the formations. Running water chuckled and chimed. Hundreds of feet high, the stacks of Arcdur resembled dishes cooked in a monumental kitchen—one was formed like loaves of bread; further away, another towered like a pile of giant pancakes.

Ashalind's pulse quickened. These landmarks she recognised.

'We are nearing the place,' she said. 'We are close!'

Angavar only nodded, but she could perceive by the set of his features how deeply her tidings affected him. They started down the slope, their horses searching for footholds in mossy fissures. Soon they rode amongst the pinnacles of another valley. Ashalind's face grew flushed, her eyes burned as though fevered. 'Somewhere here! We are on the very threshold!' She cast about intensively, scrutinising each rock formation with utmost deliberation. 'We must go slowly. If I approach from the wrong angle, I might miss it.'

'A tall grey rock like a giant hand,' Angavar chanted softly, repeating her earlier words, 'and a slender obelisk leaning towards it, coloured as the lip of a rose petal. Both monoliths capped by a lintel-stone shaped like a doorstep. Near at hand in a granite hollow, a dark pool of water fed by a spring.'

Fleetingly, Ashalind wondered at the random events or the thread of destiny that had drawn her to this particular place and time over the span of more than a thousand years.

The Faêran riders drew in at either hand. The muted ringing of their bell-hung bridles recalled the unstorms that would never more blow across Erith to waken its past.

Between the pinnacles, a dark smear appeared in the eastern sky. Like a patch of smoke borne on a current in the upper airs it approached rapidly, eventually interpreting itself as a great, wheeling flock of birds. Raising his hand, Angavar came to a halt, and the whole retinue drew rein. The goshawk fell out of the sky, stooping to latch its talons onto the leather band encircling Angavar's wrist. As Angavar drew his hand down, the bird flapped, regaining his balance before folding his wings. He hissed and whistled urgently, his gold-orange eyes as bright as burning coins. Ercildoune and Roxburgh rode up beside their leader, who called out to the Faêran in their own tongue. Many of them pointed to the sky. In grim tones Angavar said, 'It is he. The Raven cometh.'

And there was a sting in Ashalind's heart, as though the utmost tip of a whip had lashed it.

'What now?' she breathed.

'He approaches too near to the Gate. It is essential he is not nigh when it is flung wide, lest in his rage and vengeance he devises a way to slip through ahead of me and close it against us. I will *not* be exiled a second time!'

The birds flew closer now. Their hoarse croaks scarred the wind. Crows, rooks and jays were they, and ravens, their plumage glossy black.

Now that she understood him more intimately, Ashalind glimpsed the tide of raw emotion surging behind the stern set of her lover's features. She surmised that although he was aroused to anger by the sight of the Raven, his brother in altered form, he also desired that sight, for he had loved Morragan, and mourned him, in his own way.

Again Angavar's voice rang forth and again the Faêran hearkened.

'Let us drive the Raven forth!' cried Roxburgh in fury, standing in his stirrups and shaking his fist towards the skies. 'Let us hunt him hence!'

The face of Ercildoune grew pinched with alarm. 'Hunt and capture,' he growled urgently, 'ere some mighty harm befalls us.'

'Sooth, yet such a task is beyond the reach of mortals,' said Angavar swiftly. 'I will do it, with half my knights.' To Ashalind, he added, 'Goldhair, this hunt is no enterprise for thee. Thomas and Tamlain shall remain at thy side, with the rest of the Faêran and the Dainnan knights. While I am gone, continue to seek the Gate. I will return anon.'

With a sudden, graceful gesture, he flung Errantry into the air. The goshawk soared up.

Horror caught hold of Ashalind. It came to her that should Angavar-Thorn ride away now, she would never see him again.

'Do not leave me, my lord,' she begged. 'I pray thee.'

From his saddle, he leaned close to her ear. His breath was warm and sweet against her cheek.

'Why so doubtful, *eudail*?' he asked softly, wonderingly. 'Be unafraid. Half the knights of Eagle's Howe shall surround thee, led by the first among my knights, Dorliroen and Naifindil. And yet, what can there be to fear?'

'It is not for myself, but for thee . . .'

He laughed. 'What can hurt me?' Taking her chin in his hand, he kissed her roundly. 'I must not tarry. Already the flock veers to the south and away. Farewell for but a moment.'

His steed sprang forward with a sound like the rushing wind.

Just like that, he was gone.

Fifty Faêran lords followed him, and Faêran ladies besides. At preternatural velocity their steeds raced among the stacks and towers and soon were lost to view. A gasp arose from the servants of Ashalind's retinue. Shading her eyes with her hand, Ashalind peered at the empty lands where the Faêran had vanished. She thought a second vast company of birds beat their way up from the chimneys, as though startled by the riders, to fly off in pursuit of the Corvidae. Hooked were their beaks; and their wings smote the air with mighty strength. They were birds of prey—hawks, or perhaps eagles.

'I conjecture my lord is drawn to his brother,' Ashalind said aloud, in troubled tones. 'Perchance that is why he goes after him, even though the flock has already turned aside. Yet Morragan now lacks his former strength, so why do the crows and rooks follow in his wake? Are they unseelie? Do they mean to work us ill?'

'They are only true birds, colleen,' replied Maeve One-Eye, who had drawn near, 'not wights! They are neither threatening us nor helping the Raven, but merely accompanying him. Like others they are drawn to him, but for a different reason: to the birds, he is one of them but with an aura of gramarye such as they have never known, and they are fascinated, compelled.'

'I mislike this business,' grimly said Thomas of Ercildoune.

'Pshaw!' snorted Roxburgh. 'There is naught to mislike about it, Tom, only that I have been thwarted in my desire to hunt the Raven.'

'Ride on, Ashalind,' cried Alys. 'We follow.'

As she could find no reason not to go on, Ashalind did so, casting many a backward glance. At her side rode Alys. The Dukes flanked the ladies, while behind them came Sianadh and the two carlins, their wands slung at their backs. Mounted on mettlesome black steeds, four stalwart young riders came also—the eldest sons of Trenowyn. The Dainnan rode close by, their horses not outpacing those of the Faêran who had remained with the mortals.

The sky of Arcdur took on an ominous look. A dark stain was creeping in at the edges. A hush fell across the land, and as if night had fallen, or a bitter frost, the song of birds no longer rang out.

The monoliths that now towered around Ashalind did not seem familiar, but she was experiencing a growing sense of significance that brought with it a certainty that the Bitterbynde Gate was close by.

A rumbling started up beneath their horses' feet. The ground shook.

The horses propped and pranced, snorting their disquiet. Images of the death throes of Tamhania flashed into Ashalind's thoughts.

'What's amiss?' shrilled Alys.

But the Faêran knights knew.

'The Cearb comes this way!' cried the Lord Dorliroen, peering into dark valleys between rocks.

Naifindil's horse reared. 'And with it, the last lords of the Unseelie Attriod!' he shouted.

Their blades glittered, sliding from the sheaths. 'We are ready,' called the knight-lords of Faêrie, but they were laughing now, flourishing their swords above their heads so that the supernatural metal sang a song of death.

The rocks and the soil shuddered at the coming of the Cearb, the Killing One—he who wore the three-cornered hat and possessed the ability to fling hills, and move the very ground—yet he was not the only unseelie lord that now appeared. The waters of Arcdur welled in their springs as the Prince of Waterhorses approached. Scorpions and vipers scattered at the sight of Gull, largest and swiftest of all spriggans. These three Princes of Unseelie had sworn vengeance against the mortalfolk who had taken up arms against them. And yet they were greatly outnumbered. It appeared certain their onslaught would lead only to their destruction.

'A madness is with the wicked ones,' Ashalind heard Maeve One-Eye murmur in astonishment.

Indeed a madness seemed to be upon the very fabric of Arcdur. The stones walked.

Or else, they appeared to be walking. As if they had uprooted themselves from their age-old positions they waddled from side to side, impelled by subterranean vibrations. Pebbles bounced and rolled along. Small fissures began to unseam themselves.

'Fear not, Lady Ashalind!' said Lord Naifindil, riding up to speak with her. 'We shall prevent these monsters from reaching thee. The Dainnan warriors surround thee, and the two carlins also. They will protect thee while we indulge in the pleasure of defeating those who dare to challenge us. Prithee, ride on in peace, fair mistress! Seek the Gate!'

Ashalind perceived the Faêran were beckoned by the opportunity of a skirmish. 'Go to it!' she said. He bowed, murmuring a courteous reply, and wheeled his steed about, before cantering away.

The remaining Faêran knights rode forth to meet their foes while the mortal retinue gathered around Ashalind. The standing stones of Arcdur obstructed a clear view. Between the tall, broad-shouldered monoliths, little could be seen of the encounter between eldritch wights and Faêran, save only flakes of smashed granite jetting high in fountains, and sundry flashes of brilliant light.

But, even as the mortals watched, these signs of conflict were moving further off. Ercildoune scowled. 'Three wights pitted against more than two score Faêran knights!' he said. 'By rights the clash should be decided in a trice. Yet it appears that instead of engaging, those corrupt plague-sores are deliberately drawing the Faêran away from us. What they hope to achieve by such strategy, I cannot guess. They are mad! We have been made secure from all peril of eldritch origin.'

'Methinks the appearance of the Raven was also a ruse,' said Alys with suspicion, 'intended to lure Angavar and his bonny knights from us so that the wicked ones could strike. Could we have been so easily gulled?'

'Is it that Angavar himself has been beguiled?' barked Ercildoune, made short-tempered by frustration. 'No wiser counsel have I ever known than his!'

'I suspect his judgement was clouded,' murmured Ashalind.

'Fain would I join the Fair knights in battle!' Roxburgh shouted furiously, but he had given his word to remain at Ashalind's side and would not be forsworn. Even as the last words left his lips, a vast crack unclosed in the stony ground right under their horses. Three of the Dainnan riders slipped sideways into it and vanished.

'We stand upon a delving of the Fridean!' cried Ercildoune. 'Ride to safety, all!'

Generated by the violent percussions of the Cearb's footsteps, the foundations of Arcdur were disintegrating, collapsing into hungry crevasses. Close beneath the surface the ceilings of Fridean tunnels were caving in, for throughout this region of Arcdur the ground was perforated, honeycombed with wightish caverns and rights-of-way. Ashalind and her companions looked about desperately for some sign of firm footing, but, hemmed in by natural architecture, could not discover which direction led to safety. Everywhere they turned, rock and gravel was dropping away, massive stones were toppling. Riders, undermined, were sliding into abysms. The carlins drove their wands into these cracks. Great grappling roots thrust forth like muscular fingers, driving through the shifting soils to grasp the particles and hold them together. Yet the gramarye of the two Daughters of Grianan was not sufficiently swift or encompassing. Horses and men floundered as the unstable ground subsided beneath them. Ashalind and her companions were rendered helpless against a peril that was not directly of eldritch origin.

Far off, several of Angavar's Faêran knights saw what was about and swerved their horses, veering away from the attack and racing toward the stricken riders. A misty light, like that which clung about the Faêran, now bloomed all around the struggling mortals, enfolding them. They were lifted, so that their horses' hooves no longer slipped and sank into the treacherous ground.

In the confusion, Ashalind was separated from her mortal bodyguard, but two Faêran lords rode up to her and led her steed to solid ground. The mare stood trembling and sweating beneath a tall arkenfir. One of the Faêran knights held the reins.

'Lady Ashalind, you must stay here while we put an end to the enemy,' he said. 'The roots of this fir tree go deep and grip hard. They bind the rocks together with strong force. Who bides beneath these boughs stands upon sound foundations. Do not move from this place, no matter what happens. As long as you remain here, you shall remain secure until our return.'

With that warning they left her alone and rode away to join their comrades.

But even as the mortals were being plucked free from the dis-integrating foundations of Arcdur, the greater number of Ashalind's Faêran guardians had finally joined battle with two of the lords of Unseelie. Only the Cearb somehow still evaded them.

At this, Ashalind wondered. So many against so few—with such odds, the skirmish would soon be over. The Cearb seemed curiously elusive—conceivably, their delight in the thrill of the chase had caused the Faêran knights to prolong their enterprise longer than was necessary.

Unexpectedly the Cearb himself, a massive figure clad in tri-corne and black coat, emerged from behind a cluster of boulders close by. He strode past, producing his curiously shattering effect, and the terrain began to crumble in places that had previously appeared secure.

Falling stones slammed into the ground, throwing thick clouds of dust into the atmosphere which blotted out the scenes of chaos surrounding Ashalind. No matter how hard she stared, she could barely make out the figures of riders moving in the haze, or the receding back of the Cearb as he moved away without noting her. It was like looking at reflections through breath-misted glass. Only the trunk of the arkenfir, towering close, seemed real. Out of the fog issued the ringing shouts of the Faêran, the shrill war cries of the rook-youths and a stream of bellowed curses in Ertish.

The fog swirled and came together in a blot. The blot dissipated like smoke, and where it had been stood seven duergars, the leader holding a whip.

They pinned Ashalind with their baleful eyes and stepped forward.

'Avaunt!' she cried. Her mare threw up her head and made to run off, but Ashalind held her head hard, pulling on the reins. 'You cannot frighten me,' she snapped at the unseelie dwarves. 'I stand in a protected place and from here I shall not budge. Be off!'

The duergar leader grinned, raised its arm high and cracked the whip. In panic, the mare reared on her hind legs, and by the time Ashalind had steadied her, the wights had disappeared.

The ears of the mare flicked and swivelled. New sounds grew amongst the clamour. They did not arise from within the land-bound fog but instead pierced it from without and above, cutting across all other noises as scythes sever murmuring rushes.

Three strident calls grated against the sky—three creaky doors, three unoiled hinges—like a guttural keening of strange children, hoarse prophets predicting the end of the world. A trio of huge black birds flapped out of the fog. Crazed with fear, Ashalind's mare jumped sideways, threw her rider off and dashed away. Dazed, Ashalind grabbed hold of the arkenfir's stem and heaved herself to her feet. Like a triad of tombstones the hoodie crows perched sombrely, with folded wings, atop a monolith. One by one their black beaks opened like pincers and snapped shut. The eyes of these manifestations seemed not to be eyes at all, but empty sockets into which one dared not look for fear of being drawn into the unspeakable regions of madness beyond. Ashalind felt utterly alone, abandoned and vulnerable. There came over her an urgent desire to flee.

'Get you gone,' she sobbed violently. 'Macha, Neman, Morrigu—do you think I do not know you? Do you think I do not know you are trying to drive me hence? You shall not have your will of me. Here I stay!'

For one long moment the Crows of War regarded the mortal with their profane vacuums of eyes. Then, as if in answer to a signal, they extended the great arcs of their wings and flapped their way slowly, deliberately, into the sky.

The sounds of conflict had ceased. The encounter was swiftly over and the dusts of aftermath were settling now, revealing the broken landscape and a ragged pool of water lying spilled at the foot of a pile of granite boulders. Ashalind glimpsed riders, both Faêran and mortal, cantering back towards the arkenfir where she stood. She fancied she heard them calling her name, but could not be certain. The sensory battering of noise, choking dust and turmoil she had experienced had been overwhelming. Exhausted by confrontations with the wights, she felt wrung out like a mophead, wishing only to find some haven. For a fleeting instant it seemed to the beleaguered damsel that her lover had abandoned her. She felt that she could endure no more fear, having expended her strength and been left vulnerable.

Close by, the water in the pool stirred. Out of it climbed a one-eyed man with a huge, lolling head. His torso was growing out of a horse's body. Stinking white vapour poured from his mouth. Completely devoid of skin, his entire surface was red raw flesh, in which blood, black as tar, ran through yellow veins, and great white sinews, thick as horse tethers, twisted, stretched and contracted as the monster moved, stretching out his extraordinarily long, single arm.

At this first actual sight of Nuckelavee, Ashalind's courage failed her. The vision she had seen in Morragan's looking-pool, and all the well-known tales about this monster, burst upon her mind with the impetus of sheer horror. According to the practice of the Faêran, Angavar had defeated but not destroyed the creature. By far the most hideous of all unseelie wights, this abomination had slain the parents of Prince Edward. Uttering a half-smothered cry she fled, darting and dodging amongst the stones.

As she ran she could hear her name urgently being shouted, but louder still was the rampant clatter of eldritch hooves on disintegrating stone, and a rhythmic hissing as of a steam kettle boiling. Underfoot, the ground was treacherous, mazed with cracks. Out of them, like maggots from a disturbed corpse, scuttled the small, light-fearing denizens of the underworld whose dwellings had been disturbed by the quakes. Ashalind's blood roared in her ears like tormented bulls. Heat scalded the nape of her neck as though the blast of Nuckelavee's breath were already singeing her flesh. She dared not slow her progress by glancing back to find out how close he was, but in the recesses of her mind she took some courage from the sounds of grating and sliding that came to her as Nuckelavee's hard hooves slipped on the broken ground. Surely this labour must impede his progress! Still, her shoulders tensed against the blow that must soon fall from his flayed fist, crushing her against jagged edges of granite.

Wildly, as she ran, she scanned her surroundings for some hope of rescue. Between the towers and stacks glimmered a satin sky of the palest blue deepening to indigo in the east. Fine strands of cloud streaked it like chalk marks. Straight ahead loomed a tall grey rock in the shape of a giant hand. A slender obelisk leaned towards it, coloured as the lip of a rose petal. Both monoliths were capped by a lintel-stone shaped like a doorstep. Near at hand in a granite hollow welled a dark, spring-fed pool.

Seemingly just another rocky crevice among many, it stood motionless and unnoticeable in the deep shadows of afternoon, as it had stood for many lifetimes of kings: the Gate she had left behind. Yet not quite as it had always stood—a crack was pencilled down one side of it where it remained slightly ajar.

Here was a safe haven to lock out what pursued her.

Her fingernail slid swiftly into the almost invisible opening. At her touch, the massive portal swung gently aside as though it were feather-light. A shadowy haven lay within, but even as a flying pebble dislodged by eldritch hooves rebounded off the gatepost, the refugee hesitated, struck by that familiar sensation of having forgotten some matter of crucial importance.

In that elusive moment, beneath the unstable ground near the Gate, a thin barrier of silt responded to the Cearb's vibrations and gave way. A handful of gravel poured from a pocket. This undermining shifted the stones which had roofed that pocket. On the surface above, a boulder which had been balancing precariously atop a stack now tilted. Motivated by its own momentum, it crashed down. The shock of the bouncing impact split open new crevices. A rat jumped out from a fissure and ran over Ashalind's foot.

It was too much.

Fear and revulsion spurred her. With a scream of outrage she slipped inside the Gate, kicked aside three strands of hair and a broken knife, and slammed the portal shut.

Slumping against a wall, Ashalind rested to regain her breath. A radiance, ambiguous and strange, illuminated a distorted passageway sealed by a door at either end. The vaulted ceiling was cracked. In places it sagged down like a bag of water. As the walls approached the nearest portal they melded into rough-hewn granite. At the far end where they met the silver Realm Door with its golden hinges, they transmuted into living trees whose boughs interlaced overhead. This, the fateful Gate-passage between the Realm and Erith, had not altered.

On the floor lay the haft and snapped-off blade of the horn-handled knife Ashalind's father had given her at their parting. Nearby was the shrivelled leaf of an eringl tree. In the uncertain gloom, it was impossible to make out the three strands of hair which had faithfully served to keep open the gate during her travails in the world of humankind.

'Gate, oh Gate,' whispered Ashalind, between two realms.

A sound of sweet, sad singing circulated in Ashalind's head. She grew calm, and with tranquillity came the recollection for which she had been striving, just before she had set foot inside the Gate-passage.

'Fear no harm from wights now, Betrothed,' Angavar had told her, *'nor from any mortal creature. For when I am with thee, thou'rt safe from all harm. When I am not, I shall leave thee in the care of others who can protect thee, or else thou shalt bide in some secure place.'*

Once, Sianadh had instructed, 'Put fear aside, for only then will ye see your way clearly.' His words had proved apt. Terror had been her undoing, for it had driven out rational thought. Neither the duergars, nor the Crows of War, nor Nuckelavee could possess the power to scathe the chosen bride of the Faêran High King, if only she had trusted his word and stood her ground. As for the scuttling rodent (at the thought of which, she flinched), it was no more than a *lorraly* creature hurrying to shelter.

As soon as the girl in the Gate-passage reached these conclusions, she thought of something else. How long had she been lying there? Perhaps five minutes? Perhaps ten? Lunging for the Erith Door, she flung it wide.

Beyond, the land of granite towers and riven rocks lay naked to the night. It seemed empty, frozen, scoured of all living beings. White stars frosted a sky so black it seemed to suck out the essence of her being. Their light bleached the flanks of the monoliths, carving enigmatic shadows in secret crevices and deeply cloven interstices.

Some unknown measure of time had passed.

She was alone.

A profound pang of loss and grief tore through the very core of Ashalind's spirit. She cursed the legacy of humankind, that fear should ever drive out reason and set the world awry. Her cry rang out over the desolation of cold stone and clear water and dark pine, but it could not summon what had passed forever.

It could not turn back Time.

12
THE BITTERBYNDE
Part II

'I'd teach you of her looks and of her ways,
Her lilting voice, the tincture of her hair,
Her lucent eyes as bright as Summer days.
I'd teach you this and more, but she's not there.'

OLD TALITH SONG

In the soft sibilant eventide belonging to the land of stone and pine, a wind the colour of water crooned along gullies and canyons, whistled through chimneys and narrow fractures, piped in clefts and rifts and sang amongst soaring columns. Under its caress the tiny beards of mosses nodded. A small rain fell from belts of arkenfirs where each needle was beaded with a glister of water-drops condensed from the mists. It fell on the surface of cold, black waters that lapped new margins of fused glass and congealed stone. Ripples unrolled like ribbons of platinum. A lake, where no lake had been before.

Not far from the lake's edge there reared a tall grey rock like a giant hand. A slender obelisk leaned towards it, coloured as the lip of a rose petal. Both monoliths were capped by a lintel-stone shaped like a doorstep. As softly as the sighing of the wind, someone stepped from the shadows of the rocks. Her hair streamed out, lustrous, a swathe of gilt threads. Her eyes were two green flowers brimming with dew.

'What have I done?'

Stooping, she placed some glinting strands carefully in the shadows at her feet. She set her hand on a lofty slab and it shifted, sliding into place. Then she walked along the shore, into the night. In crevices of stone, the wind's breath carried away her final words like a passing thought which brushes against the brain and is almost remembered.

'I must find him.'

But she had not been quite alone.

One single fluke of fortune had at that very moment chosen to strike a man whom Fortune appeared to have cast aside. He was a vagabond, a cowled wanderer who lived each day, each year of his life on the borders of lunacy, tormented by fear. Hunted by minor eldritch wights that were held at bay only by his desperate trickery, he was also banished from the haunts of humankind, subject to a king's warrant that he be arrested on sight. Once he had lorded it at the Court of the King-Emperor, wielding power with an uncompromising hand. Now he stooped, creeping like a shabby and demented beggar through the remote places of Eldaraigne. It was he at last who stumbled accidentally upon good luck. Finally, at the exact time and place that would best realise his vengeful dreams, he was there.

This outcast was observing Ashalind from another shadow, spying from a distance, carefully noting her every move. He watched until she was out of sight. Furtively, he glanced over his shoulder, as if he expected pursuit. It seemed his expectations were well founded. Not far from where he stood, the stones—or the umbras of the stones—were alive. They were swarming towards him with a fluid movement, humping and lumping. Once they paused, lifting their heads as though to taste the air.

The watcher glided swiftly to the place from which Ashalind had departed.

So that it might be more easily marked, she had propped the

Gate open wider this time—wide enough that a gaunt man might enter easily, if he turned sideways.

Which he did.

As the tattered hem of his cloak disappeared, several of the bobbing, crouching rock-shadows flowed in after him.

For a while, the rest of the spriggans snuffed about where his trail had ended. Then they too vanished, dissolving into the landscape.

Ashalind stepped around the shore of the new lake that had formed during the unknown quantity of time she had lain inside the Gate—formed, perhaps, within one of the subsidences caused by the quakes. How long had it taken for such a wide depression to fill with rainwater? And why were the rocky margins melted, as though from the heat of a volcano? She had no idea, nor did she care to ponder. One purpose only possessed and drove her—to find Angavar again.

In the lee of a scaffold-sized boulder stood a stained rag of a tent and the blackened remnants of a campfire, unexpected and somehow grotesque against the clean lines of the landscape. It appeared deserted. The abandoned campsite of some mortal hermit could offer no succour, no evidence of her lover's where-abouts, so she passed it by.

For three nights and three days she wandered through Arcdur, drinking from its clear springs and streamlets, finding nothing of substance to sustain her, as once before. The land was broken and jagged. The split faces of the rocks were pristine—no moss or lichen had taken root, and for this sign she wept with thankful-ness. Perhaps she had not been gone for too long after the quake, after all. Slowly she wended over miles, until her feet were bleed-ing, her knees bruised from many tumbles. Yet she met no living thing, no bird, no insect, not even a solitary wight. Once, while she slept, there came a strange dream of fleeting beauty, and she thought she must have dreamed of the Faêran Rade at Hob's Hill.

At sunset on the third day, she glimpsed upon a distant hill a tower not built by upheaval nor shaped by wind and water. It looked to be a man-made edifice, yet its height was less than the towers usually built in Erith, not tall enough to be either a watch-tower or mooring turret. If men had raised it, perhaps they dwelled there still. The sight gave her new strength and she hastened up the slope.

Yet when she came at last under the shadow of the tower, she encountered neither mortal nor immortal—only silence and stillness. There was no sign of human activity, save for a few crumbs of mortar and clean chips of stone lying about the outskirts.

The tower's base was constructed on tall, open arches facing four directions. Grilles of iron covered them over. Peering into the gloom beyond the diamond-shaped perforations of these lattices, Ashalind made out a pale form lying stretched out on a raised table of stone. It lay quite still, as though unalive. The sun's last rays slanted lower, piercing the dimness. They described a statue: a figure asleep on its back, the hands crossed over the breast. Roses of white marble were piled like ice crystals at its head and feet. Yet this was no sleeper—this was an effigy of the dead, recumbent upon a catafalque. The tower, then, was a monument, a mausoleum.

Ashalind slumped against the iron trellis and as she did so, it swung ajar. She stumbled into the chamber of the statue. The gate squeaked once and fell silent again, resting on its hinges.

There is something about the statue of a human form which draws the eye. The girl glided towards the catafalque and stood looking down at the tranquil face. For a moment or two she remained thus, before the significance of what she beheld penetrated her weary mind. Then she simply sank to the floor next to the plinth. Hours later, when darkness had long since covered Arcdur in velvet, she remained slumped there, beside the stone effigy, the perfect image of herself.

The night wasted away. In the morning, the silence was broken by the clatter of hooves, the tinkling of bridle bells and the lilt of men's voices. Two riders leading a packhorse climbed the hill. The men dismounted and entered the mausoleum. Soon they backed out rapidly, ran partway down the hill and halted, staring at each other in fear and disbelief, before drawing their blades and cautiously approaching the tower a second time.

As they entered the open lattice they whistled and rang bells. They jingled their iron harness and muttered a few rhymes.

'Sure and it's the lady, no other,' they said in hushed tones.

Ashalind opened her eyes and asked for food, which they gave willingly after they had satisfied themselves she was neither wight nor illusion. Yet they were still half afraid of her.

'How came you here, lady?' they inquired.

'I came through a Gate,' she said, as bewildered as they. The shock of discovering her own tomb had rendered her numb, light-headed, detached and uncomprehending. She must have wept during the night, for her face felt stiff as a mask of plaster, her eyes stung raw with salt.

'What gate? This iron one?'

'No. A Faêran Gate.'

The two men exchanged another significant glance.

'His Majesty must hear of this,' said one. 'Send off the pigeons, Robin.'

Robin fetched a cage that had been fastened to his saddle bow. Painstakingly he wrote the same message three times on three tiny scraps of parchment. He tied them to the legs of a trio of pigeons and freed the birds.

'Where is Angavar?' she asked.

Their grim faces closed, as though they had drawn shutters across them.

'Lady, we shall take you to His Imperial Majesty, King Edward,' they said guardedly, 'but as regards all else, we will say naught.'

'I do not understand!'

'We think it unwise, m'lady. Our knowledge is limited; unintentionally, we might convey false impressions. It will be best if all the answers to your questions are given to ye from His Majesty's own lips. We are merely servants sent to tend your—the lady's tomb.'

'Just let me know one thing only,' she begged. 'How long have I been gone?'

'Seven years it is since the lady was last seen,' they reluctantly divulged, still doubting their own eyes. Then they would answer her no more, despite that she pleaded piteously.

The men gave Ashalind a cloak with a deep hood attached. They set her upon the best of the three horses, then led her through pathless Arcdur to the coast. A Seaship came to meet them and as they waited for the rowboat to pick them up from the beach, Ashalind's rescuers bade her pull the hood up over her head and face.

'If we are to keep ye safe,' they warned, 'your discovery must be known only to us. There be too many persons of doubtful character who might be interested in news of the whereabouts of a lady such as ye. We do not know who can be trusted among the crew; therefore, we trust none. Hide yourself.'

She did not quarrel with them. It seemed, after all, a familiar thing to do.

In fair weather, with a stiff nor'-easterly following, the ship set sail for the south. It had not long departed from the Arcdur coast when something happened which set the teeth of the crew on edge and started their spines crawling, and made them look askance at the hooded passenger. Some muttered that she had brought ill luck; others suggested she was some simulacrum, and ought to be cast overboard.

What happened was this: the seas rolled calm and flat and the skies were clear, when suddenly there arose all around a sound like the sighing of many voices and a rustling as of yard upon yard of clean silk. With that sigh came a rush of air, and all those on board felt as if a throng passed close by, lightly brushing them with soft fabrics. The sun's light mellowed to the colour of a rose in amber, tinting the sky and sea from horizon to horizon. The curve of every wavelet became a camellia petal. At the same time a fragrance drifted down the breeze, a scent of wildflowers so sweet and evocative it was nothing less than heartbreaking, and many of those who breathed it fell to their knees on the deck, sobbing. The ship surged forward on the crest of a wave and then the sigh passed with the strange light, away across the sea, leaving behind the creaking of the rigging and the slap of water on the hull.

It was as though a lamp had gone out.

After many hours, the flower scent faded.

None could guess what it might mean, but all were certain of one thing: that after this, the world could never be the same. Neither did any man speak of the phenomenon, despite that it had touched all of them deeply, or because of it. But they suspected the passenger. To her good fortune, not all on board were common sailors—some were King's men and Dainnan knights. They had pledged protection to the passenger and she was let alone.

The ship sailed without further event to Caermelor, where it was met by mounted guards. From the harbour they carried the hooded girl in a closed litter, ever cautioning her not to show her face. The guards rode close around, but she peeped through the curtains of watered satin. The city had changed during those seven years. Gone were the Mooring Masts and the great Tower of the Stormriders. No Windships bobbed high at anchor.

'What is the meaning of this?' cried Ashalind, but no man would look around or give reply.

'Keep within, my lady,' Robin nervously admonished, tying the curtains shut.

With all speed she was brought, hooded, before Edward. She found him in the solar of the palace, his knights and musicians and servants having been dismissed from his presence. Only a page boy loitered half asleep and overlooked in a corner, awaiting his liege's instructions.

Where a young prince had stood, now stood a grown man of three and twenty years. Edward's glance was grave and thoughtful, weighty with significance. On beholding him, Ashalind threw back her hood. They looked upon one another and neither found word to speak.

Edward reached out his hand. His fingers were trembling.

'Sit by me,' he said hoarsely.

Side by side they sat at the tall window. Its arches framed grey clouds rolling in from the west, bringing rain. Dusk was drawing in. An owl wheeled past on wings as silent as thought.

'Do you know how long I have waited for you?' asked Edward.

She nodded. Dread was an imminent flood, barely dammed by fortitude. 'Seven years, methinks. And Angavar? What of Angavar?'

But Edward had a monument raised in Arcdur and it was inspected now and then by his servants, so that no stain should mar its snowy marble, and no weed should take root, or vine climb the walls.

'And now you have come back,' said Edward, ending his tale. 'And I will tear down that bitter memorial that I may unremember the last seven years and be blithe.'

Something was tapping or flapping at the window.

She said, 'But can it be that Angavar sleeps forever? The Gate is open again—I left it propped ajar. Where is the Coirnéad? It must be sounded at once, to waken the dreamers. All is not lost! The Realm can be regained and I shall ride with Angavar to see my own family!'

Edward looked long at Ashalind. After a time he said, 'But do you not love me?'

Startled, she said, 'Of course I love you, Edward. You are as dear to me as my own brother.'

A swift shadow of pale wings crossed the chamber.

Unexpectedly, Edward leaned forward and kissed Ashalind's mouth.

As he withdrew his lips from hers, she remained as waxen and still as a doll.

He smiled. She showed no reaction.

'What is my name?' he murmured.

She hesitated, perplexed, then shook her head. His smile did not fade. 'It is Edward,' he said clearly, as though speaking to a small child, 'and you are Ash, my beloved, my betrothed.'

Behind the windowpanes, a white owl flew away.

'Am I?' she said. Her eyes were wide and innocent and empty as a new babe's.

'Oh, yes.'

For seven years the people of Erith had struggled to find ways to repair their way of life, which had collapsed now that the traditional lines of communication and trade had been severed. For the unmaking of sildron had affected everyone—peasant and lord, merchant and thief, baker and armourer, carlin and wizard, aristocrat

and prince, child, woman and man. It was as though the bones supporting the nations had been taken away, leaving only the
struggling flesh.

After the Namarran wight-wars, followed by seven years of
hard work and suffering, the people were eager to hear good
tidings.

Bells pealed joyfully across Caermelor. The King-Emperor was
to take a bride, at last. Yet this bride was not to be the one they
had expected—it had been deemed by one and all that the popular Lady Rosamonde of Roxburgh would become their Queen.
Instead, Edward had chosen the Lady of the Sorrows.

The known lands were rife with talk of Ashalind's return.
Famed for her beauty, she had survived seven years lost in the
wilderness. The lady had endured her share of misery, they said,
as befitted her name. It was a sorrow for her that he to whom she
had first been handfasted (whose name must be spoken in whispers) had disappeared out of all knowledge. And 'twas a further
shame the lady had endured such trials in the wilderness, for
although she had returned alive, she was no longer hale. So fragile was she, she must be kept in isolation, tended by the King's
best wizards and dyn-cynnils. Until her strength returned, she was
to receive no visitors nor step outside the walls of Caermelor
Palace. But her beauty had not faded, so it was rumoured, and the
young King-Emperor was greatly enamoured of her, to the dismay
of the Lady Rosamonde, who, it was said, had loved him unswerv-
ingly since the days of their childhood.

The seasons turned.

Late at night, Ash was seated in the library in the company of
two ladies-in-waiting. Often she could be found among the books
and scrolls, searching—for what, she did not know. Information
of some kind, knowledge . . . Hours ago, the ladies had fallen
asleep. Ash herself was nodding, when a fluttering in the wall-
tapestries caught her eye. She looked up to behold a small face
which appeared both old and young, like a child burdened with
wisdom beyond its years. Beneath the face, a beckoning hand.
Ash rose to her feet. Smoothing the heavy folds of her gown of

purple velvet, she tip-toed across the chamber to investigate. A young man was holding up a corner of the arras. One of his shoulders humped higher than the other, and he stooped.

'Come with me,' he said mysteriously, one finger on his lips.

Amused, she inquired, 'Who are you? What do you want? How did you come here?'

He shook his head. 'Follow Pod and you will find out.'

She, untroubled by bad memories, knowing only kindness and perhaps tedium, feared nothing. Stepping into the gloom behind the wall-hanging, she saw him duck into a dark opening, like a narrow door in the stone wall. After him she went, along hidden, dusty corridors in the palace walls and up narrow flights of stairs, directed by the light of his candle. The corridors branched at many junctures but her guide did not hesitate, pressing on as though certain of his bearings, as though this strange *between* place was home territory to him. After a long time he halted in the passageway and pushed on the wall. A panel swung forth, opening onto a confined chamber bereft of furnishings, lit by a fitfully flaming brand in a wall-sconce. Ash followed him into the room.

A slit of a window appeared to be the only other aperture. It afforded a glimpse of black sky sprinkled with a frosting of silver. A cold draught pierced the window like a sliver of ice. The air blowing in was fresh and clear, tasting of mountain streams under boundless stars.

Two figures waited therein: a young Feohrkind woman dressed in the fine clothes of the gentry, and a little fellow with thick, curly hair. A pointy beard sprouted from his chin. On seeing Ash, the young woman rushed towards her, then stopped short. Her arms dropped by her sides. She curtsied awkwardly.

Ash smiled. 'An intriguing scene. What is this play about? Tell me of your game. Who are you?'

The young woman curtsied again and spoke. Her voice sounded strained, tense as a wire. 'I am Caitri Lendoon, my lady. I was your friend, once.'

'Were you indeed? But Edward has not told me about you . . .'

'Perhaps he does not tell you everything, m'lady.'

This time, Ash frowned. After a moment her expression

cleared. 'I suppose there has not been enough time yet to recall everything to me. He is so busy and there is so much to learn!' She paused, as if sniffing the air. 'How sweet is the breeze from the window . . .'

Caitri spoke earnestly. 'I have come today from open fields,' she said. 'They are thick with yellow dandelions. And the white butterflies were rising like steam, blowing in drifts across the meadows as though a wind had shaken clouds of blossom from an orchard. And the sun was sinking down on the one hand, in bright pink and gold, while on the other—beyond dark-green belts of pine—the sky was piled high with blue-black thunder-heads. Long shadows striped the grass. Golden stretched the field, white-hazed against the storm's purple wall.'

'How entrancing is the picture you paint. Long has it been since I walked out,' said Ash, glancing towards the slot in the wall.

'How came your memory to be stolen away, m'lady?'

'I was lost in the wilderness. I fell and my head hit a stone.'

'No, no! You entered the enchanted portal a second time, and, as before, following your exit you were kissed by one who was Erith-born!'

'Your words make no sense. But wait—what business is this of yours? I am curious to know your purpose. Enough of your questions! Who are these two fellows with whom you keep company?'

'He is Pod, m'lady,' said Caitri, gesturing to Ash's erstwhile guide, 'and this is Tully.'

The goateed little man bowed briskly. The flickering shadows laved the lower part of his body, so that he could not clearly be seen.

'I wish to tell you a tale,' said Caitri.

'Go ahead, my dear, but make it short, I pray you.' Ash lifted the hem of her velvet gown free of the dust flouring the floor. 'This room is close and chilly, more like a cupboard than a room.'

'It is a secret place, m'lady, and the way for mortals to find it is known only to Pod. We have brought you here because there is much you must learn before you are wed to Edward. You may have been misled.'

Ash frowned again. 'I mislike this conversation,' she said, abruptly turning to leave. But Pod barred her path with his wizened form. 'Step out of my way, prithee, sir,' said Ash coldly. 'I will hear none of this. Why I followed you in the first place is a mystery to me.'

'Because,' he said obtusely. His mouth snapped shut.

'That is no answer. Out of my way, I say.'

'Wait, I beg of you, my lady,' said Caitri. 'There may never be another chance. I will be succinct.'

'Very well.' Seeing that she was not going to be able to shift the obstinate Pod, Ash acquiesced.

Caitri began to speak, clearly and fluently.

'The House of D'Armancourt is an honest House by long reputation. I feel certain there have been no lies told you, yet there may have been many false impressions conveyed by omission. You were once betrothed to another.' Ash's sudden intake of breath hissed through her teeth. 'This other,' continued Caitri quickly, 'thought you dead when you were lost in the wilderness. In his grief at losing you, he and his retinue passed beneath a green hill, and there they fell into a deep sleep of enchantment which they call the Pendur Sleep. Rightly, they thought never to be woken in Erith, and in fact there was no way to waken them, for the Coirnéad, the horn which might have done so, was sundered when sildron was unmade, and may never be sounded again.'

'An enchanted sleep? Who was this lover you claim was mine?'

'He was the High King of the Faêran.'

Ash laughed uncertainly. 'You astonish me.'

Caitri met Ash's eyes squarely. 'Aye, ma'am, 'twas the High King of the Land Beyond the Stars who loved thee. Can you tell me truly, that even now, even under the spell of the Bitterbynde Gate, you have not felt a hint of it? Some subtle tapping at the blind windows of memory? Greater was his power than any force, and great was the love between you as the love of the moon and the tides.'

Ash retorted, 'Speak not thus. Pray, complete your tale speedily, that I may leave this melancholy cell.'

'Even so,' acceded Caitri in disappointed tones. 'Not long before this very night a strange thing happened. It was just before your ladyship was brought back to the city—indeed, it must have occurred while you were sailing from Arcdur. No doubt you felt it, and perhaps also others on board your ship. All the world felt it. Weird it was, piercing like crystal blades, with a beauty that burned. There was a fragrance of flowers. It was the Coming of the Faêran.

'For by an odd twist, all the gates to the Fair Realm were reopened, and through them the Fair Ones poured into Erith like a rainbow flood, and they went to Eagle's Howe where their King slept among his knights, and they bore him away, still sleeping.'

'No man saw it, but the wights say his people took him in a boat across Lake Amarach, through the mists which ever twine above the surface of that water. In the lake's centre rises an island, and on the island they passed through an open Gate into the Fair Realm and were seen no more by Erith-dwelling mortals.'

'A fetching fireside tale,' said Ash, 'no doubt learned from a wandering jongleur or Storyteller. How came these so-called Gates to suddenly open?'

'The wights know, and one will tell.'

The little man with the pointy beard stepped forward. His goat's legs and hooves were now revealed to Ash, who recoiled. 'Do not fear, m'lady—he is not dangerous,' assured Caitri. 'In fact, he is a dear friend. As are Sianadh and Viviana and Ethlinn, and all who conspired to bring us here. Oh my lady, if you only knew . . .'

Tully bowed once more. 'Wean, the full story was quo' tae me by yin who kens it weel. Somehow a wayward wizard—an escaped prisoner o' Caermelor—fand his entry intae the Realm. He crept in by the Geata Poeg na Déanainn. Some spriggans who were hunting him chased in after. When the Faêran of the Realm clapped e'en on this touzled birkie—the first and only traveller to come from Erith syne the Closing—och, the news spread like unbound sheaves in a heigh hurly, ye may be sure. To gain importance for hisself, this wizard, naming hissel' Sargoth, tell'd the Faêran he had opened the Gate wi' a wee finger-bone he had fand among the stanes of Arcdur and then had tossed awa'.'

'I do not follow you, sir,' said Ash. 'Much of your speech is unfamiliar.'

'Och,' muttered the wight, 'my brogue's thickened again. I hae been too lang awa' frae mortalkind.'

Caitri explained, 'Tully says a wizard got into the Fair Realm by the Gate of Oblivion's Kiss. When the Faêran discovered him, he claimed to have opened the Gate by himself, using a bone.' Clasping her hands in an attitude of earnest beseeching, she added, 'This wizard, Sargoth, held an old grudge against you, my lady. Indirectly, you caused his downfall, as well as that of his niece, Dianella. No doubt he saw you make your exit from the Gate, but he lied to the Faêran, to spite you. Shortly thereafter the Fair Ones, perceiving him to be a spiteful rogue of the kind with whom they desired no truck, threw him out of their Realm. I heard tell some vindictive wights were lying in wait for him, and carried him off. No one has heard of him since.'

Ash shrugged impatiently. 'Continue.'

The urisk said, 'But within the Fair Realm, the spriggans that had followed him from Erith tell'd the Password to the Casket of Keys. For a thousand years it had been common kenning among tham thegither. What they could bicker, the Faêran unlockit a' the Gates. They gaed intae Erith tae bring back their braw king and his bauld knights.'

'He says the spriggans told the Password to the Faêran. This enabled them to open all the Gates. They came into Erith and took their King back with them,' said Caitri.

'Of course. I understood.'

'When Angavar King gaed back tae his Realm he waukened,' continued the wight. 'Then he lookit aboot at his bonny kingdom and was blythe, but the Faêran could not fail to note the sair sorrowing which marred his blytheness.

'I'll dree no reminder of Erith,' quo' Angavar, and he ca'd for the Gates atween the warlds tae be closed again, this time truly foriver. Yet first he ca'd oot of Erith his brother, whose form had been bent to the cast of a Raven, for the King was niver so cruel as to coup his ain kin who had been brought low. The Raven Morragan feeled the pull o' unbarred Faêrie and came winging like an arrow tae the open traverse. But while the black bird flied in at the Realm Gate, a white owl flied oot intae Erith and the Gates clapped thegither.'

'You say,' said Ash, 'that this King could bear no reminder of Erith and ordered all Gates to be closed for all time. That before they were closed, he allowed his Raven brother to enter the Realm but at the same time a white owl flew out. Of what relevance is this?'

'Self-banished,' said Caitri. 'Easgathair White Owl, Gatekeeper of the Faêran, exiled his geas with him, so that the Lord Morragan, dwindled to a bird but still able to form utterances, would never be able to invoke that last boon.'

'What boon? What Gatekeeper? It makes little sense.'

'Easgathair was once the Gatekeeper of the Faêran. He believed he deserved to be exiled as punishment, because of the shame he had brought upon himself. He considered the blame for all the troubles of the Faêran lay at his feet, for it was he who, long ago, had granted two unspecified boons to Crown Prince Morragan. One boon had been fulfilled, but the other remained. The Gates were being locked again; however, the Raven-That-Was-Morragan could ask that they never be reopened.'

A wistful expression crept over Caitri's fine features. 'If Easgathair the Gatekeeper is not present in the Fair Realm, Morragan's second boon can never be fulfilled and Angavar High King has the option of opening the Gates, if ever he changes his mind. Yet alas, I fear such an alteration of a passionate, wounded heart will never come to pass.'

'And if all this happened in a Realm to which we no longer have access, how could you have learned these matters?'

''Twas the Gatekeeper hisself who told me this tale,' concluded the urisk. 'Though he be in owl-shape, yet urisks may still hold converse wi' him.'

In the wall-sconce, the flaming torch sputtered and gasped. Ash turned her face away from its light. She paced the chamber: three steps east, three steps west.

'So this is your story, is it?' she murmured at length. 'That I was betrothed to an immortal being who shall never be seen again? That these Fair Ones of legend are gone forever? That in Erith there flutters, immortal, a white owl which is not in sooth a bird but a seeming-thing of gramarye?' She shrugged again. 'Of what use is this intelligence to me? Even if 'tis true, which I doubt, how may any make use of it? 'Twere better left unsaid. Allow me my happiness, prithee. Do not spoil what I have left to me.'

Muffled sounds rumbled through the walls. 'Methinks my absence is discovered,' said Ash. 'Let me go, before your hiding place is uncovered and yourselves are discomfited.'

Pod backed into the hole in the wall, giving way before her.

Urgently, Caitri began again to speak, and this time the words tumbled forth as if somersaulting from her mouth in their eagerness to be heard.

'King Edward is our worthy sovereign, yet one flaw mars his goodness: his desire for your hand in marriage overrides his cognisance of good and evil. It makes him willing to put aside the Lady Rosamonde, and to forget his loyalty to the Faêran King who aided him and his family in their time of need. He is even willing to trick you, my lady, in order to secure you for himself. There is no doubt in my mind that from the first moment he saw you he loved you. I have friends among the palace servants. There is one who overheard what passed between you and His Majesty when you returned from the mausoleum in Arcdur, while your memory was still intact. The King-Emperor told you Angavar slept forever, implying he was therefore unattainable. Then, in order to find out if you were willing to accept that state of affairs and take him as a substitute, he asked you if you loved him. He hoped you might accept the idea that the Sleepers could not be awakened, but he was wrong. So upon you he bestowed the salute of love, bringing on you once more the bitterbynde of the Gate.'

'How can you spout such nonsense?' cried Ash. The young woman's words had aroused such a tempest of conflicting passions she thought she teetered on the brink of madness.

But Caitri's eyes brimmed. Unchecked, the salt water coursed down her cheeks. 'Edward is our sovereign now,' she said rapidly, 'and no one dares gainsay his decrees. Yet, to be safe, he decided to keep you sheltered from your old acquaintances until you are wedded to him. He—and others close to him—has been beguiling your thoughts, much as you were misled in Isse Tower when old Grethet deluded you. You have been bewildered! Trusting His

Majesty, you believe all he tells you, and he says you are not ready to go out into the wider world yet. The Lady Rosamonde, who has loved him all her life, was desolate at hearing he had passed her over, and has vowed never to marry another—'

But Ash interrupted. 'Enough of your treasonous and disgraceful lies!' she burst out, making for the exit. 'I comprehend them not, and will endure no more!'

Yet she hesitated before she left the room, apparently struck by second thoughts. 'I deem you all acted in good faith,' she said, 'thinking your extraordinary behaviour beneficial in some manner. Therefore, take this.' Tossing a purse of coins on the floor, she stepped through the opening. Her velvet skirts softly swept the floor.

Caitri stood without speaking. She stared at the gap in the panelling, her hands pressed tightly against her mouth. She could only recall, streaking the dust on Ash's face, the glimmering tracks of unbidden tears.

Epilogue

'On my word
I want you,
And it will be so
While I have life.'

LOVERS' VOW

When the Gates were Closed for the second time, it is not known for sure whether they were ever again opened. It was said in tales that they were. Once.

The reign of Edward lasted many years. Certain it is that the shang unstorms never more came and went, except within the violence of the Ringstorm roiling around the waist of the world. Certain it is that sildron-powered ships no longer flew, nor did Stormriders rule the skies, and that their once-great Houses declined, becoming squabbling, land-bound clans.

It was maintained (and indeed it was set down thus in the annals of Erith) that the bride of Edward, King-Emperor, was a damsel of great beauty, although her ways were strange, quiet and remote, and the marriage was childless. She outlived her husband by many years. When he died, a distant relation of the House of D'Armancourt came to the throne and Edward's widow retired to a country estate, where she lived for an extraordinary length of time. Her beauty, though it faded in the end, faded slowly.

But others added a fanciful twist.

They avowed that she who became the wife of Edward, King-Emperor of Erith, was not his heart's choice but a substitute, and that he never loved her as deeply. According to their version, his first bride was stolen away in the very hour they were to be married. On the day of the Royal Wedding, into the midst of the ceremony walked a tall stranger, more beautiful than the night, and a white owl flew above his shoulder, and no man could touch either of them. Before the marriage vows were exchanged, the stranger demanded a boon of Edward, and to the amazement of all those present, it was granted. Whereupon the stranger took the bride in his arms and kissed her.

Then the whole Court stood back, staring in astonishment. For where the visitor had stood, a great eagle rose up. By its side flew a white seabird, and the two were linked by a golden chain. The roof opened like a flower to let them pass.

They flew away and were never seen more in Erith.

Afterword

Whenever something indefinable, something wonderful, is reached for with a sense of it being almost within the grasp, just beyond the fingertips, then the Other Country, filled with limitless possibilities, has been glimpsed. Eternal happiness and unflawed contentment do not reign there, for it is restless—nor is it devoid of sorrow; but ecstasy that soars can be found there, and sweet joy.

It cannot be said for certain whether this estate is a condition of existence or a region with definite or indefinite boundaries in which that condition can be achieved. And if the roads that do lead there from the outer world are not plain to see, there are inner roads, which go the same way. Some locate them easily; others never find them.

Acknowledgements

The fairies . . . all set great store by golden hair in mortals. A golden-haired child was in far more danger of being stolen than a dark one. It was often a golden-haired girl who was allured away to be the fairy bride . . . sometimes, too, the fairies adopted girls of especial beauty, and above all golden-haired, as their special charges; and when they could not protect them they avenged their wrongs.

A DICTIONARY OF FAIRIES, KATHARINE BRIGGS

'Ellum do grieve . . .' The chorus of a traditional Somerset folk song collected by Ruth Tongue in *Forgotten Folk Tales of the English Counties*, Routledge & Kegan Paul, London, 1970.

'I walk with the owl . . .': Quoted from 'The Life of Robin Goodfellow', a seventeenth-century pamphlet republished by JO Halliwell-Phillips in *Illustrations of the Fairy Mythology of the Midsummer Night's Dream*, Shakespeare Society, London, 1845.

Finoderee: '[I can] clear a daymath in an hour and want nothing better than a crockful of bithag afterwards.'
    'Cap for the head, alas poor head!' etc . . .
    '. . . [He whisks] horseloads of stone and wrack about the countryside like a little giant . . .'

'. . . [he folds in] wild goats, purrs and hares along with the sheep.'

The quotations above, and the inspiration for Finodoree's tale, are from Walter Gill's *A Second Manx Scrapbook*, Arrowsmith, London, 1932; also from anecdotes told by Train in his Account of Man and quoted by Keightley in *The Fairy Mythology, Illustrative of the Romance and Superstition of Various Countries*, Bohn Library, London, 1850.

The poem 'The Nimble Mower' is translated from 'Yn Folder Gastey', a traditional song about Finoderee, or Fenodoree as he is sometimes known. The translation, by Walter Gill, is quoted from *A Second Manx Scrapbook*, Arrowsmith, London, 1932. This poem can be viewed on the Internet at http://www.dartthornton.com

The Burry Man: Inspired by an actual ceremony that takes place in South Queensferry, West Lothian in the United Kingdom, every year on the second Friday in August.

Beating the Bounds: Inspired by an ancient custom once an integral part of daily life in Britain, which still flourishes to this day at occasions such as the Sheriff's Ride at Lichfield, Staffordshire, and at other places, including Berwick-upon-Tweed; Morpeth, Northumberland; Laugharne, Carmarthenshire, and Richmond, North Yorkshire.

The Pumpkin Scrambler: Also inspired by a colourful British custom that survives from olden times.

'If Ye Call Me Imp or Elf . . .': Adapted from *Popular Rhymes of Scotland* by Robert Chambers, W & R Chambers, Edinburgh, 1870.

The Shock: '. . . a thing with a donkey's head and a smooth velvet hide . . .'

'. . . seized [the thing], it turned suddenly around, snapped at [his] hand and vanished.'

The quotes are from *County Folk-Lore*, Volume 1, Gloucestershire. ES Hartland (ed), 1892, Folklore Society County Publications. The episode of the Shock is inspired by this book.

Gentle Annie: Inspired by a description in *A Dictionary of Fairies*, Katharine Briggs. Penguin Books, 1976.

It: Inspired by *Shetland Traditional Lore*, Jessie Saxby, Norwood Editions, 1974.

Bawming the Thorn: No resemblance to the actual ritual as performed every year in the English village of Appleton Thorn is intended, other than the adorning of the tree.

Burning the Boatman: Inspired by 'Burning Bartle' (not intended to portray the custom as performed annually in West Witton, North Yorkshire, England). The chant, as given here, is derived from the ancient version, still sung during the performance of this living tradition:

> 'At Penhill crags he tore his rags,
> At Hunter's Thorn he blew his horn,
> At Capplebank Stee he had the misfortune to brak' his knee,
> At Grassgill Beck he brak' his neck,
> At Wadham's End he couldn't fend,
> At Grassgill End we'll make his end,
> Shout, boys, shout!'

The Hooden Horse: Inspired by the many hobby horse ceremonies and customs still practised in the United Kingdom.

The Bullbeggar: Inspired by *County Folk Lore*, Vol VIII, collected and published by Ruth Tongue.

The place names in Chapter 3: Drawn from the English countryside; for example, 'By Kingsdale Beck we go,' said Arrowsmith, 'and past Churnmilk Hole. By Frostrow and Shaking Moss, and Hollybush Spout.'

The Wood-Goblins: Inspired by Christina Rosetti's magnificent poem 'The Goblin Market', 1862.

The Coillduine: Inspired by the imagery of early twentieth century clairvoyant Geoffrey Hodson, in *Fairies at Work and Play*, The Theosophical Publishing House, Wheaton, Ill., USA.

The Siofran Feast: 'The spy was intrigued at their unglamoured feast; the horns of butterflies, the pith of rushes, emits' eggs and the beards of mice, bloated earwigs and red-capped worms, mandrakes' ears and stewed thigh of newt, washed down with pearls of dew cupped in magenta flowers.' This menu is partially drawn from the poem 'Oberon's Feast', written by Robert Herrick (1591–1674), published in 1647.

The Ganconer/Love-Talker: A wonderful poem about this deadly supernatural seducer was written by the well-known Irish poet Ethna Carbery (1866–1902). It has been reprinted in *The Four Winds of Eirinn*, an anthology of her verse, and can also be viewed on Ms Dart-Thornton's website, at http://www.dartthornton.com

Viviana's song: 'All around my hat I will wear the green willow . . .' etc is a traditional English folk song.

The Two Kings: Inspired by the traditional Welsh fairy-story about Pwyll, Prince of Dyved, and his encounter with the faêrie king, Arawn.

Nuckelavee: Based on an article by Traill Dennison in the 'Scottish Antiquary', which was reproduced in *Scottish Fairy Tales and Folk Tales*, Sir George Douglas, Walter Scott, London, 1873. For the sake of accuracy, the anecdote herein is partially quoted from this source.

The Tale of Thomas Rhymer, Duke of Ercildoune: Adapted from the traditional 'Ballad of True Thomas' which tells the story of Thomas Rymour of Erceldoune. It can be found in *The English and Scottish Popular Ballads*, Child, FJ (ed), Little, Brown; Shepard, Clark & Brown, Boston, 1857–8; definitive edition: 5

vols., The Folklore Press in association with the Pagent Book Co., New York, 1957. The ballad is based on a fourteenth century romance which can be read in *Fairy Tales, Legends and Romances Illustrating Shakespeare*, by W Carew Hazlitt, F & W Kerslake, London, 1875.

The Tale of Tamlain Conmor, Duke of Roxburgh: Adapted from another beautiful traditional ballad, 'Young Tam Lin', of which there are many versions. The fullest version is #39A in *The English and Scottish Popular Ballads*, Child, FJ (ed), Little, Brown; Shepard, Clark & Brown, Boston, 1857–8.

Scottish Vernacular: Learned from *Bawdy Verse and Folk Songs Written & Collected by Robert Burns*, Macmillan, London, 1982.

Battle Scenes: Researched in *The Wars of the Crusades 1096–1291*, Terence Wise, Osprey Publishing P/L, 1978. Information was also gleaned from the World War I diaries of Squadron Leader W Palstra.

The Coronation Feast: Inspired by menus from actual medieval feasts, recounted in *The English Medieval Feast*, WE Mead, 1931; and *More Medieval Byways*, LF Salzman, 1926.

The musicians in the pie: Adapted from a document by Olivier de la Marche, fourteenth century chronicler.

The Battle of Evernight: Also draws inspiration from the great fairy love story of Ireland, 'Midhir and Etain', which has prompted many poets and dramatists to produce works based thereon.

Some words from the Elder Tongue

briagha: beautiful

caileagh faoileag: sea-gull damsel

cirean mi coileach: literally, 'cockscomb, my rooster'. It means 'cocksure boy'.

cochal: the husk or appearance of food, after the *toradh* has been removed

eudail: darling (fem.)

fallaise: a beautiful, falling torrent

ionmhuinn: beloved

nathrach deirge: literally, 'dragon's blood', is a draught to warm and nourish the traveller

rade: a processional cavalcade of Faêran riders

sabhailte: safe

seirm ceangail: bind-ring

siofra: (pl.) small, human-like wights. Although they can be mischievous, they are harmless and not overly cunning. One of their favourite activities is to mimic human behaviour.

toradh: the nutritional value of food

uhta: the hour before sunrise